KNIGHT OF CYDONIA

Malamas, Athena

Knight of Cydonia

ISBN 978-0-9811797-0-4

This is a work of fiction. Names, characters, places and incidents either are products of the author's imagination or are used fictitiously.

Cover design by Athena Malamas

Book design by Kate LaRue

Apollo Publishing

Toronto, Ontario

To my rat pack — especially Pork Chop

CONTENTS

I.	SHAKESPEARE	1
II.	DUCK, DUCK, *GUSE*	12
III.	PURGATORY	32
IV.	A MILLION DOLLARS & HORSES	54
V.	BLAKE LANDING	64
VI.	KNOCK, KNOCK	78
VII.	THE KING	88
VIII.	OVER MY HEAD	96
IX.	POETRY	112
X.	FIRST IMPRESSIONS	126
XI.	VETO	141
XII.	DÉJÀ VU	165
XIII.	WHITE LIES	184
XIV.	Q & A	211
XV.	EPITHETS	246
XVI.	DINNER TALK	274
XVII.	*DER KUß* BY GUSTAV KLIMT	291
XVIII.	WHAT'S THIS	333
XIX.	THE DARK NIGHT	360
XX.	THE BRIGHT LIGHT	375
XXI.	STAY	390

The Crystal Cabinet

The Cabinet is form'd of gold
And pearl and crystal shining bright,
And within it opens into a world
And a little lovely moony night.

Another England there I saw,
Another London with its Tower,
Another Thames and other hills,
And another pleasant Surrey bower...

— William Blake

SHAKESPEARE

He said that I had two options: *to go or not to go*. Truth be told, I didn't know what *to go* meant.

A few moments ago my father, Vasilios Ellias, calmly asked something of me that I couldn't believe. As I gazed at his stoically configured features I tried to imagine what he was thinking, but his thoughts were impossible to make out. I kept my expression equally neutral while I digested his proposition and subdued the rational side of my brain, which bellowed he had finally lost his mind. Instead, I conjured up fragmented memories of my childhood that always seemed to hang in the periphery of my heart.

I often wondered how Vas had had the time or patience to raise two crazy rug-rat daughters. You see my father is, well, a *genius* and when I was six years old he won the Nobel Prize in physics. I'm being generous when I say I have a limited idea of what his theory entails, but I do know it has something to do with explicating the asymmetry of matter and antimatter in the universe. When I was growing up, his world consisted of two entirely independent and often colliding sects: there was family and there was work. I used to grapple with the dichotomy and questioned which one, if he had to make a choice, could he live without. I always believed that family came first and his work came second, but when Vas stood by and let my mother leave, I bitterly found that I had been mistaken and I've never questioned the fact since.

Now, looking into my father's face as he awaited my response, I saw another place, another time and with a nagging uncertainty, another man.

"Is Pork Chop coming?" My voice sounded so strange, almost childlike.

"Sofia is already there."

I puckered my forehead, unable to conceal my confusion. "But she just left a week ago to see Nanny."

"Yes, she went to see your mother to say…good-bye."

I was speechless as my brain processed this information. A small part of me was starting to panic. I hadn't heard from my sister in days, which was unusual. She hadn't answered my text messages, my e-mails or my calls.

"Is Sammy there, too? They left together to see her."

My father rose from his desk and walked over to the coat stand.

"Yes, Samuel is with her," he replied, pulling on his jacket.

I don't know if it was his leaving or something instinctual inside me, like a sixth sense, but my panicked feeling was growing and the rising hair on my arms was a good indication that I was afraid.

"When do I have to decide? What should I pack? How do we"—I paused as I struggled with my phrasing—"*get there?*"

Vas walked toward me and answered my questions decisively.

"Decide today. Pack what you like. Don't concern yourself with *how* we're getting there."

"How long will we be gone?" I asked hesitantly.

His eyes lingering on my face, Vas stopped and let out a slow breath before he made his way to the door, leaving my last and most important question unanswered. Then, turning the antique brass handle to leave, he slowly looked back at me over his shoulder.

"Indefinitely."

I flicked on the lights and knew something was wrong. The portrait I had painted of Pork Chop was gone from her desk and had been replaced by a dust-lined square. Her bed looked vacant without grandma's quilt, which usually nestled at its foot. I ran to the dresser and frantically yanked open a drawer.

It was empty.

Time seemed to stagger as I stared down into the hollow piece of furniture. The small butterfly I felt in my stomach spawned violent offspring as I frantically pulled open others. Everything was gone. I threw open her closet door and the clink of empty hangers hitting one another echoed in the empty space. My mind was reeling. *What was going on?* And then I saw it. There was a green envelope taped to the back of her door. I darted toward it and tore it down. It simply read *Gustav*.

That was me. When I was younger I was terribly tomboyish and wore my hair in a short bob with crooked bangs. My sister always had a weird sense of humor and started calling me Gustav, Guse for short, after a page boy she read about in a folktale set in the Middle Ages.

But having odd nicknames is not uncommon in my family; they tend to originate in comical family stories. I call my sister, Sofia, Pork Chop. The story for that one still lives in infamy.

When I was seven we had a barbeque party at our town house in West London celebrating my mother's new exhibit. Pork Chop was a plump child with an appetite suited for two, sometimes three, and couldn't wait for the guests to arrive to start eating. When she snuck into the kitchen, she accidentally left the kitchen gate open and our King Shepherd, Pippin, found his way in. Nan spotted my sister in the pantry, covered in barbeque sauce, just as the bell rang, marking the arrival of our first guest. Pip was a smart boy and had dined and dashed by that time, leaving in his wake a trail of meatless bone. Our cousin Alex went around ranting and raving that Sofia had eaten all the pork chops. The name has stuck ever since.

To my mother's utter annoyance, I call her Nanny because people used to mistake her for our *nanny*. My father is Greek, although he is often mistaken as Russian, with wavy, dirty-blond hair and blue eyes, but my mother is Asian. Neither my sister nor I look like either of our parents but are instead a fusion of both. We have big deep-set eyes, like my father's, but they're brown like my mother's. Pork Chop's hair is dirty blond, while mine is light brown. There's nothing really distinctive in our appearance that resonates with a European or Asian heritage or even a pleasant mix of the two. We usually just pass for "white folk."

I call my father Vas, short for Vasilios, though I usually address him as Dad to his face.

I flipped over the envelope and broke the seal on the back. Inside was a sheet of white paper folded in half with a single phrase written in Pork Chop's chicken-scratch.

Go with Vas.
Don't keep me waiting.

I kicked her bedroom door, trying to think of reasonable explanations, the whys and the hows, but my mind drew blanks. *Where was she? What the hell was going on?*

Finding no firm ground to stand on in the maelstrom that was my mind, I took shelter in the lone cave that remained: denial. I wasn't sure that two plus two equaled four at the moment, but I steadied my feet and headed down to my own room to pack. I buried my thoughts and apprehensions. I told myself that I was going to see Pork Chop soon. That was final and that was all that mattered.

I was relatively calm as I folded a sweater once, then twice, and neatly placed it into my luggage. I didn't dwell on the fact that I didn't believe I was going anywhere. My mind had become a machine and it was not only keeping my fears at bay, but also keeping my emotions in check; I missed my sister. She was my best friend, although she only held that position by default. Growing up, we were shuffled between London and various parts of Canada, so we never managed to keep many—*any* friends in my case. We didn't develop accents either.

Both my sister and I were homeschooled from a young age and received our high school diplomas when we were only sixteen. I turned nineteen a few months ago and am trying to finish up my undergraduate studies in art history and classical civilizations at Cambridge. Pork Chop studies there, too, in mechanical engineering. I was never one for math. She was never one for history.

My sister and I could finish each other's sentences, but the two of us were still like night and day. She was not only the more attractive one, with her button nose, heart-shaped face and soft features, but she was also the more social one, which accounted for the countless boyfriends she went through. That is, until she fell for Sammy.

Not just anyone deserves the title of genius, but Samuel Fields does. With an unbelievably high IQ, he was a research student who worked with my father when he was fifteen. Sammy isn't only supremely intelligent and talented, he's also quite good-looking, with a charming face, crystal-clear blue eyes and sandy-blond hair. It took him two years to work up the nerve to ask Pork Chop out. She had been crushing on Sammy for the longest time and was thrilled. They have so much in common. They love the same music, the same writers, the same everything.

He wrote her a brilliant piece, reminiscent of Bach, for her eighteenth birthday a couple of months ago. It was a melodic and intricate composition that my sister let me listen to after a pathetic amount of pleading on my part. Sammy's practically become a member of the family and I can hardly think of one without the other now.

I, on the other hand, have never had a boyfriend. I surmised that I was too complicated compared to girls my age. It didn't help that I wasn't as lucky as Pork Chop when it came to the looks department either. With an unexceptionally proportioned oval face, finished off with a slightly pointed nose—a trait from my father—I have always thought my features too angular to ever be considered pretty. I only kept my boyish hair for a short period of time in my youth and it has been long ever since, too long, according to Pork Chop. It practically reaches my waist and has become stringy from the weight. My lips are too small and slightly crooked, though I've often been taunted by my family for having a "big" mouth. My mother always said that my artless smile matched Vas' perfectly.

I used to tease Nan that she had to love me more than Pork Chop because I was the uglier one. Like any mother, she said that she loved us in different ways but in equal measure. I hated when she said this. It just didn't seem honest. Everyone has favorites—colors, books, movies. If I were my mother I would love Pork Chop more. My sister is just more lovable.

Nanny would say that I was *gaga simou*—stupid—for thinking such things.

"Athena, I love both of you. My children are my joy. My life," she'd insist. "And stop saying that you're ugly. You have a beguiling face that is all your own."

"Sorta like the ugly duckling?" I had asked sarcastically.

Nan snorted. "No! That tale is frivolous and doesn't make sense to me because the duckling was never ugly. Beauty is a process and I see it growing and changing in you everyday. The only kind of duckling you are is a special one. My duckling," she had declared tenderly, reaching over to squeeze my nose.

Though I was confident of my mother's love for me I wasn't as confident when it came to her estimation of an attractive face; it often resonated with the beauty one found in the distortions depicted by Picasso.

A few hours later I had my bags lined up beside the front door and I waited, in an almost zombielike state, at the bottom of the stairs. I could hear the faint hustle and bustle of London city life that went on outside the confines of my home, but everything seemed worlds away as I waited and waited for Vas to return.

I winced as I groggily woke and immediately felt the effects of my distorted sleeping position. I had fallen asleep at the base of the stairs waiting for Vas.

"Dad!" I called out.

Only echoes replied.

I started toward the kitchen as the front door opened.

"It's time to go." My father casually walked in and lifted my bags.

"Where have you been?" I rushed after him as he bounded out the door carrying my luggage.

"We don't have much time," he said lightly, too lightly, as if he was trying to overcompensate for something, trying to make it seem like nothing out of the ordinary was taking place. He loaded my bags into the trunk of his Jag and was back up the steps to our town house before I could get a word in.

Catching him at the front door, I yanked at his jacket sleeve. "What do you mean, we don't have time? What's going on? Dad, are you *okay?*"

He pulled out of my grasp, picked up the rest of my stuff and skipped down the steps.

"I'll explain everything soon."

Vas led me to the car and I sagged down into the passenger's seat. As he got behind the wheel and floored the gas pedal, I felt myself teetering on a precipice and regardless of which way I turned I was sure that the ground beneath my feet was going to crumble.

Had he gone mad? Where was Pork Chop? What did he mean when he told me not to concern myself with *how* we were going to get to our destination?

Vas looked over at me while we waited at a red light. "Everything is going to be all right. I want you to call your mother." He pressed a button and before I knew it I heard Nanny's distinct accent on the speakerphone.

"Yes, Vasili?"

"Maria, how are you?"

"Good." My mother's reply was perfunctory.

Vas took a deep breath. "Maria, we're leaving today. Athena's with me. She's coming…Thank you. This wouldn't have been possible if you didn't stay behind to cover for us."

A cold silence followed. It was my voice that broke it.

"Nanny? Nanny, are you there?"

After a brief moment my mother answered.

"I'm here. Vasili…take good care of them. Athena,"—her voice was choking up—"I love you. I love your sister."

"You sound like you're saying good-bye. Stop being so dramatic," I snapped.

I needed to maintain some semblance of self-control and the only way I knew how to do that was to seem nonchalant and sarcastic. I could feel my tear ducts waiting, waiting for me to surrender. I had never cried in front of Vas before.

The car stopped. We were at London Bridge.

"Maria, we're here. Take care of yourself."

"What do you mean, we're here? Nanny, do you know what's going on? Do you know where Dad thinks we're going?"

"Athena, I love you; kay. Love you so much."

I could tell she was crying now and it was all I needed. The tears started flowing. The most painful thing I had ever experienced was witnessing my mother cry. We were oceans apart, but I didn't have to see it to feel it.

"I love you, too, Nanny. But I don't understand—"

My father cut me off. "Good-bye, Maria."

It was happening all too fast. The line died. My father was out of the car and unloading my bags. I got out, too. It was nearing dawn and the sun had just started to rise. Vas looked at the horizon with a troubled expression on his face and then briskly came over to where I stood to pull me toward the edge of the bridge.

"Jump," Vas ordered.

I had been willing to play along all this time. I had quieted the voice in my head that shouted something was wrong, but that willingness came to an abrupt halt.

I stared at him incredulously. "What do you mean, *jump?*" I hadn't known I was capable of reaching such a pitch.

He gestured over the edge. "Athena, think of this as a door."

I tried to tug my arm out of his grasp. "What kind of door?" My voice was hysterical.

Vas glanced at the horizon again and mumbled something inaudible. Before I could offer any further protest he picked me up and hauled me over his shoulder.

"To the future."

Then he dropped me.

¤ II ¤

DUCK, DUCK, *GUSE*

I flailed my arms and feet in expectation of hitting water until I realized that I wasn't falling at all but lying on a hard surface. I tried rolling to my side but stopped as I felt an ache in my bones that demanded I lie still. Slowly, my eyelids fluttered open and I managed to lift myself onto my hands and knees. Just as my vision cleared, I saw it coming—what looked like a double-decker tank was speeding right toward me. Perhaps it was my brain going into overdrive that caused my immobilization, but for whatever reason, I couldn't move.

With the tank only a few feet away, I suddenly found myself

being slammed into a railing and crumpled to the ground with a loud *thud*.

I must have been disorientated because I was sure my body was encased in stone.

"*No.*"

My heart thumped as I heard the male voice—distorted as if the person to whom it belonged were in pain. I opened my eyes and realized someone was holding me, but everything was a blur, including his face.

"*Athena.*" He choked my name.

He knew my name.

I reached out to touch him, afraid and confused, but I fell still as my fingers brushed against his skin—the flesh of a baby molded over rock.

"*Why…*" His voice was edged and it frightened me, making my breathing uneven.

Something brushed against my forehead and then it felt like a metal blanket unwrapped itself around me.

"Guse! You okay?"

I tried to sit up as I heard her voice, elated because it was, without a doubt, none other than Pork Chop.

"No!" I groaned, waiting for my head to stop spinning.

"Really? Or are you just complaining?"

I felt Pork Chop's arms come around me and a small smile splayed across my mouth—my sister was covering her concern under layers of sarcasm.

"Where'd he go?" I asked, resting my cheek against her

shoulder.

"Vas is coming," she assured me. "Sammy is picking him up."

I shook my head and immediately regretted it. "I didn't mean Vas," I said wincing from the violent pounding.

"Who do you mean, then?"

"The guy."

"What guy?"

I let out a frustrated breath. "The one who just saved my life."

Pork gave my shoulder a few brisk pats. "Guse, I think you might be delirious. There's no one here but me," she said, helping me to my feet.

"Didn't you see what happened? The tank would have killed—" I took a sharp breath in, finally taking notice of my surroundings. I was still on London Bridge, but it was not the same London Bridge I had just been on. There were illuminated lanes that ran twenty, thirty, sixty feet above my head—each a different color. My eyes trailed over to the city skyline and I saw buildings, draped in fog, climbing the skies endlessly.

"Two thousand two hundred twelve," Pork Chop said quickly.

2212.

My eyes grew wide as comprehension slowly dawned on me.

My sister held her hand up to my face. "How many fingers am I holding up?"

I frowned. "Three," I answered flatly, still distracted by her revelation. "I'm not crazy. He threw me out of the way and he was…hard, like bone."

"You were lying right here when I spotted you." Pork Chop

pulled my head down to inspect my crown. "You must have bumped your head or something." She shrugged. "You're just confused."

"I heard him say my name!"

"You probably just heard me calling you."

"No," I insisted. "It wasn't you because he called me *Athena*."

Pork Chop pursed her lips. "You must have imagined it; I didn't see anyone around. Let's go home? I've been waiting for hours around here."

I was still unsure of what had just happened and, coupled with the fact that my muscles were aching, I was in an irritable mood and my temper flared.

"By the way, thanks for letting me in on this. Did it ever cross your mind to tell your only sibling that you would be traveling to the *future?*"

I turned away from her. I wanted to argue but the question itself was ridiculous enough that I wasn't sure I could hold my foul disposition—what with wanting to laugh at it all. A part of me still couldn't believe it. "I mean, you took Sammy and left me behind? I'm your sister! This is unforgivable!"

"Stop overreacting. Let's jet."

Too late. She knew I was being dramatic. I grudgingly followed her as she headed off the bridge and pretended to limp a little, hoping to make her feel bad.

"You're not off the hook. I will expect serious compensation for this," I cried haughtily.

"Whatever!" she yelled over her shoulder.

As I trailed her, a fast-moving object buzzed past my head. What looked like a flying car was traveling atop one of the illuminated laneways.

"Pork Chop! What the heck was that?"

She looked up briefly and then continued walking, as if the sight was nothing out of the ordinary.

"I'll fill you in when we get home. Technology has changed, Guse."

Behind her back I mocked her know-it-all tone.

We turned off the bridge and I was captivated by the vehicles whizzing by me on the ground way. The designs were truly innovative, but not unimaginable—I didn't come from the seventeenth century and knew the possibilities technology offered. I was more excited than overwhelmed.

Pork Chop slowed her pace. "*Load,*" she called out.

Two light beams momentarily blinded me and I heard an engine start. It took a few seconds for my eyes to adjust, but once they did, I was astounded by what I can only describe as a vehicle that resembled the batmobile—except it was silver. I recognized the Japanese emblem displayed on the hood and was surprised the car company still existed.

"Is this our ride?" I asked.

"No. This is *my* ride," she replied impishly.

"You're such a dork, Pork."

My sister had always had a soft spot for fancy cars. I didn't even have my driver's license.

The car was impressive, though. Its sleek shape, encased

in silver plating and lined with chrome finishing, belied truly technologically advanced automotive design and customization. The doors rapidly slid open and Pork Chop eased herself into the driver's seat.

"Guse, get in."

I clumsily crawled inside. As the doors locked into place, it was like being sealed into a tomb—I hated small spaces. My mind didn't dwell on my claustrophobia, however, as it was thoroughly distracted by the holograms that glared into my eyes. The 3-D stereo system was the biggest attraction.

"*Home.*"

Pork Chop had barely uttered the word before the car shot upwards. If anything, I expected a forward momentum and was taken aback when we started rising instead.

"What do you think?"

I was watching the street fall away under us.

"I'm not sure what to think. What is this thing called?"

"It's just a jet-stream model. Most car manufacturers make them. But they're uberexpensive."

I could tell.

"Where did you get it from? How did you afford it?" I asked perplexedly.

She giggled and then gave me a look, as if I should know the answer to that question.

"Sammy."

Flying home, to wherever that was, we sat in silence. I couldn't stop replaying the voice I had heard on London Bridge and was thoroughly engrossed by the world that sped by. Pork Chop seemed lost in thought. I had so many questions and I wanted answers, but I decided not to press her for them just yet. I thought back to what Vas had told me before he unceremoniously threw me off London Bridge. It was still hard to wrap my head around it, but I just traveled to the future and, if I understood my father's cryptic answer, there was no going back. In the coming days there were going to be some major adjustments in my life and I wanted to relish the little peace I found riding silently with my sister. Come what may, I wasn't alone, and that was enough. For now.

We turned into a wide landing space that jutted out beside a red brick building lined with colorful stained glass windows. It was so tall that the top was entirely obscured by a dense veil of fog.

"We're here," Pork Chop announced.

I heard an audible pop as the airtight doors unlocked and slid away. I climbed out of the car and felt my knees buckle. We were high up, at least thirty stories, and I had a terrible, almost incapacitating, fear of heights. It took all my willpower to walk toward the main entrance instead of degradingly crawling there on my hands and knees.

Pork Chop couldn't resist. "You scared, Guse?" she asked mockingly, unable to resist the taunt when my fear was etched so clearly across my stricken face.

"No," I shot back.

She laughed quietly to herself and then said, "*Store.*"

The car instantly reversed, parked itself in one of the many cubicles that lined the far side of the unloading dock and vanished as it was swiftly lowered into the ground.

My sister's taunting attitude was driving me crazy. Walking through the lobby, I had a serious inclination to give her a good kick in the derrière. If it hadn't been for the magnificence of the intricately carved wooden paneling, that cradled the most exquisite stained glass windows I had ever seen, I would have done so and I would have done it really hard, too. It's just that I was too distracted to follow through.

To my utter dismay the elevator was entirely made of glass and the city below us was completely visible in all its miniature glory. Pork Chop burst out laughing as she witnessed the blood drain from my face. She was seriously trying my patience.

"Guse, I've missed you!" she managed.

I clenched my teeth and gave her the evil eye, sure that before the night was over I would be guilty of siblicide. I noticed then that we weren't moving.

"What floor are we on? How do we—"

Pork Chop cut me off. "Fifty-three," she said breathily.

Before I knew it the doors were open, Pork Chop was walking down a corridor and leaving me behind.

All the doors on the floor were distinct and had peculiar designs. Unit 532 had a small garden patch around it, which I thought unusual, but not as unusual as unit 535, which had a small fountain and fish. Pork Chop stopped in front of unit 537.

"This is us," she said.

I watched as she typed in a code on a keypad located to the right of the plain metallic door. A handle appeared from within and extended toward her. She held it for a brief moment and then turned it. "After you." In a showy fashion she gestured for me to enter first.

The foyer was open-concept and I immediately recognized the artwork that adorned the walls. The back of the unit, as expected, consisted of stained glass windows and there were twin-winding staircases that led to the higher levels of the flat. I looked up and saw that there were at least five or six floors. A peculiar chandelier, a conglomerate of geometrical shapes, hung from the ceiling.

"Nice, huh?"

I swiveled around to see Pork Chop leaning against the staircase railings, eyeing me smugly.

"How did you pull this off in so short a time?" I asked, furrowing my brow.

"Let's sit down. I need to explain a few things," she answered, heading into an adjoining room.

Something was up. I could feel it. It just didn't make sense—the car, this flat—she had left only a week ago…I narrowed my eyes suspiciously. What did my wily little sister have up her sleeve?

The room was completely devoid of color with stark white paneling encasing the spacious area.

"Is this supposed to be the kitchen?"

Pork Chop's face brightened. "Guse, you gotta see this." She held out her hands, mimicking the movements of a conductor.

"Kitchen. Load," she said gleefully.

The previously innocuous panels transformed into what I estimated to be a microwave, oven, stove-top, sink and some other mechanical-looking devices whose function I couldn't determine. Cupboards magically emerged from the wall. Stockpiles of food lay behind delicate glass frames and the once-desolate center island was now filled with every conceivable appliance.

"Tea, please," Pork Chop ordered, taking a seat around the counter. Two cups rose up from the smooth surface as I sat beside her.

"Tell me everything," I said impatiently.

"You know I have missed you. *So much.*"

This wasn't what I was expecting. If I was deficient emotionally, my sister was even more so and I was stunned by the look on her face. In all of her eighteen years I had never seen such a display. I tried to lighten the mood with my sarcasm.

"Aw, you missed your big sister. Geez, it was only a week."

"*Big* sister," she said uneasily, fingering her teacup. "Sammy and I arrived in two thousand two hundred *ten*. We've been here for almost two years. Technically, I'm the big sister now. I'll be turning twenty in December."

I blinked at her dumbly.

Pork Chop slid off her seat and paced around the counter. "I'll try to keep it short and sweet. Vas and Sammy had a breakthrough and, after a few tests that confirmed their findings, they sat down and tried to figure out what they wanted to do." She stopped and looked at me. "Can you imagine the power to travel through time?

It's"—she whirled around trying to find the right word—"mind boggling!"

I sat unmoving in a detached silence. I was feeling so many things at once, my emotions were a blur, but one thing I was certain of was that I was angry.

"Ultimately, after careful consideration, Vas decided he couldn't give the world what he had discovered. He said he wasn't sure if humankind would ever be ready for time-travel. Sammy decided that it was something he had to experience. There was a chance that he would never come back because the process was so finicky and he asked me to come with him. There was no way I couldn't accept. Sammy's my life. You know that."

There was a touch of pleading in her voice but I didn't respond to it. The sting of knowing I played a secondary role in my sister's life hurt—my pride more than anything—so I remained silent and still.

Pork Chop tilted her head to one side and pursed her lips, showing her annoyance at my stoicism. "Look, there was no time! We were so busy making final preparations and I knew you would come. I had so many things to think about and then there was Nan…" Trailing off, she turned away and started rearranging things in one of the cupboards.

I knew she needed a break, a sign of my understanding, but I relished the anguish my coolness was causing her and mentally tried to swat the little fly that buzzed, *"You're evil,"* in my head. Damn conscience.

Pork Chop stopped fidgeting and leaned against the oven.

"Sammy miscalculated the timing. We were supposed to arrive only a month or two ahead of you and Vas. Instead, it's been nearly two years. As you can see, we're quite well-off. When we got here, Sammy sold the Pollock for a fortune—the painting being miraculously rediscovered after two hundred years and in mint condition."

Pork Chop raised her hands in defense as my mouth dropped open.

Not the Pollock!

"We had to sell something and you know I've never been a fan. After quickly getting acquainted with the ins and outs of this world Sammy invested," she continued. "He recalculated the coordinates and we anticipated your arrival today. You might be amused to know that you are looking at *Professor* Sofia Ellias of the University of Cambridge. Sammy is a professor, too."

"What!" I exclaimed in disbelief. "Why would they hire you? What do you teach?"

"*History.* I teach cultural developments of the early *twenty-first* century. A bit of a pro, if I say so myself."

"You gotta be kidding me," I scoffed.

"Nope. Sammy teaches the history of scientific development of the same era. We were shoo-ins, you could say."

After moments of silence passed, Pork Chop started to bite her nails, waiting for me to say something. I got up and walked along the immaculate floor and decided I couldn't hold back any longer.

"So tell me! How have things changed? Are we in Orwell's

Nineteen Eighty-Four?' My eagerness to know rapidly drowned my bitter mood. "Any nuclear wars? Who's the president of the United States? Are there people living on the moon? Aliens! Were we invaded by aliens?"

My sister waved her hands. "Just sit down and I'll give you the lowdown."

I eagerly sat across from her. "My answers," I said hurriedly.

"First, no aliens. Second, no actual nuclear wars, but according to what I read there were a couple of close calls. Currently, the president of the United States is—get this—Harriet Jensen. Her husband, Robert Jensen, is the *first gentleman*. She's actually the eighth female president of the United States." I felt an excitement in me that I had never know before. "We do have extensive space stations on both the moon and Mars, but they're purely scientific colonies," she went on. "The biggest thing you may notice is that we're not living in some godforsaken polluted hell as was foretold by environmentalists of our day. Greenhouse gas emissions leveled off around eighty years ago and fossil fuel technology has long since been *extinct*. Get it? *Extinct—fossil* fuels."

"Yes, I get your lame jokes, Pork Chop," I said tartly.

"You never get anything," she shot back. "Anyway, the hydrogen fuel cell has not only been developed but has also evolved in unbelievable ways." My sister yawned and spread out across the sofa. "*Blanket. Load,*" she murmured lazily. A blanket emerged from the side of the couch and Pork Chop draped it over herself.

I spread out and repeated the command. "*Blanket. Load.*"

Nothing happened.

My sister laughed. "Our operating system isn't programmed with your voice command. Sammy will do it when he gets back. *Blanket. Load.*"

A blanket appeared beside me just as it had for Pork Chop and I snuggled under it.

"What about artificial intelligence? Do you have a robot? If you do, you better have named him C-3PO."

Pork Chop returned my playful smile. "No, I don't have a robot. Everything nowadays runs on operating systems, but the kind of artificial intelligence you're talking about is really rare."

"How come?"

"It's a long story. I'll tell you tomorrow."

I raised myself up on my elbows. "No. Tell me now," I insisted.

She rolled over and stretched, laying the back of her hand on her forehead. "Urgh, fine," she relented. "No one's sure about the details or the exact date, but at some point the military developed a prototype of a robot that could mimic human cognition. What followed was reportedly something akin to Shelley's classic tale—he penned *Frankenstein*, Guse, if you didn't happen to know that."

I wanted to smack her. "Shelley's a *she*, you moron."

"I was just testing you," my sister retorted complacently. "After some kind of general meeting that took place among the International Scientific Council Governing Artificial Intelligence, the government passed a bylaw banning the design of all A.I. robots until researchers could find a way to make the robot dependent on a human counterpart and be programmed to follow two necessary code sequences: command and termination. The robot had to follow orders and would have to self-destruct if its human counterpart died. So, scientists developed what they call sTell:R boTs. They're also commonly referred to as boTs. The cognitive power source for the boT was developed externally from its body and scientists hoped to implant this into the human brain somehow, but the studies were disastrous, to say the least."

Pork Chop stopped and turned her head to look at me. I was hunched over the side of the couch like a child eagerly anticipating the climax to a late-night bedtime story.

"What happened after that?" I asked eagerly.

"Scientists gave up on human research and focused on Supras instead. To their delight, Supras could physically accommodate the boTs' hardware and ergo they are the only ones who have them. I've heard of getting ac:To boTs on the black market, but I think it's just a scam."

I straightened. "Wait, what are Supras?"

"Supras are kinda like…the X-men. To a certain degree they're mutants."

My face went blank. "Huh?"

"Okay, that's the wrong word." Pork Chop scratched her head, trying to find a better way to explain. "I mean they don't look freakish or anything; they look human—they are human."

Comprehension eluded me.

"You know about genetic manipulation, right?" she asked, sitting up. "It was just starting to take off around our time, but it was still regarded as taboo. Over the last two centuries things have drastically changed." She stopped and bit her lip. "Before

I tell you about Supras, you should know that about eighty-five percent of the population today is an evolutionary product of genetic enhancement that, over time, has bred out undesirable qualities in our species. About fifteen percent of the population has recessive genes that produce what are now considered adverse traits. And then there are Supras. They make up a teeny tiny fraction—I think there's only a couple thousand of them, if that, in the entire world. Their DNA is considered the epitome of human biology and they have something akin to…superpowers."

The skeptical part of my brain couldn't resist. "What kind of superpowers, exactly?"

"I know, I know; it sounds crazy, but just imagine something that an ordinary human could do and drastically enhance that ability. All of their senses are highly developed. Strength, speed—you name it, they got it. Their bodies can recycle waste and can amass stores of energy. I don't even think they have to breathe. Their organs work faster, more efficiently and are more durable. Their skin is immune to UVA and UVB rays and is a thousand times more resilient to penetration than ours. And, to answer your first question, the reason Supras are the only ones who have sTell:R boTs is because, well, we dinky normal humans can't endure the physical burden the boT places on the body."

I raised an eyebrow quizzically.

"Apparently, the internal hardware of the boT—think of it like a power switch to turn their thoughts on and off—is actually *built into* a body cavity of the Supra. I heard that it's put next to the heart. It harnesses solar power to fuel itself, but the life of the Supra is needed to generate cognition. The boT would essentially go brain dead if their Supra counterpart died. Your average human can't house the apparatus because it produces such a high voltage of energy that it would fry us from the inside out. I won't get into the details about what is rumored to have happened during the human trials." My sister let out a breath. "Sammy tells me that the Supra and the boT can even exchange thoughts through coded sequences. It's the closest thing we have developed to telepathy," she added.

"Mutants," I muttered in disbelief.

"They're not mutants," Pork Chop emphasized, shaking her head.

I didn't respond as I digested what she told me.

"Guse, focus." My sister clapped her hands. "The point of all that is—alas—this Jedi Master shall never have a boT of her own for a faithful companion."

Oh, please.

"Alas, indeed," I said sardonically. "What are ac:To boTs?" I asked, remembering the other snippets of information she had given me.

"They're radical, meaning they aren't tied to a Supra and there's nothing external controlling them. It's been said that ac:To boTs can be much more powerful than normal sTell:R boTs, which is scary considering how strong regular boTs are. I forgot to mention that boTs can take on almost any shape or size. It's freakin awesome."

My eyes grew wide. "Have you seen one?"

"Uh, no." My sister fidgeted with her blanket, making me think she was nervous for some reason. "But I would like to."

I eyed her warily for a moment, but brushed off her unease. "Why don't you just get an ac:To boT then?"

"Truth is I'm not sure they exist. There are rumors and what not, but the successful construction of one has never been confirmed. It's supposed to be really difficult to produce an ac:To boT because the technology required is much more complex. They don't look different from regular boTs so often scam artists just build robotic dummies and try to pass them off as the real thing. Believe me, if there was a way that I could have a boT I would have one by now."

It was so much to take in. I crossed my arms and drummed my fingers along my forearm.

"Have Supras tried to take over the world?" I asked seriously.

"Oh. My. Gosh. Seriously, you're such a stupid head."

"What?" I countered. "That's a perfectly valid question. I mean what's stopping these superhumans from enslaving the human race or from destroying government institutions and erupting in complete anarchy?"

Pork Chop walked over to me and started hauling me up.

"Where are we going? Have they? Are we in danger? What kind of world did your stupid boyfriend suck us into?"

She rolled her eyes as we headed for the stairs. "Listen, Guse, Supras may be strong but they are small in number and you need to understand the advances in military technology; it wouldn't be that easy to take over the world," she said, smiling. "Besides, there are other things you need to worry about." She gestured for me to keep climbing as we reached the landing of the second floor.

"What do you mean by that?"

"You'll see soon enough."

I stopped mid-step. She tried to push me up but I held myself against the railing.

Pork Chop groaned. "I take it back. I didn't miss you at all. You're so annoying. You're exhausting my brain."

"I'm not taking another step until you tell me."

She put her hands on her hips and looked at me for a moment. "Fine. This is the last thing I'm going to answer before I knock you out." I acquiesced with my silence. "First, your room is through there." She pointed up at the door to my right. "Second, you may have been a smarty-pants in our time but—I hate to break it to you sis—you're pretty much a dumb bum by today's standards. So, you have been registered in London's Haverston College of Higher Education. You're going back to *high school*."

I flinched at the word.

"Considering you never actually went, I'm sure you'll enjoy the experience. Sammy gave you the benefit of the doubt and thought you could handle senior year. Personally, I thought you wouldn't be able to handle the curriculum at all, but you look too old to pass for a middleschooler, even now when kids develop at a much faster rate."

"Whatever," I shot back, irked by the glee in her voice. "High school with a bunch of kids is going to be a breeze."

Pork Chop waved her finger in front of my face. "Ah, ah,

ah. First of all, these aren't just any kids. They're much more developed, both physically and intellectually. And second of all, my child,"—she tried to pat my head condescendingly before I ducked out of the way—"you've always been so competitive. I'm not sure your ego will be able to handle the inferiority you're going to feel to these modern-day adolescents."

She was full-out mocking me now and I shot her some serious cut-eye.

"Just wait until you see some of the girls. Thank god and all his angels that I have Sammy. I'm not sure how runts like us would ever catch a guy with competition that steep." Pork Chop cocked her head at me. "And you've got it worse than me since I got the good genes in the family."

"God had to compensate because he forgot to give you a brain," I snapped, brushing past her on my way to my room.

"Seriously, Guse. We got it bad."

"I'm going to sleep," I answered over my shoulder.

"Sweet dreams," she called out, again in that condescending tone. "Oh, and third of all, you've never had a knack for numbers. Just you wait."

My room was empty except for a large bed that rested beside the color filled window and a barren desk that stood against the far wall. I was sure that there were hidden features lurking throughout, like in the kitchen, but the last thing I was going to do was ask Pork Chop. I meant to check out the washroom but, exhausted, I drifted toward the inviting bed instead.

¤ III ¤

P U R G A T O R Y

"**W**ake up, sleepy head!"

I rubbed my eyes and rolled over. It took me a few moments to register where I was. It was about dawn and small streams of colorful light were shining through my window. I tried to find the source of what I now recognized as my sister's voice.

"Everyone's downstairs eating breakfast. Hurry up and get ready, you're going to be late for school!" she sang, in an irritating voice that was coming from a large speaker at the far end of the room. I was certain that it hadn't been there last night and made a mental note to ask Sammy about the other hidden features of my room.

The voice bellowed again. "Guse, get up! Wednesdays are casual days so you don't have to wear your uniform."

I noticed the zipped-up garment bag hanging beside my bedroom door.

"Ah!" I groaned, running my fingers through my hair. "God, kill me now."

The lights came on automatically as I entered an ordinary-looking washroom, outfitted with a large metallic sink, shower, tub and toilet. I opted for finger-brushing my teeth and mouthwash after the toothbrush I picked up started rotating so fast I was sure it would give me a root canal. It sounded like a drill, too, and that was enough of a psychological deterrent to make me shove it back into the cabinet.

I dreaded what the day might bring and sat half-asleep on the toilet. Conceding that I didn't have much time, I reluctantly pried my eyes open and reached behind me to feel for the flusher, but there was nothing on the austere surface. Annoyed, I turned halfway around, thinking there had to be some kind of latch or switch.

"How the heck do you get this thing to *flush?*" I said aloud.

The water instantly drained from the basin, toilet paper shot out at the end of a mechanical arm that moved in an up-and-down wiping direction and a noxious substance sprayed into my eyes, momentarily blinding me. The seat then started to mechanically rise and then lower itself and I fell off, smacking right into the floor. I heard my sister's voice above the commotion.

"Gustav! Hurry up!"

As I lay slumped on the ground, peering up at a monstrosity of a toilet that continued to bury me under a mountain of toilet paper, I thought of how, in the span of two days, it couldn't possibly be healthy to think so often of murdering one's only sibling.

I collected myself and opted to skip the bath. Someone had brought up my bags and I rummaged through them for fresh clothes. Overcome with a sudden urge to see my family, to see Vas, I quickly got dressed. I slipped into a pair of boots, threw a light sweater over my T-shirt and hurried downstairs.

They were indeed all there, sitting merrily around the counter, chatting as if back in our old town house. It would have been the conventional picture of my family having breakfast except for the fact that the kitchen literally looked alive. All the inanimate contraptions I had observed the night before were moving to and fro, stirring with a life of their own.

They all stopped talking as I entered.

Vas smiled at me. "Here she is."

I thought my father's eyes looked anxious, but I could never really tell.

"Hi, Dad. I'm glad you made it," I answered awkwardly, unsure of what else to say.

"Yes, we made it," he said, unsmiling, studying my face.

"What's for breakfast?" I asked brightly, taking a seat next to Pork Chop. I felt tense. I was never entirely at ease when I was with Vas. Our conversations were often strained because I was always so self-conscious about what he was thinking.

"Pancakes." Pork Chop shoved a plate toward me. "If you want something else you can just order it. Sammy's already adjusted the programming."

That would explain the toilet.

"Good to see you, Guse," Sammy greeted, in his ever cheery voice. He stood and picked up a tanned leather bag that was perched on the seat next to him. He handed it over to me. "We got you everything you'll need. Sof is going to drop you off before making her way to Cambridge."

I took the bag from him grudgingly.

"Dad, I really don't think this is necessary. It's so unfair. If Pork Chop can be a professor, then so can I."

"Athena doesn't know what she's talking about. She needs to learn how to read programming. She needs to learn about the society we live in. I think it will be good for her. I learned all this with Sammy ages ago."

I shot my sister a furious glare. "No one asked you, thank you very much."

Vas waved his hands in the air.

Damn. That usually meant the case was closed and to be quiet. My father hated arguments.

"Athena, your sister's right. We live here now and the most important thing is for you to be educated. Education is power. Knowledge is power. You know that."

I slumped down in my seat.

"Well, how are you going to educate yourself? I don't see you enrolling in some stupid College," I countered.

"I'm an old man. You're young. This experience will be good for you and, besides, my dear, you are not as educated as I am. Don't worry. I'll be fine. But as for you,"—he pointed his finger at me—"to school you go."

I crossed my arms. Case closed.

Leave it to Sammy to conveniently change the topic of discussion. My father and he quickly got into an intense conversation regarding the miscalculations of the coordinates they had devised.

"Sammy, in a nutshell,"—I interrupted them—"what exactly happened last night? How was any of this possible?"

Sammy shrugged. "According to the time space continuum—"

"In English," I requested.

"In a nutshell, Guse, Richard Dawkins was wrong."

"Fair enough," I answered, rearranging the napkin on my lap nervously. "Can we ever go back?"

"Not likely," Sammy said slowly.

I nodded.

I hardly touched my breakfast before Pork Chop announced, "Let's go, guys."

"Where are you going?" I asked Vas.

"He's going to sit in on a couple of my lectures and meet the dean of the university. I'm going to recommend your father as an associate professor in my field. He's qualified, don't you think?" Sammy said with a smile. He had an endless amount of enthusiasm for everything and could always brighten my mood.

I picked up the bag he had given me and followed my sister out of the kitchen.

"Sleep well?" she asked casually.

"Yeah. Everything was fine except for one small thing."

"What, Guse?" Sammy asked.

The front door slid open and we walked out.

"Oh, just that the toilet tried to eat me!"

We took two cars because Pork Chop's car was only a two-seater. Sammy and Vas rode together. Pork Chop was still chuckling to herself as I climbed into the passenger seat.

I glared at her. "I'm so glad that you find such a traumatic experience amusing. I bet you knew that damn toilet was wonky."

"Come on, traumatic? Don't you think you're acting like a bit of a drama queen?"

"It nearly gave me a heart attack," I said seriously.

"That's because you're a natural-born chicken—easily excitable."

I reached over and tried to smack her but she swatted my hand away.

"Don't worry. Knowing Sammy, he'll have it fixed by yesterday."

As we worked our way downtown, I was surprised at how many vehicles filled the laneways both above and on the ground. After about a twenty-minute ride, due more to traffic than distance, Pork Chop pulled up in front of a large building designed in the classical style and perched atop an expansive glass structure. Squinting, I tried to translate the Latin inscription that was carved into the façade of London's Haverston College of Higher Education—looming ominously before me.

"Okay, get out. I'll pick you up at six."

"Six!"

Pork Chop shoved my shoulder as a loud honk sounded behind us.

"Classes end around three-thirty, but both Sammy and I have late lectures, so I can't make it before six. I'm sure you'll have a lot of catching up to do so you can work in the school library until I come and get you."

"Geez, thanks, mom," I said sourly, as I got out of the car.

"Try not to be such a loser. Make some friends, Gustav!" she called out.

I truly believed my sister was a freak of nature—half hyena. Her laugh made your insides curl.

Walking toward the College, I immediately felt short. At five foot five, I never thought of myself as such, but climbing up the main stairs, it was as if I was among giants. I was by far the shortest in the crowd and I realized Pork Chop hadn't been kidding last night. Everyone was dressed in sleek attire and was ridiculously well kept. Tailored jackets, shiny boots, squeaky-clean sneakers, immaculately ironed shirts, pressed skirts and pants filled my mind. Fashion trends had definitely evolved but, surprisingly, they weren't completely indiscernible from the attire of my day.

I looked down at my appearance and grimaced. I didn't really fit in. My long, wavy hair was frizzy, I knew my eyeliner was smeared and my clothes, although completely normal to me, looked odd compared to what most of the other students wore. I thought I probably resembled a cut-out from a history book documenting what would now be considered outlandish attire of early twenty-first century youth.

I was never one to care about what people thought, but I had never been to high school and had never experienced the infamous cruelty of teenage cliques. I always thought my mental fortitude was admirable, but it had never really been tried or tested. As I passed by a gaggle of girls, screeching laughter followed me and I winced at how hard it was to ignore. I tried to boost my confidence by telling myself that they could have been laughing at anything or anyone and, that honestly, I couldn't be bothered if they were laughing at me anyway.

I was just about to make my way through the main entrance, when something stopped me—a strong breeze making the long strands of my hair whip around my face. My movement was slow as I turned to glance back toward the edge of the unloading dock. I'm not sure why I did it. Perhaps I was feeling a bit melancholy and thought I might be able to catch a last glimpse of Pork Chop's car if she had found herself stuck in a bottleneck. But my eyes didn't look along the lane of vehicles and they didn't search for the flash of silver of her car. Instead, as I stood atop the stairs I let my gaze float without direction over the mass of students. A violent gust of wind suddenly blew right through me.

And then *they found me.*

Eyes so sharp, they cut. It was as if they were a pair of black holes propelling me toward them. I staggered down a step and a wave of students pushed through me, momentarily blocking my line of sight. I strained my neck over their tall bodies, but it was pointless; I couldn't see a thing. Shoving through them, I scanned the terrain for the host of the black onyx set. But *he* was gone. So, too, was the charge in the air—something tangibly electric had died. Then again, it could have been the weather; the wind had instantly stilled.

More students packed themselves against me and I hesitantly headed inside, brushing the encounter from my mind. I didn't have time to think about figments of my imagination. I wasn't wearing my glasses, which wasn't unusual, considering I rarely wore them, and my eyes were probably playing tricks on me. I have a very weak grade so I don't really need them to see and only wear my glasses when I have to, for exams and what not. It's not an aesthetic thing— if it was I would have gotten contacts—it was a preference borne from the fact that, for me, not wearing glasses was like wearing a pair of rose-colored ones; everything resembled an Impressionist painting and I liked it that way.

The grand foyer was filled with students rushing to get to class. Statues of old men covered the walls and stared down at me as if casting judgment. I headed toward a large map on a stand in the center of the domed entrance hall. It showed that I was at division 1001. I had biology first period and had to get to room 1302, which meant heading up three floors. I saw several elevator stations but opted for the stairs instead.

After a few short detours, I finally came upon room 1302. Most of the seats had been filled already, which was expected. It was nearing the end of September and Sammy had said that the College was already three weeks into the semester. I decided to wait at the front of the class for the teacher to appear. The name on my schedule read *Ms. Spaltor.*

I gazed across the classroom and tried to ignore the dirty looks and snickers of the contemptuous student body that sat before me.

It was hard, though, because all eyes were turned toward me. The desks were shaped like boomerangs and a student sat at either end. 3-D holograms of various parts of the human body were suspended in midair against the walls. A large, illuminated white screen hung at the front of the classroom with a smooth metallic desk and chair in front of it.

The school bell rang and the class quieted down. I tried to think of something to occupy my mind while I waited, but I couldn't, so I settled for staring at my feet.

With a bang the classroom door flew shut. A young lady scurried by me and plopped her bag and jacket onto the desk. I gathered she was Ms. Spaltor. I thought she looked young—too young to be a teacher—but there was something in her demeanor that exuded a certain maturity which made me think her youthful appearance belied her age. Her hair was done up in a neat chignon and she was dressed in a gray tweed suit with shiny black pumps.

"*Chapter four. Load*," she said in a smooth yet stern voice.

Holograms appeared in front of each student and materialized on the white screen at the front of the classroom. Ms. Spaltor pulled a small stencil from her bag and started to introduce the chapter—oblivious to my presence.

"Today we are going to go over the complete genome of the human spinal cord. I expect you to have reviewed—"

"Excuse me." It was better that I interrupt sooner rather than later.

She stopped and glared in my direction and my cheeks started to redden. She was silent so I continued. "I'm new to the class and—"

"Sit down."

I was momentarily taken aback. "But I—"

She cut me off. "Sit. Now," she snapped, as if I was a dog to whom she was giving a command.

I bit the inside of my cheek, irked by the order, but decided to hold my tongue and looked for an empty spot. The single vacant seat was at the back of the class and I hurried toward it. Without missing a beat Ms. Spaltor carried on.

Working up enough nerve to survey the students around me, I noticed that not a single head was turned in my direction—everyone was playing close attention to our teacher and the images she was introducing—with the exception of one. The girl sitting across my table was looking straight at me and was smiling.

"Hi," she mouthed, waving.

I was more taken aback with this reaction than I was with Ms. Spaltor's. I was so dumbfounded that I didn't know how to respond. The girl timidly pressed her lips together and started to turn away after I failed to reciprocate her friendliness.

"Hi," I quickly mouthed back.

She smiled brightly before swiveling around to face our teacher.

She had straight, black hair that fell past her shoulders, and she was delicate and fine boned with big, black eyes. She had an exotic look with luminescent white skin and small, thin lips. I recognized the designer emblems on her clothes and bag. It appeared that some fashion houses had stood the test of time.

Students began to dissect the holograms in front of them using the same small stencil Ms. Spaltor had pulled out of her bag earlier.

I looked around the desk for one I could use. I didn't have to search long before one came rolling toward me from the opposite side of the table. My friendly neighbor was smiling at me again and gestured for me to pick the tool up.

"Thanks," I whispered.

The holographic image immediately came apart as I held up the thin metal stick. I spent the rest of the class trying to listen to Ms. Spaltor's in-depth analysis of the human spinal cord, but mostly I played around with the device, getting a feel for the mechanism and figuring out how to use it.

At one point I heard a small giggle and looked over to find my partner laughing at me. She waited for Ms. Spaltor to turn her back before demonstrating one of the functions of the tiny tool. Following her instructions, I managed to open a separate file and dissect a few vertebrae.

The bell rang, the holograms disappeared and students automatically started to file out.

"Hi! I'm Sue," she said walking around our desk. "My friends call me Boe, though. You can keep that." She pointed to the tool I held, which I had intended to return.

"Thanks. I'm Athena. I'm new."

Boe grinned. "I can tell. What other classes do you have?" she inquired.

"I have physical education second period and then math. After lunch I have history and then communications last period."

Boe clapped her hands together. "Oh, good! We have history together. You can have lunch at our table if you like. We eat at the northeast corner of the hall."

I was grateful to have found anything akin to a friend.

"Okay, sure. I'll see you then."

I wasn't very social and people often misunderstood my aloofness as haughtiness. What's more, for some reason the natural composition of my features resembled a frown and I always looked broody unless I consciously changed my expression. Boe didn't seem to mind or notice. She waved back at me as she headed out of the classroom.

"See you then."

I may have lucked out and gotten out of gym class because I was called to the main office to fill out registration and other miscellaneous forms, but sitting in math class, I was anything but lucky. I hated to admit it, but Pork Chop was right. Math was a disaster. For all I knew, Mr. Mulbrach was speaking in an obscure Native American dialect. Everything flew over my head—in one ear and out the other. I tried to follow along, but the equations were too complex. I thanked god that we did our work on flat screens instead of on suspended holograms like in biology; I couldn't fake comprehension if my equations, which looked like a children's scrapbook filled with random symbols, were floating in the air for all to see. What made it worse was that the person sitting beside me failed to acknowledge my existence.

My head was pounding and the migraine I developed in math showed no signs of retreating as I shifted along with a crowd of students eager to get lunch. I just wanted this day to end.

I heard the buzz that emanated from the lunch hall from two

floors away. As I got closer, the noise from all the chatter of students catching up on the daily gossip became almost deafening. I shuddered as I thought of how my name might be thrown mercilessly into conversation.

Once through the commanding archway, I realized that the students alone didn't cause the commotion. The vast lunch hall was filled with zooming gadgets flying in every direction. I could barely see the ceiling through the dense mass. Small gizmos were carrying trays of food and placing them in front of the students, who were seated at metallic benches that lined the room meticulously.

There weren't any stations to purchase food and I gave my tummy a little rub as it let out a mild growl. I was hungry and I hadn't brought a lunch with me. Standing idly in the doorway was making me nervous so I quickly looked around for Boe. She was at the northeast corner of the hall, just where she had said she would be, and I started to pick my way through the crowd. Boe saw me approaching and waved to me.

Every seat at the table was filled except the empty seat beside her.

"Everyone, this is Athena," Boe said cheerily.

I hadn't expected them to welcome me with open arms, but I was affronted at how maliciously they eyed me. Looks of pure venom. I slid into the seat next to Boe. She seemed unaware of her companions' hostility as she made introductions.

Devonne was an ebony-skinned girl whose unfriendly expression contrasted with the graceful features of her face. Beside her was Tia, a striking looking girl with a creamy mocha complexion, across from whom sat Richard and Forbes. Richard looked like your typical prepster, with short, wavy blond hair and ocean-blue eyes to match his sun-kissed tan. Forbes looked European, with dark eyes and slick black hair that was neatly gelled.

"Let me think, what do I want today?" Boe asked herself. The table was eerily quiet. *"Arugula salad with chicken. Sparkling water. Lunch. Load."*

There were a few mumbles of disdain before similar lunch orders were given. "What are you having?" Boe asked me, ignoring the sour faces that surrounded us.

"I'm not sure yet. I'm not really that hungry. I had a large breakfast." It seemed my stomach had been waiting for me to denounce my hunger before releasing a growl so loud that I'm sure the entire hall heard.

Boe looked at me thoughtfully.

"You should try the chicken salad. You'll like it. It's very good. *Chicken salad. Lunch. Load."*

"I'm sure I will. Thanks."

Just then a floating tray lowered Boe's salad and drink in front of her before folding up and zooming off. My chicken salad arrived in a similar fashion a moment later.

I thought Boe was making an effort to lighten the mood because she continuously chattered about the weather, the crowded unloading dock and her previous classes, including her dissections in biology. When she looked to me for confirmation regarding the latter all I could manage was a resigned nod.

It didn't take a social scientist to figure out that I was seriously unwanted at the table, so I finished my chicken salad quickly and tried to excuse myself.

"I think I would like to explore the school a bit more before my next class." I directed this at Boe. I was sure everyone else was elated about my early departure.

"Wait. We have history next. We can walk to class together. I can show you around," she offered.

Devonne and Tia looked incredulously at one another before turning their acid gaze on me.

"Okay," I said hesitantly.

Boe had barely touched her lunch.

"See you guys later," she said in an artificially cheery tone—her voice notching up an octave.

The buzz of students chattering dimmed as we left the hall, and I tried to relax.

"I'm sorry about the others," Boe said quietly.

"Don't worry, I'm used to it. I don't make friends easily." I didn't want her feeling sorry for me. There wasn't reason to, anyway; I didn't care what those shallow people thought.

I stiffened as Boe reached out and gently wrapped her arm around mine. I was about to protest, thinking her gesture was meant to offer me comfort I didn't need, when she whispered, "Neither do I."

Boe suggested the conservatory as our first destination and led me down never-ending hallways as we made our way through the building.

"Are you from London?" Boe asked.

"Uh, sort of. I spent some time here as a kid, but I actually grew up in Canada. I just recently made London my permanent residence with my father and sister."

I didn't like talking about myself, so when we reached two large doors that read *Dresden Conservatory* I took the opportunity to change the subject. "Why did you pick the conservatory to show me first?"

"I love plants," Boe replied off-handedly. "They remind me of my mum...She loved to garden."

It didn't escape my notice that Boe used the past tense when she referred to her mother. I bit my lip, understanding that she was dead.

"I like to garden, too," I said awkwardly.

Boe gave me a small smile as we walked inside.

The conservatory was massive and bright; rays of light poured in from the glass ceiling. I was amazed at the plant breeds that I encountered; some I had never seen, studied or heard of before.

I took a whiff of a plant that smelled like rotten eggs and wrinkled my nose. "Man, that stinks."

Boe looked at me with a peculiar expression on her face.

"What is it?" I asked warily.

"I'm sorry. I'm being rude. It's just you're so..." She trailed off, trying to think of the right word.

"Odd," I suggested.

"No! Refreshing. You're so curious about everything."

I grinned at her. "It's okay, my sister constantly reminds me that I'm a bit of a loser."

"You're not a loser! I like you which means you couldn't *possibly* be."

"Thanks," I offered, touched by her sincerity. "I just want to say that I'm definitely grateful for your company. I have the feeling it's going to be tough getting to know anyone around here."

"You're telling me," she said despondently.

"What? It seems like you have plenty of friends—"

Boe cut me off. "Those aren't my friends! It's hard to explain, but those people are the most superficial, self-absorbed snobs you can imagine. I hang out with them to keep up appearances and because our families associate in the same social circles. But that's it. They can't appreciate anyone or anything that's different. I take myself to be an excellent judge of character and I knew the instant I saw you that you weren't like those plastic dolls you met today. And besides, you're funny. I like you." Her voice was casual, as if she was stating obvious facts.

I was quiet at her outburst.

Boe smiled uneasily. "Sorry about that. Sometimes I have this need to vent."

I nodded my head. "I get it."

"I'm glad we have class together," she said in a merry voice—one that I was getting accustomed to. I guess everyone had their own way of composing themselves to ease uncomfortable situations.

"Science isn't exactly my forte, Boe. I hope I don't drag you down for our labs."

She laughed. "Athena, that's not *possible.* If you're concerned about your mark, don't be. I'll make sure you ace biology."

"I appreciate the vote of confidence, but I don't think that's going to happen."

"Yes, it will."

I puckered my forehead and stared at my ethereal friend. "Because I'm going to study really hard and do all my homework?"

Boe waved her hands. "If you want to."

I understood her innuendo, unsure of how she could do it, but it wasn't something I desired.

"No, I have to do that because it's the only way I would want to ace biology."

She scoffed. "It's up to you, but just know that I've got your back."

"I'll keep it in mind."

"I meant to ask"—Boe held up a rose hybrid for me to smell—"do you happen to know my brother?"

I shook my head, certain that it wasn't possible. "I don't believe so."

"Are you sure?"

"I'm pretty positive, Boe." I would have bet my life on the fact considering I just traveled two hundred years into the future.

"But he was looking at you so strangely today. I could have sworn he knew you."

"Today? I'm sorry, I don't remember you introducing him at lunch."

"He wasn't at lunch. My brother doesn't go to the College."

A crease developed on my forehead. "But you said when he saw me today."

"Yeah, for some reason he drove by the unloading dock this morning and I spotted him staring at you."

Then I remembered the dark eyes.

"Staring at me?" I said unevenly, feeling the rise of color in my cheeks.

"It was really weird." Boe frowned.

"What does he look like?" I asked, doing my best to sound relaxed.

"He doesn't really look like me, but he has the same skin tone and black hair." Boe sighed. "Forget it. I'll ask him about it later. He was probably looking at something else and you just happened to be around."

"I'm sure that's it," I insisted.

"Maybe his name will ring a bell. It's Blake Dresden."

My pulse quickened; I realized why Boe had taken me to the conservatory—the *Dresden* Conservatory—but that wasn't the only reason I felt uneasy and I couldn't explain why that was.

"Sorry." I let out a cough. "Don't know him."

We took our seats in history class just as the bell rang. Our teacher, Mr. McGradie, a young-looking man with wavy, brown hair, dressed in a blue jumper and pressed black pants, was already seated at his desk when we arrived.

"Nuclear War. Today we are going to discuss the repercussions and developments stemming forth from the threat and real possibility of nuclear war."

Text pages appeared on our flat screens as Mr. McGradie stood and walked around his desk. "I asked you to review this section for today's class. Any volunteers?"

A single hand shot up. It belonged to a girl who wore her curly hair in a neat ponytail tied with a red ribbon. She sat in the first row.

"Ah, Eleanor Mattimore. Statement, please."

The girl immediately rose from her desk and faced the class to recite what can only be described as a definition of the words "nuclear" and "war" fused together. Her mechanical answer showed her reading of the text but didn't demonstrate any range of analytical understanding of the issues. She sat down looking thoroughly pleased with herself.

Mr. McGradie rubbed the bridge of his nose and took a breath. "Something a bit more original, perhaps."

I couldn't see Eleanor's face, but I think everyone noticed her back visibly stiffen. No one else volunteered an answer so Mr. McGradie chose at random.

"Jeremy Lefton. Statement."

The boy two rows in front of me, who had been playing with his fedora on his desk, let out a whistle as he stood. Mr. McGradie crossed his arms to let Jeremy know he wasn't in the mood for his antics today. I guessed that he was the troublemaker of the class.

"All right, all right," Jeremy cooed. "Here's my statement: war is and always has been a *necessity* to mankind." He continued in the same arrogant monotone throughout his entire speech and I was sure my eyes would find themselves permanently fixed in a cross-eyed position from the frequency of rolling them.

"Athena Ellias. Statement."

My eyes grew wide at the declaration of Mr. McGradie's next victim. I wasn't sure I had heard correctly, but when, for the third time that day, I found all eyes resting on me, I rose hastily.

"Statement. Now, please," Mr. McGradie repeated.

I racked my brain. I didn't know what kind of definition he

was looking for. I didn't know what was considered "correct." For some reason all that came to my mind was Hemingway's *Notes on the Next War.*

"'They wrote in the old days that it is sweet and fitting to die for one's country. But in modern war there is nothing sweet nor fitting in your dying. You will die a dog for no good reason.'" It was the answer of an art student—obscure and a long shot.

I sat down slowly to make sure that I didn't miss my seat and fall clumsily to the ground. I was expecting a few snickers so I was a shocked when I heard none. The class was so silent I thought I would have been able to hear a pin drop. Everyone was turned in their seats, staring at me. I raised my eyebrow inquisitively at our teacher, who eyed me fixedly from the front of the classroom.

"Aisha Santos. Statement." Mr. McGradie's voice seemed to bring everyone back to their senses. They shifted around and turned their attention to the girl who sat behind Eleanor.

I let out a quiet breath and looked over at Boe. She was smiling and gave me a thumbs-up. I shrugged my shoulders and smiled back.

Boe and I parted ways after history and I told her I would meet her out front after my communications class.

If math had been a disaster, communications was a tsunami. Not only did communications entail the study of various languages, including three dialects of Chinese, which everyone seemed to have mastered, but also memorizing and then communicating coded sequences. Urgh! Pork Chop was right *again.* I stared down at my screen, the images in front of me were nothing more than a blur, and one desolate thought echoed in my mind: *I'm doomed.*

¤ IV ¤

A MILLION DOLLARS & HORSES

I met up with Boe in the grand foyer after the final bell. Students were rushing out and we found ourselves crammed in the entryway.

She raised her voice so I could hear. "Do you drive?"

"No. My sister dropped me off. She's picking me up a little later. I'll probably just stay in the library and study."

"What time is she coming?" she asked.

"Six," I replied.

She furled her thin eyebrow. "Why don't you come hang with

me? I can drop you back here before six." I hesitated. "Come on. It'll be fun. I'm meeting my guy a little after five. I'd like you to meet him."

I assumed she meant *boyfriend* but I didn't ask for clarification. What the heck.

"Sure."

We walked around the unloading dock and stood near the edge. I could already feel my knees buckling.

"What's wrong? You look a little pale."

I waved my hand. "It's nothing. I just have a small fear of heights."

She gave me a quizzical look before turning away.

"*Getty. Load,*" she said smoothly.

"What's Getty?" I asked.

"My car," Boe replied with a playful grin.

I rolled my eyes at the fact that Boe referred to her car by name.

I heard the sound of an engine roaring as a sleek red car pulled up in front of us. If Pork Chop's car was impressive, the vehicle that stood before me was obscene.

"Get in," Boe offered as the doors slid open.

I walked toward the passenger seat and gingerly sat down.

"Is there anywhere you would prefer to go?" she asked.

"I'm really new to town so I'll let you decide."

"I'll take you to the Boardwalk. It's a fun place to hang out."

We flew around town for about ten minutes before we stopped on a wide landing that lay beside a long cobblestone boardwalk that stretched on endlessly. What's more, it's entire length rested on top of glass buildings.

The vibrant area was filled with various shops and vendors. 3-D holograms drifted about, small gadgets whizzed around and a light fog hovered at the edges of the walk. It really felt quite fantastical. It was silly, but I wouldn't have been surprised to see a famous boy wizard fly around the corner at any minute with his mechanical broomstick and wand.

One of the vendor's signs that read *Popping Candy Apples* caught my attention. That was something I definitely wanted to try so I ventured over. I had left my bag in Boe's car but had the tiny chip Sammy had given me. He had explained in the elevator that if I needed anything I could use it. It was sort of like a miniature credit card—paper money wasn't used anymore.

"I've never had a popping candy apple before," I said excitedly.

Boe looked at me in surprise. "Really?"

I nodded earnestly as we walked up to the stout vendor who had a thick, bristly mustache. I asked him the price for one apple.

"Half a mill," he grunted.

I wasn't sure what that meant, but I was certain that Sammy would have given me enough to afford a measly candy apple.

"Two please." I handed the chip over to him, hoping he knew what to do with it. The man threw it into a small, black machine. The chip shot out and he handed it to me.

"Thanks," Boe managed, in between bites.

"Don't mention it."

"But you know, Hot Spot, the booth we passed, makes them

double the size and half the price. I think they're only about a quarter of a million there and they taste way better."

I gagged and Boe looked at me worriedly. I waved my hand to reassure her that I was fine as I coughed out a small candy shard.

"I just choked. I'm fine."

She nodded in understanding and turned to focus on devouring the sweet.

My eyes grew wide as I digested what she had said. *Quarter of a million.* That was one freaking expensive candy apple. Then again, if I took inflation into account, it would make sense that a million dollars wasn't worth as much as it had been, but it still baffled me.

Boe pointed to a vacant bench as we reached a quiet area of the Boardwalk and she took a seat.

"Hey, Sue. I see you're with your new *friend*."

I was licking my fingers when the male voice startled me. I looked up to see a tall, handsome young man walking toward us. He was dressed in a well-fitted white jacket and black pants. His eyes were a vivid green and were accented by the sandy, light brown hair that fell into them. Two guys and a pair of girls accompanied him. I only recognized one of them; Boe had introduced me to Richard at lunch. The girl who had her arm wrapped around him had a crown of beautiful, curly blond hair that ran past her shoulders, and a milky-white complexion. Beside her stood a girl with long, black hair, almost as long as mine but not quite, and dark, almond-shaped eyes. She clung desperately to the other male, who bore similar traits. They were all exquisitely attractive.

"Actually, we were just leaving," Boe said curtly, standing with a worried expression.

I got up, too, sensing the anxiousness in her voice.

"Don't leave on account of us. Your mother would be so disappointed to see her only daughter forgetting her manners. Where's our introduction, Sue?" the green-eyed man asked in a grim voice.

Boe clenched her jaw and narrowed her eyes. I'm not sure if the play of light that danced around her face made my mind play tricks on me, but Boe looked absolutely terrifying.

"Back off, Charlie," she said in a threatening tone.

The young man, apparently named Charlie, pressed harder.

"Sue, stop being a stick in the mud. Why don't you let your friend decide?" Turning his gaze on me, he showered me with a breathtaking smile. "I'm Charles Astor. It is a *pleasure* to make your acquaintance."

I eyed him carefully. There was something about Charlie Astor, besides the fact that Boe obviously disliked him, that rubbed me the wrong way. I acknowledged his introduction with a slight nod.

He exaggeratedly took a step back and slapped a hand across his chest. He spoke directly to Boe. "I'm amazed at the company you keep, Sue. She's obviously not only a *runt* but a *mute*, for god's sake."

The group behind him laughed and my temper flared. It is always in the most dramatic moments of my life that all my words seem to desert me. What I often end up doing is quoting the words of others. I can't explain why some writers' words emerge more predominantly than others or why I don't bother thinking about what I'm going to say before I say it.

Stepping firmly between Boe and Charlie, I thought of Cowper's *The Task*.

"'I would not enter on my list of friends, though grac'd with polished manners and fine sense…the man who needlessly sets foot upon a worm.'" I pointed my finger at Charlie's fine-looking face, trying to buy some time to figure out how my eloquent yet nonsensical quote had any relevance to the situation.

"I may be a worm,"—*Dear god, I was an utter idiot and had just called myself a worm*—"but the point is that you should be ashamed of yourself for picking on people to make yourself feel better."

Mental cringe. Mental cringe. I sounded like a forty-year old teacher scolding a naughty second-grader.

Charlie held his palms up in mock submission and let out a snort of a laugh.

"You got the worm part right. Sue, where did you find this one? She's feisty."

I shot him a furious glare but clamped my mouth shut. If I kept talking I was never going to get out of the hole I had just dug for myself. Charlie shoved past me and attempted to throw his arm around Boe's shoulder, but she averted him with an astounding quickness.

"Come on, ditch her, Sue! Let's go riding. Charlie has a new steed. You used to love horses," Richard called out.

"Richie's right. I rode it here. Say the word and I'll load."

Boe shook her head. "Not interested, Charlie. I have to take Athena back."

Charlie glided around Boe as she came up beside me.

"*Athena*, is it?"

I gave a slight shudder as he purred my name.

He smiled slyly, eyeing me over his shoulder. "She can come, too, if she likes. She can ride with Jasmine."

"Get real, Charlie. I'm not riding with her," the dark-haired girl shouted out defiantly.

"Fine. Richie can ride with you. Sue's little friend can ride on her own." Charlie winked at Richard. "Hey, what do you say? You think you could manage some riding?" he asked me snidely. "Come on, Sue. I'm sure your friend has never ridden before and there's a first time for everything," he sang.

"As a matter of fact Mr. Astor I have ridden horses all of my life," I declared with defensive pride. "I would be more than happy to go for a ride if not for the distaste I have acquired for the accompanying riders. With the exception of Boe, of course."

Charlie twirled to face his pack of brutish friends. "Oh, oh, *excuse me*. It seems we have a prorider in our midst." As Charlie pivoted back around to face me the laughter of the others came to a sudden halt. As if confronted with some kind of apparition, he froze and a look of concern replaced his mocking grin. Standing beside Boe was a very tall, well-built young man with the most captivating hazy gray eyes. It was as if he had come out of nowhere—his presence gave even me a start. Boe, however, didn't seem surprised.

"Is there a problem here?" His voice was husky and rough.

Charlie crossed his arms as his gang flanked him.

Boe rested her hand gently on the young man's arm. "They were just leaving, RJ."

"There you go again, forgetting your manners. Sue's friend here just offered us a demonstration of her superior riding skills," Charlie said contemptuously. "*Sith. Load,*" he commanded.

"I'm warning you, leave her alone, Astor. She can't handle it and you know it."

I knew that Boe was trying to protect me but my pride could only take so much.

Charlie shot me a quick glance before he pressed on. "Are you calling your *friend* a liar? Tsk-tsk. It's obvious she's never ridden a day in her life. It's just *deplorable* that she had to conjure up some ridiculous lie to hide her evident inferiority."

That was it.

"Do not speak of me as if I'm not present! Look, you miserable excuse for a—" My mother put hot peppers in Pork Chop's mouth when she was twelve as punishment for using profanity, thus I have never been inclined to use the really bad swear words. It was pathetic how I was such a Goody Two-shoes. I didn't mean to be, but it was something ingrained in me from my upbringing. Damn parents.

"What, runt?" Charlie snapped.

"You—vomitous—poohead,"—I truly pitied my articulation—

"I don't have to justify anything to you; I said I can ride and I can."

Charlie forcefully grabbed my arm before I could turn away.

"Prove it," he sneered, holding me so tight he was bruising flesh.

The next thing I heard was the growl of an engine. Emerging through the fog, over the edge of the boardwalk, was the most daunting motorcycle I had ever seen. There was a distorted horse's head molded over the front of the bike and the wheels were encircled in a bright blue incandescent ring that appeared to be spinning. The front handlebars were covered in intricate switches and buttons, and a vast array of gears were visible through a layer of clear glass that wrapped around the side of the bike.

Before I realized what was happening, Boe stood between Charlie and me, and my arm was set free.

"We're leaving," she declared.

Charlie looked at me. "*Liar*," he rasped.

"Stop it, Astor. I don't care if she can't ride. It's sad that you get off on intimidating those who you think are lesser than you. Reality check, you're a deadbeat." Boe's voice was grinding as she spoke through clenched teeth.

Jasmine took a step forward. "Watch your mouth," she warned. Richard and the other two promptly started to encircle us. Neither Boe nor RJ seemed bothered. I, on the other hand, was on the brink of hyperventilation.

"Look, I'll ride the stupid thing," I interjected nervously.

It couldn't be that difficult. Pedal meant *go* and handle meant *break*, right? Or was it the other way around?

"Athena, you don't have to do this. It's okay," Boe offered

sympathetically.

I shook my head in disagreement and started walking toward the bike.

"Yes, I do. No one calls me a liar. Besides, it can't be that hard…" I trailed off as I stood at arm's length from the intimidating vehicle.

Boe grabbed my shoulder. "No, you're not doing this," she said firmly.

I shook her hand off. "I'll be fine."

I quickly climbed onto the bike, as Charlie looked on, determined to prove myself. I would ride around in a circle and loop back. No big deal.

The bike hummed beneath me.

Boe grabbed my forearm. "Athena, get off!"

I tried to break her hold on my arm but her grip, like Charlie's, was solid.

"RJ, tell her how dangerous it is." Boe turned to the gray-eyed young man at her side. He looked at Boe and then curiously at me. Before he got a chance to say anything, Charlie grabbed Boe and yanked her away.

"Runts gotta learn the hard way."

The situation escalated in the blink of an eye. RJ pounced on Charlie. Charlie held Boe. Richard and the others smothered the three of them. Then I heard Charlie's voice sear through the air.

"Manual. Racer. Load."

And they disappeared behind me.

¤ V ¤

B L A K E   L A N D I N G

I was holding on for dear life and I couldn't see a thing. The bike took off so fast I wasn't able to securely position my legs. My hair was blowing in my face; I tried to spit out a mouthful. Everything was shrouded in a haze and I couldn't tell what direction I was traveling in.

Suddenly, I broke through the fog and found myself looking down at an expansive cityscape. Trembling, I desperately tried to grasp the bike's rigid body. I had almost managed to reposition myself when an unexpected turn threw me forcefully to the side. I tried to use the momentum to swing myself back up onto the seat but another rapid swerve unbalanced me. I had only one hand gripping the handlebars and I knew I couldn't hold on for much longer. The bike took a sharp turn and my hand slipped free.

In the briefest of brief moments the words of Dylan Thomas filled my mind: *"Rage, rage against the dying of the light."*

It didn't seem likely, however, that my rage was going to stop the light from dying, let alone stop me from so doing. I started to flap my arms and legs crazily, before I was swooped up and firmly planted back on the seat of the bike.

At first I wasn't sure what was happening. My mind and my body were momentarily two distinct entities. They seemed to fuse together when I registered the solid form molded against my back. Two soft yet firm hands took hold of my own and folded them over the bike's handlebars. I didn't think my breathing could come any more rapidly, but I reached a new level of hyperventilation as I felt a face bury itself close to my ear. A waft of warm air tickled the back of my neck before I heard the voice.

"oC, load her."

That voice. It was male, melodic and cool, not quite American, not quite British and one I recognized, even though it wasn't as strained as the first time I had heard it—on London Bridge.

He lightly pressed my fingers against the handlebars, indicating that I should hold them tighter. "You can register commands now."

The softest skin brushed against my face and I shivered, knowing I had felt it before.

He abruptly lifted his hands away and I sensed his legs loosen around the bike.

"I don't know how to do that!" I said, panicking. I wasn't sure I would be able to get back to the Boardwalk without his assistance.

I tried to turn my head to catch a glimpse of the stranger behind me but I didn't get a chance. He pulled his face close to mine again and wrapped his hands around my waist. I gulped and felt heat rising in my cheeks. My heart was beating so fast I thought if I didn't fall to my death I was going to die from cardiac arrest. Sliding his hands from my waist, he boldly pressed my thighs into the bike, making me light-headed.

"*Automatic. Load,*" he ordered.

The bike fastened onto my legs and my seat deepened. Startled by the movement, I reflexively let go of the handlebars. His hands shot up and placed them firmly back on. I felt him breathe out against my neck, as if in frustration. I angled my head wider this time, again trying to catch a glimpse of the rider behind me, but I only caught his lips as they brushed against my cheek. "*Primary Station. Return. Load.*"

As quickly as he appeared, he disappeared. The weight against my back vanished and it was replaced by an airy lightness. The bike wheeled around and, at a much slower pace, started to head back into the fog. The city vanished below me and soon I couldn't make out anything more than a foot in front of my face. But I wasn't paying much attention to where I was going, anyway. There was only one thing I could think: *who was he?*

My body felt numb and my brain was trying to sort out too many things at once, which is probably why it took me a few moments to realize the bike had stopped and was parked in front of the now deserted Boardwalk. My knees gave way as my feet hit the cobblestone and I had to hold the curb for support. I looked around anxiously.

What happened? Where were Boe and RJ?

I didn't have to wait long for an answer. I soon heard the familiar rumble of an engine—I was beginning to develop a serious aversion to that sound.

Boe's red car materialized out of the fog and she stuck her head out the window. "Are you okay?"

I nodded reassuringly. "I'm fine. Don't worry about me. What happened? Are you okay? Where's RJ?"

She blew out an exasperated breath and puckered her forehead. "Don't ask."

I heard the clapping and the sound of multiple engines before Charlie, Richard, Jasmine and the other two, whose names I didn't know, appeared behind Boe. Charlie was the one applauding as he stood atop the seat of Richard's bike, which closely resembled the one that had just nearly got me killed.

"See, Sue. No harm done."

In a flash, Charlie jumped from the back of Richard's bike onto his own. I stared at him for a moment as he murmured a command and easily maneuvered the bike around.

Had my eyes been playing tricks on me? Not only did Charlie seem to move at a fast-forward pace but he was also able to *suspend* himself in the air to reposition his feet before he landed. Dumbfounded, all I could do was blink until I noticed that Charlie was staring at me.

"Feisty." He grinned smugly.

My first instinct was to stick my tongue out at him, but I decided to take the high road and shot him a contemptuous look instead.

Richard and the others took off as Charlie turned his bike away.

"Always fun to play with runts. See you around, Sue!" he called out, as he followed his friends.

Boe narrowed her gaze as she watched them take off. I heard her murmur something but couldn't quite make out what she said. I glanced at my watch. It was a quarter past six. Pork Chop was not going to be pleased; she hated waiting.

"I have to follow them to make sure that RJ doesn't cause any trouble."

Boe looked agitated and it worried me.

"I understand. I'll wait here for you to get back."

She turned her head away from me and cocked it slightly, as if she was listening for something. "Urgh! Too late. He's already causing trouble." She shook her head in frustration.

"I'm sorry, Boe. Don't worry about me, I'll get back to the College on my own."

I felt guilty. It was all sort of my fault. Even though I had no idea where I was or how I would manage to get back to the College, I didn't want to impose on Boe. She obviously had other things on her mind as a direct result of my stupidity.

"No, Blake can take you." Boe looked past my shoulder to something behind me.

The fog had spread and covered the Boardwalk in a dense blanket. Squinting, I followed her line of sight and spotted the *someone* she was looking at. I instantly knew it was him.

Leaning against a streetlight, beside the bench Boe and I had sat upon earlier, he was staring fixedly in my direction. His presence seemed to consume the air around me for I found it difficult to breathe—and I needed to breathe because I wasn't sure my heart could sustain the rapid pumping without oxygen much longer.

He pushed off the pole and walked toward me. He was lean and his body moved with graceful precision. Although he wasn't overly muscular I knew his supple build belied a strong body and my heartbeat quickened as I remembered the way he had touched me on Charlie's bike.

I had seen my fair share of handsome faces that day, but the one that held my gaze did not have the kind of handsomeness you often encounter. Dark hair loosely framed his face and his features seemed to have been perfectly chiseled from a rare piece of the finest marble. He wore a pair of commanding boots and was dressed in dark jeans and a black jacket.

He stopped a short distance away from me. My eyes swam across his face before they landed on his penetrating deep eyes. Then it hit me. Blood drained from my cheeks as I felt a bond— corporeal and irrational—chaining me to the dark stranger.

"Athena, this is my brother Blake. Blake, this is Athena. Can you take her back to the College? I know if you go after RJ you're bound to cause more harm than good."

I was still staring at him. You would think I would look away, if not for the blushing then from common decency, but it was as if I was having some kind of out-of-body experience and had absolutely no control over my mental faculties. Blake remained tensely silent. His eyes hadn't left my face.

"Blake, come on," I heard Boe plead, followed by a muffled noise behind me. "Damn it! He's determined to pick a fight."

The word *fight* broke me out of my zombielike state but I still didn't turn toward Boe, even when I sensed the movement of her car behind me.

"Athena, I'll see you tomorrow in class all right? Blake, you're taking her," she said adamantly.

I felt a stream of air against my back and I knew she was gone, which meant only one thing—I was *alone* with *him*. And I was terrified. The high pitch of my panicked voice was deafening inside my head. *"Boe, come back! Don't leave me!"* I didn't know what to do. I wanted to look away. I wanted to speak. I wanted to move. I wanted to breathe, but I didn't. I couldn't.

"Can we go now?" My question was practically a whimper and I winced at how my nervousness came ringing through my voice.

Blake narrowed his eyes for a moment before walking silently to the edge of the Boardwalk.

"Let's go, oC."

I furrowed my brow, puzzled as to who or what *oC* was. I had heard him use the term earlier as well. There was no one around, though, and it seemed like he was talking to himself.

With astounding speed, a black vehicle, resembling something I was sure the military used, appeared in front of Blake. Maybe oC was his car? In the time it took me to take two steps, Blake had managed to seat himself in the driver's seat and swivel the car around so that the open passenger door faced me.

He stared impassively across the dashboard as I hesitantly approached the vehicle. If not for the spots of white I noticed splayed across his knuckles, you would have thought he didn't care whether I entered or stood immobile on the Boardwalk indefinitely. My tension stemmed from anxiety, fear and nerves among other things, so I doubted we suffered a similar affliction. I wagered the strain Blake showed was due more to irritation.

Without looking at him, I lowered myself into the passenger seat. As soon as my bum hit the soft leather, my door slid shut and we jetted forward.

I knew we were going fast as the city zoomed by. This only caused my tension to mount. I sat stiffly in my seat with my hands clutched tightly in my lap. It took a while for me to notice the quiet. The car's engine was barely audible. I scanned the interior cautiously and thought my first estimation of the car had been dead-on because it was like I was sitting in a cockpit; the car seemed armed for battle. We made a sharp turn but I hardly moved an inch in my seat and I gathered this was truly a "high-performance" kind of car.

Although I was sure any attempt at conversation would increase the level of awkwardness I felt, there was something nagging at me that I had to get out.

"I want to thank you for helping me earlier on Charlie's bike."

I stopped abruptly and held my breath waiting for his reply. Silence answered. "I hope Boe finds RJ and everything turns out all right," I continued. " I didn't mean to cause so much trouble. It's really all my fault."

"Yes, it is."

I froze—doubly stunned—stunned that he had answered me at all and stunned at the answer he had given.

"Well, yes. I mean it was my fault to a certain degree, but I was just standing up for myself," I replied, a little more assuredly.

"By lying," he shot back coolly.

"I did not lie," I declared with vehemence.

"Your ability speaks otherwise." He spoke without the slightest change in his demeanor, remaining unfazed even though my voice had started to rise.

"I said I've ridden horses all my life and I have. It's not my fault if they inferred—incorrectly, might I add—that I meant bikes or motorcycles or whatever they're called. I meant horses as in the animal; the living, breathing kind." My temper gave me nerve so I turned to look at Blake and instinctively backed an inch into my seat. He was glaring at me with a curious look on his face, similar to the one RJ had worn before I sped off on Charlie's bike.

"Anyone would assume that they were referring to jet-racers," he said, turning his eyes back to the road.

"Assume makes an ass out of *u* and *me*," I quipped, followed by a severe mental cringe. I sounded like a five-year-old. Couldn't I come up with something better?

"No, just out of you."

My mouth dropped open as I stared at him indignantly.

"I'm not even going to dignify that with a response. The fact is that I didn't lie. And I'm sure Boe meant well, but there are times in life when you have to stand up for yourself and—"

"Prove that you *cannot* in fact ride a jet-racer," he interjected.

"I did manage to, didn't I?"

He shot me a sideways glance. I raised my eyebrows and lifted my chin, daring him to say otherwise. Even though I had admittedly needed some assistance, I still *technically* rode the damn thing. Vas always said that I would make a good lawyer; winning or losing a case all came down to the technicalities.

"I suppose you did ride it, but at a price," he said briskly.

It took me a moment to register that he wasn't referring to his rescue but rather to the confrontation between Boe and Charlie. He had me there. A wave of guilt washed over me. I shouldn't have let things escalate the way they did. I should have just kept my mouth shut.

"'Against a foe I can myself defend, but Heaven protect me from a blundering friend,'" I mumbled to myself, recalling how upset Boe was when she went after RJ.

The buildings we passed started to look familiar and in no time at all I found myself shadowed by the towering entrance of the prestigious school. My door slid open and I climbed out.

"Thompson was a biomathematician and I doubt he had many friends for reference. Boe could do far worse than a blundering friend like you. It was D'Arcy Thompson you were quoting, yes?"

I blinked several times before slowly turning to face him. He cocked his head and raised an eyebrow, letting me know he was graciously waiting for my response.

"Uh-huh." I nodded, silently reveling at his etherealness. Shadows contoured his features and the chiaroscuro effect evoked a hauntingly beautiful face. Da Vinci himself would have been honored to render his likeness on canvas. Then I became all too aware that he was also looking at me. My cheeks warmed as I thought of what Blake's assessment of my features would be. My self-esteem had taken a beating all day and my insecurities paralyzed me.

"Athena."

He said my name. It was ridiculous but I can't describe the feeling that poured over me as my name escaped his lips.

"Yes?" I squeaked. I held my breath as he leaned toward me and opened his mouth to speak but, before he could, the blast of a loud horn startled me and I fell against the still-open passenger door.

"I believe your ride is here," Blake said calmly.

"Gustav! Let's go!"

I pulled myself up and latched onto the side of the car and nervously tugged at my shirtsleeves, trying to regain my composure. I frantically took a step away and then turned back toward the car as my mind searched for the best way to salvage my dignity. I wanted to seem calm about the whole thing, but for some reason I could only manage to produce frantic movements. It was clear that I was entirely humiliated because my mind veered into idiotic mode. I endeavored to pull the car door down, until it dawned on me that it would do so automatically. I then flittered my hand up and down, torn between whether or not to wave good-bye. After miserably failing to appear cool about the whole thing, I decided to make a quick exit and sprinted to Pork Chop's car.

I banged my head as I ducked into the silver vehicle.

"Who's in the car? Where'd you go?" she asked curiously. Pork Chop was looking in the direction of Blake's car.

I nervously tried to find the seat belt. "Nowhere. I made a friend. She took me to the Boardwalk. Let's go. How much money did Sammy load for me on the card? Is a million dollars a lot of money? Where's Sammy? Where's Vas?"

My sister looked at me inquisitively as I sped through my explanation and layered on the questions. I raised my eyebrows and smiled innocently. "What?" I asked, trying to sound casual.

She narrowed her eyes at me. "What have you been up to, Guse? Were they mean to you at school? It's okay, you can tell me. Did you run away?" She was asking me in that mock tone of hers.

"Ha. Ha. You're so funny, Pork. Really."

"I'm not falling for it. You're hiding something," she accused.

I rolled my eyes. "My friend's name is Sue Boe. She is real and does not live in my head. Look, you're late, and I'm hungry, so let's go," I urged, as I looked fervently at Blake's car. It hadn't moved. My sister followed my gaze.

"Aren't you going to introduce me to *Sue Boe?*"

I cringed and clenched my teeth. "*Can we go, please?*"

She made a face. "Touchy, touchy. I don't want to meet your

dorky friend, anyway. I'm not nosy like you. I'm just a bit curious because that model hasn't even been released yet and it has custom finishing."

She was referring to Blake's car.

"So, what's the big deal?"

"It's not a big deal, it's just that your friend is probably rich. Very rich."

I sat back, relieved, as Blake's car silently zoomed off.

"Can't we afford one of those?" I asked.

"Of course," Pork Chop replied snootily. "It's just I don't think Sammy would approve of spending such an excessive amount of money on a car. And we are talking *excessive* here."

"How excessive?"

"Let's just say if Sammy and I got married"—she winked at me— "he would say it would be a ten-year anniversary gift. But I tell you now, it had better come at the one-year mark or there won't be a ten-year anniversary."

"Does the Vatican still exist?"

Pork Chop gave me a funny look. "Why?"

"Because I'm going to make a request for Sammy's canonization. Only a bloody saint could put up with you for that long."

Pork Chop gave my shoulder a light punch as we pulled away from the College.

"It's the gospel truth and you know it."

"Your jokes are so lame, Guse. You should just stop now before you make a further fool of yourself."

"What's for dinner? I'm starving."

"That reminds me. Sammy and Vas are going to be home late. They're meeting with Logan and the dean. Sammy wants me to come but I really don't want to."

"Who's Logan?" I asked.

"He's a friend and also a professor at Cambridge—that is how Sammy and I met him. He's also the vice president of ViAno believe it or not. His father heads the company and he works with him."

"What's ViAno?" I asked.

"It's a leading development company that is focused on producing innovative technologies to minimize impact on the environment. Anyway, do you want to come to dinner?"

"No! Why would I want to do that?"

"Come on, Guse," she said sweetly. "Please."

"No. No. No."

She wasn't going to sucker me into going to some boring dinner, and the last thing I had in mind was to do my sister a favor; I will still a bit cross with her.

"Fine. *Home. Load.*" She sounded miffed.

Excellent.

¤ VI ¤

K N O C K , K N O C K

As Pork Chop dropped me off on the unloading dock she again pleaded for me to come. I adamantly refused.

"Last chance."

"I'm not going," I replied, as I climbed out of the car.

"Fine. I'll remember this, Gustav." She let out a huff of defeat but her expression quickly changed to one of smug satisfaction. "Did Sammy give you the code for the door?"

"No. What is it?"

She smiled slyly. "I guess you have two options: endure dinner with the fogies or sit here all alone waiting for us to come home.

And there are all sorts of *psychos* around here. You could get, dare I say it, *abducted*." She chuckled.

"I would rather take my chances with the *crazy people* than endure a second more of your obnoxious company." Pork Chop made a face. "Just tell me the code because I'm not going," I insisted.

"Fine. Nineteen-fifty-three," she said impatiently. "Nan's birthday." With that, she made a quick U-turn and sped away.

I repeated the code in my head. Before I could start conjuring up melancholy thoughts about the date my sister had chosen, I realized I was missing my bag and had left it in Boe's car.

Sammy had put a list of commands on my desk—one hundred pages worth of them. I decided to try my hand at different functions. I started in the kitchen. There were thousands of combinations so I chose at random. I was astounded at how specific some of the commands were; I could control the exact number of salt grains that went into my salad.

After exhausting my brain in the kitchen, I decided to venture into the library next. I was browsing the collection when I heard something akin to a telephone ring and ran into the hall.

"Yes? Hello? I mean, *Answer. Load.*" I wasn't sure if the command would register so I was pleased when several screens emerged: one beside the staircase, another beside the kitchen entrance and one beside the door behind me. I was encircled by screens on which Pork Chop's face appeared.

"Guse?" My sister's squinted eyes relaxed as she turned to Sammy, who was waving to me in the background. "Sammy, you were right. She did manage to answer the phone."

"Very funny, Pork. Obviously I would know how to do that."

She laughed. "We're going to be home late so don't wait up. Are you okay by yourself?"

I gave her some cut-eye, with my arms crossed. "Seriously, you're getting on my nerves. Of course I'll be fine." I was actually nervous about being alone, but I wasn't going to admit that. "The place has an alarm, right?" I tried to ask casually.

"See, Sammy, she's scared," Pork Chop teased.

"Excuse me. No, I'm not. I just want to know in case I decide to go out or something."

"Guse, no one believes your lies. The place does have an alarm though, so you don't have to worry about someone breaking in and attacking you," she retorted sardonically.

"Look, I don't care if you're turning twenty in a few months. I'll be twenty in January so let's get one thing straight. Think of our family as a hierarchy. Technically, Vas is at the top, but I'm his right hand—the second head of the family. You" —I pointed to her face— "are my subordinate. Got that, Pork Chop?"

"Please! First of all, you're going to be a disgrace to the Ellias name when you flunk high school and second, *technically*, I've told people that you are a bit younger than your oh-so-mature nineteen years and that I'm a tiny bit older than my near twenty."

"What do you mean a *bit* younger? A *tiny bit* older?"

"Don't worry about it." Her voice had a singsong tone that I immediately disliked. I heard voices in the background getting louder. "Gotta go. Call if you need anything."

"Yeah, if you need anything just call, kay?" Sammy called out from behind her.

I gave a short wave. "Kay, bye," I said, determined to get answers from Pork Chop later.

The screens went black and receded into the walls as I stood silently in the foyer. I had turned to go back into the library when I thought I heard a knock on the front door. Who would be visiting at this hour? The last time I checked, the clock on the kitchen wall said a quarter to nine. A second knock followed. I frantically ducked, looking for a place to hide, as if the visitor could see me from behind the front door. Another knock came—more forcefully this time. I squatted down behind the staircase and hoped they would go away. An electronic operator's voice caught me off guard.

"Command to answer."

"Huh? *Answer*—no!" I shook my hands as the keypad on the front door became illuminated. I prayed that there was some sort of manual lock I could hold down, but the door slid open as I lurched toward it. Falling to the ground, I froze as I stared at spotless black boots. My eyes slowly trailed up past a pair of long legs and a firm torso to finally rest on *his* sublime face. My mouth dropped open as if I was going to offer an inquiry or explanation. Boe's arrestingly handsome brother seemed to wait for whichever one I chose. Neither came.

It took me a while to notice my schoolbag in his hand. Without blinking he held it out over the threshold. I gulped and slowly got up off my knees and gingerly took it from him.

"Boe wanted this brought back to you." His voice gave me goose bumps.

"Thanks," I said, averting my gaze to a spot on the floor. Blake didn't make a move to leave so I braved a look at him. I wasn't surprised to find him staring at me. I probably looked like a dimwit.

"Do you want to come in?" I blurted out, without thinking.

"No," he answered firmly. I raised my eyebrows at him quizzically.

"No?" I repeated his answer. Then why wasn't he leaving?

"Are you alone?" he asked.

"Well…yes."

He brushed past me and ever so lithely walked in. Just like that, a hive full of bees erupted in my head; my mind was literally buzzing.

He stopped to examine one of my sister's favorite paintings. Time ticked by as Blake carried on his silent observation of the masterpiece.

"The mystery of his work is profound," he finally murmured.

I admired Monet's work a great deal, but I didn't revere it like Pork Chop. I gave Blake a quick sideways glance before turning to the canvas splashed with vibrant colors.

"'Everyone discusses my art and pretends to understand, as if it were necessary to understand, when it is simply necessary to love.'" I don't know why I said it; it just came with such force to my mind. "That is, in the words of the artist himself," I said meekly, my cheeks burning red.

My chest collapsed as Blake stepped in front of me. Cocking his head to one side, he wore a look of consternation. I didn't dare breathe as his narrowed eyes roamed my face, as if in search of something. Looking thoroughly disturbed, he turned away from me and headed toward the back windows.

To my surprise, the stained glass windows slid apart and revealed a wide balcony as Blake drew near. A cool breeze filled the room and sent chills up my spine. I planted myself against the window frame as Blake made his way to the railings. It was so strange to have him here. Strange and exhilarating.

"Do you go to the College? I haven't seen you—"

"Boe likes you." His back was turned to me so I couldn't see the expression on his face. "But it might not be in your best interest to befriend my sister."

Is that why he had come here tonight, to tell me to stay away from Boe? I recalled Pork Chop's comment about Blake's car and how Boe had mentioned her family's *social circles*. It became all too clear to me. Blake didn't like the fact that his sister was associating herself with a *runt*—that's what Charlie Astor had called me, wasn't it?

"I don't think Boe needs your approval regarding her friends and I sure don't need the permission of an arrogant, self-righteous, meddling brother to hang out with her. Who do you think you are? People like you and Charlie Astor might think you're better—"

Then, he was in front of me.

"That's not what I meant."

I took a step back. "I know *exactly* what you meant."

He seemed unperturbed at my accusatory tone. In the span of two steps he closed the gap between us. Was he trying to intimidate me? If he was, it was working. He was so close I was sure he could see how fast I was breathing.

"It might be difficult for *you* to associate with Boe. Charles Astor is a perfect example."

I furrowed my brow and shook my head. I took another step away as Blake drew closer, and I found my back up against the window. I was trapped. I was confused. What was his concern?

"Is Boe okay? Is anyone injured?" I scanned his face worriedly. Maybe something had happened to them and he blamed me for it? If he did, I couldn't deny that I deserved it.

Blake took a slight step back and peered at me curiously.

"Well, are they? Is that why you're here?" I continued. "Tell me." I touched my fingers to my forehead as the migraine that had subsided earlier in the day came back with full force. Blake didn't say anything.

"I'm sorry," I murmured, thinking the worst had happened to the pair. "You're right, it was my fault. Please tell Boe that I didn't mean for things to get out of hand."

Boe was really the only friend I had, and by the looks of things she was the only friend I was going to make at the College. If someone had gotten hurt, I wouldn't blame her for keeping her distance from me. Feeling unnerved and vulnerable, I tried to move away from Blake but he grabbed my arms and pulled me close to him. His boldness alarmed me and I struggled lightly to get him to release me.

"Boe's fine." He paused. "Both Boe and RJ can take care of themselves."

I couldn't mask the confused look I wore.

"Then why are you…" I trailed off as he slid his hands up my arms and rested them on my shoulders. It was like being hit by a shock wave; electrical currents reverberated throughout my entire body. Blake moved his hands sinuously past my shoulders. My lungs gasped for air as his fingertips teased the sensitive flesh peaking through my shirt collar. Wrestling my gaze from the ground, I bravely lifted my head to look him in the eye. My knees felt weak—the same feeling I get when I'm too close to a ledge or find myself really high up—because Blake gave off an unbridled intensity that left my mind blank. His fingers traced my jawbone and swept over my cheeks before starting to comb through my hair.

It was all too surreal. All too extreme. I barely knew anything about him. What's worse, I didn't care. I felt an abandon with this stranger that was so alien to me, dangerous, even, and yet I didn't question it. Blake pulled my head closer to his and I let my eyelids fall shut in fervent anticipation of what was coming. In one swift movement his lips brushed over my jaw and nestled beside my ear.

"Athena," he whispered roughly.

And then he was gone.

Blake vanished so quickly it was as if the night breeze had blown him away.

My body was chilled and I couldn't stop shivering even after I climbed into bed. My thoughts were unsettled and I couldn't sleep. It was as if my brain was trying to piece together a puzzle. Tossing and turning, I called to mind how Charlie had jumped from the back of Richard's bike onto his own. I recalled how RJ had appeared out of thin air and how Boe had evaded Charlie's advances. And then I thought of Blake. There was something so mystifying about him. Blake. Blake. Blake. Blake. Blake. Just having him in my head, thinking of him, ignited new shivers—shivers born not of cold but of something else. My eyelids flew open as the final piece of the jigsaw came into place: *Supra*.

Staring glumly out my bedroom window, I pushed the thought of Supras to the back of my mind. What clouded my mind instead was guilt.

I hadn't been able to sleep so I decided to look up the commands for my room. To my utter disbelief, I found my collection of books from Nan's place arranged exactly as I had left them, my Waterhouse prints, my paintings, my photographs, my Audrey Hepburn DVD collection, my fencing equipment, my shoe collection—everything was there, concealed behind the austere walls, waiting for me to discover them.

I knew that Pork Chop had done all this for me because she wanted the transition to be easy. I was touched at my sister's caring, but I really couldn't give her all the credit—Pork Chop could be thoughtful but she was terribly disorganized. Sammy, however, is super-organized and I was sure he had helped in putting everything together. Although I never openly admitted it, I loved them both very much. I loved my family very much—they were all that mattered.

I couldn't help the tears that started to stream down my face as I thought of the one person my family had lost—the one person we had left behind.

Nanny was gone forever.

I guess it took a while for it to hit me because I hadn't really thought of her as *dead*. She had been alive and well a mere day ago. But the sun of 2212 was setting and the realization that she had died centuries ago was dawning. The revelation was excruciating.

I let out a low whimper and crumpled onto the floor. I didn't cry so much as heave gutturally, feeling as if a limb had been mercilessly torn from my body. The bond between mother and child was so strong—I knew it then. As I felt the loss cut deep, I was sure, more sure than I had been of anything in my life, that Nanny could feel me suffering two hundred years in the future. She could feel her baby's pain.

I hadn't really had a chance to say good-bye and I needed to tell her so many things. I wanted her to know how much I loved her—a love beyond words, beyond measure, beyond death. I wanted her to know that without her a part of my life would always be barren—an irreparable tear in the fabric of my life.

"My children are my life. My joy." That's what she had told me.

I let out a dejected cry as I thought of what Pork Chop and I had stolen from her and from ourselves: a mother's joy and our mother's life. As I lay miserably on the floor, I tried to remember her face, her voice, her laugh, her warmth, everything that resonated with *Mommy*.

¤ VII ¤

THE KING

A glare of light in my eyes woke me up and I hesitantly turned onto my stomach anticipating pain—sleeping on the floor would guarantee a stiff back. To my surprise, there was no pain and I wasn't on the floor. I was in my bed. I guess I had managed to drag myself onto it in the middle of the night, but I didn't give it much thought. The last thing I needed was to dwell on last night. The torrent of grief that had swept over me had dimmed, but there remained a hollowness in my chest where my pain still echoed.

I managed to hoist myself out of bed and was halfway to the

washroom when I stopped in my tracks and pivoted to face the spot on the wall where Pork Chop's voice had bellowed from yesterday morning. A crease developed on my forehead as I caught sight of the time on the small monitor above it. It was a quarter to ten in the morning and I was seriously late for school. I made my way to the kitchen and called out to the three of them, but nobody seemed to be home.

Where was everyone?

Just then—as if it was an answer to my unspoken question—there came a knock on the door. Usually I would have been much more cautious in answering but I wasn't thinking clearly and a part of me imagined a tall, dark and handsome figure standing behind it.

"Answer. Load," I replied hastily.

Startled, I took a step back when I found myself face to face with a stranger. A peculiar look passed over his face, but was soon replaced with a bright smile.

"You must be Athena. I'm Logan Leger, a friend of Sam and Sofia's."

The stranger was tall and immaculately dressed—a disparity with his blond tresses, which were gelled into disarray. With chiseled features, he was very handsome, and the color of midnight blue gleamed from his almond-shaped eyes.

Logan Leger. His name sounded familiar.

"I had the pleasure of meeting your father last night. A philosophical physicist always makes good company." He grinned as if impressed by his own wit. "Unfortunately, the dean had to leave early on in the evening and asked to meet with the three of them this morning. Sofia mentioned that you were new to London and, seeing that I live not too far from here, asked if it was possible for me to give you a ride to the College."

"Aren't you a bit late?" I asked, raising an eyebrow.

"If I didn't know better, I'd say that was a complaint," he replied, feigning offense. "And here I thought I was being generous by letting you sleep in."

I waved my hands in the air dismissively. "I didn't mean it that way. Look, you don't have to give me a ride."

"I believe I do."

"No, you don't. I'm not a child. Sorry if I sound blunt, but my sister has been treating me as if I am one lately and I've had about enough." I knew I was being rude, but I was not in the best mood and I was taking my angst out on *her* friend. "Mr. Leger—"

"Logan, please."

"Logan, I'm sorry that my sister has unnecessarily inconvenienced you. I do *not* need a babysitter and from what I've been told you would be an expensive one, anyway."

He grinned at my attempt at light humor. "You have a ride, then? I was told that you couldn't drive."

"That's beside the point."

"Is it? Forgive me, but I was under the impression that that was exactly the point. Are you telling me that you have some other means of transportation in mind?"

Thinking about it, I didn't have a ride to the College. It was really the last place I wanted to be, but I couldn't afford to fall any further behind and, more important, I was scared of what staying cooped up would do to me, considering my fragile state of mind.

I shrugged my shoulders. "No, actually, I don't have a ride—"

"It's settled then. I'll take you." He didn't ask my permission so much as confidently expect my approval. "Get dressed. I'll wait for you at the unloading dock. See you in, say, five minutes."

I didn't like being told what to do, especially by a pompous friend of my sister's, but he was at the elevator by the time I took three hostile blinks so I decided to let it go.

My uniform consisted of a navy-blue tunic and white blouse. I threw them on quickly. I was grateful that there was no tie—I had never learned how to tie one—but there was a neck cuff that I couldn't figure out how to put on, so I just stuffed it into my pocket. I hopped into a pair of tights and slipped into black flats. It looked like it was going to be an unusually sunny day so I grabbed my solar-shield glasses and Tilley hat before heading out. Pork Chop thought that the glasses and hat made me look like a senior citizen, but I didn't care. I have a strong aversion to the sun—I don't want cataracts and I don't want wrinkles.

My schoolbag was beside the front door where I had left it. I picked it up and flashbacks of Blake holding me last night flooded my mind. I shook my head a couple times, hoping the physical movement would knock the thoughts right out. Thinking of him only reminded me of how much I wanted to see him again. *Pathetic.* There was no way I was about to become a feeble airhead over someone I barely knew.

Logan was parked by the side of the unloading dock in a small, silver roadster. It wasn't as intimidating as some of the other vehicles I had come across, but the engine roared as I approached and I knew that there were other features that compensated for its size. Logan was rubbing his chin and grinning as the door slid shut beside me.

"What's so funny?" I asked dryly.

"Nothing. Shall we?"

I slouched down in my seat as the car veered away from the loading dock. I felt horrible. I had barely slept, my eyes were red and I had already missed my first class. In my head I vented to myself: Pork Chop should have woken me. But, on second thought, I conceded that it was better that she hadn't. She might have noticed my eyes.

People always thought of me as emotionally barren. It was hardly true, but I would never go out of my way to set the record straight. I didn't like to show my feelings because it made me feel safe to think that people couldn't see me. I often thought of myself as a fortified penitentiary, meant for imprisonment and dissuasion of entry—I didn't like to let people in and I didn't like to let things out. Pork Chop has never really seen me cry; at least, not since we were kids, and I knew there was a part of her that wanted me to break down, hoped that I would, so that we might suffer together. If it helped her cope, I shouldn't care about mere appearances. Giving whatever comfort I could offer to my sister should be the only thing that mattered, but instead I feigned allegiance to the age-old philosophy of the stoics. Instead, I chose the selfish road. Instead, I chose to suffer alone.

Nanny.

I could feel the burn in my eyes. The thought of her was so poignant, so painful. I couldn't afford to break down now. Not in front of Logan. Not in front of anyone.

"Don't look so miserable. Education is supposed to be fun." Logan's tone was one used for children.

Perfect. This was exactly the avenue I needed to pursue to keep my emotions in check: anger.

"Did you go to Haverston?" I asked flatly.

"No."

"Then you don't know what you're talking about," I snapped.

Logan's mouth twitched. "I take it you haven't received many warm welcomes."

"I didn't say that." I was hoping he wouldn't press the conversation after picking up that I wasn't in the mood for one. "I don't think I have to be there, that's all. It's not the right place for me," I said coldly.

"Yes, Sofia told me that she thought it would be hard for you."

"Seriously, I want to kill her! How come she gets to sit on this high horse telling me what to do?" I was talking more to myself than to Logan. "What does being older have to do with it, anyway? She isn't that much older than me."

"I think a decade gives her a bit more experience."

"What do you mean a decade?" I asked confusedly.

"Isn't that right? Am I off by a year or two? I thought I remembered Sofia mentioning some plans for your seventeenth birthday sometime in early January."

I didn't know how the hell I passed for sixteen, especially with all the wrinkles I was developing from the ever-deepening crease on my forehead. I could have pulled off being twenty-five in my time. Pork Chop had told them I was *sixteen*. That meant she told people she was *twenty-six*.

Why couldn't I be twenty-six? Why couldn't I be a professor? Why did I have to go to the College? My thoughts resembled those of a spoiled child, but still, *why?*

Logan was looking at me, awaiting my reply.

"Age is just a number." I let out an exaggerated breath. I was done talking. "Do you mind if we turn on the radio?"

Logan gave me a funny look. I raised my eyebrows questioningly in response.

"You're a bit odd, just like your sister. Turn on the *radio*." He said this last bit as if he were repeating the last line of a joke. "You two have a similar sense of humor." He chuckled lightly. "*Music. Load.* What would you like?"

I wasn't sure how to digest his remark, but I really didn't care.

"It doesn't matter. It's your choice."

"What kind of music do you like?" he asked.

"I like everything."

He ran his fingers through his hair. "I thought you wanted to listen to music?"

No, I wanted him to stop talking. It took all my willpower to maintain my manners.

"I do."

"Liking everything means liking nothing."

Huh? What did that mean? And he thought I was odd.

"Excuse me?"

"You haven't listened to *everything.*"

What was wrong with this guy?

I raised my hands in mock surrender. "I don't care. You can choose."

He wouldn't relent. "Your choice or no choice."

"Ugh! Fine. I choose…" I obviously didn't know any modern bands so I said the first thing that popped into my head. "Elvis." I have no idea why Elvis Presley came to mind. I wasn't even a huge fan. I didn't mind his music but there were a whole host of bands that I would have preferred listening to at the moment. I guess I was hoping that Mr. Presley still held the status of "classic" nearly two hundred and fifty years after his peak.

"Song selection?"

I hit my head against the headrest. Logan laughed gingerly and I shot him a sharp look.

"Whatever. No music. Forget it." I made sure to enunciate the annoyance in my voice as I crossed my arms over my chest.

Just as I was beginning to appreciate the silence, *Jailhouse Rock* boomed from the speakers. I jumped in my seat at the unexpected blast. I ground my teeth and kept my eyes on the lanes ahead. The thought of going back to the College didn't seem so bad if it meant the end of this exhausting car ride. I wanted to smack Logan's grin right off his beatific face.

¤ VIII ¤

OVER MY HEAD

It didn't take long to reach the College. Logan pulled to a smooth stop beside the unloading dock and I turned to get out, but my door didn't slide open. I took a deep breath and looked over my shoulder. He was rubbing his chin again and looking at me amusedly. He reminded me of Pork Chop and how she often found my "antics" comical. The last thing I appreciated at the moment was being a source of entertainment for this pest.

"Can you open my door, please?" I said curtly.

"I can tell that I have offended you. Let me make it up to you. How about I take you around London this afternoon? I'll let Sofia know that she needn't pick you up."

My eyes grew wide as I dissected his offer.

"*Why?* What do you mean?" I demanded.

He raised his hands. "No strings attached. God, you're worse than your sister. I'll pick you up at four?"

My door slid open.

"What? No! Thank you for the offer, but I don't need to see London. I've seen it, thank you. So, thank you for the ride, but—"

"That's the third time you've said thank you so you must really mean it. Actions speak louder than words, so they say: you can show me how *thankful* you are when I see you at four today."

One thing I did not respond well to in members of the opposite sex was unwarranted cockiness.

"Whoa, whoa, whoa. Let's back up here. First of all, I take back all of those thank yous. Come to think of it, I don't thank you for anything. And I will not be seeing you at four today. Did my sister put you up to this?" I asked irritably.

Logan's grin widened. "I guess you could think of it like that. For as long as I have known Sofia there are but a few topics that are constantly the center of conversation; one being her concealed adoration for her sister, *Gustav.* I have been looking forward to meeting you for some time."

I was surprised by this intimate piece of knowledge and the sincerity I heard in his voice. Not wanting to show any vulnerability I layered my response with sarcasm, as per usual.

"I hope I have met your expectations."

"Of course, any gentleman would reply that you have

indubitably surpassed them." Logan beamed.

I frowned. "I don't see a gentleman anywhere. Besides, there's no need for diplomacy here. You've driven me to the College as my sister asked. There's nothing more for you to do." He leaned over the passenger seat to look closer at me.

"Nothing more I need to do with regards to your sister's request, but there is a great deal more I would like to do."

At his words, I started to blush. "Good-bye, Mr. Leger," I replied haughtily, and turned abruptly.

"I'll be here waiting at four sharp."

"Wait all you like," I shouted over my shoulder.

As I entered the main foyer I took a moment to collect myself. I was supposed to be an inferior kind of human in this future age, but in just over a day I had encountered more male attention than I had in my entire nineteen years. What was the world coming to?

I marched toward the physical education center and was overcome by a feeling of dread. What Pork Chop said was true; I had an aversion to losing. As I entered the complex and spied the kind of athleticism I was up against, I cringed at the fact that—crap—I was in for some major losing. Big-time.

"Uniforms in the change room. Suit up!" Mr. Ballin hollered. He was one intimidating gym teacher with a clipped mustache and icy glare. "Now!" he shouted.

His bark startled me and I shook before jogging toward the change room.

"Ow!" I cried out, as a pair of shorts, a T-shirt and a set of shoes fell through a shoot in the entryway and whacked me on the head. I gently rubbed the spot, where I was sure a little bump was soon going to develop. Picking up the scattered items resentfully, I realized they were all exactly my size.

Girls rushed by me as I headed down the corridor. Some were coming, but most were going as I entered a large, cavernous room, with a single, long bench that divided it in two. I recognized the same plain, white paneling that lined our kitchen and figured that meant there were things lurking behind these walls, too.

I wasn't sure where I was going to leave my stuff and was about to ask someone for help when a really tall girl scurried by me and stopped a few feet away.

"*Locker. Open. Load,*" she ordered.

A locker emerged from one of the panels and slid open. The girl dumped her belongings inside. "*Locker. Close. Store,*" she called, as she headed out of the room. The little cube slid shut and vanished.

The area soon emptied and once I was left alone I walked over to the panels and slid my fingers over the stark surface.

"*Locker. Open. Load,*" I said hopefully, thinking that a locker had been programmed for me. I eagerly looked around but nothing happened. Damn. I repeated the command, louder this time, but still nothing appeared.

"You have to give an initialize command before that will work."

I jumped at the voice of the unnoticed stranger standing in the change room doorway.

The girl had emerald-green eyes, an attractively proportioned face and long, blond hair. She eyed me quizzically.

"Yes of course, an initialize command."

I had no idea what that was so I stood nodding my head as if that was indicative of my knowing.

"Well?" she asked.

"Well, what?" I answered.

"Aren't you going to initialize your locker?"

My mind was trying to come up with some sort of excuse to cover my obvious ignorance when she added, "You know, *Initialize. Locker. Load.*" The innocent smile on her face told me that she was giving me a way out.

"Yeah, I was just about to do that." I cleared my throat, an embarrassed sound. "*Initialize. Locker. Load.*"

To my left, a locker appeared and the door slid open.

"Thanks," I mumbled. "Are you in my class by chance?"

"No. I'm not a student. I work here as an athletic coach from time to time. I'm Corinne."

"I'm Athena."

"Listen, you better get ready or Mr. Ballin is going to have you lapping for the rest of the hour."

"Thanks again," I said, as Corinne moved to leave.

She threw me a brief wave in response. "Just as a piece of advice, Athena, try to ignore some of the girls today."

"I'm sorry," I said, unsure about her comment.

"There's nothing wrong with being a little different. Only if you're a freak of nature like a Supra, should anyone care."

"Sure," I offered awkwardly, puzzled about Corinne's dark tone.

"Nice to meet you, Athena." She turned her back and left.

"Nice to meet you, too," I whispered.

I undressed quickly and loaded my stuff into the locker. *"Locker. Close. Store."* The little safe slid shut and merged back into the wall and I ran out of the change room.

"You!" Mr. Ballin stood apart from the group of girls with his finger threateningly pointed in my direction.

"Yes?" I tried to answer firmly.

"Laps until that bell rings. Do. You. Understand?"

I pursed my lips, debating whether or not I should argue over the order. I had a problem with authority, especially when I thought I was being treated unfairly, but it was my first gym class and I thought it wouldn't be good to start off on the wrong foot. Sometimes you had to swallow your pride when choosing your battles.

"Move!" Mr. Ballin barked.

"I don't think her stumps can manage."

I glared at the girl who'd spoken and realized that it was Tia speaking to Devonne.

"I don't think she could even manage a lap. Bets, Dev?" she continued.

"I don't know, Tia, I think they might be able to hold her up for—I'll be generous—a lap and a half," Devonne sniggered in reply.

Their giggles sounded like malevolent cackles. Witches.

I was sure if I had a weaker mind, their words would have been poignant enough to make my nerve crumple right there and then, but instead the insult only increased my resolve.

"Are you deaf?" Mr. Ballin howled. "I said laps until that bell rings."

"Yes, sir," I answered sharply.

I started lapping the complex and didn't stop until I heard the ding of the school bell. When it finally rang, I swore I could hear angels singing. The truth is, I wasn't sure I could have gone on for much longer.

"These stumps can manage just fine, thanks," I said icily, albeit a bit breathlessly, as I brushed past Tia and Devonne on my way back to the change room.

I felt like it was a victory; a small, insignificant one, but I had to take what I could get.

I was exhausted after gym and decided to take a brief detour to the conservatory before math. As I absentmindedly passed through the rows of greenery I found myself thinking about the suspicion I had that Blake, Boe and the others I had met last night were Supras. For some reason I couldn't wrap my head around it. When Pork Chop described them to me I had imagined that they would be more obvious to spot. She said they looked completely normal, but a part of me couldn't shake the images that "mutant" evoked. Remembering the contours of Blake's face and Boe's delicate beauty, I could hardly call them mutantlike—they were more godlike than anything.

I squatted down on a stool and leaned against something that resembled a palm tree. Closing my eyes, I tried to sort out where this left me. If Blake was a Supra he would be completely out of my reach—an angel on earth—and there was no way I could ever deserve him. I prayed that I was wrong, as I remembered the way he had looked at me last night; there was something indescribable about his soulful eyes. Boe was another matter. I didn't care if she was from another planet; if she wanted to be my friend then I held no objections.

The sound of glass shattering caused a violent contraction in my chest. My eyes flew open and I shot up so quickly the stool toppled to the ground. The glass from the conservatory roof was raining down in torrents behind me and a storm of crystal shards was headed in my direction. I started to run for the exit when there was a downpour a few feet ahead of me. Ducking under the closest table, I covered my head as splinters sprinkle the ground. The conservatory was thrumming and I sensed multiple things zooming around, stirring the trees near me. I cautiously peered out from under the table and spotted what I can only describe as black robotic ninjas hovering above me. With closer inspection they seemed too agile for robots and I surmised that there were people behind the suits.

They were covered in metallic armor and their faces were hidden under black masks with slanted slits for eyes and railed mouthpieces. They each stood atop what looked like a small unicycle that was attached to their ankles. The pedals were immobile, though, and instead of wheels blue light orbited between their feet. I had seen something similar on Charlie's bike last night.

I bit my lip and ducked my head back down. Oh, man, they looked scary and *mean*. Not good. Especially not good considering they had just smashed into the College's conservatory uninvited and were probably here to cause some serious trouble. As I lay unmoving and hidden, I thought smugly to myself that when I died Pork Chop was going to be crushed with guilt. It was all her fault! She was the mastermind behind making me go to this damned school.

The trees swayed wildly as the intruders zoomed by. The thrumming that filled the room vanished and I gathered they had left the conservatory. My thoughts raced as I assessed the situation. I had to get out of here, but I had no clue as to how I was going to do that.

Carefully crawling out from underneath the table, I swept aside layers of glass with my feet as I reached for my schoolbag. Sammy had given me this earpiece device that was supposed to be a phone. I needed to call him—there was no way I was going to call Pork Chop. I didn't want her coming for me. It was terrible to ask Sammy to put himself in danger—Pork Chop would never forgive me if anything happened to him—but I had no other choice. There was only one option between the two of them: Sammy. Pork Chop was dear to me in inexplicable ways.

As I closed my hand over the earpiece, something flew into the conservatory and I stiffened, sensing it station itself over my head. I turned slowly, sure I was about to meet my demise, but the black figure didn't attack. It looked me up and down and then tilted its head to the side, making an assessment. Suddenly, it jerked forward. My palms slammed against the ground as I fell back and glass shards pierced my hands. I ignored the pain and scurried across the floor, bracing myself for the assault, but it didn't come. The ominous figure made its way toward the exit and zipped right over me instead.

"Stay here," it ordered, its voice raspy and mechanical.

Obviously I wasn't going to stay put. I wasn't sure if what the figure had said was meant to keep me out of harm or to keep me here until it came back with the others to—mental cringe—*kill* me. I got up hastily and stuffed the earpiece into my pocket just as the lunch bell rang out. Blood drained from my face as I realized where the intruders were headed.

I could have hidden like a coward, knowing a massacre was about to take place, but as images of corpses, guns and one particular bloodied face filled my head I found myself sprinting toward the lunch hall.

I had to find Boe.

Breaking into the hallway, I was crammed between bodies. At first I thought that mayhem had already broken out, but I soon recognized the carefree chatter that passed between students when class ended.

Why didn't anyone know what was going on? The blast in the conservatory had been anything but quiet.

Boe was in the northeast corner of the lunch hall, as usual, but as I approached her I knew something was wrong. The table wasn't as full as it had been yesterday; I noticed a few familiar faces seated at alternate tables. The remaining faces I recognized were standing behind Richard. Boe stood alone, opposite them.

Richard glared at me as I ran up beside her. "Look who it is. Boe's pet has arrived."

"Don't talk to her like that, Richard. I'm not in the mood to be patient today. Cross me and I'll be damned if I don't teach you a lesson myself." The sharpness of Boe's voice made my stomach clench.

"Aching for some more action, Sue?" Richard taunted. "Last night's brawl got you all riled up? Your boy must be rubbing off on you. Eager to fight, are we? Not to worry, the next time Charlie meets RJ Valcrest, somebody won't be walking away. boTs or no boTs," he said in a low voice.

Boe was clutching the edge of the table and her knuckles were so white they almost looked transparent.

I didn't have time for their bickering.

"Boe! We have to get everyone out of here. I was in the conserv—"

"Who the hell do you think you are to prance in here and interrupt our conversation? Look, *runt*, you're going to get what's coming to you—"

"That's enough!" Boe's voice was razor sharp and I took a step back as she crushed the table edge with her hands. The suspicions I had were confirmed before my eyes. *Supra.*

Boe looked like she was going to make a move toward Richard so I stepped between them.

"Boe, listen to me—" Before I got a chance to finish, Richard swiped me with his arm and I found myself hurtling across the hall. A group of students cleared themselves out of the way as I steeled myself for the impact, but Boe was at my side in an instant and she carefully set me down. Sammy would have said *"holy monkeys!"* She was fast.

I was about to tell her what had happened in the conservatory but she was gone in a flash. Whipping around, I saw that Boe and Richard were atop one of the lunch tables surrounded by a herd of onlooking students. I momentarily forgot about the danger we were all in as I gawked at the scene before me. They moved so quickly I could barely keep up and I was getting dizzy from looking to and fro. I would have thought that they were dancing if not for the jarring sound I heard when they collided with one another.

Catching Richard with a roundhouse kick, Boe sent him soaring across the room. He got up, unfazed, and leapt back toward her. Their arms and legs moved with a precision I had never seen.

With a snarl, Richard threw himself at Boe but she sidestepped his advance. Grabbing him, she wrapped her leg around his arm and planted her foot firmly on his neck. Richard tried to grapple his way out of her hold, but Boe just squeezed harder.

Richard's voice was hoarse as he cursed on his knees. "Go to hell, you—" He didn't get a chance to finish; Boe tightened her grip and cocked her head to the side—a mannerism that reminded me of her brother.

Still swearing, Richard finally relented. "I won't touch the runt" —he choked as Boe twisted his arm— "I won't touch *her* again."

Boe seemed pleased with the answer and let him go.

I was already pushing my way through the crowd, trying to get Boe's attention.

"Boe! Boe! Please! They're coming! They came through the conservatory. A dozen or so of them." I was going to elaborate but she seemed to process what I was saying before I finished. She looked at Richard and both their eyes widened. Then she was beside me, pulling me toward the back entrance of the hall, with Richard at our heels. Only a few other students had gotten up and were following us, as if they had also been informed of what was coming. Some students still stared at us but most had gone back to their lunches and we couldn't just leave them.

"Boe, what's going on? We have to warn everyone."

"They're not coming for them," she said bitterly.

"What do you—" I was cut off by the ringing of a blaring alarm. Everyone froze for a fraction of a second and then chaos erupted. Students starting pressing into us and I tripped, forcing Boe to practically drag me along. With a loud *bang*, a huge metallic door slid shut over the lunch hall's entrance, causing students to run toward the back exit instead.

Richard had gotten ahead of us, along with a couple of the other students, and were only few feet away from the exit when the black cloud of bodies swarmed in.

"WiiGiis!" someone cried out.

Boe stiffened and murmured something before the leader of the clan shot out a whizzing ball that grew blindingly bright and then exploded. It felt like a jet took off inches from my face but there was no heat and there was no fire. Shaken, I staggered a few steps back and caught sight of bodies falling around the hall in slow motion. My chest heaved as Richard's body crashed onto the floor a dozen feet away from where I stood. I realized that the only students who had been affected by the blast were the few who had initially made their way to the back exit with Richard and—Boe! I stretched out my arm, praying to find her there. She wasn't. *"They aren't coming for them,"* she had said. Then I remembered how the black figure had left me unharmed in the conservatory. I had gotten it all wrong. These intruders weren't here for the students; they were here for the Supras!

Frantically scanning the heads around me, I looked for her jet-black hair, hoping she hadn't been affected by the explosion. I started toward the other end of the hall when my foot got caught on something on the floor. I looked down to find Boe's inert body crumpled in a heap.

"Boe!" I whispered worriedly. I crouched down beside her and cradled her tiny body. I could barely make out a pulse, but I didn't know if you could actually feel a Supra's pulse.

The small black army dispersed and started to scour the room. I assumed they were picking out their prey so I had to hide Boe fast. She wasn't heavy at all and it was easy for me to drag her body underneath one of the lunch tables. As soon as I was safely undercover, I heard a collective intake of breath. Students had shirked away from Richard's comatose body and left him helpless against the dark figure that approached him.

The crisp sound of boots hitting the floor made my heart spasm. Two other pairs appeared soon after.

"How many?"

I gave an involuntary shudder. It was the same raspy, mechanical voice that I had heard earlier.

"Four."

"Where's the last?"

"There were only four."

A slight pause.

"Sonar readings assured five."

"Escaped, then."

"Or hiding," one of them hissed.

"List the captives."

"Akawa. Elstead. Renaro." One of the boots pushed over Richard's body so that he lay faceup. "Coleridge."

"We'll take only three. Which one shall we eliminate?"

Oh, god. I gulped. I glanced over at Boe beside me and noted how peaceful she looked—a pixie in a deep slumber. I prayed that they didn't find her. Shifting out from underneath the bench, I looked over the tabletop to get a better view of what was going on. Students were hunched down on the floor in small groups surrounding the three WiiGiis that stood over Richard.

One of the WiiGiis squatted down beside him and slapped his face roughly. Richard didn't move. The WiiGii discharged a small gadget from its forearm and held it to Richard's ear.

"Wakey, wakey."

Richard let out a tormented groan and slowly came to. Satisfied, the WiiGii stood and returned the gadget to the open cavity in the forearm of his suit. Now semiconscious, Richard tried to raise himself on his knees.

"WiiGii," he sneered. "You're going to pay for this, you piece of—"

One of the two figures that had been standing back lunged forward and viciously grabbed him by the neck. Richard was barely able to defend himself; he struggled in vain. It was so strange considering the amount of strength and speed I had seen him display just a few moments ago when he fought with Boe.

"Ah, Coleridge, I'm going to enjoy watching you die. Any last words?"

Without hesitation Richard spit into the dark face. I heard a low growl before the WiiGii's metallic hand collided with Richard's jawbone. Then followed a short but brutal beating that left Richard's body motionless. I had to shut my eyes, unable to watch the brutality. I hated violence.

The WiiGii walked toward his two conspirators.

"Well?" he snarled.

"Kill him quickly. We'll get the others." The two suits zoomed off toward the other end of the hall as the one that remained slithered toward Richard.

"With pleasure."

¤ IX ¤

P O E T R Y

I raised myself onto my feet and made my way around the table, thinking to myself: *today is the day you're going to prove yourself an utter idiot.* Was I trying to be a hero? Was I really willing to put myself in danger to help *Richard?*

Homer's epic poem flittered into my head and all I could think about was that haunting passage in the *Odyssey* when Achilles tells Odysseus about his morbid existence in the Underworld. The Greek hero sacrificed his life for a noble cause—love for his comrade—but when Achilles meets his old friend in the land of Hades he desolately admits that he would rather live as a beggar among the living than a prince among the dead. Basically, death sucks no matter what you die for.

I tried to force the depressing scene from my mind and tried to convince myself that I wasn't going to die. I had to believe this or the fear was going to paralyze me. I was standing up for what was right. *Right?*

I doubt I could have mustered enough courage to face the dark devil that stood before me if I had thought I was defending Richard alone. WiiGiis were attacking Supras, which meant they were also attacking Boe. Taking a deep breath, I stepped in front of Richard—unmoving at my feet—and the WiiGii abruptly fell back into a defensive crouch, surprised by my sudden appearance.

"You can't do this!" I frantically looked to the other students huddled around me. "We can't let him do this," I pleaded. The students greatly outnumbered the lone WiiGii and there was strength in numbers. "Please help me. Are you just going to sit around and—"

"Yes, they are," the WiiGii hissed. "Do you know why?" I shook my head dumbly. "Because scum like Coleridge don't deserve to live. Everyone knows about his family's *plantations*. They take and treat life as if they are gods. Save your righteous virtue for someone who deserves it."

"Aren't you doing the same thing?" Confidence surged in me as I heard strength in my voice. "What are you, judge, jury and executioner? No one stands above the law."

"'*Silent enim leges inter arma*,'" he purred.

I knew the saying was Latin and tried to recall my rudimentary knowledge of the language. *Arma...Arms.* Cicero! I had trudged through Latin 101; I barely remembered anything, but I knew my quotes and I knew the perfect foil.

"Laws may be silent in times of arms but I feel Cicero would stand as *my* ally, for he would say, 'I prefer the most unjust peace to the justest war that was ever waged.' He holds peace above justice. Killing Richard is wrong and won't accomplish anything."

The WiiGii was silent for a moment.

"You're as blind as justice herself, kid. This isn't your fight." The voice was still harsh, but less menacing. "They treat you no better than a dumb animal and you're ready and willing to defend them?" A touch of puzzlement in the inhuman voice.

"Yes, I am."

I stared into the fearsome slits and tried to imagine human eyes peering out of them. There was a living, breathing person in there, someone who might still have a conscience, and I had to hold on to that image. I had to believe I could reason with the WiiGii.

We both stood still, two opponents taking part in a duel, waiting for the signal to draw weapons. The problem was that I was unarmed and was surely going to get shot in the head. The only weapon I possessed was the sword of a sophist: my wits and my words. As the WiiGii's hiss perforated my bones, I was sure that wits and words weren't going to be enough.

"Are you really willing to *die* for a Supra?" It made my death sound prophetic, like it was written in stone. "Back down and you don't get hurt. Make your choice."

It was the second time today a choice had been demanded of

me. I hadn't been sure of my first one, which led to an unbearable car ride with Logan and Elvis Presley. I didn't know what the consequences of my actions would be this time, but I had a feeling it was going to be far, far worse.

I felt a tug on my hem and stepped back as Richard tried to hoist himself up at my side.

"Here, take this," he choked, and held out a small, silver tube. "Press the green button to neutralize its suit."

I took the thing from his shaking hand and images of a light saber popped into my head. *Focus, you idiot!*

The WiiGii let out a venomous chuckle. "You want to fight me?" it asked scornfully. "This isn't a game, little girl. Step aside. The Supra is the one dying today. I don't need your blood on my hands, but if it comes to that I won't hesitate. Last chance. What's it gonna be?"

I was breathing fast as I clutched the tube and stretched out my hand, as if holding a foil in preparation for a fencing bout. I was so focused on the threat before me that I hadn't registered that the students who had been huddled around us had slowly dispersed, and there were now frantic movements coming from the entrance of the lunch hall.

Hope surged in me as I realized that help must have come. I needed to delay for only a while longer. The WiiGii, too, seemed to sense the precariousness of the situation and started moving toward me. I knew then that help would come too late; I would be dead by the time it arrived. I still had time to back down. I could stand aside and let it kill Richard. I would be a coward but at least I would be alive. But I knew that if I did, I would forever be left with an uncertainty of self and conscience. As the WiiGii's footsteps drew nearer, I knew that my mind had been made up. Even though I was trembling with fear I held my head high as I watched my destroyer come for me.

They say that life is full of crossroads and that you discover who you are by the roads you choose. With my feet firmly planted, I was sure that when I spoke the words of Jonathan Swift I would hear the sweet ringing of truth and was proud of the road I chose.

"'Hated by fools, and fools to hate, be that my motto, and my fate.'"

The WiiGii stopped dead in its tracks. My heart skipped a beat as I scanned the surface of the mask, looking for a trace of some hidden humanity that would make it rethink its course. Then I noticed that the WiiGii's attention was captured by something directly behind me. Then it charged, crazed with determination, and mayhem erupted. I pressed the green button and a wave of electrical current shot out of the small tube. The sheer power of it propelled me forward with so much force that I thought I was going to ram right into the WiiGii as it plunged toward me. Just as we were about to collide, I was pulled back and thrown to the floor.

As I hit the ground, I saw a robot the likes of which I had never seen before fly past me. Towering over the WiiGii, it gave off a blue glow and looked to have an arsenal of weapons at its disposal, as they were prominently displayed across its body.

Throwing out a small, whizzing ball, the WiiGii drew back and then an explosion sent a stream of powerful air currents blasting through the lunch hall. The robot enclosed itself in a glowing egg shape and floated innocently just over my head, as the WiiGii yanked out a small stick that mechanically assembled itself into a large spear.

I realized Richard had his arm around me, but I didn't have time to register the awkwardness because another robot immediately appeared. It wasn't the appearance of the second robot that captivated me, though; it was, rather, the insuperable figure of Blake descending like a conquering angel from a large hole in the ceiling. He was falling fast but didn't seem preoccupied with bracing himself. The ground shuddered from the force of his landing, the solid surface cracking under the pressure. Blake was unaffected as he bounced into step—his knees barely moved from the impact. Without so much as a blink, he shot toward me and pushed me low to the ground.

"Stay down!" he ordered, with an edge in his voice.

The sound of the WiiGii and Blake colliding made me cringe. The robot that accompanied Blake rushed to his side but he dismissed it with the slightest wave of his hand and it flew off.

Where was it going? It needed to help him.

With a blinding flash, an electrical current shot out from the end of the WiiGii's spear and, like a torpedo locked on its target, pursued Blake ruthlessly. My mouth fell open as Blake leapt off one of the lunch tables and twisted in the air to avoid the blast. He was so fast and moved with an inhuman dexterity; the abilities that I had seen Boe and Richard display were nothing in comparison. Blake ducked, turned and "back-flipped" out of the way, but no matter how fast he was the deadly stream followed him. I cried out something unintelligible just as the beam was about to slice right through his chest. With astonishing calmness, Blake tapped his boot on the ground and a blue light immediately illuminated his sole. He swiveled his legs around just in the nick of time and his foot *cut* through the charged beam, extinguishing its current. He executed this with a prancing vigor that left me in absolute awe.

The other WiiGiis started to gather from around the hall, greatly outnumbering Boe's brother. Filled with a need to help him, I hoisted myself up, hoping to cause some sort of diversion. Before I could take a step, Richard grabbed my ankle.

"Where do you think you're going? It's not safe. Just stay here," Richard whispered urgently.

"Let go of me. I need to help him," I said, as I tried to yank my leg out of his grasp.

"What! He doesn't need your help. Do you know who that is?" he asked incredulously.

"Richard, let me go." I shook my leg more forcefully.

"No. You're being—"

"Get Coleridge!"

Richard's grip slackened as he heard the WiiGii's order and I fell back. Instead of hitting the floor, I felt myself being lifted. Richard and I were dumped back onto the ground halfway across the hall in mere seconds. Blake was crouching down in front of me.

"Keep her here, Coleridge. If they touch her, WiiGiis will be the last thing you need to worry about." He was speaking to Richard but his eyes never left my face.

"WiiGiis aren't worth worrying about, Dresden," Richard

sneered. "And you might want to tell Boe's friend here that you don't require any *assistance*. She thought a diversion was in order."

"You're outnumbered. You could get hurt. This isn't your fight," I said adamantly, trying to justify my behavior.

"Seriously, what's the matter with you?" Richard asked me, looking thoroughly perplexed. "I think he can take care of himself. Besides, a few scrapes and bruises are exactly what Dresden deserves, if the WiiGiis can manage."

"How about we skip the fighting altogether and just give them Richard?" I replied snidely, narrowing my eyes at him.

Blake shot Richard a contemptuous look. "Sounds like a plan," he answered coolly. "That is, if Coleridge here can't manage to keep you out of harms way."

"What's she to you, Dresden?" Richard asked curiously. "You seem a little too eager to protect her."

"She's Boe's friend," Blake replied curtly.

"Boe!" I rose as I thought of her underneath the lunch table. "I hid her—"

"Bloody hell. Boe's fine. Just *stay here*." Blake grabbed my shoulders, shoved me against Richard and then he was gone.

"Jackass. I hope those WiiGiis pull up their socks and get a few blows in."

"He's saving your hide, you ingrate." I elbowed Richard in the gut and immediately regretted it. It was like elbowing a brick wall. I rubbed my arm tenderly, trying to mask the pain.

"Get real. He's doing this out of duty. Keep in mind, the WiiGiis didn't just attack me. If they did, I doubt Dresden would lift a finger to help. He thinks he's above everyone and everything. He's just pissed because his sister was involved," Richard retorted, sounding disgusted.

"Look who's talking, you hypocrite. I don't know why I didn't let the WiiGii kill you. I can just imagine what a *plantation* is. Do you use *runts* like me for slaves, for experiments, is that it?" I asked harshly.

"That WiiGii doesn't know what it's talking about," Richard shot back defensively. "My father might work with Astoral Corporation but he would never have anything to do with that shady business. They have no evidence. Charlie says it's just a conspiracy against his dad's company and against Supras. Plantations are myths and if they do exist my family has nothing to do with them."

Richard and I stared at each other—neither willing to concede defeat. "And…you're not a runt," he added slowly.

"That's not what you thought yesterday," I said through clenched teeth.

"You've changed my mind." He spoke in such a quiet voice I wasn't sure if I had heard him correctly, but I didn't press the matter.

"So what are plantations?" I inquired, trying to change the subject.

"Exactly what you think they are except worse. That's what they say."

"Are you a Supra, Richard?" I asked out of the blue.

He smirked. "Isn't it obvious?"

"How come you're so weak? What did the WiiGiis do to you?"

"First of all, I'm not weak." He scoffed. "And what they did was detonate a sTell:R bomb."

"What's that?"

Richard puckered his forehead. "You've never heard of a sTell:R bomb before?" I shook my head. "Where are you from, exactly?" Richard asked quizzically.

"It doesn't matter." I brushed off his query. "Just tell me what the bomb does."

"It de-stellarizes a Supra's boT. Depending on how strong the boT is and how strong the Supra is, the effects vary. Most are knocked unconscious. Some are just weakened while their boT re-energizes, like me, for example."

"You have a boT?"

"Of course I have a boT. I'm a Supra," he replied with a grin at my wide-eyed expression.

"Well, where is it?"

"Burning a hole in my pocket."

"No, seriously, where is it?"

"Like I said, it's in my pocket. boTs constantly change their shape. Do you think Dresden's boT goes around looking like a military weapon all the time? I'm surprised that you're Boe's friend and you don't know this, Athena."

I was taken aback when he said my name. It sounded weird coming from him and my cheeks suddenly felt warm.

Richard cleared his throat. "Hey, do you want to see it? My boT, I mean." I nodded my head. "Don't touch it, though, because it will burn your skin right off."

"It doesn't burn you?"

Richard paused and looked at me with a funny expression on his face. "No, it doesn't burn me," he said, shaking his head.

He was about to dig in his pocket when he froze and stared past me with narrowed eyes. Richard startled me by pulling me close to him, as if he was trying to shield me. Then I saw the WiiGii lunge ferally toward us and, without thinking, I pressed the green button on the tube that I still held.

I landed with a hard *thud* and got the air knocked right out of me. My lungs didn't get a chance to recover before a cold hand clutched my throat and made my airways constrict.

"Let her go! It's me you want." I heard Richard call out.

I tried to struggle but the grip was too tight. The mechanical hand was closing like a compressor. I was sure then that I wasn't going to suffocate to death—the WiiGii was just going to snap my neck in half. I was starting to see stars when a fuzzy image of Blake manifested at my side. With unmasked fury he severed the WiiGii's arm in one swift action. Any doubts I had that it was human were laid to rest as blood sprayed from the lifeless limb and writhing body. I was still choking, though. As I tried to yank the severed arm off my neck, I saw Blake clench his jaw. I was scared that he was going to rip the arm off without giving any thought to how he would surely break my neck in the process. I took a step away as his hands moved to my neck and I nearly tripped over the WiiGii's feet.

Blake narrowed his eyes at me. "I won't hurt you," he said coolly.

I would have protested further but as I saw the armoured limb fall to the ground I was left speechless. Blake's hands were so gentle that I didn't even feel him remove the arm.

"Blake! I've got her." I recognized RJ's voice. He was standing on the lunch table beside me and he held Boe's limp body in his hands. He quickly glanced at me, then at Blake and shot toward the hole in the ceiling.

Without permission and without pause, Blake impetuously pulled me to his side and took off after RJ.

I was nauseated with fear, desire and indecision all at once. My hands stung as I grasped his shoulder and the lapels of his jacket, but I barely noticed because he was *flying!* I guessed it had something to do with the blue light emanating from his boots and I made a mental note to myself that I wanted a pair.

I was trembling but was only vaguely concerned for my safety. He held me so tight against him that I could barely breathe. I didn't want him to loosen his grip so I tried to mask my shortness of breath, but failed miserably.

As we flew beside the College, I worked up enough nerve to look at him and, prompted by my attention, he turned to meet my gaze. Overwhelmed, I took a sharp intake of breath thinking of how he could own me with just a look.

Out of the corner of my eye I saw his sTell:R boT coming toward us as it changed its shape, morphing into some kind of cubicle. Blake took his free hand and gently tucked my head against his shoulder when the boT engulfed us. He deftly repositioned himself into a sitting position and I found myself perched on his lap. I didn't have time to process the awkward predicament because we were shortly lowered through the roof of Blake's car. The boT split, separating me from Blake, set me into the passenger seat and immediately transformed back into its original shape and flew off ahead of us.

As the College passed out of sight, I turned to Blake and asked more shakily than I intended, "Where are we going? Is Boe okay? I don't know what—"

"Boe's fine."

As with our previous conversations, I found myself waiting for more to follow. Several moments ticked by and I realized he was finished. I deserved more of an explanation than that.

"Boe's fine." I repeated his statement. "You're sure? Well, fine, that answers my first question. But you still haven't told me where we're going."

He remained unreadable and utterly still—a lifeless two-dimensional shape that sat against the blurry backdrop of London passing by.

"Look, I don't know what the hell is going on. I don't know what the hell just happened. I don't know where the hell you're taking me. I don't know who the hell you think you are to treat me like this. And—what the hell happened to my hands?"

I had been numbering the list on my fingers when my bloodstained palms caught my attention. I held them up incredulously for inspection and saw that the blood had gushed down all over my forearm. It looked bad. It had probably been the rush of adrenaline that prevented me from feeling the cuts. As I tried to close my fist I could feel small shards of glass and debris stuck in the wounds. *When had this happened?* Then I remembered the glass from the conservatory.

I held my hands to my chest and my breathing became uneven. I was pathetically squeamish when it came to blood and needles. I couldn't even watch the popular medical dramas on TV because some of the content was just too graphic. Pork Chop loved that kind of stuff and when she hogged the television and forced me to watch it with her I was constantly plugging my ears and covering my eyes. She took some kind of masochistic pleasure in hearing bones crack and watching bullets being removed from gun wounds. I couldn't handle that kind of thing.

I don't know why—maybe it was the terrifying events of the day catching up to me—but I started to shake, a precursor to a complete breakdown from shock. Maybe Blake sensed the authenticity of my reaction because it broke him out of his hard mold.

"We're going to get your hands taken care of. We're almost there." His voice sounded strange, anguished almost.

I dismissed the thought and attributed it to my obvious delirium. I didn't even look at him. Images of my raw hands were invading my mind and causing my tear ducts to fill. It wasn't so much the pain, although it hurt badly; it was more a psychological response.

I remained acutely aware of Blake's presence but he became no more than silhouette beside me. Everything seemed to fade. I lay my head back and started humming something incoherent. I was trying to clear my mind but the harder I tried the less able I was to focus.

¤ X ¤

FIRST IMPRESSIONS

Don't cry. Don't cry. Don't cry.

I assumed that we were in Blake's room—if you could call it a room at all; it was bigger than our old town house and I marveled at its grandeur. Like the rest of the house—it was really more like a palace—the ceilings were covered with marble moldings and displayed an array of different motifs from ancient mythology to modern robotics. The back wall was filled with rows of books that ran right up to the ceiling. A winding staircase cascaded down the wall. The same crystal windows that encased the rest of the residence made up one entire side of the room, with white fluid sloshing at the sides—liquid curtains that seemed to defy gravity. I could see three floors above my head. An assortment of lab tables, gadgets and miscellaneous items were scattered along the marble-tiled floor.

I sat on a stool that automatically adjusted to my height and Blake stood beside me. He gently examined my hands and then picked up a terrifying needle. There wasn't anything particular about the needle that made it terrifying—all needles fall under that category. People say that if you don't look, it's easier to handle, but I'm the type of person who likes to know the ending of a book before I read it; I like to know what happens in a movie before I see it. Freud says we should always try to analyze ourselves if we are to overcome our neuroses. I always thought this tendency of mine marked me as a control freak. It was as if knowing bestowed upon me some measure of control. So naturally, I sat fixated on the needle that approached my hand. The hyperventilation quickly followed.

"Athena."

I looked up as Blake said my name.

"Huh? Yeah?" I said dazedly.

Blake leaned down and moved his head toward me. He was so close. Our faces were less than an inch apart.

"You have to calm your breathing or you'll pass out." His voice was melodic, deep and unmistakably commanding. I certainly felt faint, especially when he brushed my face and pressed his lips against my ear. "You don't like needles, I take it?" He moved his head back so he could look at me. His brow was slightly furrowed. "I would think a girl like you wouldn't be bothered with something so trivial. Jet-racing, showdowns with WiiGiis and you're afraid of a little pin prick?"

He was so damn hard to read. I couldn't tell if he was teasing me or insulting me. Or both. I blinked rapidly as I fell out of my stupor.

"I'm not scared of a needle," I declared proudly.

"Oh, I know. You just took one effortlessly."

I opened my mouth to say something but stopped and looked down. Blake wasn't holding the needle anymore.

"I told you. No problem," I said, clearing my throat.

Blake just nodded his head—his expression still unreadable.

My hands were numb so I couldn't feel any pain but when he started cleaning my wounds I had to turn away. I couldn't bear to see him clean out the glass from the flesh and I didn't want him to see me grimace when he did it, either. Looking over my shoulder, I scanned the room and tried to imagine Blake in the meticulous space: living, reading, passing the time. I was so curious about him.

"Is this your room?"

He didn't answer. Maybe he hadn't heard me, but I thought it was more than likely that he was simply ignoring the query.

"Yes," he finally answered.

"Do you read?" I inquired, without thinking, wanting to capitalize on his decision to speak to me.

Ugh! I was such a *stupid idiot*. Of course he read.

Blake cocked his head at me and quirked an eyebrow. "Yes, I do."

"I mean, these books are all yours?"

"Yes."

"Do you like to read?"

What the hell was the matter with me? I sounded like a buffoon. I was just trying to keep the conversation going and for some reason all I could manage to ask was the same frivolous question that would most likely lead to the end of our little exchange.

"Yes," he answered, without pause.

"I like to read, too." I nodded my head stupidly and inwardly cringed at the awkward silence that ensued. "Are you a university student?"

"No."

"Do you have any other siblings besides Boe?"

He didn't answer methodically like before. "Yes."

"Sister or brother?"

"Brother."

"Older or younger?"

"Older."

"I have an older sister as well." I pursed my lips as a smug-looking image of Pork Chop appeared in my mind. *Older* sister be damned. "How close are you guys in age?"

"You're done."

I was taken aback by his brisk comment. I thought I had offended him somehow until I realized that he was referring to my hands. They were clean and wrapped in bandages.

"Thank you."

Blake crossed his arms and leaned his hip against the table. "No, *thank you.* For Boe."

"She's my friend. Helping her was a given, so you don't have to thank me."

"Yes, I do." He was quick to refuse me. "I'm in your *debt.*"

I got off the stool and stood to face him.

"No. You're not in my debt. Just forget it."

"Too bad," he said coolly.

His arrogance piqued my pride.

"Look, you don't owe me anything. The WiiGii would have killed me if you hadn't…We're even. If you owe me anything it would be an apology. If I recall correctly, the last time we met you told me to stay away from Boe. That I wasn't good enough to be her friend. So—"

"You misunderstood my intentions. Boe has a tendency to attract trouble and it would be unwise for you to associate with her."

"No, I think I understood your intentions perfectly. I know people think I'm just a runt or something and since you are, well…some kind of superhuman, and I guess Boe is, too, you didn't want me—"

He cut me off. "Is that what you think?"

"Well, yes."

"Let me clarify myself then since you are *dead wrong.*" He grabbed my wrists and turned my palms up. "Today is a perfect example of why you should stay away from Boe."

I struggled lightly for him to release me, but he didn't.

"I don't see how that's your concern. I'm not your problem."

Blake let out a breath, his gaze so intense that it cut right through me.

"Yes…You. Are." He spoke as if the words burdened him.

I was afraid at how our exchange was escalating. Like our previous encounters, the mask of passivity he wore so quickly slipped away, like he couldn't hold it in place.

I furrowed my brow. "No, I'm not. I'm nothing to someone like you. Let me go," I countered.

Instead of acquiescing to my request he tugged me closer.

"You're so quick to judge me. You think that I would meekly submit to conventional expectations and shun a human being for something that is entirely out of their control? You believe that I would think that—do that to *you?*"

He made it sound as if what I just said was ludicrous, an impossibility that he would ever judge me that way.

"What am I supposed to think? Students at school treat me like a leper and for some reason Boe doesn't. She's actually nice to me and then you tell me to stay away from her and….you always look so irritated with me. If you weren't so indifferent I would think that I repulse you or something. It's like you can't stand me."

Blake's indignation was almost violent.

"*Repulsed.* No…never…What I can't stand is not being able to…"

Heat burned through my veins as he slowly released one of my wrists and smoothed his hand across my jawbone. His eyes wandered down my face and rested vehemently on my mouth. Ever so slowly he ran his finger along my lower lip and gently traced it as he pulled my head closer. With more daring than I ever thought I was capable of, I pushed myself closer to him and Blake's eyes became hot—fervid—his finger passing roughly over my lip so he could slide his hand into my hair. I raised myself up on my tiptoes, wanton for his touch, as he bent his head toward mine. His mouth started to open and I felt his sweet breath on my face. My hands were still numb so there was no pain when I balled them into fists to clutch his shirt.

Blake's lips were practically grazing mine when he stopped, stood still and cocked his head to the side, distracted. Setting his jaw, he looked like he was deliberating over something. All the while I waited, fraught with desire. His grip suddenly tightened around me and he gently jerked me forward. He didn't kiss me but his lips shifted over mine as he spoke.

"You're definitely *my* problem."

He held me for a moment longer, unwilling to let go, before he darted with incredible speed from the room.

I stood frozen in place as my mind lingered on Blake's parting words. I was *his* problem. What the heck did that mean? I took a few deep breaths trying to get my head straight. I was so inexperienced when it came to interaction with the opposite sex. I was so overwhelmed, confused and conflicted all at once. It was all so new. Staring at the door Blake had just passed through, my heart rate accelerated at just the thought of him returning.

Where did he go? And why in such a hurry? Worried, I immediately thought of Boe, but Blake had reassured me that she was fine. Maybe he was lying to keep me calm.

"She's fine. She's fine. She has to be fine. Breathe deeply, Athena," I said aloud as I rubbed my forehead anxiously. I turned to sit back down on the stool and nearly tripped over myself as I caught sight of two robots floating aimlessly above the center of the table. I was sure that the room had been empty a moment before. I gathered that these were the two sTell:R boTs I saw earlier in the lunch hall although they took on slightly different shapes. One of the boTs gave off a blue glow and looked like an odd assortment of geometriclike shapes. Its head was sort of pyramidal and what I took to be its torso was long and cylindrical with two shapes resembling cones at its base. Small mechanical wings flanked its sides with two tiny clamps for hands at the ends. Looking at the other boT, I thought it unsurprising that since the first one was small and lithe that the second would be wider and stocky. Its head was shaped more like a cube and sat atop a wide bowl of a torso upon which four spherical balls jutted out. It gave off a green glow.

I leaned over the table to get a closer look and made an exaggerated wave. "Hello? Uh, can you hear me?" I jumped back as the green boT abruptly gave the blue boT a nudge. "Hello?" I repeated. "I'm Athena." I felt a little ridiculous introducing myself.

Wide eyes blinked open as the blue boT came to life. The conelike shapes at its bottom started to spin rapidly as it moved forward and reached out to me with its small hand.

"Greetings! I'm oC. It's so nice to meet a friend of Blake's!"

I was dumbstruck as I watched the mechanical head speak to me. Its voice was distinguishably male, distinctly English, surprisingly juvenile and deliriously enthusiastic. I liked it at once.

"I wouldn't call myself a *friend* exactly," I explained nervously.

"You must be! Blake has *never* brought anyone home. He seems to like you very much." He sounded so assured.

Without warning the green boT shot out a spherical fist and hit oC square on the head before returning to its immobile position. Letting out an uneasy laugh, oC pressed out his hands to excuse himself and gave me a slight bow before he whipped around to face the other boT. Tilting his head from side to side, he looked like he was carrying on an animate conversation, but he didn't utter a word aloud. I raised my eyebrows in wonder as I recalled that Pork Chop said sTell:R boTs were able to communicate in an almost telepathic like way. Both Boe and Blake did the same thing sometimes, often looking like they were listening to an invisible telephone.

"You saw how she stood up for that boy, Richard Coleridge, today. It was quite admirable and shows her fine character. Come now, Blake is quite fond of her you know and she must really be something considering his affinity to that depressing twentieth century philosopher; other people may be hell but she's an apparent exception!" oC evaded another jab from the mute boT.

My cheeks started to burn as he nonchalantly spoke about Blake's *fondness* for me. Two days ago I was a normal teenaged girl. My life hadn't been conventional exactly, but it hadn't been exceptional either. Now, two hundred years in the future, I found myself in the fantastical house of a demi-god and had his talking robots for company. *What next?*

"oC, is something wrong?" I asked hesitantly.

His hands fluttered rapidly. "I'm sorry, Athena. It's just going to take some getting use to—having you around that is."

I couldn't see myself, but I was sure my face had taken on a shade of purple. Mortified at how oC kept emphasizing that I was going to become a fixed presence in Blake's life, I didn't pay too much attention to the nervousness in the little boT's voice.

"I take it your boT friend doesn't like strangers. That's understandable. I'm uneasy around new people too. What's his name?" I asked curiously.

oC squeezed his eyes shut and slapped his hand over his head. It was so odd looking that I was about laugh.

"WHO YOU CALLING A *HE?*"

The clearly female voice sounded like an angry southern gospel singer, except I was pretty sure she wasn't interested in preaching. The boom of her voice made the room rattle.

oC flew in front of me, acting like a shield, and held out his hands in supplication to the green boT, who was taking on a menacing looking shape. Armaments folded out of her massive robotic frame and warfare weaponry flanked her mechanical limbs.

I wanted to hold my ground and pretend that I wasn't scared but, honestly, all it would take from the livid boT was a snap of her treacherous fingers to annihilate me, so I pathetically hid myself behind oC.

"vIBee, she didn't know! An honest mistake. No need to get angry now," oC told her, using a soothing tone.

"Don't you *vIBee* me, oCTon. Did you see how she went around inspecting us like we were goods on display? I'm gonna teach this runt some manners!" she screeched.

oC transformed himself and tried to grab the female boT as she lurched forward, but she managed to zoom past him and came toward me as I ducked out of the way.

"vIBee, I'm sorry!" I frantically crawled around the table. "You're obviously a sheeee!" The tabletop was blasted into bits and I covered my head as the debris flew across the room.

Psycho boT.

"Don't you call me *vIBee* you little piece of—"

"vI! Blake's not going to be"—oC dodged around vI when she tried to swipe him—"happy about THIS!" oC's voice was shrill with panic.

I scurried across the room and threw myself behind a nearby couch, but it was obliterated to pieces a few moments later and left me exposed on the floor. oC shaped himself into a large, flat mesh sheet as vI sped toward me, hoping to bar her path.

"oCTon, I'm warning you. You had best move aside."

"I cannot let you hurt the girl. This is completely uncivilized behavior. She has done nothing to you."

"I won't hurt her too bad. I'm just gonna *play* with her."

oC cringed. "I can absolutely not allow it."

"Fine boT, have it your way."

I gasped as vI blasted right through him.

"vI, how could you?" oC asked soberly as he reassembled himself.

Wracking my brain, I remembered that Pork Chop told me that boTs were programmed to follow commands for human protection.

"*vI. Stop. Load,*" I shouted, dragging a chair in front of myself.

She froze immediately. I wiped my brow as undulated relief swept over me and lowered myself over the arm of the chair. It seemed no matter where I went I found myself in perilous trouble these days. "oC, are you okay?" I asked, exhausted. The feeling of security quickly faded as I noticed oC frantically shaking his head at me and waving his hands as if in warning. Just as I took notice, vI swiveled around to face him. oC's arms immediately stilled and he hid them behind his back.

"Did she just *Stop. Load.* me?" vI howled.

oC's head began to chatter.

"Did *she* just *Stop. Load. me?*" If vI sounded angry before, she now sounded furious. "OH, NO SHE DIDN'T!"

"vI, she didn't mean to offe"—vI punched oC so hard she sent his detached head flying across the room—"eeeenndddd yooouuuu!"

I hurled myself out of the chair, but vI's pincers grabbed a fistful of my hair and yanked me to the ground.

"Who'd you think you're *Stop. Loading,* girl?"

"Ow! Ow! Ow! Ow! Ow! Let go of me you crazy robot!" I cried out as she dragged me across the room.

"Now you calling me crazy!" she said derisively.

Multiple sets of claws sprang out of her metallic body; one wrapped itself around my ankle and flipped me upside down, while the others lifted my arms at various angles and titled my head backwards and forward.

vI's belligerent voice pierced my eardrum as one pincer banged on my head.

"Knock. Knock. No surprise, nothing there!" She laughed. "I don't see what's so special about this runt. Flimsy arms and legs. Wouldn't call that face pretty." vI squeezed my cheeks together and I thought my jaw was going to crack.

"Hey!" I shouted. "Put me down this instant," I demanded, struggling against the onslaught of invasive pincers.

"How'd you like being inspected, missy? You rotten no good little—"

"I get it!" I snapped. "You don't like me. The feeling is *very* mutual. Now put me down or I swear I'll—I'll—I'm going to detonate a sTell:R bomb just like that WiiGii did today in the lunch hall!" I tried to make my threat sound intimidating, but it sounded lame even to me.

"Those bombs don't work on me you moronic cockroach, but let's get one thing clear: are you threatening me?" she asked contemptuously.

"Yeah. Yes I am!"

"Good. When they find your body I'll just say that you were threatening me and I had no choice but to defend myself. " vI's laugh made my stomach churn.

When they found my body.

"vICeron, this has gone far enough! Don't make me stop you."

Still holding me, vI whipped around at the sound of oC's severe voice.

"oCTon, stay outta of this."

"I cannot." oC's arms and legs transformed into an armada of artillery. "Put the girl *down*."

"Make me," vI hissed, taking off toward the higher floors like an airborne missile.

The ground grew farther and farther away and bile rushed to my mouth—if this continued much longer I was going to be seriously sick.

With oC on her tail, vI zigzagged around the cavernous room, which was in complete disarray; debris was scattered everywhere, half the furniture had been destroyed and pages from massacred books drifted in the air.

A beautiful domed crystal window sheltered the topmost landing. The area was larger than a soccer field and was crowded by gymnastic equipment, an assortment of weaponry, floating holograms, a massive pile of books, an impressive art collection and various instruments, including a grand piano and cello. Dominating the far end of the room was a telescope so huge that it went right up to the ceiling. Then I saw the bed—his bed—and I knew we were in Blake's *bedroom.*

Facing a dead end, vI whipped around, her arm transforming into something that resembled a missile ejector, and aimed it at oC's head.

"You wouldn't dare!" he said, aghast. "Not in this room. Blake's already going to be furious about the mayhem downstairs."

Sure that I was going to vomit, I tried to grab my knees to turn myself upright when both boTs suddenly stiffened and tilted their heads in synchronization.

vI cursed.

"Put her down," oC pleaded.

"Oh, all right!" vI let out a huff and, with all the restraint I was sure she was capable of, released her grip on my ankle and dropped me before flying off.

I yelped as I fell the thirty or so feet to the ground, but oC caught me gently and cradled me like a child.

"oC, I think I'm going to be sick," I moaned.

"Just rest here for a moment. vI simply needs to calm down. I'm going to go find her and I'll make her see reason."

I didn't want him to leave me in case she was in some hidden wing waiting to finish me off.

"Where did she go? Is she going to come back? Don't leave me," I entreated.

oC released me into a sea of white. "Don't you worry about a thing," he assured me. "vI won't be back and I'll return in a moment."

After he disappeared, I put my hand over my eyes and tried to focus on steadying my breathing, which was like trying to steady a sailboat in the midst of a hurricane. Impossible. It wasn't because I was worried that vI was going to come back to get me, although I didn't dismiss the possibility, it was because I was pretty sure that I was going to hurl and I was in Blake's *bed*.

¤ XI ¤

V E T O

A wave of dizziness hit me like a ton of bricks as I shifted to move off the bed. I haphazardly managed to tumble to the floor and I instinctively rolled into a ball. The tiniest movement detonated an atomic bomb inside my head that effectively blew my brains to bits. I held still hoping that would deter the pounding, but something started to vibrate in my pocket. Similes of atomic bombs had been bombarding my mind so I immediately thought that vI planted one as plan B—if they couldn't find my body, they were going to find its pieces.

Fishing for the device, I struggled fervidly as if my life was on the line and conceded that every second that passed was surely going to be my last. My hand finally wrapped around the source of the vibration and, with all the strength I could muster, I threw the thing as far from me as I could. That little she-devil boT had to do better than that to finish me off.

Grabbing the bedclothes, I frantically hauled myself over the bed and scurried to the other side—a soldier on a battlefield—and heaved myself to the ground, hoping to use the massive piece of furniture as a shield. I grabbed the downy soft sheets and buried myself under them waiting for the impact from the explosion.

But nothing happened. After a few moments I strained my ears as I thought I heard a muffled voice calling out to me. I hesitated about whether or not to uncover myself, thinking it could be some kind of trick. The voice grew louder and it sounded like whoever was speaking was getting closer. It finally boomed right next to my ear and I was almost giddy with relief; I recognized Pork Chop's aggravated voice.

"Hello? Earth to Gustav. Such a dumb bum I see. Didn't Sammy show you how to answer your eFone? Just say *Answer. Load*. Use that little brain of yours!"

I threw an irritated expression on my face and pulled the covers off my head. I could feel my face blanch before quickly burning red. Blake knelt on one knee beside me holding out the little earpiece Sammy gave me. My *eFone*. Pork Chop's voice continued to bark out of the little device and suddenly her holographic face appeared before me.

"Guse, are you there? I can't see you."

Thank god. That meant she couldn't see Blake either.

"Yes," I managed to squeak.

"Finally! Where the hell are you? Load your visual feature."

I wondered whether Blake intentionally disconnected the visual function in anticipation of my reluctance to let Pork Chop see where I was or with whom I was with, or if Blake himself didn't wanted Pork Chop to know.

"Hello!" she bellowed.

Man, she could be annoying.

I cleared my throat. "Yeah, I'm here."

A muscle ticked in Blake's jaw as he scanned my face searchingly.

"Where is here? I heard about the incident at the College and thought you probably hid yourself in a locker or something and got stuck inside." She chuckled. "Such a scaredy cat, Guse. WiiGiis aren't interested in *you* okay. Logan called me though."

I was sure that Blake narrowed his eyes for a fraction of a second. "He heard about the attack and scoured the College for you. He said you were supposed to meet him and when you didn't show up he was worried you got hurt even though no injuries were reported. Where are you? Still got all your limbs?"

I was used to Pork Chop's dose of over the top sarcasm but she was making me sound like an idiotic coward and Blake was hearing every word.

"First of all, I didn't agree to meet your obnoxious friend. Second, *please*, obviously I wasn't afraid of the WiiGiis. I was completely calm the whole time."

Blake's expression didn't change as I rebuked my sister's

snarky comment.

"Whatever, where you are?"

"My friend got hurt and I went home with her to make sure she was okay."

"You don't have friends," she teased.

"I'm hanging up, Pork," I threatened, grimacing as she laughed heartily.

"All right, all right. Is your friend okay?"

"Yeah, I think so." I looked at Blake to see if something in his face would refute my claim; he simply nodded.

"Kay, give me your coordinates and I'll send Logan to pick you up."

I wasn't sure what bothered him, but Blake visibly tensed.

"I'll find my own way home. Don't worry about me. I'm a big girl."

Pork Chop rolled her eyes and let out a breath. "Fine. Call me if you need anything. You do know how to call me, right?"

"That's it. I'm hanging up on you. *Hang-up. Load.*"

Pork Chop erupted with laughter as I grabbed the eFone from Blake's hand and shook it vehemently. "*Hang-up. Load,*" I repeated, but the call didn't terminate.

"Ah, Guse, your antics really brighten my day. That's not a command you idiot. Later!" Her face disintegrated as I squeezed the little earplug in frustration.

Blake stood and held out his hand, offering me his assistance to get up. I was still a bit dizzy but my pride insisted that I refuse— the pounding in my head that returned after the short rush of adrenaline pleaded for me to accept. I was too damned stubborn though. Awkwardly getting up on my hands and knees, I ignored his offered aid and shakily managed to stand by groping the side of the bed. Blake's hand remained outstretched but he didn't move to assist me.

After running my fingers through my hair, I straightened my clothes, avoiding his gaze. He boldly claimed my face in his hands and tenderly tilted my head to the side before I could protest. vI clamped down on my jaw so hard that she probably left a mark.

"What happened?" The edge in his voice made the hairs on my arms rise.

"I—I—It was an accident." I don't know why I found myself covering for vI, but I was scared for her; Blake looked murderous. "I'm sorry about the damage. I think things got a bit out of control. I'll pay for everything." I cringed as I thought of sticking Sammy with what would undoubtedly be a catastrophically large bill. "It's sorta my fault. I think I was somewhat offensive. I've never really met a—I mean I'm not accustomed to interacting with…*boTs*."

Blake didn't look the least bit convinced as he took my hand and led me toward the bed. I followed him hypnotically and sunk down onto the edge as he laid the slightest amount of pressure on my shoulders.

"Stay here."

The next instant he was already halfway across the room. I didn't want to be left alone, but more than that, I wanted to be near him.

"No! I'll go with you," I said, jumping up to start after him. My feet got tangled in the bedclothes that lay scattered on the ground and I had to jig and jive to keep my balance. Managing to free myself without falling flat on my face, I turned back around and was startled to find Blake standing but an inch from me—man, he was fast. It was puzzling because he wore a look of inhibition, as if he wanted to catch me but held himself back anticipating that my ego would insist that I help myself.

I let out a nervous breath and gave him an uncertain half smile. "I'll go with you, if that's okay?"

His eyes narrowed as he tilted his head. "Don't be afraid. vI's not going to be a problem."

I was almost sorry for the boT at Blake's cryptic message.

"I'm not afraid. I just want to see Boe that's all."

"Boe's fine. I'll take you to see her when I come back."

"Where are you going?" I asked a little too eagerly.

"I'll be back soon."

"Look, I'm fine and I can take care of myself. If you're planning on punishing vI, don't bother. I don't need you to fight my battles for me. I'll deal with it myself. I am *not* scared of her. I see right through vI and her bark is far worse than her bite." My body cried that every word I just said was an absolute lie.

"My boTs have been incredibly *rude* and seem to have forgotten their manners. I plan on taking this matter up with them *right now.*"

"Honestly, you sound exactly like vI." Blake pursed his lips. "She didn't do any permanent damage, see." I held up my bandaged hands and turned around. "Perfectly intact. Just forget it." It was easier trying to convince Blake than trying to convince myself. I still had a serious bone to pick with the vicious boT. "Blake?"

I had never addressed him by his name before and I thought it was funny how I found the syllables so dear to me.

Blake wore an expression on his face that was hard to describe. It was almost a look of wonder, as if I had said something so profound he couldn't quite believe it. "Can I ask you for something?"

"I *am* in your debt," he whispered, moving closer.

"I was wondering…could you…" Blake's hands found their way onto my arms and started to caress their way up to my shoulder blades. "Could you…" I couldn't concentrate as his fingers splayed across my nape.

"What?" he asked, his grip tightening around the back of my neck.

There was something I was going to ask for, but my thoughts were all befuddled.

"Tell me what you want," Blake urged.

As his hand tensed around my arm, I felt a stab of pain and I remembered.

"I want a *sTell:R bomb*," I blurted out.

Blake fell still at my request and gave me a probing look. Then he smirked. I didn't get what amused him but his reaction was arrestingly attractive.

"What's so funny?"

He shook his head lightly.

"Do you know what I'm talking about? It's the thing the WiiGii threw out today."

"Yes, I know," he said smoothly. "You would like to fight your own battles wouldn't you?" Blake pulled away from me with a spark of amused annoyance gleaming in his eyes.

"Can you get me one?" I asked, biting the inside of my cheek.

"I'll see what I can do," he replied, reaching down to take hold of my hand, as if it were the most natural thing in the world.

I wasn't an overly affectionate person and had never held a guy's hand before and it was terribly awkward. Blake led me down the length of the room and slowly entwined his fingers with mine. I was glad that my palms were covered in bandages or else he would have felt how clammy they were. I don't think he would have minded though, as he gave my hand the lightest squeeze when I attempted to loosen it free. Apparently, he liked it exactly where it was—held securely by him.

Wondrous images swam before my eyes as I traversed through the enormous mansion but I didn't pay much attention. Blake's hand in mine sent pulses through my body that fogged up the windshields of my mind; I couldn't see anything for the life of me but I could most definitely feel the heat.

The same milklike liquid I saw earlier in Blake's room covered Boe's bedroom door, which was made entirely of crystal. When Blake and I approached it, an open doorway appeared as the fluid sloshed away. I was going to inquire about how it worked, but found Blake frowning. Turning to find the source of his agitation, I immediately felt the tension, so thick it was almost tangible, as I spotted Boe and RJ standing in the middle of a very feminine room. Our presence didn't seem to bother them as they stared silently at one another. They wore similar taut expressions that accented the visibly pulsing muscles that ticked across their faces.

All too aware that not only were Blake and I intruding, but my hand still lay gingerly in his, I quickly tried to tug it away—not wanting to draw attention to this intimacy—and wanted to leave the scene, but Blake tightened his grip and drew me closer.

"Blake, let go of my hand," I whispered. I vainly tried to pry his hand away but I might as well have been trying to unfold a rock. "Blake, let go," I urged.

"No."

I looked at him bewilderedly. "What do you mean *no*?" I said through slightly clenched teeth.

"I like it there." His eyes hadn't moved away from Boe and RJ and his expression was as blank as always.

"Too bad. Let go. Now."

"You like it there too. Boe won't mind," he drawled, just above a whisper.

I could feel myself start to sweat from the heat wave.

"You're crazy." I tried to push Blake back through the door as I glanced at Boe and RJ who still stood as stiff as statues. "I think we're interrupting here. Let's just stop by later."

I frowned as Blake tilted his head to the side and I pictured the three of them having some sort of telepathic conversation that I couldn't hear. That was so unfair.

Blake could have literally been fastened to the ground because he didn't give the slightest when I pushed up against him. He simply rested his hand around the base of my neck as I shoved against his chest, which was as hard as stone. His touch was so potent it made me neurotic but I was beset over how to channel the charge inside me. Narrowing my eyes, I pulled away from him and took a step back. With one hand still held in his, I pressed my shoulder into him with all my might. If I wasn't so overwhelmed I would have thought it was comical. Out of the corner of my eye I swear I saw Blake grin, as if he was delighted with my efforts, my rough touch, but when I looked at him his face wore the same subtle expression.

"Get out!"

I stopped and turned abruptly at the sound of Boe's voice. Stepping in front of Blake, I hid the hand he still held behind my back.

"We were just leaving Boe," I said quickly.

As a hurdle of threatening looking shoes, we're talking four to five inch heels at least, started shooting across the room at RJ, I realized she hadn't been talking to Blake and I.

"Athena, I didn't mean you!" she said apologetically. "My *friends* are welcome to stay," Boe admonished, glowering at RJ.

"You're acting like a bloody child, Boe. Enough of this." RJ caught a red stiletto and threw it down. "You know I'm right, that's why you're throwing this fit. Can't you ever admit that you're wrong?"

She pointed her finger at him menacingly. "Who do you think you are to tell me what to do? You don't own me RJ. I'll do whatever the bloody hell I want to do. I'm *not* leaving the College."

"You don't need the College. Why are you being so damned stubborn." RJ evaded another airborne shoe missile. "Boe, stop it. Can't we talk about this calmly?"

"What's there to talk about? My decision is made."

RJ ran his fingers through his hair.

"Well?" Boe asked fiercely.

"I have a say when it comes to your safety and I'm putting my foot down. You're not going back, Boe."

"That's it! Just go! I don't want to see you right now."

RJ didn't make a move to leave.

"Get. Out. Of. My. Face. Alexander Valcrest or the next thing I throw at you won't be a god damn shoe!"

He brushed past me as he made his way out, but I didn't actually see him leave—he was too fast. As soon as he was out the door Boe's eyes fell on the open doorway. Her look of anger quickly changed into one of displeasure.

"He's right," Blake told her.

Boe stared irritatingly at her brother. "Not you too," she replied, darting around the room picking up her vast collection of footwear.

"Why are you so adamant about the College?" Blake asked coolly.

The delicate stiletto Boe held in her hand snapped in two; I gathered she was angry.

"You know why. I want to do *normal* things. I want to be around people my age. Is that too much to ask, Blake?" Her voice was small and filled with a loneliness that I recognized. She slouched over the bundle of shoes wrapped in her arms and sat onto her excessively pink bed. Blake let me slide my hand free as I moved to go to her—I hoped Boe hadn't taken notice.

"Compromise, Boe. RJ might be able to put up with your dramatics but you know this won't work on me."

A sliver of deviousness crossed Boe's face as she grinned at her brother.

"Come on Blake, I'm not going to hide like some chicken shit. If those WiiGiis want me, well, they can come and get me. And I don't really care about going to the College, but that doesn't mean RJ can tell me what to do. Besides, all's well that ends well, right?" She wrapped her arm around my shoulder affectionately. "Thanks to Athena that is. See, I have my own personal bodyguard," Boe said, smiling at me. "RJ has nothing to worry about."

There was a miniscule change to Blake's features that almost made him appear to be scowling.

"Boe are you nuts?" I declared.

What was she thinking? Wasn't she concerned about what happened today? "You could have been seriously hurt. You should be freaking out," I said anxiously.

"Don't be such a worry bug, Athena. It takes more than a couple of WiiGiis—hiding their ugly faces behind those tacky masks—to take down this." Boe pointed to herself confidently.

I stared at her, trying really hard not to roll my eyes. If this was her way of dealing with the shock, then I had to be supportive. And this had to be her way of dealing with the shock because I couldn't fathom that she was really this unconcerned; she nearly got killed or worse.

Boe seemed to detect my skepticism. "Athena, if those WiiGiis had even touched me their heads would be detached from their bodies right now."

I didn't doubt that Boe could take care of herself; I saw her abilities myself that day, but I was still unconvinced that the WiiGiis weren't a threat to her.

"Maybe RJ has a point, Boe," I told her hesitantly.

She was about to dismiss my concern when she took notice of my bandaged hands.

"What happened?" Alarm lined her voice.

"Just a few minor cuts," I replied casually.

"You should note that Athena's a very good liar, Boe."

I glared at Blake resentfully. Still thought of me as a liar did he?

Boe eyed me wearily and then looked at her brother. She seemed to be thinking about something really hard.

"Fine! Two weeks that's it!" she said finally.

"Tell RJ he owes me one." There was a touch of smugness in Blake's voice.

"I'll tell him that he owes *Athena* one," Boe replied, correcting him.

"That would make two of us." Blake's eyes hadn't left me and I shifted uncomfortably under his gaze.

Boe turned and gave me a hearty hug. I didn't hug people often and awkwardly patted her shoulder as she embraced me.

"Lucky you," she whispered. "My guys always repay their debts tenfold." She withdrew and winked at me and I smiled uneasily. "I'll see you tomorrow, kay?"

"Sure, I guess."

With a wave, Boe bounded for the door and disappeared. A second later she popped her head back through the doorway.

"By the way, I'm taking the TX."

"Nice try, Boe," Blake told her, crossing his arms.

"Please! I want to catch him."

Blake was silent. Boe stomped her foot before turning slyly toward me.

"Athena, I will forever be in your debt if you would do something for me."

Blake pursed his lips, as if in anticipation of Boe's request. "Blake said he was in your debt, right?"

"I told him he was being ridiculous. He's not going to owe me one because he thinks that I saved *your* life," I said sardonically.

Boe waved her hand dismissively. "Hosh posh. Of course he is in your debt. Heck, the world is in your debt for saving my invaluable life."

This time I couldn't restrain myself. "Oh, brother," I scoffed.

"Athena, since we are recently acquainted, I'll let that little remark slip. You obviously don't know who I am," she retorted in mock indignation. "Getting back to the matter at hand, since Blake *is* in your debt, if you asked him to let me take his car then he would be obliged to let me."

"He's not in my debt, Boe," I said resolutely.

"Well, are you, Blake?" she asked her brother impatiently.

"Yes, I am." The edge of Blake's mouth twitched upward.

Boe squeezed her hands together as if in prayer and mouthed, "Please."

I scowled as she pouted her lips together. The last thing I needed was another pesky little sister.

"Blake," I said through clenched teeth.

"Yes, Athena," he answered, narrowing his eyes.

I couldn't tell whether I heard anxiousness or eagerness in his voice; was he apprehensive over my request or eager to fulfill it? Either way, when he said my name my heart started to race.

"Would you let Boe take your car?"

"The TX to be specific," Boe chimed in.

"We'll call it even," I said sourly.

Blake leaned across the doorframe as Boe tapped her foot impatiently. After a few moments he cocked his head lightly and Boe leapt toward Blake to give him a solid peck on the cheek.

"Luv you." She beamed. As she ran out the door I heard her holler over her shoulder, "Athena, I owe you big!"

"She owes you big," Blake repeated.

"Whatever."

This was the second time Boe had left me alone with him. I could already feel the currents in the room changing. A part of me wanted to find out where the river would carry me, the rational part of me wanted to avoid the awkwardness that was sure to follow.

"Do you think you could give me ride home?"

Blake leaned away from the doorway and straightened abruptly. He didn't answer me but just stood staring, wearing his usual stern expression. "If it's a problem I can call my sister to come and get me. What's the address here?" I started to fish for my eFone in my pocket.

"Is that what you want?" he asked quietly.

"Forget it," I said. I dug out the little earpiece. All I had to do was figure out how to get it to dial. "I guess I got one too many knocks on the head today because my mind is drawing a blank here.

I'm not up to date with all these new gadgets. Would you mind showing me how to call out?"

"You want to go home?"

I immediately got the sense that he wanted me to stay, although that could be wishful thinking. Blake was always so austere in his speech and demeanor, always talking in some kind of cryptic code.

"Well…" I didn't know what to say. "Shouldn't I go home? Boe's gone. Why else would I stay?"

He crossed his arms. "Why else would you?" he asked innocently.

If this was a game, he was an adversary I couldn't beat.

"You tell me Blake," I replied, shrugging my shoulders.

"I'll show you around." He left the room without waiting for my reply.

I lingered back for a moment not wanting to appear too eager. He was waiting around the corner for me when I emerged from Boe's room and I couldn't suppress the grin that spread out across my face. He eyed me curiously and cocked his head to the side—he did this so often I couldn't help but think he had been a bird in a previous life.

"Something funny?" he asked.

I shook my head. "Not really."

As we walked side by side down another decorous hall I was certain that he would try to hold my hand again, but he didn't.

I could feel the dynamic between us changing. I wasn't sure if it was at my instigation or if it was simply a natural progression, but I wanted to believe that my growing confidence was a sign that a part of me recognized that Blake, on some level, was reciprocating whatever I was feeling. It's funny how your mind sometimes thinks up the most random things. I looked over at him and thought of how he would be a challenging pursuit and I had never pursued anyone before; it was like jumping from kindergarten to a Ph.D in astrophysics. Nothing I had ever experienced assured me that I was up to this feat, but there was a very small voice in the back of my mind, one that I couldn't seem to quiet, that whispered I wouldn't have to try very hard. When Blake sidestepped us around a Baroque marble statue that I was about to walk directly into, I rethought that.

I still couldn't believe it was actually a residence as opposed to a place where people paid an entry fee to marvel at works found in the most prestigious museums around the world. We walked through endless galleries and Blake never left my side. When I wandered around to gaze at a certain masterpiece he would follow, never letting more than a foot of space separate us. His proximity did funny things to me so it took me a while to gather my wits to pry him for some answers.

"So you live here?" I didn't look at him, but pretended to stare analytically at a work by Gorky. It was a piece you could pretend to contemplate about.

"I do," Blake answered.

Now that I had broken the ice there was no letting up. "With Boe?"

"Yes."

"Anyone else?"

"Yes."

"Who?"

"Our boTs, naturally."

"Boe has a boT, too?"

"Of course."

"Just one."

"Yes."

Pork Chop thought I didn't have many friends because I didn't have "people" skills. She said I sounded like a pushy journalist when I conversed with people. It was sort of true. I was a curious person, so I always had tons of questions and I didn't like to talk about myself. The onslaught of questions often made people feel uncomfortable. Blake, however, seemed unconcerned with my directness.

"How come you have two?" I asked, still staring at the canvas.

"Veto."

I puckered my forehead. "Veto?"

"I'm not answering that question. Not today anyway. Next."

I turned to face him. "Why won't you answer that question?"

"Veto." He placed his hand against the small of my back and veered me toward a Waterhouse painting.

Was he trying to distract me?

"Come on," I pleaded.

"Veto," he said, trying to turn me toward the masterpiece.

"You sound like a petulant child," I said reproachfully.

He shook his head slowly from side to side. "Veto."

"Stop saying that. How come you have two boTs?" I whined.

Blake drummed his fingers over his lips as I looked at him demandingly.

"oC is really my sTell:R boT. vI is, technically, mine through association," he finally conceded, choosing his words carefully.

"What does that mean?"

He crossed his arms. "Athena, I'm going to veto any other question about the boTs. So, if you don't want me to sound like a petulant child, then I suggest you ask another."

I scowled. "I take it you don't go to the College."

"No, I don't."

"How old are you?"

"Older than you."

"How old is older?"

Blake raised one eyebrow. "I think we've determined that I'm older. Next."

"Why don't you want to tell me how old you are?"

"Because I don't," he replied coolly.

Frustrated, I headed toward an eye-catching installation.

"Where are your parents?"

"Dead."

My steps faltered as I remembered the conversation I had with Boe in the conservatory. "I'm sorry to hear that." I waited to see if he would say anything further, but he didn't.

"Are those all your questions?" he asked casually, tucking his hands into his pockets.

"What do you do?" I asked curiously.

"I do lots of things."

"I mean, do you have a job?"

"You could say that."

"What kind of job?"

"Veto."

"What!" I gave him a suspicious look. "Are you a criminal? Or do you work for some top secret government agency and you can't tell me about it?" I asked sarcastically. Blake quirked a brow and just shrugged his shoulders. "Well, I don't know if I should be hanging around with you. For all I know you could be a terrorist or a drug dealer," I retorted.

"To reassure you, let me state for the record that I am not engaged in any of the illegal activities you mentioned." He playfully rubbed the back of his neck and smirked. "I dabble with some technological research now and again."

"What kind of technological research?"

"How about I get to ask you some questions so you can throw this beloved four letter word back at me? I daresay you'll be just as inclined to veto my questions as I am to veto yours."

"No, I won't be. If you give me answers, I promise to do the same," I offered sincerely. I doubted he was really curious about me anyway.

"A promise is a promise, Athena. And I promise that my questions will be of a very, very, *personal* nature and I will press for details."

I hated how he could make my face flame. "But I'm feeling generous and I'll give you another option. Anyone will tell you that I'm notoriously impatient, but I will let you ask me questions, all night if you like, so long as you don't press me if I choose to veto," he said smoothly, cocking his head.

I slowly turned and headed into another spacious gallery. "Do you have any hobbies?" I asked, accepting his second option.

"Many."

"Like what?"

"The list is far too long and unimportant."

"I'll be the judge of that."

"Veto."

"You've got to be kidding me. I might as well not bother to ask any questions since you won't give me any answers." He just stared at me as I let out an aggravated huff. "Do you know Logan Leger?" I remembered he was slightly distracted when Pork Chop said his name earlier.

Blake looked straight ahead of him as we walked in silence down a narrow corridor.

"Why do you ask?"

"Do you know that it's impertinent to answer a question with a question? You should first give an answer," I said teasingly, knowing I hit a subject that made him uneasy.

Blake just kept walking and ignored my comment so I decided to answer his question.

"When my sister mentioned him you looked…it was as if you recognized the name."

"I did," he answered curtly.

I was just about to ask him to elaborate but he spoke first. "Logan Leger works for ViAno; almost anyone would recognize his name."

"You don't know him personally?" I asked.

Blake halted abruptly and pivoted me around to face him. "How do you feel about Leger?"

I furrowed my brow. "What do you mean by that?" I asked, confused about his query.

"When you met, did you feel anything for him?"

I stared dumbfounded at Blake, anxious about the apprehensive look on his face.

"Why are you asking me this?"

"Just answer the question," he said gratingly, making the hairs on my arms rise.

"I—I barely know him," I offered.

"You barely know me," he whispered.

It seemed like my chest was ill fit to house my heart because it was bursting painfully. I didn't understand where all this was coming from. What did Logan have to do with any of this?

"How did you feel last night on the Boardwalk?" Blake fervently cupped my face in his hands. "How do you feel about me?" he demanded.

I gulped, wondering how the tables had turned. I wished that I could turn back the clocks a few minutes and have him vetoing my questions again.

I shrugged nervously. "Well…" It wasn't a question I could bring myself to answer. "How do you feel about me?" I asked hesitantly.

Blake's breath was sweet as he exhaled. "Did you know it's impertinent to answer a question with a question?" he replied, his voice husky.

"Did you know that I'm quite impertinent?" I teased. "So, do you...like me?"

I was sure he was going to veto the question or insist that I answer first, but instead he shook his head.

"I don't *like* you," he answered sharply.

I could feel the blood drain from my face as his words slapped me across the face.

"Then I guess it doesn't matter how I feel." I snapped angrily, trying to cover the hurt.

I tried to pull away from him, but his hands came around my waist and he held me against him, my chest heaving frantically against his.

"Athena," he practically growled my name. "God...I...It doesn't matter," he declared, clenching his jaw in restraint.

"What doesn't matter?" I asked shakily.

Blake took hold of my shoulders and pushed me away.

I couldn't hide the pain on my face and I looked at him beseechingly. "What's wrong?" I asked, my lips quivering, unsure how much longer I could hold down the fort.

Blake held up his hands and backed away from me, like I was sick with disease. He turned to walk away, but I stepped in front of him and caught his gaze. And then his arms were around me, his hands pressed against my back.

"Athena. Athena. Athena," he said my name as if he adored it, which made me all the more confused.

"What's going on?" I choked.

Blake seemed to struggle over something, a sinner torn between concealment and confession. He closed his eyes and leaned his forehead against mine—the touch burned me.

"Blake, tell me?" I pleaded.

"Veto," he whispered. "Not today."

I shook my head vehemently. "Tell me. Something strange is going on here. I can feel it. It doesn't make sense. I mean you're a stranger." Blake's eyes softened. "You don't even know me," I said quietly.

A tenderness that touched my soul filled his depthless eyes as he bent down and ever so softly kissed one of my hands.

"I'll take you home," he murmured, concerned perhaps because I started to shake uncontrollably.

He turned his head to the side, the usual way he did, as if listening to some kind of invisible telephone, and then his face went blank.

"Wait here," he said through gritted teeth.

Was it vI?

"Blake, please don't hurt her too badly."

He looked at me reassuringly and caressed the apple of my cheek with the back of his soft finger. "vI hasn't come out of hiding yet. There's another matter I need to deal with."

I bit the inside of my cheek as he gently released my hands and left the room.

¤ XII ¤

D É J À V U

There was nothing definite that I feared, but I found myself helplessly afraid. I felt so small in the large room surrounded by haunting faces plastered onto canvases. What's more, each painting seemed to resonate with me; they were all to my liking—works I would have chosen for my own personal collection—and it made me feel uneasy.

Daunted by a feeling that I was being watched, I quickly exited the gallery and made my way down an arched hallway lined with black granite.

"Athena!"

"Ahh!" I jumped around to find oC wincing, apologetic for startling me.

"I'm sorry. I didn't mean to sneak up on you. I know that you have a weak heart." His round eyes grew wide, fearful that he said something he shouldn't have. "Blake asked me to come and stay with you until he returns." He spoke quickly, changing the subject.

"What do you mean I have a weak heart? Even if I did, how would you know that?" I asked, narrowing my eyes.

"I'm a very perceptive individual. I see that I startled you so I surmised that you must naturally have a weak heart and that you have a propensity to be alarmed," he offered nervously.

"oC?" I said suspiciously.

"Yes?" he answered meekly.

"Tell me the truth."

He innocently held out his small hands. "I don't have the slightest idea what you are talking about. That is the truth. I would better explain myself but you see vI dislocated my head so I suppose my wiring is in a state of abominable disrepair." He spun his head and crossed his eyes. "Oh, yes, definitely, wiring is all wrong. Don't pay attention to anything I say."

I was about to berate the boT when I felt the small vibration of my eFone in my pocket. I pulled it out and Sammy's holographic face appeared.

"Guse, you there?"

"Samuel!" oC's voice was whimsically animated, overcome with excitement.

A line creased my forehead. "oC?" My voice was more vehement this time.

The boT smacked his face and started shaking his head in indecision.

"Guse, pick up." Sammy looked worried.

"oC, you know Sammy?" He zoomed away from me and I ran after him. "oCTon!" I used the same name vI used when she was irate. "Answer me right now!"

"oC has to go now." He was so nervous he was talking about himself in third person.

"Guse, finally!" Sammy called out.

I stopped as he disappeared around the corner—the sneaky little boT had answered the call before I could catch him.

"Sammy, can you hear me?" I asked.

"Yeah, I can, but turn on the visual feature. I can't see you."

So, oC didn't want Sammy to know where I was either. He intentionally disabled the function like Blake had when Pork Chop called. They were hiding something and I was determined to find out what.

"I think this thing is broken. It doesn't work," I explained.

"Sof mentioned something about that. Look, are you okay? Where are you?" He sounded anxious and I was touched by his concern.

"I'm fine, really. I'll be home pretty soon. I'm just at a friend's house."

"What friend, Athena?" Sammy's tone was severe and he called me by my name, something that didn't happen often.

"A friend from school. Honestly Sammy, Pork Chop's rubbing

off on you. I am capable of making friends."

"Where are you exactly?" he asked crossly.

oC appeared around the corner and zoomed toward me. This time I was going to get an explanation from him.

"Sammy, I gotta go. Everything's fine. I'll see you soon, kay?"

The line died before Sammy could answer and then I spotted her behind oC.

"Time to go, Athena," oC said in a frenzy as he hoisted me up by my shoulders and flew us back through the gallery.

"Let me at her, oCTon!" vI's voice was a deceptively calm echo as she shot out pincers that snapped furiously at my dangling feet.

"Faster, oC!" I called out fearfully.

We twisted around sharp bends, shot up various staircases and through narrow passages but oC couldn't seem to lose her. vI was relentless in her hunt and she was close. Too close.

Before I knew it, we were through a door I recognized and I heard an earsplitting sound as something collided with it as it slid shut.

"Hmph. Serves her right," oC declared snootily, heading toward Blake's bedroom. "I'll be right back," he said, setting me down.

"oC, come back here," I shouted.

"Sorry, must go. Must go," he stated tersely before descending to the main landing.

I expected to hear some kind of explosion when he and vI butted heads, but the room remained eerily quiet. I waited for a while for him to reemerge but he didn't. Damn it. If Blake's resolve to avoid my questions was final, then I had to try another source. oC was the weak link and I was definitely going to exploit that; the boT was just too affable to be able to resist my pleas. I was sure of it. There was a small voice in my head that couldn't help but quip, *"You're so evil."*

At the moment I didn't care about being good. You didn't have to be a genius to figure out something fishy was going on. I got the feeling that there were sleeping dogs that Blake, Sammy, maybe even Pork Chop, didn't want me to arouse. Liars. All of them liars. Come hell or high water I was going to get the truth.

I stalked across the open space, trying to calm myself. I barely paid attention to the complex apparatuses I passed or the collection of what looked like dangerous artillery. I walked by Blake's bed and stomped around the enormous telescope. Letting out a deep breath, I stared out the crystal window and could see tiny specks of city lights buried under a foggy blanket. I cringed and backed away as I realized how high up I was.

As I turned to pace back up the room, I noticed a narrow doorway off to the side and made my way toward it. Curiosity killed the cat but I was always a strong believer that satisfaction brought it back. The wooden door stood out, it didn't fit with the modern décor, and looked like it belonged to a cottage in the woods. I eyed it warily before I tried the slim silver handle. At first it wouldn't budge, but after a brief moment I heard a click.

"Access granted." The electronic voice startled me.

Pushing open the door, I found a narrow hallway and headed inside. I can't explain it, but I got a sense of déjà vu, as if I'd been there before. The unsettling feeling in the pit of my stomach became painful as I entered a dimly lit cylindrical chamber. There was a wooden antique desk in the center with various items on its surface placed in meticulous order: there were two rows of perfectly lined pens, stacks of neatly arranged books that were sorted by size and a stack of manuscripts that looked like they were from a past century—curled at the edges and yellowed by time. I was about to inspect them when I stopped, chilled, as if I had just seen a ghost.

My feet seemed bulky and they had trouble taking steps; it seemed to take me forever to make my way through the adjacent room to the painting that hung at its center. Shaking badly, my hand reached out to touch the acrylic covered surface. My eyes stung as a collage of blue color seized me. I was staring at what had once been the skyline of New York City with the World Trade Center towers still standing. I let out a stifled breath as my fingers traced the artist's name on the bottom right hand corner. I knew this painting. I adored this painting. I demanded its inheritance over Pork Chop so many times. It was Nanny's.

She painted it early on her in career during a difficult time in her life—the inspiration for the depressing blue shades. I wanted to melt inside it. I wanted to embrace it as if it was my mother incarnate. The pain came so suddenly—it took all my strength to repress my feelings, to not think of her. If I did, I would be beside myself. Grief was something I reserved for the privacy of my own room where I could sob alone in the dark. I had to remember that I wasn't at home and I didn't have the veil of night or the luxury of privacy. Shaking my head distraughtly, I tore my eyes away from the sea of blue and hurried out of the small enclave, desperate to escape. I brushed by the solid desk and was nearly at the entrance of the narrow hallway when I stopped dead in my tracks and shuddered from a cold that had nothing to do with the temperature of the room.

I slowly turned toward the bookcase that lined the far wall and spotted the single item that stood deserted on the middle shelf. Shock, apprehension, disbelief—they were bogging down my mind. First, Nanny's painting and now… The small blue book sat erect, its spine was covered in gold lines and a red ribbon peeked out from its top. I recognized it. It belonged to a series I knew very well. My eyes fell reluctantly onto the golden volume number that still shone, although the book was worn.

As I pulled it gingerly out of place, a loud noise boomed down the passageway. I gazed wildly at the entryway, expecting vI to come crashing through at any minute. Clutching the book, I ran out, not wanting to get caught in the private chamber. I halted before bursting through the wooden door and flipped open the cover and stared down at the front page. It was so unlike me to think of the word that roared in my head. I was surprised when I heard the profanity so clearly, but I guess that's what shock could do to a person. There it was, neatly written in a familiar cursive:

This book belongs to:

Athena L. Ellias

I slammed the book shut and stuffed it through my collar. vI and oC came crashing toward me just as I threw open the door. They both spotted me at once.

"What are you doing in there, runt?" vI sneered.

I ran toward the large telescope trying to find cover. oC was wrestling with her as she shot out pincers.

"viCeron, please!" oC sounded so distraught. "Get a hold of yourself. You are jumping to conclusions."

vI snorted indignantly. "Don't you dare go patronizing me, oCTon. If you think this little piece of garbage is going to be my cipher then you've got another thing coming."

oC's eyes grew so wide they would have popped out of his sockets if he had any. He threw his hand over vI's mouth, but her voice continued to bellow out of a snapping pincer. "I don't know what kind of hold this one has over Blake, but I'm not allowing this to go any further. I'll get rid of her myself, and he'll get over it."

"vICeron, please be quiet. You've already said more than you ought to have." oC sounded exasperated as he tried to snap shut various pincers that continued to speak.

What was vI talking about?

"I ain't gonna be this runt's plaything. You got that, oCTon? You can pass that message onto your master! He can kiss my shiny round a—"

"La, la, la, la, la, la, la, la, la." oC started to sing, doing his best to drone out vI's voice. "You are not being reasonable. You know how he feels about the girl." oC eyed me wearily, not wanting to say too much.

"He just needs a woman, a plaything, to get over this small

infatuation. I'll have gals lined up around the block by tomorrow. He. Doesn't. Need. *Her.*" vI began to thrash more furiously and oC was having a hard time keeping her at bay.

I crouched beside the base of the telescope and started to make my way around it when the sound of drills made me tremble. vI gave up on pincers and was now thrusting drills at oC, who looked terrified.

"vI, he's not infatuated—"

vI slammed into the boT and managed to get free and lurched toward me. The clamp on my back suffocated my lungs.

"HE *LOOOOOOVES* HER!" oC shouted desperately.

For a fraction of second vI froze. I thought it was funny that her robotic reaction matched mine perfectly—speechless, soundless, incredulous.

"He doesn't know how to love," she replied cruelly.

oC seemed hurt by her remark. "You have no idea, vICeron. You have no idea."

vI looked disturbed by oC's quiet voice.

"It's just an infatuation," she hissed, tightening her grip around my ribcage, which was on the verge of cracking.

"You know that's not true. You and I know him better than anyone and you know that that is not true." oC's voice was barely above a hush. "He *adores* hers. He loves her so profoundly—to utter and complete distraction. It's the truth, vI."

"No. No. No. No. No. He. Doesn't. How can he? He's barely known her for a day."

My thoughts exactly.

oC hesitated. "It's complicated."

What was complicated?

"Put her down and we'll sort everything out, all right?"

vI shook her head, unconvinced. oC slowly came forward and nudged her shoulder gently.

"You won't let him separate us, right?"

I was sure I was mistaken, but I thought vI sounded afraid.

"Never. Nothing to fear, everything is going to work out. You'll see. Now give me Athena."

After a moment of deliberation, vI's grip slackened. As oC gently took hold of me, both boT's stiffened and tilted their heads—total déjà vu. It was starting to seriously aggravate me that I never knew what was going on.

"I'll take her. vI, go." oC's voice was grave.

vI hesitated for a moment. "oC—"

"Now!"

I could feel the heat vI let off as she flew out of the room at jet speed.

"What's the matter?" I asked anxiously.

"I'm taking you home."

"Why? What's wrong? Where's Blake?" The domed crystal window unfolded as oC added supports around my body and then he catapulted out of it. "oC!" I yelped.

We descended rapidly through a blanket of cloud until the boT lowered me into Blake's car. The driver seat was vacant and he hovered over it as we took off.

"oC, please tell me. What. Is. Going. On? Why are we leaving?

And"—I didn't know how to word the question—"what did you mean before, about the *complications* with Blake?"

oC faced me and literally zipped his mouth shut.

"Can you at least tell me where vI went?"

He shook his head.

"Why vI hates me?"

oC unzipped a little corner of his mouth. "She doesn't hate you, my dear."

"Yes. She does." I hugged my aching body and grimaced.

"Are you hurt?" he asked worriedly.

"I'll survive," I retorted.

"You'll grow on vI. She just needs some time," he told me confidently.

I puckered my forehead. "What do you mean by that?"

oC zipped his mouth back shut.

"Fine. Be like that," I grumbled.

I guess I was going into emotional overdrive because tears started to threaten my eyes. I tried to blink them away and hastily scrubbed one off my cheek as if it were acid.

"Are you crying?" oC asked, sounding surprised and distressed.

"No," I snapped.

"Oh, I can't stand it when you cry!" he wailed.

"I'm not—did you just say *when* I cry? When have you seen me cry before?" I asked bewilderedly.

He winced at my question. "I just meant when people cry in general. I'm a very sensitive individual."

"Give it up, oC. Stop lying to me," I demanded.

"Blake will tell you when he's ready."

"Ready for what? And what will he tell me?"

"Everything," oC answered firmly, nodding his head.

"Seriously, if you don't stop being so cryptic I swear I'm going to get violent."

oC let out an awkward cough. Was he laughing at me? The threat was pretty ridiculous; I wasn't prone to violence and I had a feeling oC knew that.

"Blake's had some kind of Romeo moment, is that it? Love at first sight and the whole shebang?"

oC looked at the car ceiling and started to whistle a tune I recognized. This was going to be trickier than I thought.

"You can stop with the act already. I know what's going on," I said tightly. "It's pretty clear that Blake's trying to woo me in an audacious attempt to keep me away from Boe. He thinks that if he breaks my heart I'll keep away from her. I can't believe the nerve of that guy and you! You're his accomplice!"

oC looked affronted. Perfect.

"I know Supras like Blake think I'm trash. It's fine. I couldn't care less. But did he honestly think that I would fall for it? I mean the guy's pathetic. I see that vI is actually the honest boT." This was outright blasphemous. "She probably saw right through this game Blake's playing and was trying to warn me. That was why Blake was furious with her—she nearly blew his cover."

"Athena, that is utterly—"

"Let me finish. They say you should always judge men by their actions. If that's the case then I don't care if I ever see the lying, dishonorable, worthless excuse for a human being, or whatever the heck he is, again! I hate him."

My words were almost sacrilegious; I felt anything but hate for Blake. It was so cliché and lamentable, but I was pretty sure I was in the "L" word. I couldn't berate myself over it now though. I needed answers. "I just feel sorry for Boe. She has to live with him."

"Are you quite finished?" oC asked sternly.

"Hardly—"

"Good, because let me tell you something, Ms. Ellias. There is absolutely no ruse. Your assertions are sheer nonsense. And, *pah*, vI honest. My god, I've never known a more deviant soul. Blake's intentions, feelings, actions"—oC cleared his throat—"are wholly genuine."

"Come on, let's get real here. I may not be as ugly as vI thinks I am, but I'm no beauty and she said herself there are plenty of eager fish in the sea. You see that was what first gave him away. No one would be delusional enough to think that someone like Blake would see anything appealing in me."

"My dear, my dear, all I can say is that 'there is no excellent beauty that hath not some strangeness in the proportion'. You are quite the beauty you just don't know it."

"I would say thanks for that, but I'm not sure it's a compliment. You're basically calling me strange. But I guess I can't really argue with you there."

"*Strange.* That word means many things. When I apply it to you it means something more along the lines of rare, a timid mare—beyond compare."

I turned my face to the window to hide my smirk at his theatrical declaration. His words were spoken with such sincerity that I didn't want to offend him.

"That is what vIBee is to me anyway," oC said in a melancholy fashion—to himself I was sure.

I couldn't help but let out a disbelieving huff. vI, a timid mare? She was more like a cow with PMS.

I think oC would have blanched if he was capable of so doing because he was instantly embarrassed about his confession. "In any event, I'm sure that is what Blake would say."

"I doubt he would be quite so poetic," I replied sardonically.

"Ah, wrong again my dear. You can bring anything out in him. *Anything*. I'm amazed by it myself sometimes."

I was both chagrinned and hopeful, ashamed for being dishonest and hopeful that what the boT said was true.

"Liar! oC, you're a liar just like Blake. Stop treating me like I'm an idiot." I turned the best impression I could do of icy eyes on the small boT. "You know they say the devil has two names: Satan and *Liar*."

oC's mouth dropped open and he fell into an odd stupor before he quickly cocked his head and gave me a puzzled look.

"What about Lucifer?"

I was speechless for a moment as I hadn't anticipated this response.

"Fine. Three."

"But what about—"

"Whatever!" oC shrunk his shoulders under my contemptuous

gaze. "You win." I held up my hands. "I'll stay away from Boe. Happy? You can tell Blake he can give up this ploy to hurt me. And you can tell him that I saw right through him all along. That jerk didn't fool me for a minute. I hope I never see his satanic face again."

I was torn by this last part. No one could ever think of Blake as satanic, but then again his face was the pinnacle of temptation.

oC let out a sigh of relief as we pulled up to the familiar red brick building and my door slid open. I climbed out of the car, but still had myself turned toward the boT. I wasn't going to let him off the hook that easily.

"I just want to say that I was so touched at how you protected me from vI, but I can see now that you were just a puppet putting on a show for your master. As far as I'm concerned you can both go to"—I couldn't say it. I just couldn't. oC looked genuinely slighted—"the bottom of the ocean to rot."

P-a-t-h-e-t-i-c.

"Is that so?" Blake's voice shot through me like a bullet, making my knees collapse, but the ground came no closer as I found myself wedged between his arms and his chest.

I could see through my peripheral vision that he was staring down at me so I leaned my head closer to his body to hide my face. Had he heard everything?

I couldn't bring myself to move and neither did Blake and I became aware that we were standing alone on the landing dock; oC had taken off in Blake's car.

As the sun started to sink in the sky, a strong wind swept through the city and then quickly died away, but the cool air did nothing to dim the invisible flame that was burning my skin. I was barely standing as he was supporting all my weight.

"Athena, look at me." His words were a whisper torn between an order and a plea.

His voice held such dominion over me that I was surprised that I didn't comply at once, but the coward in me couldn't face him. "Athena, will you please look at me?"

It was an entreaty that pierced my heart, but I shook my head childishly. Blake shifted me against his body and stood me firmly upon my feet as he gently pulled away. "You hate me then?"

I looked up immediately and moved toward him. "No! I was just—"

He cut me off. "Lying," he drawled, molding his hand against my waist while the other enfolded around my face.

"I'm not a liar."

Yes, I was.

"To the contrary, I believe *you* are the devil in disguise."

"I'm not," I mumbled, unsure of what I was talking about; I lost all coherent thought the moment I felt Blake's touch on my skin.

"Athena, I need to…" His voice was husky and I couldn't breathe through my nose. My heart was hammering madly as my mouth fell open and he pulled me so tight against him that I couldn't help but gasp. His lips tickled my ear as he let out a low growl, a sound of frustration. "I know I shouldn't…" He stiffened, as if his words gave him resolve to separate himself from me. I couldn't understand his restraint.

"But I want you to," I whispered earnestly.

His face brushed over my cheek and the look he gave me was piercing.

"You have no idea what want is." Blake pressed my head closer and my eyelids fell shut. "No idea." His lips didn't press against mine but moved, feather light, across my jawbone. His kisses moved slowly along my throat, up my cheek and finally danced over my closed eyelids. I raised myself eagerly on my tiptoes, wanting his lips on mine, but he stopped and pulled away. I opened my eyes dejectedly. Why did he stop?

"You should go inside."

I puckered my forehead, recognizing the coolness in his tone.

"Don't do that," I said quietly. "Don't do this to me."

"Do what?" he replied passively.

His indifferent demeanor hurt me, more than I liked to admit.

"I wasn't lying in the car. I know you're hiding something. You're lying to me..." My eyes started to water and there was nothing I could do. "Please just stop."

Blake's jaw was solid, his eyes narrowed, his body suddenly tense. "Stop pretending. I can't do this anymore. When you're around me I feel..." I felt so vulnerable. "It seems like you care but then you look at me...like that." A lone tear slid down my face. "Like you can't wait to be away from me."

"That's because I can't," he replied flatly.

I briskly turned to head inside, certain that I was going to breakdown. As soon as I took my first step, the book slipped through the layers of my clothes and fell through my legs. I stopped but didn't look down at the small blue book that lay open at my feet.

Blake's voice was so low I just barely made out his words.

"Is that what you want...for me to stay away? Tell me to stay away."

"No!" I hadn't meant to sound so choked up. "I want the truth."

At once his lips were at my ear. "'A truth that's told with bad intent, beats all the lies you can invent.'"

I shook my head dumbly. "I never know what you mean. What does that mean?" I asked dismally.

His body brushed down mine as he bent to pick up the aged book.

"It means I should lie to you. The only reasons I have for telling you the truth are selfish ones." Standing behind me, he encased my body with his arms and held out the blue book in front of me. He slid the red ribbon against the fold of the pages and closed it shut. "I believe this belongs to you." His voice was morose.

I shook my head dejectedly. "How is that possible?" My hand was shaking as I slowly took hold of the book.

"I need to go."

He released me and my back was whipped by the chill of him leaving.

"Blake!" I felt like I would never see him again. Filled with trepidation, I ran to the dock's edge and peered over it as I called out his name. He was gone.

A desperation I had never known before was starting to suffocate me. I think I knew how I felt about Blake the moment he came upon me on Charlie's bike. No, it was even before then. I think there was something inside of me that knew he would come; that knew he was waiting for me. Blake was always at my side when

I needed him: the tank, the bike, the WiiGii. But my need now, to see him, to hold him, to find the assurances I so badly wanted, was so much stronger than either of those times. My life had been in danger before, but now something much more fragile was in peril—my heart.

Epicureans believe that death is nothing to us. "No one is sent down to the black pit of Tartarus. It is *our life* that all those things exist which are fabled to be in the depths of hell." That's what Lucretius says anyway. I was hardly of the same mind, but I could see his point. It doesn't take much to die and once it's over there's peace—hopefully there is. Life on the other hand can be painful, it is something that often has to be endured, and my heart was something I had to live with.

Letting out a determined breath, I decided I couldn't take it anymore. I had to know. For once, I took heed of the small, irrational, voice in my head and let it guide me. The slightest surrender on my part was all it needed because it immediately doused its logical counterpart. I crawled onto the edge of the dock, certain that he would come for me. Then again, maybe the "L" word was making me insane and I was just about to commit suicide. My knees were trembling madly as I stood before the brink. I had to do it quick. If I had time to think, I would just talk myself out of it. Clutching the blue book to my chest, I took my leap of faith.

¤ XIII ¤

WHITE LIES

I jumped but there was no fall. Blake's body found mine instantly. I kept my eyes closed as I let out a sound of elation and wound my arms around his neck. I never wanted to let him go. My feet dangled above the ground, but Blake didn't put me down and I didn't want him to. I wanted him to hold me forever. He budged, trying to pull me away but I tightened my grip—strangling him if it were possible.

"I'm not letting go until you tell me how you got that book," I said muffled against his neck. When my lips brushed against his skin my body piqued with gooseflesh.

"Have you lost your bloody mind?" he asked roughly. "What would possess you to do that? "

I squeezed myself closer to him. "Do you realize"—he held me tighter—"what could have happened? How crazy that was?" His voice was edged with anger. What if I—"

"I knew you would." In truth, I hoped he would. In hindsight, my judgment had been seriously lacking. I could be dead. But I read somewhere that God favors crazy people and it must be true because I was still alive and, what's more, I was securely locked in Blake's arms.

"If my sanity is under par at the moment it's not *my* fault." I reluctantly peeled my face away from his neck, avoiding his gaze, but Blake tilted his head to catch my eye, silently demanding that I look at him. Instead I turned to look at the book that lay closed on the ground. "Tell me how…"

Blake laid the slightest pressure on my chin, an appeal to make me face him. Finally, I relented. Staring into his eyes, blood seared my face and I knew—desolately and jubilantly knew—that I had fallen, so deep, so hard that there was no going back. I had lost my mind and my heart. I didn't need a grain of sand to see the world because what I saw in Blake's eyes was so much more.

"Swear to me that you won't do anything that foolish again."

I bit my lip, contemplating whether or not I should bargain for the concession. "Swear to me," he demanded.

"I swear," I answered quickly, frightened by his fury.

Cupping my face in his hands, Blake closed his eyes and pressed his forehead against mine. Exhaling slowly, he let out a breath that intoxicated me.

"You're making a hypocrite out of me," he said, opening his eyes to give me a piercing look. "I should have known I wouldn't be able to stay away."

I didn't understand what he meant.

"Why would you want to stay away from me?" My gut wrenched as I thought of all the reasons why I wasn't good enough for him. "Is it because I'm…different?"

Blake slid his fingers over my lips, effectively silencing me.

"I can rarely ever imagine what's running through that complicated, exasperatingly thoughtful, head of yours and yet it amazes me that you still think that I don't *like* you." He pulled my face to his. "I bloody…"—his eyes were fierce—"Do you want me?"

My cheeks seared under his hands. What did he mean by "want him"? The immediate answer that came to mind was *hell yes*, but obviously I wasn't going to say that. My mouth dropped open but nothing came out; he always had the ability to render me speechless.

"Do you want me around? With you?" he asked again.

I couldn't stop blinking. You could hardly tell Blake was anxious but the slightest change to his features was so unlike him that I immediately took notice. Why was he anxious? He hardly had reason to be. I on the other hand had to constantly talk myself out of believing this was some sort of cruel joke.

Unable to voice a response, I simply nodded my head. His eyes sparkled and set my heart on fire. He was *happy* and I was helplessly in *love*.

"Fields isn't going to be happy about this," he admitted.

"Fields?" My eyes grew wide. "You know Sammy?"

"Yes."

I waited for him to elaborate. I should have known better.

"How do you know him?" I asked emphatically.

Blake looked over my shoulder toward the entrance of the building.

"How much?"

"Excuse me."

"How much do you want me around?"

I pulled away and gave him a quizzical look. I couldn't think straight with his sweet breath drowning my senses—it was quite pathetic really. I was at least pleased that my newfound condition hadn't caused me to lose my self-deprecating wit altogether. I could still acknowledge my lameness and that had to count for something.

"I want you around as often as you're willing to endure my presence," I answered half-jokingly. The truth was, I wanted him around every second of every day.

"Do you know what you're asking for, Athena? As often as I'm willing to endure your presence—I don't think you would like that amount of time. I'm a solitary animal and am not used to company."

I assumed Blake thought I was asking for too much time—time he wasn't keen to give-up. I had hoped for a different answer and winced thinking he probably took me to be needy.

Hurt, I tried to cover my feelings and took a step back to distance myself. "I was just kidding. Whenever you're free. You can call me or I can call you." I felt so weird and sounded so immature; I'd never asked for anyone's number before and I didn't even know my own. "Actually, I don't know my number. I guess I can give it to Boe when I find out." I rethought that, not sure I was comfortable letting Boe know I had feelings for her brother. "Or you can just meet me sometime after school."

In a flurry Blake's face was so close to mine that his lips brushed my cheek when he spoke. "Promises, promises. This one is so hard to keep."

"What promise?" I asked, followed by an audible gulp as his fingers entwined themselves in my hair.

His lips pressed against my earlobe. "First of all, you misunderstood my question." He wasn't answering my question about the promise. Sometimes it was so hard to keep up with Blake because he didn't follow the rules of polite conversation. "When I asked how much you wanted me around, I didn't mean how often. What I meant was, what would you be willing to do, to sacrifice, to be with me for now."

Blake's words evoked so many questions, so many separate issues that I didn't know which one to voice first.

"I don't understand," I replied.

"I'll name my terms." Blake lifted his head and his lips twitched, like he was containing a grin, as he looked at the suspicious expression on my face. "You can't tell anyone about us."

I suffered a heart attack when he said *us*. "There are some things I can't tell you, that I won't tell you. You will have to accept that. The last thing"—he hesitated—"you have to distance yourself from Boe."

I jerked my head back so I could glare at him crossly. He had anticipated my reaction.

"Boe lives in a constant zone of chaos," he said firmly, offering that as his lone justification.

"If I was to even consider those terms,"—I hope I sounded convincing because the truth is I would have submitted to any terms he named— "what do I get in return?"

"Me."

This time I had a stroke.

"You?"

Nodding, he slid his hand around my lower back and pressed me toward him.

"So, we're agreed?"

I could barely think. I was so close to capitulating when I heard a small voice in my head reminding me of what Vas dictated to Pork Chop and I since we were old enough to sign our names: always read anything before you sign it and always read the fine print.

"No deal," I whispered hoarsely.

Blake held still.

"This is a one time offer. Are you sure?"

I gasped as I felt the velvet of his tongue on my neck working down toward my collarbone. I was at his complete mercy as my legs turned to mush.

"I—I have terms."

"Name them," he said huskily across my flesh.

"Well, actually,"—Blake's tongue continued its assault down my neck—"I have questions."

"No questions," he murmured.

"Then,"—I was fearful of my own words—"no deal."

Blake's head flitted up. "Athena," he said, frustrated.

I wasn't sure I would ever stop loving the way he said my name, but I had to speak while his lips were off me.

"Why do I have to distance myself from Boe? She's my friend. My *only* friend." Blake looked as if he was going to interrupt so I hurried on. "And why should I accept your terms when they are based on a contingency: for now. How long is that, five minutes, five days, five weeks? Your offer is rather ambiguous don't you think? In light of all of this, these are *my* terms: I won't stay away from Boe, that part is completely *vetoed.* I'll accept what you won't tell me, but I'll have you know that I can be quite resourceful and if you won't provide me with the information I want then I'll find someone who will. Since I'm due to find out anyway, you might as well be the one to tell me. I won't agree to your terms because I won't make promises I don't intend to keep."

Blake cocked his head. "Is that it?"

"Yes," I said hesitantly.

"How generous of you." I couldn't tell if he was being sarcastic. It didn't sound like it though. "I can only assume that what you offered in exchange for your terms is the same in nature to that which I offered. Technically, you only named counter terms to the ones I proposed. Considering what I get in exchange, it would be foolish of me to refuse." His face was the picture of serenity.

"And what exactly do you want in exchange?"

It wasn't a real query. I understood what he implied, but I

wanted to hear him say it.

Blake brought his lips right up against mine but simply held them there immobile.

God, kiss me. Please kiss me.

"I want you," he whispered.

I let my mouth drop open against his, but didn't move as I waited for him to initiate the kiss, *my first kiss.* But he didn't. How could he not? I would have pounced on him if not for the hurt my ego felt at his ability to hold himself back. Blake stepped away and, out of the corner of my eye, I saw him pick the little blue book up off the ground. I wanted to cry. The lump in my throat had gotten so big it was practically choking me. I wanted him so much and it didn't seem like he wanted me the same way.

Blake didn't hand the book back, but tucked it into his jacket pocket.

"It's settled then," he said quietly.

I shrugged my shoulders and nodded meekly. Blake's hands were on my shoulders tugging me close to him.

"Tell me what's wrong?"

I shook my head. "I don't know. I feel so confused, as if I'm wandering in the dark," I answered dejectedly. I looked at Blake even though I knew my eyes were misty. "I need someone to turn on the lights. It doesn't have to be bright, it doesn't have to be much, just something, anything—a flicker." It was the only card I had and I decided to play it. The truth. "I have no idea what's settled. I have no idea what's going on. I'm so lost."

Without thinking, I leaned my head against Blake's chest,

wanting to feel his solidness. I wanted to reassure myself that he was real.

"I've known Sammy my whole life. We grew up together."

I stopped breathing. How could that be?

"I want you to stay away from Boe because I don't want you hurt and in the most unromantic way possible, which I thought would be to your liking, you have agreed to be my, or rather I have agreed to be your—it's a twenty-first century term that you detest, but it will suffice—boyfriend. The word is irrelevant to me, but you rather hated it for some reason," he drawled in a low voice.

"You want me to be your girlfriend?" I croaked nervously, barely focused on the question as my mind was still grappling with what he said about Sammy.

"Not exactly."

I frowned, confused. It was like he wasn't speaking English.

"But you said—"

"I don't want you to be *my* anything." Blake leaned back and tilted my face up. "I just want you to be *mine.*"

I cleared my throat, wanting to sound coherent. "Then why did you want to stay away from me?"

Blake narrowed his eyes and scanned my face ardently. "It wasn't supposed to be like this. Fields brought you back when he shouldn't have." The muscles in his face were tense. "I wanted him to stay away from you and Sofia, but it didn't work out that way. Now look at me—my hand caught right in the cookie jar."

I was trying my best to keep my breathing even but it was a lost cause.

"What do you mean Sammy brought me *back*?" I asked shakily.

Blake hesitated. "When you landed on London Bridge two nights ago, it marked the second time you traveled to the future. Your father brought the two of you here before."

I wasn't able to hold it in anymore and my breathing quickly turned into hyperventilation. I must have looked bad because Blake's expression was one of concern. "Take deep breaths. It's all right," he said soothingly before muttering something disdainful to himself.

I tried to reassure him that I was fine, but I couldn't manage anything. My lungs were thirsty for air and my brain was exploding with information.

He knew Sammy.

He grew up with Sammy.

He wants to be my boyfriend—I did hate that word.

I travelled *back to the future.*

I knew nothing but black.

I felt him holding me before I opened my eyes. He sensed my return to the conscious world because he gently started to rock me.

"Athena." Whenever he said my name it was as if my ears heard singing. I opened my eyes and met his alarmed gaze. "It's unfortunate," he declared.

I puckered my forehead. "What is?"

"It's unfortunate for you that I will have to take into consideration your fragility when it comes to revealing information as you put it."

"What? No, I'm fine." I tried to hoist myself up and realized that

Blake was sitting in the passenger seat of his car and that I was on his lap. He looked at me unconvinced. "I'm fine," I repeated, my body thrumming from being so close to him.

In a swift movement, Blake stood once again on the loading dock with me cradled in his arms. We were inside the building's entrance before I had a chance to say a word. My mind wasn't even daunted by his speed because my anxiety quashed my bewilderment—I didn't want to go home. Not yet.

I fidgeted in his embrace. "Blake—"

"I'm not giving anything else up tonight."

I continued to squirm so he gently released my legs, but still held me close. "Athena, tell me the truth. I need to know if you're all right."

"Can I have my book please?" I asked, cocking my head.

Blake raised his eyebrow. "Your book? I'm not sure I know what you mean." My feet brushed the marble surface of the lobby as Blake strode toward the elevator. "The only book I have in my possession at the moment is one that was given to me." The elevator opened and he stepped inside.

"I must have been the one who gave it to you and I want it back," I quipped in a matter-of-fact tone.

"Do you now?" Blake's eyes were both dark and dancing. "I thought it was rude to take back gifts."

I pursed my lips. "Fine," I relented, "but who marked the page with the red ribbon?"

"You did," he replied, stepping out of the elevator.

He was leaving. I can't describe the dread I felt at being parted from him. I knew I was being needy, but I couldn't help it, deny it and, at the moment, I really didn't care—well, ninety-nine percent of me didn't care; one percent, a percent that I was still proud of, mocked me relentlessly.

"When will I see you?"

"This brings us back to your previous misapprehension. I believe you said you would like to have me around as often as I was willing to endure your presence."

I blanched as he repeated my words. "I was being sarcastic," I replied defensively.

"I see." Blake nodded his head slowly. "I suppose it's irrelevant then"—he shrugged his shoulders—"but, if that were the case, you should know that I would choose to be with you *always*, but that would be impossible," he said, with a trace of disappointment in his voice.

I stepped toward him, my heart bursting, but he pressed out his hands. "They're waiting for you and I believe you have company," he said, grinding his teeth.

I wondered how he could know that. Then I remembered he was a Supra and I was insignificant.

"The world for your thoughts," Blake asked curiously.

"Why haven't you kissed me yet?" I said quickly, without thinking.

He smiled, a small glimmer of a smile. It was so odd how the simple movement of his lips incited such a moving response inside me. His smile was an unpracticed one, as if he seldom did it, but flawless all the same. It was something that didn't seem to come naturally to him because Blake wasn't the type to display anything for conventions sake or for the sake of being cordial. He was always authentic, aggravatingly existential, so when he smiled he made me feel like it was something special, reserved for me and only me.

"That's a good question. All I can say is why haven't you asked me to?" The smoothness of his voice was tinged with a perceptible edge.

"Asked you?"

"You know your mind better than I do. I won't make promises I don't intend to keep, no matter how absurd, especially when they are to you."

Was he saying that I made him promise that he wouldn't kiss me until I asked him to? That was absurd.

The elevator doors began to close.

"Till tomorrow," he said in a low voice.

I slammed myself against the doors as they sealed me inside the glass box. Blake gave me so much to think about, to worry about, to question, but there was only one thing blaring in my head as his face disappeared. *KISS ME.*

The voice struck a chord, both literally and inside me. Entering unit 537, the sound of my favorite soprano swept me into a storm of sound waves that managed to bring my head out of the clouds. I walked toward the living room, knowing whom I would find there—Vas. I smirked to myself, puzzling over why he would be listening to my favorite and not his. Vas thought me something akin to a traitor—I preferred Sutherland over Callas. I had to constantly remind him that I was only half Greek and that I wasn't blinded by nationalistic sentimentality. Maria Callas was one of the greatest opera singers of the twentieth century. No doubt about it. But, personally, Joan Sutherland was by far the better technician. Vas said that my choice showed my taste for precision over performance, as if the latter was by far the more important of the two. Listening to the squall of a crescendo, as I walked into the kitchen, I thought of how wrong he was.

My bright mood quickly died, a flame that had no time to burn, as I entered the living room. Vas was there, but so were a whole bunch of people I didn't know and three others I did: Sammy, Pork Chop and *Logan*. Nobody seemed to take note of my presence and I hoped that I could slip back into the kitchen unnoticed when Logan's eyes found mine. I froze, waiting for him to reveal me, but he didn't. He just smiled and raised his eyebrows. I furled mine, slowly backing up. I darted around the corner into the foyer as soon as I was clear.

"Not an opera fan I take?"

I jumped around to find Logan standing behind me.

"Yes I am," I declared.

"Then, won't you care to join us?" he asked politely.

"I have a lot of school work to catch up on so I don't think I will," I replied, trying my best to be genial.

"That reminds me. I brought back your schoolbag and your hat." His voice was light as if he found something funny. "I found them in the conservatory when I went looking for you. Sofia has them."

I didn't know why, but I was strangely uncomfortable. I nervously brushed a stray strand of hair over my ear and saw Logan's face change as he took notice of my wrapped palms. He reached out and took my hand possessively. *Oh, great.* He probably thought that I intentionally showed him my battle scars to get attention.

"You're hurt." Logan's voice was gentle.

"It's nothing." I pulled my hands back and headed toward the stairs, but he blocked my path.

"What happened?" he asked tersely, sounding angry.

"I cut my hands on some glass, that's all."

"Do Sofia and Sammy know?"

"I'll tell them later. They obviously have company now and I don't want to interrupt."

Logan ran his fingers through his hair. "I guess I deserve this."

"Deserve what?"

"You're angry with me. I can't deny that you have every right to be. You got hurt today and it's partly my fault."

I shook my head, confused and a bit annoyed. "How could it possibly be your fault?"

"If I hadn't given you a ride you probably wouldn't even have been at the College."

"That's ridiculous."

Logan eyed my hands somberly, looking at the evidence that refuted my claim. "There's no reason to feel guilty. It just happened. It's no one's fault," I said sincerely.

"How about you absolve me of my guilt and agree to let me do something for you?" he asked with his teasing tone creeping back into his voice.

I frowned. "I don't need to absolve you of anything. Out of curiosity, though, what exactly do you want to do for me?"

Logan's smile was very charming. "Let me take you to dinner."

I wasn't sure if the offer was of a friendly or romantic nature. I was generally quite tactless and my natural response was to berate him with questions a la Spanish Inquisition: What did he want? Why did he want to take me? What was he up to? Was this Pork Chop's doing?

I managed to reserve myself and come up with a diplomatic *no*.

"It's really not necessary."

"I'll settle for lunch then."

Was he asking me out on a date?

"Sammy and Sofia can join us if they like. The four of us can go," he proposed.

A double date?

"Uh, I don't really have any time these days with school and everything and you are obviously very busy with…whatever it is you do."

I noted to myself how weird the conversation was. I sounded so juvenile talking about school and homework. What made it stranger was that Logan looked no older than me. He could have passed for a mature adolescent or a young looking twenty-five and yet he was the head of some big company and a professor at Cambridge. It baffled me how youth and age had become so indiscernible. It seemed so unnatural, so alien.

I silently wondered how old Logan was. I suddenly wondered how old Blake was—how old I really was. I posed as a seventeen year old, not much of a difference to the nineteen I was a few days ago, but as Blake's words unraveled in my head, I thought of how he eluded to another past, another life. Grappling with the ambiguity, I thought maybe I was a forty-year old living in a nineteen year old's body. I wouldn't have been surprised. I always thought of myself as an old soul anyway. If I was forty, then at least my mind was still sharp, the cynicism of the world hadn't managed to decay it too much. Or maybe it had and that would explain why I was such a loner...

"Busy is an understatement," Logan said lightly, breaking my train of thought. "But I'll make time. For you."

I couldn't help but blush and smiled uneasily.

"Is this because you feel guilty? Please—"

"No. I *want* to take you out," he said persistently.

I was now the one feeling guilty. I felt bad because Logan was so genuine, so charming and so thoughtful and I didn't deserve his attentions. What's more, he had gone in search of me and brought my things back from the College.

"I waited outside the College for you well before four today. I believe I made this request prior to..." He looked at my hands again. I held them behind my back self-consciously. "Guilt has nothing to do with it."

I tried to lighten my tone. "You don't want to take me out. Really, I'm terrible company. Just consider yourself lucky that I'm sparing you."

"Let me be the judge of that," he replied, with an arresting half-smile.

Maybe this wasn't the best approach. Everyone knew that guys loved girls who were hard to get. I wasn't interested in Logan, but I didn't want to offend him. How could I pretend to be interested, so it didn't seem like I was playing hard to get, but uninteresting at the same time so he would give up. I wondered what Pork Chop had told him about me that made him so keen to meet me?

"I don't know what stories my sister has been telling you, but let me tell you that...*like* I'm so busy because I need to *like* go shopping for a whole new wardrobe and *like* I—I totally need to get my hair done and—"

"Perfect. I'll take you."

I rolled my eyes but couldn't help but grin as I saw amusement in his eyes; he found my attempts to dissuade him entertaining.

"Okay, I give up. Just tell me why you're so eager to take me out?"

"The truth?"

"What else?"

"Your sister asked me to."

"I knew it!" Most people would have been humiliated, but I wasn't. It was as if a burden had been taken off my shoulders. He was only doing this because of my sister.

"But, that's only because she thought that I would like you. And, upon meeting you, I decided that I do."

I shifted nervously on my feet and looked anywhere but at him. Logan seemed to find my anxiety comical.

"I'm making you nervous aren't I?"

"No, not at all."

"Is your face naturally that shade of red then?"

Was this his idea of flirting?

"I don't know what you're talking about." I turned and started climbing the stairs. "Bye, Logan. Thanks—" I remembered how he had taunted me about being *thankful* when he dropped me off at the College. "I appreciate you bringing my bag home and everything."

"What date shall I set?"

I let out a determined breath, knowing he wasn't the type to give up easily—he was too assured of his appeal and his charm and his confidence was not unwarranted; Logan was quite debonair, but he could have been an angel incarnate and still wouldn't have been able to hold a flame to Blake. Blake consumed all thoughts—everything—I didn't have anything left for this charismatic stranger.

"I have school and…I'm just going to be honest…I'm not really *available*." I hoped he would get my innuendo and not need further clarification. "I don't know what it is you're looking for but I don't think I'm it."

Logan chuckled to himself.

"Athena, let me apologize. I think you misunderstood my intentions." Logan's eyes were full of mirth. I would have started feeling a little aggravated at being his constant source of amusement, but my gut had dropped so violently that my toes could feel it. "My offer was meant to be a gesture of a friendly nature." He let out an amused cough. "You needn't be concerned with your availability."

Trying to hide my embarrassment, I lifted my chin and looked down at him from atop a stair.

"I understood you perfectly so you needn't be worried about clarifying the nature of your offer. I was, of course, referring to my schedule. You see with school and the load of work that I have to catch up on, my *availability*, is really quite limited."

Logan nodded his head exaggeratedly. *"Of course."*

"Some other time."

"I will take you up on that. Again, I'm sorry about today."

I waved my hand dismissively and started to ascend the stairs again.

"Guse! Finally!" My sister's voice was like a bell marking the start of a race—I wanted to sprint to my room. I winced as she emerged from the kitchen. There was no escaping now. "What's wrong with your hands?" Her tone was one of annoyance, but she couldn't fool me. Unlike Logan she noticed my bandages immediately, as if the moment she saw me she had done a thorough appraisal wanting to make sure that I was unharmed. Her sardonic attitude belied her concern for me.

"I got into a fist fight," I said, parrying her nonchalance by playing the smart aleck.

Pork Chop scoffed. "At least try to come up with something remotely believable."

"Seriously, I got into a fist fight."

My sister and I could go on with this kind of trivial talk forever. I was hoping Logan, who was laughing lightly, would see how tiring the Ellias girls could be.

"Then how come your face isn't smashed in?" Pork Chop quipped as she crossed her arms.

"Obviously, because *I* was the one doing the smashing," I replied smugly.

"It's so sad that I have to tell father that his first born has sunk so low that she has to hurt herself for his attentions. When we commit you to the asylum, I will be happy to inherit your shoe collection."

"It's too bad that your feet are too fat and that you won't be able to squeeze into them," I replied snidely, satisfied by the narrowed-eyed look my sister gave me.

"Your feet are fat!" she retorted indignantly.

"Really, no need to get so defensive, Pork Chop."

"I wouldn't wear your smelly shoes anyway," she replied in a huff, contorting her face into an expression of mock disgust.

To any outside observer it looked like Pork Chop and I were bickering for no good reason—but that wasn't really an anomaly for sisters. I would think that most arguments between siblings were of a trifling nature. Anyway, Pork Chop and I weren't bickering—this was our banter. Vas always thought we were in a constant state of discord, but Pork and I rarely argued about anything. Our day-to-day exchanges sounded antagonistic, but they weren't. Funnily enough, when we did argue, there was no screaming, no throwing things; there were quiet, cold silences. That's how you knew something was wrong.

I started to re-climb the stairs as I heard voices trailing toward the foyer.

"Hey, where do you think you're going?" Pork Chop was quick to ask.

"Obviously, to my room. Before I forget, where's my bag? Logan said he gave it to you."

Fluttering her hand at me, Pork Chop turned to face Logan. "See, didn't I tell you how obnoxious she is."

"Me! You are the obnoxious one. Logan, I tell you, Sammy is the holiest man I know for putting up with her." I raised my hands in mock supplication as Logan shook his head.

"Oh, no! Don't drag me into this. I know better than to offend Sofia." He smirked at my sister. "But holy doesn't sound too far fetched considering what a prayerful individual she is."

"Prayerful?" I asked skeptically, raising my eyebrow. "I don't think my sister knows the meaning of the term."

"I think you may be wrong because I believe she does. What was it you were telling me earlier?" he asked Pork Chop.

My sister looked delighted with herself. "'God, grant me the serenity to accept the things I cannot change, the courage to change the things I cannot accept, and the wisdom to hide the bodies of those people I had to *kill* today because they pissed me off.'"

Logan's amused laughter matched mine. There was a warmness about him that reminded me of Sammy. His good humor was easier to appreciate with my sister around and now that I knew he wasn't trying to court me.

"What's so funny?" Sammy asked, strolling out of the kitchen toward the three of us.

"Sofia's been reciting her daily prayers," Logan said with a smile.

"Where'd you hide the bodies Sof?" Sammy asked slyly, taking hold of Pork Chop's arm as she tried to elbow him in the gut.

Sammy's eyes anxiously raked over me. Like Pork Chop, he was looking for signs of damage and it made me uneasy.

"Hey, Guse, what happened to your hands?" He tried to sound casual but I could tell he was troubled.

"She got into a fist fight," Pork Chop said quickly.

It was funny how my sister had the uncanny ability to read my mood. She could sense that I didn't want to talk about what happened today and she was mediating the conversation so that it didn't get too serious and too focused on me.

"How did you get home?" I wasn't the only one who noticed how weird Sammy sounded. It was as if he was interrogating me like a suspicious parent.

"My friend gave me a ride," I said in a relaxed tone, looking Sammy straight in the eye. It was ironic how Vas always told Pork Chop and I to never lie, but at the same time taught us how to— with the eyes.

"I thought you said that she got hurt." Sammy's voice was lined with doubt.

"She did, but like I told you before, she's fine. It was nothing serious."

I knew I was technically lying, but I didn't feel too bad about it. I may have been a liar but I knew that it took one to know one.

"What's her name?" Sammy asked sharply.

"Geez, Sammy, you sound like a prosecutor." Pork Chop's comment was an attempt to bail me out of the interrogation. Logan was quiet.

I promised not tell anyone about Blake, but that didn't mean I had to lie about Boe. Besides, I already told Pork Chop her name.

"Her name is Boe." I watched Sammy's eyes acutely to see if the name meant anything to him. If it did, I couldn't tell. "I have so much reading to do so I'll fill you in later, kay?" I skipped up the steps not waiting for a reply. "What's for dinner?" I asked glancing back at them.

"Gruel," Pork Chop declared.

I rolled my eyes and ignored my sister's snarky remark. I wasn't really interested in the menu anyway. My stomach was empty but my anxiousness had diminished my appetite—I wouldn't have been able to force a cracker down. I only bothered to inquire at all because I didn't want anyone to suspect that there was anything wrong with me.

Before my bedroom door slid shut, I was already commanding my book collection to appear. On the fourth shelf from the top sat a perfect block of blue. I started with book one and ran my fingers along the base of the volumes until I came to volume seven. Pressed up against it was volume nine. Volume eight was missing. I pushed the two books apart to create an empty space between them. As I traced my finger along an invisible book spine, I couldn't recall when I'd lost it or when it had gone missing. Keeping my eyes on the vacant space, I backed up and sat down on my bed. Thinking of Sherlock Holmes, I decided that a bit of deductive reasoning was in order.

Blake said he knew Sammy and that they grew up together. How was that possible? Blake also said that Pork Chop and I had been to the future before. If that was true, how come I didn't remember anything?

Prompted by the memory of my sister and I riding in her car the first night I arrived, I thought of the answer to my first question. I remembered her looking at me and saying one word: *Sammy*. If Blake knew him all his life then the only explanation that made sense was that Samuel Fields was not from my world. He was from the future.

Another thought occurred to me—a nagging suspicion—since Blake was a Supra, could Sammy be one, too? It was a possibility. There was no way to really tell.

I started to pace the room and wondered if my sister knew anything about this. I wondered…how much was she hiding from me if she did?

Vas. I thought of the role my father played in this. How much did he know, if anything at all?

My mind was still traveling down the path of deduction so I didn't dwell on my tentative anger because there was something more important provoking my attention. Something Blake said that made my stomach churn and made the blood drain from my face.

He said he wanted me for now. I didn't know what *for now* meant and it worried me. What troubled me more was that he said that he had wanted Fields to stay away—he hadn't wanted me back in the future at all. But why?

Watching the final rays of sunlight melt into the sky, I stuffed the last remains of spaghetti into my mouth. I felt stifled so I opened my windows and was unsurprised to find a small balcony. I sat on the window seat and was a motionless, sober figure as I gazed into oblivion.

Pork Chop had come up to tell me that the guests were staying for dinner. I had vehemently told her that I didn't want to join them. She said that it was either dine with them or starve. I had chosen the latter. She brought up a tray of spaghetti five minutes later.

Among the guests were the Dean, a few associate professors and a couple of friends of my sister's whom she wanted me to meet. I didn't think there was any way I could manage to plaster a plastic smile on my face. I could be social and friendly but it was really hard for me to be when I was being insincere. So I declined. I hated abandoning my sister again. Whenever we were forced to attend dreary dinners or family affairs, we were the source of each other's entertainment, able to communicate with silent jokes and innuendos that nobody understood. I'd make it up to her another time. I just couldn't be bothered today. I could only manage so much.

I took a shower and hoped that it would calm my nerves. But it didn't. I changed into my pajamas and turned off my room light before going back to the window to sit and think in the dark. My long hair was tangled and I yanked a comb through it—taking my angst out on the wet locks.

I hoped that Pork Chop would stop by my room before she went to bed so I could ask her a few questions, but it was late, nearing eleven o'clock and I could still hear the faintest trace of voices and laughter so I guessed that we still had company over.

I was shivering and my hair was stiff from the cold, but I didn't move from my seat by the window. I felt strangely melancholy and my mood, like the bitter air, was shrouded and gloomy. As I listened to the sounds of the city, I could feel my eyelids get heavy. Then, just as the noises around me started to fade, out of the shadows I heard it: the timbre of a warm fire that kindled my spirit. The sound wafted up from the balcony below and eased my rigid body.

I got up, pulled my down sheets off my bed and wrapped them around me and slowly walked to the edge of the balcony. Laying down, I pressed my face to the cool, hard surface. I didn't have to guess from where the soft melody came—Sammy was playing.

The deep vibrations of the cello echoed such emotion, such feeling; Sammy played brilliantly, vividly, beautifully.

Soon, I lost myself in the resonance of the piece. The final note came too soon and as it wavered into nothingness, I felt the return to the bleak, starless night. The void the music filled was again hollow as quiet descended, but the song of ivory keys dancing quickly washed the emptiness away. My lips twitched as I smiled privately to myself; Pork Chop had decided to grace our guests with her playing. And grace us she did. My face was numb as I pressed myself harder against the ground, but I didn't care. It was as if she were playing the strings of my very heart, of my very soul. Deeply morose and delicate, the notes were the language of the stars and of the cosmos. It made you think of the unthinkable, of infinity, and for just a moment that's what I wanted, to forget where I was. I wanted to float aimlessly, a morsel in time, and lose myself in the vastness of the universe.

The keys commanded her. The music demanded that she play with purpose, with passion, and she surrendered herself to it. I yielded in much the same way—soon lost in a place beyond the edges of this world.

¤ XIV ¤

Q & A

I was getting carsick as I tried to focus on the moving figures that emanated from the electronic magazine I held in my hands. It was well into the afternoon and Pork Chop and I were headed to some shopping center. My sister woke me up twenty minutes ago and announced that I was excused from school. I thought it a late declaration considering what time it was—school was already near over. Since she was free for a few hours, she insisted on going shopping.

When I opened my eyes to a new day I was surprised that I managed to sleep for so long, but was more surprised that I was in bed—that was the second time I anticipated a sore body but found myself buried under the comfort of my sheets.

The thoughts that overwhelmed me last night were still festering in my head, but Pork Chop's voice kept rushing me to get ready so I barely had time to think because all I cared about was finding a way to mute the damned speaker or I was set on yanking it right out of the wall.

As soon as I got into the car, Pork Chop gave me a bunch of magazines with small tags that marked specific pages and asked my opinion on which dress I preferred. The magazines weren't filled with pictures, but instead each page was like a small television screen that played short commercials—I tried my best to hide my excited curiosity because I knew that this sort of technology was probably equivalent to the innovativeness of a sticky-note from our time.

Looking down at another extravagant gown, I felt my head slowly start to spin. I closed my eyes and laid my head back.

"Which one do you like?" my sister asked impatiently.

"Can I look at these later? I'm getting car sick."

"Honestly, Guse, you need to toughen up."

"Car sickness is genetic. It's not my fault."

Pork Chop scoffed. "No, car sickness is psychological. You need to see a shrink."

"Why did I agree to come with you? I should have known I would have to endure this."

"Because you *looove* me." My sister chuckled.

"No I don't. I only came because I decided to take pity on you considering how much you missed me."

"Missed you? Please! I missed Vas. Being an only child would have been a dream come true. I vividly recall begging him to give you up for adoption at an early age."

"Correction. I was the one who wanted you given up for adoption."

"Don't steal my jokes, Guse, just because you can't come up with something original. I will admit, though, it is difficult to match my wit," she said, raising her chin.

"It is difficult to endure it," I replied derisively.

"Can you just tell me which one you like?"

"Why do you need a dress like this anyway?"

"*We* need dresses for the University's Governor's Gala, which honors faculty for social contribution and academic achievement."

"They're honoring you?" I hoped that my sister heard shock and not resentment in my voice. I was always the more academic one between us and my ego was hurting thinking that Cambridge was honoring her.

"No, they aren't awarding me anything, but they should be!" she huffed. "I'm presenting Logan with the Giller Prize and will be making a speech. And of course, Sammy is being presented the Modellin Prize for his theory on the political continuum stemming forth from the escalation of nuclear warfare."

"Hey, what do you mean *we?*" I asked suspiciously.

"You're coming, obviously."

"No I'm not. Why do I have to come?"

"We can get dressed up and it'll be fun. Come on, Guse. It will mean a lot to Sammy."

"It's going to be so awkward," I whined. "Besides, they're not honoring you. Sammy won't care if I don't come."

"Yes, he will. Can you stop being such a lame-o all the time?"

"When is it?"

"In two weeks."

"I'll think about it."

My sister smiled mischievously. "If you don't go then I'll drag you to that stupid school dance that the College has every year, which happens to be on the same night as the Gala."

"What?"

"I'll tell Vas that it is important for you to network especially because you're a newbie at the College. I'll convince him to make you go. Sammy and I will be your chaperones. You want awkwardness, I'll give you awkwardness. You just try me, Gustavo."

"Earth to Porkie, Sammy's going to the Gala. They're presenting him with an award. I doubt he'll bail for a high school dance," I said, refusing to take the bait.

"That's what you think. He hates this kind of stuff. He's going because I want him to thank me—dedicate his speech to me. But he'll go where I go."

I scowled. "Why do you want me to come so much?"

"Because it'll be fun," she replied cheerily.

"No, it won't be. I'm not a fun person. You never have fun with me at events like this. I never dance. I don't drink. I'll just mope at the table the whole night."

"That's not true. I recall you sipping some champagne and Greek dancing at Tina's wedding."

I gave my sister a hard look. "That's because you dragged me up there and I didn't want to offend the bride—our cousin. That reminds me, I still haven't forgiven you for that."

Pork Chop made a face. "Just come."

"There's going to be no one my—our age there. I doubt Vas could make me go anyway, but even if I had to, a measly school dance seems a whole lot better than dinner with a bunch of fogies." I crossed my arms stubbornly.

"What do you mean fogies? Guse, let me clarify something. Age is not exactly perceived as it was in our time. I can see that you haven't been doing your biology homework because I think people in kindergarten are taught the human phases."

"You lost me," I said impatiently.

My sister rolled her eyes. "Basically there are now four life stages for a human being: *Alphaphase, Betaphase, Gammaphase* and *Deltaphase*. You with me?"

"Not that hard to follow. Four phases got it."

"Don't be so snarky, I'm just trying to educate you." She reached over and tried to swat the back of my head. I attempted to swat her head in retaliation but she shoved my hand away. "Don't distract the driver!" she shouted.

"Forget it. I'll wait for biology class."

"Just listen. Each phase is designated for a particular age range. Alphaphase begins from birth to the age of thirty; Betaphase from thirty to sixty; Gammaphase from sixty to ninety and Deltaphase from ninety to one hundred and twenty. There's also Omegaphase, but you don't have to worry about that because it only applies to Supras."

"What do you mean?" I said a little too high pitched that my sister gave me a funny look out of the corner of her eye.

"Omegaphase is like from one hundred and twenty to—I don't know—I think they estimate two hundred and fifty or something like that."

"Supras live for that long?" Panic was suffocating my lungs.

"Apparently," Pork Chop said nonchalantly, as if the topic was of little interest to her. "Anyway, most of my friends, including my associates at Cambridge, are Betaphites, meaning they are somewhere from thirty to sixty years of age. The thing is—you've probably noticed this—they all generally look the same age."

My sister nudged my shoulder. "Hello, earth to Gustav. Are you listening to me?"

I managed a nod. I could hear my sister, but I wasn't focused on what she was saying. All I could think about was how much I hated math. Why did one plus one always equal two? There was no way to manipulate the numbers and the figures in my head were burning into my brain. *Supras lived for two hundred and fifty years. Which meant...*

"In today's society people barely ask for your age, just your phase," my sister continued. "And in terms of relationships, phases that either precede or follow one another are considered *compatible*. Meaning, an Alphaphite who was like twenty could possibly date someone who was forty or older—a Betaphite. People generally start to age once they are a Gammaphite because the booster shots are not as effective...I'm dying of cancer and have six weeks to live. Got that, Guse?"

My sister finished speaking so I nodded again. "Guse!"

I jumped in my seat as my sister gave my face a light slap.

"Hey! Whatcha do that for?" I said angrily.

"You weren't listening to me. I'm trying to explain something important here. What's wrong with you?" she asked, annoyed.

"Nothing. You'll be dead in six weeks so I was just thinking about what I was going to do with your room," I replied quickly, hoping to hide how uneasy I felt. "Go on. I'm listening."

"Hmph. I'm not sure if I should waste my breath considering you have apparently developed an attention deficit disorder, but I'm going to tell you because you have to remember this detail if anyone asks you about Vas."

"Vas?"

What did any of this have to do with him?

"As I was saying, people don't start to age until they are a Gammaphite. Do you remember the age range?"

Sections of my brain were simply not working. I was going to relent and ask her to repeat herself, when, miraculously—considering the state of my mind I thought it pretty miraculous—I remembered.

"Obviously, sixty to ninety years old."

"Good. I was starting to doubt your ability to use your ears. Now, with regards to Vas, just like we had to adjust your age a bit, we also had to adjust his age because he looks so old."

"What do you mean? He looks great for his age." My father was only forty-five, a young looking one at that.

"Not really. The Dean is fifteen years older than Vas and he looks much younger."

"What? How is that possible? Does everyone nowadays get face lifts or something?" I asked, torn between cynicism and disbelief.

"We have these things called booster shots. They stimulate cell regeneration so people don't age as fast, but the effectiveness diminishes when you become a Gammaphite."

"How old did you say Vas was?"

"Seventy-five."

"Seventy-five!" I exclaimed.

"Yeah."

"And people believe that?"

"Haven't you been listening? Man, talking to you is like talking to a door knob. That's how old Vas looks like."

"But then how do you distinguish people who are twelve from people who are fifty? And does that mean people those ages can date—get married? That sounds so messed up, not to mention pedophilic," I said critically.

"It took me a little while to get used to, but it's not that extreme. Someone who's twelve will look younger than someone who's fifty and an Alphaphite reaches the legal age of adulthood at sixteen so that much hasn't changed. Distinction of age really comes down to one thing now: the noggin."

"Huh?"

"It's kinda funny because the world has become so superficial on some levels, obsessed with aesthetic beauty, but at the same time, society has developed a new found appreciation for intelligence and for maturity. Once you start to meet more people, you'll know what I mean. People often exude their ages through their knowledge, attitude, interests, and their speech. Age hasn't quite become a number because it still marks a certain threshold for individuals— the time they've had to build up life experience and everything that comes with it."

I slumped down into my seat dejectedly. The day had started out bright and fresh, but was slowly being shrouded under a dark veil. I needed to focus on anything but the topic of discussion or else talking to my sister—talking to anyone—would soon become nothing more than conversations with shadows. I was falling into a morbid depression and I didn't know how to get myself out of it.

"Is the biology lesson over?" I was forcing the sarcasm hoping to hide how disconcerted I was.

"For now," Pork Chop replied with a sigh.

"How do you turn on the radio?" I needed some music to lighten my mood.

"Get with the times, Guse. There is no such thing as a radio anymore. We have digital programming so there's no need for them. They became obsolete decades ago." Pork Chop pressed a few buttons and holographic images appeared. Then I remembered how Logan had given me that funny look when I asked him the same thing. I did need to get with the times. This admission only added to my dour mood because I was sure that it would take me a lifetime to do it.

Pork Chop didn't bother asking me what I wanted to listen to; she would make the selection herself. I couldn't help but smirk at her song choice. My sister could be so egotistical sometimes and naturally chose a song bearing her name.

Looking out the window at the passing sights, I found it so strange that the city didn't seem that alien to me. It wasn't the techno-vision of the future often prophesized in my time. Some buildings were still made of brick, some of stone, then some were made of glass and metal—it was a mesh of all sorts that wasn't unfamiliar.

"Do you ever drive on the ground?" I asked my sister, interested in exploring the city.

"Sometimes; if it gets too muggy traffic control blocks off the laneways inside the city. It happens quite often actually. We've had pretty good weather lately so there hasn't been a need. People don't have a choice but to drive on ground when the weather sucks and since this is London, it happens more often than not. The traffic is a nightmare. Sammy literally has to drag me to the campus on those days—practically every day starting after mid-October to early summer. That reminds me, I won't be able to drive you to the College because we have to leave much earlier. We're going to have to work out some sort of car pool situation."

"Why don't I just opt for home schooling instead?"

"Talk to Vas," Pork Chop stated innocently.

I crossed my arms. "I swear, I'm gonna get you back for this one day."

My sister ignored my remark. "Which one do you like?" She gestured toward the stack of magazines that lay in my lap.

"I don't know. They're all right."

"Just all right?"

I shook my head and flipped through the topmost magazine. I had to give her something or I knew she wouldn't let up.

"I like this one, but you didn't mark it."

Pork Chop took her eyes off the road for a brief moment to eye my selection. She tilted her head toying with the image of herself in the dress. The gown had a silk bodice that flared out into a sleek taffeta bottom. There were no sleeves but elegant shoulder pieces cut in an empire style, with delicate, crystal embroidery.

"Yeah, I like it too, but it doesn't suit my figure. I'm bustier than you and my shoulders aren't quite so broad. That dress suits your straight frame better. Who's it by?" I lifted the magazine for her to take another look. "Typical. That's going to be really expensive."

"I didn't say I wanted it. I just said I thought it was nice." I perused another magazine trying to find the pages with tags and finally found one I liked. It was a sleeveless, deep sapphire dress. The contours of the gown marked a flawless execution and high degree of craftsmanship. The bottom was made up of soft silk and muslin with exquisite embroidery tracing the top of the gown down the side and flared full out at the back. It was a dress fit for a queen. Perfect. Pork Chop would love it.

"This one."

"Yeah, I liked that one too. You don't think it's too much, do you?"

"When have you ever been concerned with too much?"

"True, but I think I might be concerned with the price tag."

"How much we talking here?"

"So many zeroes that it supersedes your mathematical abilities."

"For a dress?" I said disapprovingly.

"Hey, I deserve it. I work very hard. And I'm only following your example. You were always the big spender."

"I don't spend that much," I said defensively. "And besides, I've never spent this much."

"It's not as bad as it seems. I assume you've figured out by now that the value of money is not quite equivalent to the value it used to be."

"I bought a candy apple for a million dollars and nearly choked on it. Yeah, you could say I got it."

My sister spit out a laugh before carrying on. "When I say the dress is expensive, I mean it's basically as much as a designer dress would have cost in our time. Maybe a little bit more."

"So a lot more."

"Maybe a poor person's yearly salary." Pork Chop's voice was teasingly apologetic.

"Don't you feel bad about spending money that isn't even yours? I gather your yearly salary can't possibly cover your lavish spending. Where's your pride?" I asked in mock indignation.

"When it comes to spending Sammy's money, my pride is exactly where it always is—buried underneath my closet. Haven't you ever heard of the saying, 'what's mine is yours'?"

"Yes. It is reserved for married people," I retorted.

"Sammy doesn't see it that way and he hates money. He thinks it corrupts everything it touches. I'm actually doing him a favor by spending it, you see."

"You know, I don't think I've ever heard of a Saint Samuel. Sammy will be glad to be the first."

Pork Chop proceeded to stick her tongue out at me and I returned the gesture.

Buried under layers of silk and taffeta, I was sprawled out on a chair in the fitting room as Pork Chop went through another dress.

"Just pick one already," I said impatiently.

"I have to weigh my options."

There was something wrong with every dress she tried on: too showy, too subdued, too fluffy, too simple, too big, too small, too red, too white—I was sure she went through every color of the rainbow—too ordinary. We hadn't even left the ground floor yet.

"Why don't you try some on? I told you that you need one, too."

"And I told you that I'm not going." It wasn't that I didn't enjoy shopping or trying on gowns for fun. Usually, I was much more the shopaholic than Pork Chop. But I just didn't feel like it. Any enthusiasm I had these days was fleeting because I couldn't hold the thoughts, constantly scouring the peripheries of my mind, at bay for long. Worries, apprehension, suspicions, doubts always came veering into my head with such force that nothing seemed capable of fighting them off.

"Guse, are you sick?"

"No, why?" I asked, surprised by the question.

"Because you're acting strange. You seem…distracted."

"Are we done here? I don't think you're going to like any of these." Ignoring my sister's query, I held up the bundle of gowns that lay folded in my arms.

"Fine. Let's go upstairs." Pork Chop turned to change out of an awful teal gown she had tried on. "Crap. I didn't realize it was so late. We got to move it."

"What's wrong?"

"I'm going to be late if we don't hurry."

"We can come back another time."

"I don't want to make another trip for nothing. We'll go now."

I convinced Pork Chop to take the escalators instead of the elevator by challenging her to a race. My sister and I thrived on familial competition. The escalator steps were made out of glass sheets that weren't physically connected together but were adjoined by a faint blue glow that covered the base of each step. I hadn't realized that we had to run up six floors, but I was pretty fit so I thought nothing of it. I had always been more athletic than my sister and thought it was going to be an easy win. So, I was shocked when I came rolling up to the top floor and found Pork Chop leaning against a glass railing looking idly at her nails as if she had been waiting for me for hours.

"How'd you do that?" I asked in a huff.

Pork Chop pointed to me. "Loser!" Then she pointed to herself. "Winner!"

"You cheated!" I accused.

"Don't be a sore loser."

I narrowed my eyes at her. "You've taken those booster shots that you mentioned in the car, haven't you? I've noticed you lost weight, too, but you still eat like a cow."

"I do not eat like a cow!" she cried.

"Sorry, wrong animal class—Pork Chop," I joked.

"Whatever. You're just mad cuz I beat you. La la la la la."

It never ceased to amaze me how my sister and I simply failed to mature.

"I will not accept that. Cheaters don't win. Cheating is an automatic forfeit." Quickening my stride, I came up beside her. I guess she knew what I was about to do because we both tried to boot each other at the same time.

"Can you control yourself, Gustav? We're in a public place."

"Cheater," I muttered.

I knew Pork Chop wasn't going to find anything in the high-end store, as she eyed a terribly tacky gown. I was going through a rack of clothing, when I saw a sales lady approach us.

"Excuse me. Unfortunately, I don't believe we have what you are looking for. I believe the plus size stores are located on the sub-level."

I puckered my forehead and looked at my sister who turned to face me.

"*Excuse me,*" Pork Chop and I said at the same time.

"I believe my articulation was crystal clear. I'm afraid we don't carry what you are looking for." The woman's hair was pulled so tightly over her head that it stretched her face unnaturally. She gestured with her hands toward the entrance of store, indicating her desire for us to leave.

"And how, pray tell, do you know what we're looking for?" Pork Chop asked briskly.

It took me a while to figure out the saleslady's hostile attitude had nothing to do with clothing size—I was a size six and looking at Pork Chop, she could probably squeeze into a four now—and had everything to do with our old jeans and rundown sneakers; we didn't look like we could afford anything in the store.

"Whatever it is, we don't carry it," the ice queen replied curtly.

I'd never had the urge to slap anyone in my entire life until that moment. Looking at Pork Chop, I was worried that she was likely going to be the one to do it.

"Let's go," I said, giving the witch a cold stare as I reached out to take my sister's arm.

She pulled away from me and I was sure that she was going to send the women careening across the store, right into the massive shoe display behind her.

"What are you doing?" I asked Pork Chop nervously, putting myself between her and the saleslady.

Pork Chop's lips twitched. "Seriously, Guse, I wasn't raised in a barn. I'm not going to start a fist fight." I frowned at her. "I just have one thing to say to *you*." Pork Chop lifted her index finger and pointed it threateningly at the unfazed black-hearted hostess. "Did you know that it would take me forty two muscles to frown and stomp out of here instead of using just four to extend my middle finger"—at which my point my sister did—"and tell you to bite me!" Pork Chop wheeled around on her heel and walked with her head held high out of the store. "Now we can go."

The woman crossed her arms and looked at me like I was dirty.

"That's right," I told her. I felt the need to say something as well. "What you did is against the law and I'm going to report you and…you just wait!" But why? Why did I have to say things?

I just sounded stupid.

"Guse!"

"So there," I concluded and turned to leave, trying to hold my head high like my sister.

"What did you say to her?" Pork Chop asked once we were away from the store.

"I said I was going to report her because what she did was against the law."

"Okay, you just humiliated yourself."

"No, I didn't. How she treated us was completely unjust. I wasn't going to stand for that."

"Fine, but why did you have to sound like a buffoon?"

"I didn't," I snapped.

"I think ya did," she said teasingly.

"Athena!"

Pork Chop and I were just about to head into an elevator when we turned to find the person calling my name. I recognized the voice and she wasn't hard to spot. She was like a lightning bolt in an open field. People stopped and turned their heads and made way for her like she was royalty. She was utterly graceful and perfectly balanced, although she ploughed toward us on four-inch heels.

What was Boe doing here?

"Hey, Boe." I tried to sound cheery as I looked at my sister nervously. "What are you doing here? Why aren't you at the College?"

"I guess the same reason you're not. WiiGii attacks are a good excuse for playing hooky, right?"

"Yeah, sure," I replied uncertainly. "This is my sister Sofia. This is Boe," I said with a touch of haughtiness in my voice, not because I was proud that Boe was my friend, although I was immensely so, more because I was alluding to the inside joke that I couldn't make friends.

"Hey, nice to meet you," Boe said sweetly.

"Same here. I can't believe you're actually real. Most of my sister's friends live inside her head."

"Hey!" I exclaimed.

Boe laughed lightly. "No, I'm real. Where are you guys headed?"

"My sister's taking me home because she has to head back to work."

"That's too bad, but why don't I take you home instead so we can hang out?" Boe suggested eagerly.

Pork Chop turned to me. "I don't care; it'll save me time. Guse, you want to stay?"

"Of course she does," Boe said certainly.

Pork Chop smiled at my friend's enthusiasm. I could tell my sister liked her.

"Yeah, okay," I agreed.

"Kay, see you at home. Nice meeting you, Boe." Pork Chop waved as she headed into the elevator.

"Adios," I called out as the doors closed. "What are you shopping for?"

Boe motioned for us to head toward a set of escalators and shrugged her shoulders lightly.

"I don't really need anything."

I furrowed my brow. "Then what are you doing here?"

"Hanging out," she replied quickly.

I narrowed my eyes at her innocent face. "Alone?"

"Uh-huh."

I don't know why, but I thought that maybe it hadn't been coincidence that I'd run into her.

"Boe," I said her name questioningly, "how come you're here?"

"I love to shop," she offered.

I gave her a skeptical look. "Is that the real reason?"

"Okay, I was following you."

"Following me? From where? Why?"

"Actually—correction—I was informed that you were here and was asked a *favor*." She said this as if she was trying to redeem herself.

I puckered my forehead. "A favor?"

"And by the way, you needn't worry about the saleslady. She's already been fired. I can make a foreclosure on her house happen, too, if you want."

"You saw that? And, no, it's okay; a foreclosure is not necessary." I hadn't meant to sound so serious, but I couldn't help but match Boe's tone. She didn't sound like she was joking.

"It was a good thing I had to keep hidden because I would have told that moron to do more than just bite me. Come to think of it, we should go find her so I can put her in her place." I recognized the hardness in Boe's expression. It was one I had seen a few times now. Boe's temper could be scary.

"The sentiment is much appreciated, but really unnecessary. Anyway, you said something about a favor."

Boe beamed. "I did."

"What was it? Who asked…"

She raised her eyebrow smugly as I trailed off. The warmth in my face was a blush.

"He wanted me to intercept you for him."

Fire—my cheeks were flaming.

"I'm sorry, Boe, you lost me."

I shrank away as she wrapped her arm around my shoulders.

"Athena, don't be so timid. You can confide in me. I must say that I'm a little surprised. I can't remember my brother liking anyone before. I don't really get it." I turned to Boe wondering where she was going with this. "Not because you're not likeable. I didn't mean it like that. It's just Blake's so…morbid. He *hates* people as a general rule." oC had said the same thing. "It's really weird for him to like anybody, let alone someone so fast and a friend of mine. You could say he doesn't hold my friends in the highest regard, except for RJ, but that doesn't really count because he knew RJ long before I was born and—"

"Uh, Boe?" I interrupted her side note. I couldn't think about anything besides the fact that Blake wanted me intercepted and that Boe was only here because she was doing him a favor.

"Yeah."

"You don't have to do this. I don't know why your brother asked you—how did he know I was here?" The snippet of information Boe gave me earlier made me wonder about who exactly was following me.

"He's here."

My heart thumped.

Boe bit her lip trying to suppress a giggle.

"What's so funny?" I asked conscientiously.

She patted my shoulder. "Oh, Athena, I think everyone in London can hear your heart pounding."

"I'm really out of shape. I'm still recovering from running up the escalators." I secretly wondered if she was joking or if she could really hear it. "Are we going to meet him now?" I asked, feeling very hot, like I was wearing five layers of clothing.

"Not yet. Since I'm here, I might as well do some damage to his bank account. Besides, I said I owed you one for the TX. I've decided to take you on a no holds barred shopping spree so you can outfit yourself according to your station. He can have you after I'm done with you."

I had never known such shame. If Boe could in fact hear my heartbeat, then she would have noticed it accelerate when she referred to Blake having me.

"My station? And what exactly is that?" I tried to cough out the high pitch that had crept into my voice.

"My BF," she said merrily.

"Boe, I met you two days ago. Isn't it a bit soon to christen me your best friend?"

"Hosh, posh. I'll make you a deal all right." I rolled my eyes. "I have something you want, so just hear me out."

"You do?" I asked suspiciously.

"How about we go shopping for a bit and I give it to you in exchange?"

I raised my eyebrow. "And what exactly is it that I want?"

"Let's shop and I'll *talk*." Boe raised her eyebrow in return, waiting for me to get the innuendo.

I cocked my head at her. "Information?" Then the light bulb lit up in my head.

"That's right," Boe replied, nodding roguishly.

"Deal," I answered firmly.

She immediately ushered me toward a designer store—the last place I wanted to go.

"We have to be quick because he's getting impatient," she explained.

I silently pondered if blushing could actually burn flesh.

I was sorting through a stack of clothing that Jeanie had assembled for me. When Boe and I had entered the store we were immediately greeted by the jolly stylist. She knew Boe personally because she greeted her with a hearty hug and called her by her first name: Sue. I wondered if anyone actually called her Boe. No one I met called her that except for Blake, RJ and myself.

When Boe introduced me, Jeanie did a quick assessment. She worked in retail and you could tell she was very good at her trade because she was the epitome of diplomacy and social skills. Regardless of what Jeanie saw in me, the fact that I was Boe's friend was enough. She welcomed me like she had known me for years.

I told Boe that I would agree to shop on two conditions: that she talk, which was already agreed upon, and that I would pay. She brushed off the second condition as she inspected a dangerous looking mini-boot. When I reiterated it, she ignored me. I decided to press the issue when checkout time came.

I threw a silk top over my head and shimmied into a skirt that was too clingy for my taste, but Boe said I had to try on a few things before she would answer anything. She was devious that one.

"Question time, Boe." I walked out of my dressing room to find her standing in front of a gigantic mirror wearing a tight black outfit with matching pumps that were lined with silver studs.

"Like it?" she asked.

"Boe, you could make a rag look good."

"I know." She smiled at her egotistical remark. "But I think it's too dominatrix. I'm torn for what look to go for this season. Sleek and seductive or girly and soft."

I grinned at how seriously Boe was contemplating her options. Someone who didn't know her might think she was just full of herself—vain and egocentric—but being a diva was just a part she liked to play. There was more to Boe than that and I knew she was very much like still water; to the eye she might look shallow, but I knew the pool ran deep. Looking at her poise in the mirror, I thought that putting up with the shallow part would be worth it, if I got the real Boe some of the time. And from what I gathered she reserved this side of herself to those select few whom she truly cared for and trusted.

"You said you would give me information." I sunk down into a black suede chair and crossed my arms.

"Okay, fine, but ask your question while you change into another outfit. I can hear you perfectly."

"You can?"

"Of course." She motioned for me to move. "Chop, chop. We haven't got all day."

I sprang back into my dressing room and started peeling off my clothes.

"Okay, question one: what abilities do you have?" I felt like I was talking to myself. "How old are you? What are WiiGiis? Why did they come after you and the others—"

Boe threw open my door and shoved an outfit at me. I was timid, never one to change in front of other girls in gym class, so I grabbed a bunch of clothes to shield myself. I only had on a bra and underwear.

"I'm not looking! Try this one on. I think it will suit you and, sheesh, one question at a time."

I frowned and took the pieces of clothing from her. A few moments later I hopped out of the dressing room. "Are you satisfied? Now. Tell. Me."

"Yup, I was right. It looks perfect."

I let out a breath of frustration. Boe rolled her eyes. "You asked about abilities first. I'll start with my hearing. Not only can I hear you perfectly from inside the dressing room but I can also hear every conversation inside this store as if they were taking place right beside me. I can hear voices in the adjoining stores and on the rest of the floor, but they're just murmurs."

"Doesn't that get annoying?" I asked.

"Not really. You have to remember that I was born like this. Abilities aren't something you have to get used to. It is something that is assumed instinctually. What I hear sounds normal to me because I've never heard anything else. That's the thing that people don't get about us. They think Supras don't live *normal* lives, forgetting that normal is something quite relative. If I couldn't hear the conversations taking place in the next room, or if I wasn't as fast or as strong as I am now, I would feel *abnormal*, because being me is all I have ever known. I can no sooner put myself in your shoes than you can put yourself into mine."

Glancing down at the near five-inch pumps Boe was perched on, I thought she had a point. Boe followed my gaze and giggled.

"What are the biggest differences between us?" I pressed, eager for information.

Boe pulled on a tweed jacket and inspected her reflection. "Well, we don't produce energy the same way. We don't have to consume food and our respiratory system is much more efficient. I don't have to breathe nearly as often as you do."

"Really?"

Boe nodded. "I think Supras have to take a breath every week— or is it every two weeks? I don't know. I breathe all the time so I'm not sure how long I can go without doing it. Oh, and we don't have to go to the washroom."

"What?" I could hear the disbelief in my own voice.

"That was the issue that sparked that huge controversy, remember?"

I furrowed my brow. "What controversy?"

"Athena, have you been living under a rock your whole life?" I shrugged apologetically. "How could you not know about the biochemist Pearson Averson? He was the one who made that infamous comment pushing the dualism between Supra and human and said the difference between the two was that Supras were homeostatic systems and that humans were creatures who wallowed in their own filth." Boe shook her head disapprovingly. "Total jackass. Anyway, I can't believe you didn't hear about that. There was a huge uproar."

"It just slipped my mind."

Boe eyed me suspiciously. I hurriedly changed the subject not wanting to dwell on my ignorance. "How old are you?"

"Sixteen."

"Really?" I asked, puckering my forehead.

"Yeah, why?"

"It's just…you seemed…older."

"Nope, I'm sixteen. I know ages are a tricky thing with us considering our life span," Boe replied casually, slipping into a new jacket.

I gulped nervously. "And how long is that exactly?" I prayed Boe didn't hear the tension in my voice.

"I don't really know. Scientists estimate approximately two hundred and fifty years, but I'll let you in on a little secret." Boe's voice fell to a hush.

"What?" I whispered, leaning on the edge of my seat.

"They're not actually sure. You see, no Supra has ever really died, at least not from natural causes. There's been speculation that Supras might be able to live forever." Boe leaned in closer. "If that's true, it's a good thing that Supras can't be produced anymore."

"Produced?"

Boe looked at me wide-eyed. "You don't know?"

"Know what?" I asked anxiously.

Boe shook her head, dumbfounded at my lack of understanding. "You don't know how Supras were developed?"

I raised my eyebrows indicating that I didn't. "I wasn't exactly carried in a womb for nine months and then delivered by my mother," Boe quipped sarcastically.

"You weren't?" I asked, unable to conceal my surprise.

Boe frowned. "Athena everyone knows that Supras were developed in embryonic sacs that were housed in only three facilities in the world: Switzerland, Washington and Japan. Right?" I just nodded. "I'm a Switzer and so are Blake and Bach."

"Bach?"

"My eldest brother." Boe suddenly straightened. "You asked about WiiGiis next I think."

I noticed how Boe grew tense when she mentioned her older brother, but I was too engrossed with what she told me about Supras to care.

"Wait, could you go over how Supras are made? And what do you mean they aren't produced anymore?"

"Athena, do you seriously not know this?"

I shook my head. Boe wore a skeptical look but continued anyway. "Human DNA is manipulated so that sperm and ovum carry Supra genes." She sounded like an impatient teacher telling students how babies were made. "The phases of development are completed after two and half months. A human cannot be used as a host to carry the baby so it has to be developed artificially. After the first stage of development the synthesizer has to be implanted into the chest cavity or else the Supra will die."

"What's a synthesizer?"

Boe looked at me incredulously.

"I'm sorry," I offered, "I was home-schooled and I never really covered the subject of Supra," I said in my defense.

"How could you not learn about that?" Boe made it sound like I just told her I wasn't taught the alphabet.

I shook my head impatiently. "I don't know. I just didn't."

"A synthesizer," she said, as if explaining what a heart was, "is the nuclear apparatus that stimulates the homeostatic condition inside the Supra. It is also the source of cognitive conduction."

The look on my face must have bellowed *huh* because Boe elaborated without my asking. "Cognitive conduction is how boTs and Supras communicate. And the reason Supras cannot be produced anymore is because of the elemental sources that are needed to make the synthesizer. It's found deep, near the Earth's core. We used up all the resources the Earth had and it's non-renewable. You have to remember that it took a long time to perfect the mechanism. By that time, materials were scarce. That's why the Supras that do exist today are extraordinarily wealthy. Only the richest of the rich could afford to create offspring as Supras. Scientists have tried to find other sources but to no avail. Many consider it impossible. Besides, the leading scientist, Jovan Feldenheim, disappeared shortly after Supra generation took off and his research was lost. A lot of people believed he went into hiding after speculation arose that there was an interest in doing human studies to see if synthesizers could be made for the human populace." Boe pursed her lips. "Honestly, I don't know why you're so curious about this. When I offered you information, I thought you would be more interested in secrets about my brother."

I blanched as Boe shoved me toward the dressing room. "No time. No time. Try on the beige, then the black. More shop, less talk," she ordered.

Staring at my blank face in the mirror, I couldn't bring myself to move. Eventually, I managed to pull on random pieces of clothing in a state of distraction.

Boe laughed at me when I emerged from the dressing room.

"What?" I asked.

"Your buttons are all mismatched. Didn't you look at your reflection?"

I looked down at myself and saw that the beige jacket I was wearing was all distorted. "We're just going to have to come back another day. I'll ask Jeanie to put some items aside as they come in. Did you like anything?"

"No," I replied, turning to change.

"I liked the second outfit you tried on and the black one. We'll get those."

"Fine, but I'm paying Boe," I called out as I shimmied out of the designer gear.

"Athena, stop it. I'm paying."

"Boe, I got it."

She didn't respond. After no reply came I knew that she had

left. Damn. She was checking out. I roughly yanked on my clothes, eager to catch her. A small part of me felt guilty because the prices on the tags were huge. I would be totally humiliated if the chip Sammy gave me got declined, but my pride was stronger and I was determined to pay. I threw open the dressing room door and sprinted toward the cash. Boe caught me by the arm.

"I said I'm paying," I insisted.

"You said you didn't want anything. There's nothing to pay for."

I was about to protest when Jeanie came over and gave Boe a hug and then hugged me next. Boe rolled her eyes when I showed signs of discomfort.

"Thanks for everything, Jeanie," Boe said sweetly.

"Anytime, Sue. I'll have the orders sent out today, no problem."

"What orders?" I asked suspiciously.

Boe waved to Jeanie and grabbed my arm to walk me out of the store.

"My orders. Relax," Boe answered calmly.

"I don't believe you." I narrowed my eyes at her fine face.

"WiiGiis are a terrorist group bent on ridding the world of Supras," Boe went on, changing the subject. She was good because I forgot about the orders.

"Why would they want to do that?"

"Because they think Supras are discriminate beings who have too much control in the world. I will be the first to admit that there are some pretty shitty Supras out there. You've met a few." I knew she was referring to Charlie Astor. "But that doesn't mean we're all bad. WiiGiis seem to believe that all Supras are inherently evil.

They think we all need to die."

"Aren't you concerned about that?" I asked anxiously.

"Whatever. I can't be bothered with them. I think that answers all your questions. I still can't believe you didn't ask me to give you something juicier."

"Juicier?"

Boe reached over to give my cheek a gentle squeeze, but I flitted her hand away.

"Athena, your cheeks flare too easily. It's so much fun to tease you because you're so shy."

"Am not," I shot back.

"Then I'm sure you wanna know"—she looked at me mischievously—"boxers or briefs?"

"No!" I exclaimed, mortified.

Boe started to laugh and gave me a nudge. "Or maybe neither!"

"I'm not participating in this conversation." I tried to quicken my pace but Boe matched mine easily.

"At least let me give you something. How about his favorite color? Or his favorite poet?"

I looked at Boe and sighed. "It's black and a tie between Blake and Browning."

Browning? I thought it was Emily and not Robert she was referring to, but I considered both of them too soft for Blake. I assumed she meant Blake as in William Blake.

"Where are we going now?" I asked as we headed toward the exit.

"I have to take you home—to my home—because he's threatening me now," Boe replied, annoyance lining her voice.

"How exactly does that work? How can you hear him?" I asked curiously.

"Supras cannot communicate directly with one another. It's a common misunderstanding people have. Supras can only communicate with their boT. I hear Blake because he tells oC something and then oC tells kO.

"kO?"

"Yeah, my boT."

"Is that a girl name or a boy name?" I wasn't going to make the same mistake that I made with vI, though I suspected that most boTs were probably not as sensitive as she.

"kO's a he," Boe said sentimentally.

"Where is he?" I wondered, looking around.

"Right here." Boe pointed to what looked like a pin the size of quarter on her jacket.

"Can he hear us?" I asked, eyeing the small piece of metal.

"Of course."

"Can he see us?"

"Of course."

My mouth dropped open. "In the dressing room—"

"He turned off his visual features. kO isn't a peeping tom, Athena."

The pin blinked yellow twice. "See, he's offended that you would think so lowly of him."

"I'm sorry, kO. I didn't mean to offend you," I said quickly, trying to be polite, although it was really weird talking to Boe's jacket.

Boe scoffed in frustration. "He's so edgy today. I don't know what you've done to my brother."

My stride quickened. "I haven't done anything."

Boe ignored my comment. "kO's loading Getty. Is there anything else you wanted before we leave? Although, I think Blake is going to have a mental breakdown if he sees us go into another store."

"Sees us? How can he see us exactly? Through kO?"

"No, he's around here looking right at us."

I tried to look calm as I fervently surveyed the rows of stores. "How long has he been here?" I asked nervously, unable to spot him.

"Since the start. He was the one who was following you." Boe was trying to hold back a smile. "Athena, you don't have to ask. Yes, he heard everything we were talking about."

Boxers or briefs.

"Boe! Why didn't you tell me?" I exclaimed.

"I wanted to see what you were going to ask me," she said with a laugh.

I tried to smack her shoulder but she evaded me and came up beside my other arm in an instant. "You're so cute when you're embarrassed."

I let my face fall and I gave Boe a reproving stare.

"Come on, it's no big deal. Besides I'm sure Blake himself is disappointed you didn't ask something more personal about him."

I was so tired of being the source of people's amusement. Normally, I really wouldn't have cared; I took it all in good fun, but when it came to Blake I found myself on edge. I didn't like the fact that he heard everything, saw everything, because it made me insane thinking about what he thought.

I didn't say a word on the ride to Boe's house. I wasn't really mad, just nervous. Boe made the occasional cheery comment and danced in the driver's seat to the music that was playing, but I barely noticed. I only started to pay attention when we pulled up in front of a large gate that opened onto a private driveway.

The first time I was there, Blake hadn't gone through the main entrance and I never saw the exterior of the house. As I looked out the window, my mouth dropped open in awe. The building was so palatial that you couldn't see the entire structure in a single view. It looked like an entire Chateau had been resurrected from the ground and magically stood upon a glass base that ran stories above street level with the grand house making up the peak of the building. The front entrance wasn't modern at all, but was classically designed with arched windows, corinthian columns, ornate sculpting and marble figures. I guessed that was a trend in the city because many of the historic buildings maintained their original façades and most often modern extensions arose on top of them—London hadn't lost its history even in the face of modernity.

The passenger door slid open and the inside of the car was invaded with a cool mist. I shivered as I got out, but Boe didn't follow suit.

"Aren't you coming?" I asked.

"No, I'm meeting RJ. We have to go shopping again, kay?"

I crossed my arms. "That's not likely, Boe."

"Don't be mad. I'll tell you next time, I promise. No harm no foul, right?"

"Fine," I said softly.

"You have to come over after school one day. I won't be back for two weeks so you have to keep me posted on school gossip."

"What do you mean you won't be back for two weeks?"

"Don't you remember the other night I agreed to compromise? I'm taking a leave of absence from the College for two weeks. RJ thinks it isn't safe for me."

"Oh, no." Not only did disappointment fill my voice but dread did as well.

"Hey, talk to RJ," Boe said apologetically. "I'm sure you'll be fine. If anyone messes with you, just let me know."

"Thanks." I looked around the empty loading dock. "Um, am I just supposed to wait here?" I asked awkwardly.

Boe grinned. "Yup. You can go inside if you like, but he's here and I don't think you're staying." Boe winked.

"What do you mean?" My voice hiked up a pitch.

"Let's just say that this wasn't the only favor I was asked. I must say Athena, my brother is quite in my debt."

"Why? Tell me," I demanded.

"It's a surprise."

"Boe—"

"Gotta go." The passenger door slid shut and Boe reversed the vehicle. Before driving off she lowered her window. "Bye Theena!"

A deep crease developed on my forehead. Sometimes I wanted to squeeze her little neck when she talked to me with that annoyingly cheery voice.

¤ XV ¤

E P I T H E T S

I couldn't see very clearly because the mist obscured my sight and I couldn't spot Blake anywhere. Boe said that he was waiting so I stayed on the loading dock thinking he would appear. After a few moments, I thought maybe he hadn't arrived yet and decided to go inside. I turned around only to find him standing at arms length from me.

My eyes found his and I was lost, so lost it was frightening. I thought it was so unfair how my body betrayed me so quickly. I couldn't slow my heartbeat or hinder my breathing. I couldn't wash away the scorch marks on my cheeks or calm my nerves. The complexity of being human baffled me. I didn't get how it was possible to think and feel so many things at once. Blake on the other hand looked serene in his perfection, which made me feel that his presence meant far more to me than my presence did to him.

"I've been waiting for you," he admitted.

I didn't say anything and just let his words, spoken in a velvet voice, linger in the air. I just wanted to look at him and memorize the contours of his face.

"I missed you," he whispered.

The stab in my chest was so acute. I wanted to laugh and cry at the same time.

Blake took a step toward me and then another. We stood chest to chest but he didn't pull me to him. "Did you miss me?" he asked softly.

I closed my eyes as he brought my face to his and trailed it with kisses—first on my forehead, then on my cheek and then the tip of my nose. "Tell me that you missed me," Blake demanded lightly.

I opened my eyes and then my mouth, but I was incapacitated and I couldn't speak.

"Say it." His finger was as hard as stone but as soft as baby's skin as he ran it over the bottom of my lip.

I gulped. His touch wasn't enough. I needed to feel him too and slowly lifted my fingers to trace his jawbone. Blake reached up and pressed my hand against his cheek, venerating my touch.

"Tell me," he urged huskily.

I nodded my head, hoping the answer would be sufficient, and a small smile splayed across his lips, making me feel like I didn't have kneecaps.

"I think it might rain. We'd better get going before it does. I have a surprise for you."

Blake's declaration caught me off guard because I had just decided to kiss him when he spoke. Swooping me up in his arms, he sat me into the passenger seat of his car and a moment later he was in the driver's seat. My stomach tightened at my disappointment. Clearly Blake's feelings weren't as potent as mine because I could hardly breathe around him and yet he never seemed perturbed.

"A surprise? I don't like surprises," I said quietly.

"I know. But you'll like this one," he replied smoothly. I looked at him, questioning his confidence. "Trust me."

I sighed and looked out over the dashboard. We were already zooming through the City. "Can we listen to some music?" My heart was still thumping madly and I felt terribly self-conscious when I remembered that Boe said she could hear it, which meant that Blake could too.

I stole a glance at him, only to find him looking out toward the city with his lips pursed. He was contemplating something. Then I heard the first few bars of a song that sounded vaguely familiar, but I couldn't place it. My eyes widened in surprise when the lead singer bellowed my name. Blinking rapidly, I badly wanted to laugh because his song selection was too funny, but I suppressed the urge. The song made me think that there were many facets of Blake that I didn't know.

"Something funny?" he asked.

I shook my head. "Nope."

"Is there a problem with my taste in music?"

"No, not at all," I replied, doing my best to keep my face neutral.

Blake cleared his throat. "I'll let you choose the next one."

"How do I search?" I asked, inspecting the 3-D hologram besides me.

"Tell me and I'll play it."

"Can't you show me?"

Without taking his eyes off the laneway Blake reached out and touched the holographic image. A search menu came up with sort options with categories for artist, song title and period. Without waiting for his instruction—I wasn't sure any were coming anyway—I typed in the song that I wanted.

"You didn't have to do that today." Blake spoke just as I was about to press the play button.

"Do what?"

"Interrogate Boe."

"I didn't," I replied, furrowing my brow. Blake was tense all of a sudden and it made me nervous. He seemed fine a second ago.

"You could have asked me, but I assumed you were trying to make a point."

"What do you mean by that?"

"You were trying to prove that if I don't give you the answers you want then you'll find other sources. That's what you said last night, remember?" Blake clenched his jaw and his grip tightened on the steering wheel.

"I wasn't trying to prove anything. I was having a *private* conversation with my friend." I wanted to berate him for eaves dropping but I held my tongue.

"If you're so eager to know about Supras, I'll show you our abilities firsthand. Say the word and I'll line up with RJ and Boe and put on a freak show just for you." His voice was like ice, chilling my bones.

"I don't think you're freaks. Where's this coming from?" I demanded. "You can't honestly believe I think that way, because if anyone's the freak it's me and I know it." I crossed my arms and turned to look out my window, not wanting him to see how hurt I was.

I hadn't even noticed, but the city had already slipped away and we were zooming over countryside. Forcing a small smile, I was glad that the English countryside hadn't changed—it was still country covered with hills and pastures of green velvet. Nature had a way of touching the spirit, something I could never really fully comprehend, and I needed its soothing qualities. I was thankful that wherever Blake was taking me it was away from the metropolis.

The day had been cloudy from the start, but small patches of sunlight managed to sneak through as we descended and drove on paved ground.

The spots of white on Blake's knuckles hadn't receded and he continued to look stressed.

"What are you thinking?" I asked quietly, hesitant to speak.

He looked at me slowly, wary to meet my eyes.

"That I don't deserve you. That you shouldn't be here—"

"You said you have a surprise for me." I wasn't going to give him the chance. I was scared about the tone of his voice. If I let him go on I knew the day would come to an end much to soon. I wanted to be with him for as long as I could and if that meant I had to push things to the back of my mind then I would.

"Blake, can you at least tell me where we're going?" I looked at him helplessly, silently pleading to let him drop whatever he was going to say. "Since you're so fond of deals can I propose one of my own?" He cocked his head. "I'll let you surprise me on one condition." Blake raised his eyebrow inquisitively. "That you take me home when I ask to be taken. I want to spend the day with you. All day. And I don't want to keep worrying that you're going to back out on me. Deal?"

Blake leaned over to take my hand and sighed before kissing my knuckles.

"Deal. Perfect timing because we're here," he said without expression.

We were in the middle of a long road surrounded by towering trees.

"Where are we?" I asked, glimpsing out the car window.

"At my family's estate."

I couldn't see the main house or anything beyond the thick brush as the vehicle's doors slid open. Blake was at my side helping me out of the car by the time I planted my first foot on the ground.

"Close your eyes." I couldn't help but smile at the trace of excitement in his voice.

"Why?" I asked suspiciously.

"Because you'll know before we're there and it will ruin the surprise." Blake turned me around, wrapped one arm around my waist and rested his hand on my stomach. It tickled a little but I held back a giggle. Blake's other hand came over my eyes and made my pulse quicken.

"That really isn't necessary. I won't peek," I offered playfully.

"Yes, *you will*."

I scoffed even though he was right. Of course I would peek. I was the type of person who wanted to know the end of a book before I read it.

I was about to take a step forward when Blake held me against him. "Wrap your legs around mine. It'll be faster if I run," he whispered against the back of my neck.

Damn hormones. My body started to thrum.

"It's fine, I can walk," I said breathlessly.

Blake took his hand away from my eyes and I thought that he relented, but I was wrong. He hoisted me up and wrapped my legs around his. I didn't have time to protest because an instant later he had his hand over my eyes again and the other against my stomach as he raced us toward our destination.

A few minutes later he slowed to a walking pace. I wasn't even curious about the surprise. I wasn't even wondering where he had taken us. All I thought about was my body pressed against Blake's, so it took me a while to notice the familiar odor.

The light from outside faded and I knew that we just entered a barn. Not only could I recognize the scent, but I also heard movement and the distinct sound of *horses*. Blake removed his hand from my eyes and peeled my legs off him.

"What's the surprise?" I asked with a timid smile spread across my face.

"You know that saying, 'A horse! A horse! A kingdom for a horse'?"

"Yes," I answered slowly, my eyes still closed.

"Did you also know that there are many epithets associated with the goddess *Athena*." Blake's lips moved against my cheek. "One of them was *Athena Hippia*, meaning horse, because she invented the chariot and was said to be the goddess who first tamed horses for men to ride."

"Thanks for the mythology lesson, but I already know this," I replied teasingly.

Blake chuckled lightly and the sound was heaven. "Of course you do. Well, think of what a predicament I found myself in trying to find a horse fit for a goddess."

I turned my head and Blake's lips brushed against the back of my neck, covering my body in gooseflesh. Taking my arm, he pivoted me around and held out my hand. I sensed the warm air as the powerful animal—I could tell it was strong and proud already—breathed out a greeting. Its black coat—I knew it would be black—was the softest I had ever felt. I still hadn't opened my eyes.

"What's his name?" I asked quietly. I knew it was a he.

"Persafelis. Persy for short," Blake answered against my ear.

The name was perfect. Something I would have chosen. "Open your eyes. He's *yours*."

The finest of thoroughbreds, he stood at least eighteen hands tall. He was utterly black—black as the deepest night, but his eyes were the light of day—warm and welcoming.

"Persy," I whispered his name, stroking his neck gently.

His ears shot forward as if he recognized my voice. Turning, I looked at Blake over my shoulder. It was too great a gift—one I should have refused, but I couldn't bear to do it.

"It's too much," I said softly.

"It's not enough." Blake's somber voice matched his expression. There it was again—the dark quality that so often crept into him, but I was determined to dampen it.

"Do you ride?" I asked, trying to be playful. He sighed. "Where's your horse?" Blake glanced down the extravagant barn and for the first time I noticed the tiled floor, the iron gates that lined the stalls and the exquisite mosaic ceiling. This was a barn good enough for my stead. "What's your horse's name?" I inquired curiously.

"Familiar with Homer?" Blake asked, crossing his arms. "He's named after the horse who was endowed with human speech before the Furies struck him dumb because he forewarned his master about his death at the hands of a god."

I started walking toward the far end of the barn.

I furrowed my brow. "Why did you choose that name?" I half-whispered.

"You know it?" Blake asked casually.

"Of course I do, but why Xanthus?"

"For a few reasons. First, Xanthus and his brother Balius were said to be the fastest horses on earth, as fast as the West Wind. Boe's horse, as you can imagine, is named Balius. If you didn't know, my sister happens to be quite the equine lover. The second reason"—Blake quirked his eyebrow and I raised mine in return—"I thought it fitting considered I fell for a god. A goddess, actually."

I blanched red and nervously bit the inside of my cheek while Blake looked at me unfazed.

I let out an awkward cough. "Tack up. Let's go for a ride. We'll see whose stead is indeed as fast as the West Wind."

Blake cocked his head, eyeing the look on my face.

"I'll get their bridles, but I don't need tack. Do you?" he asked innocently.

Was that a challenge?

"Bareback it is," I announced with childish pride.

Blake shrugged out of his jacket and threw it over the stall door. His shirt was well fitted—too well fitted—and you could make out the lean contours of his body. I gulped as my eyes followed his receding figure. He came back an instant later with two bridles in his hands and handed me one, then headed toward Xanthus' stall.

Persy lowered his head for me without fuss and bridling him was the easiest thing. I heard the barn doors creak open and caught sight of Blake heading out with Xanthus—a horse as white as Persy was black.

There was a chill in the air and I buttoned up my jacket after I left the barn.

"I'll give you a leg up," Blake offered, coming around behind me.

"Kay," I answered, doing my best to sound casual. I would have insisted on mounting myself but Persy was too tall and there wasn't a mounting block in sight. I took hold of Persy's withers as Blake bent down, just far enough to grab the back of my calf. I prayed that when I shivered he assumed it was from the cold.

"Ready?" he asked. He didn't wait for me to answer but lifted me like I was made of straw.

I slid my legs around Persy, settling myself on his back and noticed that Blake was already atop Xanthus. Moving away from the barn, we headed toward an open field that lay sprawled behind the main property. My nerves were making me tense, and I was horribly stiff. Feeling the suppleness of Persy's mouth, I tried to loosen my grip. I didn't have soft hands and it was my greatest flaw as a rider.

I could see the main house from where we rode and it was grand indeed. I was sure it housed at least fifty rooms, if not more. The grounds were impeccably maintained and the façade was charmingly aged.

I slowed Persy to a brisk walk. Xanthus, instantly, matched his stride.

"Is Persy really mine?" I asked, glancing at Blake.

"Yes he is," he replied in a matter-of-fact way.

"Was he mine before?"

I pulled Persy to a halt when Blake answered with silence.

"You had a horse named Persy, but he's not the same one you're riding now. He's a descendent though."

Everything Blake said always sounded carefully composed and it made me tirelessly suspicious.

"What happened to him?"

Blake straightened. "He died."

"How?" I demanded.

"Old age," Blake replied in a flat voice.

"*Old* age?" I repeated his answer disbelievingly. "How old was he when I had him?"

Blake nudged Xanthus forward and the horse picked up speed.

"How about we ride to the downs and back. It's getting late and we should head back soon."

I didn't answer him right away, but just stared at his back.

"How much time has passed since I left?" I asked hesitantly, knowing my voice sounded uneven.

"Does it matter?" he answered, indifferent.

I let out a breath and shrugged. "I guess not," I answered sharply.

Blake could be both fire and ice and I couldn't keep up with the constant change of temperature. One instant he was soft and hot and the next he was cold and hard. During the car ride earlier he acted the same way. I just wanted him to tell me what he was thinking. I wanted him to stop hiding things from me. But I was also scared to press him because he always made me feel like I was on thin ice.

I wasn't wearing a helmet and I hadn't ridden for weeks, but my frustration gave me nerve and I was overcome with the desire to race—really fast. Blake may have been a Supra, but he could only go as fast as his horse and I put my faith in Persy. We would race and I needed to win. I had to win.

The wind picked up and the traces of sunlight that danced across the open fields vanished. All that was left was a cloudy coolness, but the weather didn't bother me.

"Blake, let's race to the downs and back." I vaguely remembered driving by them earlier.

"Athena—"

"Winner names their prize." I didn't wait for Blake's reply and I booted Persy forward. He was like a racehorse taking off at full speed, but he didn't take a single stride before Blake rolled me onto the dewy grass. Persy stood a few paces beside us; having stopped the moment I left his back.

"We're not racing." Blake wore an uncompromising look, but I couldn't be bothered by it. His immaculate face was just inches from mine and it only made me want him more, fueling my illogical desire to race him.

"Yes, we are," I said stubbornly.

"You don't need to race me…I'd give you anything you want."

I wanted to believe his words, spoken so sincerely, but I couldn't. He could take them back a moment later and probably would.

I pressed my hands against his chest and narrowed my eyes. "To the downs and back."

"You're not racing me," he replied firmly. There was something in Blake's voice that irked my ego. He made it sound like racing him was a ridiculous notion—child's play.

"You don't think I can win?"

Blake pursed his lips, frustrated by my answer. "What I'm saying is that I'm not going to race you. Just tell me what you want."

"I want to win fair and square, so you'll be honor bound to give me what I ask for."

"What do you want so badly?" Blake whispered, the lines of his face softening.

I wanted him. I wanted the truth. The two seemed inextricably intertwined.

"Bloody race me, Blake. Race me like you want to win—like you want it badly."

The softness that had started to melt his features hardened—his eyes were ruthless.

"Wait here." Blake ordered, raising himself off the ground.

I moved to sit up, but he pushed up against me and lay me back down. "I said don't move."

There was no refuting him this time. His gaze was feral and it commanded me like I was no longer master of myself. I didn't dare move after he vanished, but just lay dumbstruck, starring up at the hazy sky. When Blake lifted himself off of me, it was like he peeled away a second skin, making my body tingle where he had lain.

Blake hoisted me to my feet in what seemed like no time at all. Smoothing back a hair that had been billowing around my face, he planted a sleek helmet on top of my head. I just looked at him dumbly as he tightened the chinstrap and noticed the vest slung over his arm. After helping me into the outerwear he slowly zipped it up, then drew a pair of gloves from his pant's pocket and slipped them into place. Blake took such care with each finger, as if he was wrapping something delicate. While he dressed me, his eyes never wavered from my face.

"To the downs and back. Winner names their prize." Blake's voice was a grating whisper.

I didn't even manage a nod before I was back on Persy. This

time, however, I found myself seated in a saddle. I stole a glance over at Blake who sat atop Xanthus, still bareback like a wild god.

Finding my stirrups just the right height, I fitted my boots into them and took a deep breath. To the downs and back. Xanthus took off, sprinting against the howling wind—a sign sent from the heavens to mark the start of the race. It seemed Blake was going to play fair, which meant nobody was going to let anybody win without a fight. Excellent. I shifted into a strong half-seat and booted Persy forward.

Blake and Xanthus were but a dark blur racing across the open plain. Breaking away from their course, I decided to take a shortcut over a fence. It was risky because it came after a sharp turn and Persy would have to jump it at an angle but I trusted him. He flew over it easily. I granted that Persy could have flown over the measly fence even if I was the worst rider in the world. We headed toward another fence, a bigger one this time. I gave Persy a few half-halts to control his power and his stride. He cleared the fence with as much ease as the first time—his hind legs were indomitable. I slowed his gallop to a strong canter as we made our way through a patchy area and saw Blake and Xanthus come roaring up beside us.

The horses, fighting like the majestic animals they were, rode head to head battling for dominance. The cold air was bitter and harsh against my face, but I didn't feel the burn. All I felt was the rush of blood to my head and the hunger for victory. It was fitting that the words of a famous racecar driver kept playing in my head. "Winning wasn't important. Winning was *everything*."

Riding fearlessly across the downs, I didn't hear the voice of caution in my head as Blake managed to get ahead a few strides. I rode neck or nothing and I didn't care for the consequences. My focus was complete, but I still marveled at what a fine rider Blake was. His form was sublime and easy. You could tell his hands were made to guide the mouth of a horse. His mastery of the skill and of the animal were so complete it made me doubt myself for a moment. I reached down to give Persy a quick pat on the neck—a boost to reassure myself. I doubted anyone could match Blake's riding abilities, but I rode Persy and that turned the scales.

As we circled back around, Blake maintained the lead. I couldn't catch the few strides he had been able to secure ahead of us. Leaping over a tall fence, we rode into the last field. I needed to make a move soon. I gave Persy a strong kick and he threw himself forward. *That's my boy.* I knew that he was an intuitive horse. He could sense the nearness of the end. Persy was also a proud animal and wanted the victory as much as I did. The finish line wasn't too far off and I saw Blake look at me through the corner of my eye. He spurred Xanthus on and gained more ground. Persy had to act or we would lose. And act he did, accelerating with such power, such strength, such will, that his fierce gallop overtook his powerful adversary in a few strides. Just when I was certain that victory would be ours, a shadow rocketed over my head. It happened so fast I thought my eyes were playing tricks on me, but then I saw Xanthus cross the finish line—horse without rider—and then Blake appear at his side. I blinked rapidly, unsure of what had just transpired and pulled Persy into a canter as we approached the main property. Blake was once again on Xanthus and was riding away from us.

He cheated.

My knees buckled as I dismounted, a sure sign that my legs were going to be sore, but I didn't care. Horse and rider were nowhere in sight as I unlatched Persy's girth. I hefted the fine saddle from his back and turned to head into the barn, but found Blake barring my path.

"You cheated," I accused and moved to step around him.

Blake mirrored my move, unwilling to let me pass. His hands came around the saddle so quickly that my muscles didn't have time to react before he lifted the weight off my hands. I looked up at him as he carelessly discarded the fine piece of riding equipment. I turned, determined to get it back, but found that it was nowhere in sight. Furrowing my brow, I got a glimpse of a black blob sprawled in the middle of the open field we just rode through.

Blake swiveled me back around to face him. "I'll name my prize now," he declared callously.

"Forget it," I shot back. "You didn't win. I won by default so I should be the one naming my prize."

"You never stipulated the rules, Athena. In such a case, I surmised that there were none. You wanted to race me because I would be honor bound to give you what you asked for. I expect the same." His voice had a hard edge that made me uneasy.

I shook my head. "Then the race doesn't count. I'm not scared of a rematch, but this time I'll make the rules crystal clear."

Blake grabbed my arms. "I won. There won't be a rematch. There's one thing I want and, regardless of what you say, you're bound to do it."

I tried to wriggle my way out his hold, but his grip was ironclad.

"You're going home," he said flatly.

I didn't understand what I did. I wanted to spend the rest of the day with him, willing to endure his sour mood, but if he couldn't stand being with me any longer then I wasn't going to force him.

"Fine," I agreed soberly. "Are you at least going to give me a ride or should I call my sister to come and pick me up?"

Blake jerked me closer to him. "No, you're going *home*."

I started to panic, knowing he didn't mean unit 537. "I'll call Pork Chop," I said quickly, "she'll come and get me." I tried my best to play dumb.

He shook his head. "You can go first. I'll make sure she follows as well. The sooner you're back, the better."

I thrashed for him to release me. "I'm not going anywhere," I exclaimed bitterly.

"It's what I want and you don't have a choice," he replied, bowing his head.

"I don't care what you want." I felt trapped. "Let me go," I demanded. "You're hurting me," I lied, helpless against his strength.

Blake released me and took a step back, wearing an expression of self-loathing on his face, as if the thought of hurting me disgusted him. My heart cracked, knowing I inflicted it upon him, but I needed to protect myself—I was in danger of losing my mind. "Blake, you weren't really hurting me," I offered apologetically, taking a step toward him, but he backed away.

"Let's go," he said briskly, whirling around to walk off.

As his receding figure got smaller and smaller, Blake's gait remained even and quick-paced, marking his lack of concern for whether or not I followed. And I didn't follow. I couldn't move. Some deep part of me knew that if I pursued him I would have to face something I couldn't quite handle, so my body remained immobilized.

When my feet eventually started to move, it was as if some force beside myself was manipulating my limbs. I didn't head after Blake, but instead tramped across the slick field to retrieve Persy's saddle.

The barn was warm and I lingered there, unwilling to face the cold that awaited me. I absent-mindedly ran my fingers across the iron rails of the stalls as I walked up the aisle—thinking of how I was going to find another way home—when I felt the soft fabric. My heart jolted as I realized that Blake had forgotten his jacket. Closing my eyes, I lifted the piece of clothing and buried my face in it. It still smelled like him—an unmistakable smell that I couldn't dissect, but would know anywhere.

My frozen body reached a new level of stillness as I heard the barn doors open in front of me. Raising my tear-stained face, I met his gaze straight on. As the distance closed between us, we were two beings standing at opposite spectrums being inexorably pushed together by some force neither of us really understood.

Blake looked pained and it killed me. I was sure that he was going to confess something by the expression on his face, but he didn't. He slowly reached toward me and my heart hammered fiercely. I wanted him to touch me, to hold me so badly, but instead he briskly took his jacket and slipped into it. It was like being gutted with a butcher's knife.

"We're leaving," Blake said, keeping his well-bred voice carefully inexpressive.

"Tell me something," I blurted out. Blake stopped in front of the barn doors with his back turned to me. "Why do you want me to go back?" I asked, trying so hard not to cry.

"I just do," he replied quietly. He hadn't moved and I couldn't see his face.

"*Why?*" I pleaded.

Blake turned his head, but didn't move from where he stood. "That's what I want. It's reason enough." His voice was distant and cool.

"I deserve a better answer than that." I spoke so low, I barely heard my own words, but I knew Blake heard them. "You said you wanted to be with me. I don't understand. What's changed?"

Blake hung his head and didn't respond right away. "I feel responsible for you being here when you shouldn't be. Athena, I do have feelings…I do care, but I've decided that I don't want to live with a liability and I don't want to live with the guilt should you get hurt…I want to be *free* of you," he hissed, running his fingers through his hair before pushing through the barn doors.

I gently flicked away a tear that rolled down my cheek. I was so numb that I couldn't even muster enough anger to berate myself over crying. I peeled off the vest he put on me and drew off the pair of gloves he so softly pulled over my fingers. I let the items fall carelessly to the ground.

The gravel crunched under my boots as I walked down the long and winding drive. It felt like I had walked for miles and yet Blake's parked car had not come into view. He was well ahead of me and I froze mid-step as I saw him come to a stop. After several moments, he still hadn't moved so I walked on. He turned and I stopped again, casting my eyes on a distant spot past his head. I was hurting so badly and I couldn't bear to look at him.

"What's the matter?" I asked, brushing strands of hair behind my ear with a hand that wouldn't stop shaking.

Blake's steps were slow and careful—the steps of a tight rope walker. "I'm trying so hard...but I can't..." He balled his hands into fists. "I can't do this," he said angrily.

"Do what?" My voice was strained as he came up beside me and I braved a look at him.

Blake glared at me with vicious eyes. "Can't you just *go?*" he shouted.

I took off at full speed, sprinting across the gravel path. I couldn't bear it anymore. I dashed past his car and kept running, wondering why he hadn't caught up to me yet. It only poured salt into my wound when I realized he was going to let me go—he wasn't going to come after me.

Then I stopped, slid over the rocky surface and toppled over. I barely hit the ground before I hoisted myself up and started running back to him, pushing my lungs beyond their known capacity. I couldn't run from Blake. I could run and run and run but every road, every path, every avenue would lead back to him. Running away simply meant taking a detour—winding up the mountain instead of climbing straight to the top—the destination was always the same though.

I would have run right into him if he hadn't taken a step back to buffer the impact. I was glad he did because he was as hard as steel and I was sure something would not have gone unbroken.

"You're not sending me back!" I looked at him fiercely. "I am sick and tired of people telling me what do. I am sick and tired of being lied to." I pointed my finger at him and pressed it against his chest, but quickly withdrew it as my finger jammed against his concrete body. "But more than anything, I am beyond sick and tired of feeling that what I want isn't important."

Blake looked at my sore finger and frowned. I stuffed my hand into my jacket pocket and raised my other one. "Nobody seems to ask me what I want. Everyone is so keen on making decisions for me that they completely forget that it's my life. There's a philosopher—I can't remember which one exactly—who says everyone looks out into the world through their own cave. This"—I pointed to my head—"is my cave and I am the only one living in here. Since I seriously doubt that someone or something is going to become my bunk buddy anytime soon, everyone who thinks they can tell me what to do can go—*jump in a lake!*" For some reason, the common saying that Vas frequently used popped into my mind.

Narrowing his eyes, Blake smothered my fire with just one look. I gulped as he took hold of my hand and pulled me into the dense mass of trees.

"Where are you taking me?" I demanded. The forest ground was uneven and muddy and I had to concentrate on my footing.

"Tell—" I tripped over a fallen log, but Blake held me up and kept moving until we entered a clearing.

"This is what you want?" he asked coolly.

I puckered my forehead as I looked onto a small lake.

Blake released me, threw off his jacket and pulled his shirt over his head, revealing a chest so immaculate, so smooth, I was sure it surpassed the finest rock the earth could produce. I fell back against the bark of a nearby tree and my eyes grew wide as Blake yanked off his boots. He shot up into the air and dove like the most nimble of athletes. There was no splash when he entered the serene pool but just the soft rippling of water. I barely noticed, though, because all I could focus on was two things: the *thud* of Blake's pants falling to the ground and the thudding of my heart—on the brink of exploding.

My eyes fervently scanned the liquid terrain as I made my way to the lake's edge. I was filled with feelings I had never really experienced before and it was overwhelming.

"Am I forgiven?" His voice sounded from directly behind me.

I hastily turned to meet him. Blake had left no space between us, his wet chest pressed against my jacket, and I felt lightheaded—I could see that Blake wore no shirt but I couldn't tell anything about what he wore below the waist.

"I—I didn't mean—I didn't mean to literally jump in a lake." I couldn't help it when my voice came out in gasps.

Blake reached up and tucked a wisp of hair behind my ear. "You should be clear next time. You see, I have this…problem," he admitted slowly, bringing his hands around my face. They were wet and cold, but my skin flamed beneath his touch. "I can't help but do anything you ask."

Confusion. Confusion. Confusion. I was always in an annoying state of confusion when I was around Blake.

"What does that mean?" I asked shakily.

Blake looked over my face, caressing me with his eyes. I was sure I was going to pass out of I didn't manage to get more oxygen into me.

"Athena, I can't refuse you," he said almost resentfully.

I stared at him, perplexed. "Yes, you can."

"No I can't." Blake pressed me against him, his voice demanding. "Do you know what I am?"

I nodded, knowing he was a Supra.

Blake shook his head, denying my answer. "You have no idea."

"You're a Supra," I said quietly.

"I'm nothing," he confessed, "because I'm not *free*." Blake pulled my head to his, raising me on my tiptoes. His lips were so close to mine they nearly touched. "There is no choice, no action, no breath I take that you don't have power over."

My mind was reeling. I couldn't make sense of what he was talking about. Was he saying that I held something over his head, like a device that could control him or possibly his boTs? That was lunacy if I ever heard it. But then it made perfect sense. Blake had pursued me the moment we met, but fervently wanted me gone. And he insisted that Sammy be kept in the dark.

"I can't remember anything from before. I don't know what it is I have or what you need from me. I swear, Sammy's never told me anything. Please believe me. I would never do or use anything that would hurt you like that," I said desperately, confused and practically choking.

Sliding his finger over my mouth, Blake groaned in frustration and pressed his head against my forehead. After a brief silence, he leaned his head back just enough so that he could look at me.

"Do you know what existentialists believe?" He didn't wait for me to reply. "That *anything* can be justified on behalf of freedom and we have a duty to pursue it."

I lowered my eyes, ashamed. "I told you, I don't know what you're talking about, but I'll help you in anyway I can… Just tell me how and I vow to set you free."

A brief silence followed my lingering reply. Slowly taking my hand in his, Blake splayed my fingers across the base of his neck.

"Can you feel my heartbeat?" he asked softly.

I couldn't feel anything except the pulsing of my own blood through my veins as my fingertips touched his muslin skin.

"I can't feel it," I murmured.

His face softened and he pressed his hand over mine, desperately wanting me to feel the rhythm of his life.

"Can you feel it now?" he asked, an urgent whisper.

"No," I said quietly.

Blake pushed my hand down past his neck and spread my palm against his bare chest.

"What about now?"

Keeping my eyes locked on his, I shook my head slowly.

"I'm sorry," I answered.

"Don't be." He sighed. "How could you feel my heart since you're breaking it?" His hand caught my face. "Athena, just listen to what I'm saying." Blake shook me gently. "My only duty is to you. You are my everything. My everything. My world entire."

His words were a harmony that hypnotized my very soul, but I was quick to refute him. "I don't believe you," I choked, not sure of what else to say. "Why are you saying this? You're just going to take it back. You don't have to lie to me to make me help you."

Blake jerked me toward him. "Help me. You can't help me— do you know what you've done to me?" he growled, his lips descending on my neck. "You have instilled the worst kind of bad faith in me—a complete and irrevocable rejection of freedom. The father of existentialism would castrate me because I never want to be free." His lips became more fervent against my skin. "I. Never. Want. To. Be. Without. You."

Blake's explanation was too convoluted and I didn't understand, but I didn't care. His hands roamed down my body and I felt like I was being raked with coals.

"Athena, you are my only conviction. A gift I should safeguard—"

"Blake—"

"But if being with me is something you want"—I nodded my head desperately—"then I can't deny you," he said slowly.

"Is it something you want?" I asked, afraid of the answer.

Blake ran the back of his fingers over my cheekbone. "It's something I need," he whispered. "Love is a bloody selfish thing. I should have stayed away from you, but I couldn't."

"Don't say that. I don't want you to stay away," I insisted, clutching his hand to my chest.

"Ignorance would have been bliss. You would have never known...but I can see that I've already condemned you."

"No, ignorance would have been painful and a lie. You saved me." I wasn't going to let him wallow in underserved guilt. "Stop thinking like that. It scares me."

Blake's face softened at my confession. "Glaukopis," he murmured.

I knew what it meant—it was another epithet associated with my name that referred to Athena's gleaming eyes. "There are none that can compare to yours." Blake slowly reached up and gently ran his thumbs over my cheeks. "Stars pale against their brightness. Every time you look at me I get lost in them." His voice was filled with a wistfulness that made my heart soar and, suddenly, there was nothing more that I wanted than to be connected to Blake in the most primal and intimate way. I was going to kiss him.

"You have that look on your face." he said, bringing his head down toward mine.

"What look?" I asked breathily.

"The one you often wear whenever you want me closer; whenever you want me to touch you. It's something I can never quite believe—that you could want me so badly."

I mentally scoffed. Who the heck wouldn't want him?

Determined to show him just how much I did, I slid my hands around his bare waist—still unsure of whether or not he wore anything below. His body was heaven and pure sin at the same time.

I pushed up against him. "You said that you couldn't refuse me,"

I whispered.

Blake's fingers curled through my hair while his other hand slid down my back. My eyelids fluttered shut as his lips trailed my jawbone. Blake opened his mouth and let his tongue caress the soft flesh of my neck and I started to shiver. Filled with an urgent heat, I wanted to feel that on my mouth.

"Blake—"

"Don't." He straightened, prying my hands away from him. "Don't ask me something I can only fail to give right now."

I started to protest but he deftly stepped away from me. All I saw was a blur of movement before Blake returned fully clothed. Disappointment swept through me; I never discovered what Blake had or hadn't been wearing and for some reason, having him dressed only heightened my desire to have him kiss me.

"You said—"

"Yes I did." He took hold of my arm and headed toward the forest.

"Well—"

"Don't ask me right *now*." Tugging me along, he didn't face with me when he spoke.

"Why?" I demanded.

Blake took one of my hands and stuffed it into my jacket pocket. He wrapped his hand around my other one and gave me a quick kiss on the forehead before moving on.

I let out a breath of frustration. "How come—"

"Because I won't stop."

¤ XVI ¤

DINNER TALK

We hadn't exchanged a single word since the lake. Perhaps we were both waiting for the other to say something first. Walking next to Blake as we entered his home, I had never wanted super powers so badly—super power actually—the one would have been sufficient; the ability to read minds.

I bit my lip as my stomach let out a growl. There was no point in hoping that the click of our boots against the marble floor could conceal the sound.

"You're hungry."

"Not really. I'll eat when I get home," I said quickly. I was indeed famished but I didn't want to eat. My hunger for food was trivial compared to the desire I had for Blake to stop and bloody touch me.

"You've barely eaten all day," Blake replied smoothly, as two ornately decorated doors opened before us.

"I'm fine—"

"You've returned." I was surprised to hear RJ's voice. He was seated across from Boe at the longest dining table I had ever seen. What's more, a boT hovered over each of their heads. My eyes trailed down the table and I gulped as I spotted oC with vI beside him.

"Finally," Boe said, feigning irritation, while she pulled out a chair that looked so weighty I was sure it would have taken several men to move it. "Athena, come sit."

I looked to Blake only to find him glaring at RJ. He placed his hand at the base of my back and walked me toward the vacant seat Boe had offered. Blake tucked the chair behind me as I sat and took the seat directly to my right at the head of the table.

"Where were you *all afternoon?* I've been waiting here for hours," RJ asked slyly.

Blake leaned back in his chair. "If I had known you were prowling around here, I assure you I wouldn't have bothered returning at all."

RJ smirked. "I see that you've decided." He looked at me and smiled. "I assume this means I can speak to her now."

Blake gave him a warning look, but RJ brushed it off. "What's new Athens?"

Athens?

Blake stood so abruptly that I cringed as his chair grinded against the floor.

"A word," he said coldly, gesturing for RJ to step outside the room.

I then understood Boe's frustration the night we encountered Charlie; it seemed RJ had a penchant for confrontation and it was likely he was going to get one because Blake looked volatile.

"Let's talk while we eat," RJ answered calmly. "Athens, I'm sure you remember iP." He signaled to his boT and it came forward. Conventionally robotic, it had a square head with arms, legs, hands and feet.

"Hey, long time no see." iP crossed the table and offered me his fist.

I smiled at the boT's warm greeting, but I was distracted because RJ spoke to me like he knew me and apparently so did his boT. iP chuckled and reached down to pick up my hand. His metal fingers molded mine into a fist and then he proceeded to give me props. It took me a few seconds to register what he was doing.

I let out a nervous laugh. "Sorry, iP. The hunger is getting to my head."

"Athena, why didn't you tell me you knew my brother and RJ?" Boe asked, turning to me.

I tucked a piece of hair behind my ear. "I guess it slipped my mind," I offered innocently, realizing that not only did Boe and I not know each from before, but she also didn't know about my past with her brother. I had thought of that first day in history and wondered if Boe and I becoming friends hadn't really been accidental, but now I knew for certain that it had been purely a coincidence—a coincidence that would put me in Boe's debt for the rest of my life, but I wasn't going to inform her of that fact—ever.

"RJ told me that you guys go way back."

"We're leaving." Blake pulled out my chair and hoisted me gently from my seat.

I didn't want to leave. I glanced at Boe and RJ and was sure that I wasn't going to have any difficulty finding a topic to discuss over dinner.

"But I'm hungry," I entreated, clutching my hand to my stomach.

Boe grabbed my free arm. "Yeah, she's hungry, Blake."

Openings in the granite table appeared and trays of food were set upon the table. Blake released his hold on me and I once again took my seat.

"Is all this food for me?" A crease developed on my forehead, as I looked at the multitude of dishes.

Boe waved her hand. "Oh, no. That's for you." She pointed to a tempting dish of spaghetti and a salad that was placed directly in front of me. I had no complaints; angel hair pasta was a favorite.

"Who's going to eat the rest?"

"I am," Boe replied, unsure about what puzzled me. "RJ's eating, too."

"You eat?" I asked, looking first at Boe and then at RJ, who was glowering silently at Blake. I noticed that iP was looking down the table at oC and I realized that they were probably communicating with one another.

"Of course I eat." Boe caught my attention by flicking me lightly on the shoulder.

"You told me that Supras don't eat though," I said absent-mindedly. My attention was divided between Boe and the silent conversation taking place across from me.

"I didn't say that. I said we don't *need* to eat. That doesn't mean we don't. Food is yummy."

I grinned at Boe's declaration, finding it amusing that the slight girl who sat beside me was going to consume enough food to feed Africa and most likely not gain an inch on her slender waistline.

"You're going to eat all this food because it tastes good?" Boe nodded her head eagerly. "Haven't you ever heard of gluttony?"

"The seven deadly sins only apply to mere mortals, Athena."

I heard a cough sound from behind Boe just as I rolled my eyes. I completely forgot about her boT.

"Athena, this is kO. My baby boT."

The miniature boT, who did look very much like a baby, let out a huff and came forward to rest his small hand on my shoulder.

"For some time now, I have wanted to express my thanks for protecting both myself and my charge."

It took me a second to realize he was referring to the day the WiiGiis attacked the College.

"Please, don't thank me for that," I insisted, waving my hands.

"Athena, you're too modest. After spending more time with me,

I'll make sure that humility of yours gets crushed with pride," Boe quipped deviously.

"Whatever you say."

"What a double standard, Blake," RJ exclaimed, holding up his hands. Blake didn't say anything in turn, but instead cocked his head briskly to the side. "You take that up with Fields."

I couldn't understand the one sided conversation. "Look at how miserably you failed," RJ continued, glancing at me with a wily grin. "And you haven't answered my question Blakie boy, where were you all afternoon?"

Suddenly, iP flew in front of RJ and oC rushed up the table in front of Blake, as both of them stood.

"Uh, guys," I said nervously.

"Boys! Sit!" Boe ordered, but neither of them moved.

Finally, RJ sat down. "Read anything good lately?" he asked me, piling some food on the bone china plate in front of him. Blake sat down stiffly, eyeing RJ maliciously. "You always had good recommendations," he said casually.

"Nothing lately, sorry," I replied, gauging Blake's reaction.

"Eat, Athena. The growl of your stomach is echoing in my ear," Boe urged, as she and RJ started consuming their own dishes.

Picking at my salad, I looked over at Blake who was now looking at me wearily. "RJ, long time no see, right?" I started. "Gosh, it seems like a lifetime, but it was only how long ago?"

Blake pursed his lips and gave me the look of an intolerant parent—I was being a naughty child.

RJ smiled. "I know what you mean. It definitely seems like a *lifetime* for sure." I raised my eyebrow at his insinuation. "But hey, you don't look so bad, just a few wrinkles around the eyes, some minor thinning of the hair, a bit wider around the waist."

I dropped my mouth open indignantly. RJ chuckled and Blake gave him a sharp look.

"Stop being such a meanie!" Boe demanded lightly. "You look fine," she reassured me, "but if you want your hair to be thicker you should cut it and you should maybe go a color darker." Her face brightened with enthusiasm. "I'll take you to the salon on the weekend and I'll give you a makeover."

I shook my head vehemently. "No thanks, Boe."

Boe was about to push the subject, but a glance at Blake silenced her. "Fine," she huffed, "but we're still going shopping. That reminds me Blake, thank you soooo much for all my new gifts. I don't think I've ever spent as much as I did today." Boe smiled smugly at her brother. Blake simply crossed his arms.

"You guys grew up with Sammy, right?" I asked nonchalantly.

"I've never met him," Boe answered. "I only know him from his pictures."

I puckered my forehead. "Pictures?" I could see Blake tense out of the corner of my eye.

Boe nodded. "Yeah, that's how I recognized your sister today." Boe frowned at my wide-eyed expression. "What's wrong?"

The pang in my stomach was so acute—a mix of hunger and anxiety. "You have pictures of Sammy and my sister?"

"RJ does." I followed Boe's gaze as she looked over at him, sipping a glass full of some thick green liquid. "How come you don't have any pictures of Athena?" Boe asked him.

RJ looked at Blake, who sat with his chin in his hand and his arm propped over the armrest of his chair. "Athens, you should know why I don't have any photos of you," he said, looking directly at me. "You hate taking pictures."

"I do." I wasn't affirming his answer, but was repeating his statement in disbelief—shocked that he knew this about me.

"Besides," RJ went on, "the breakup wasn't very pleasant and Blake here didn't want any pictures of her."

Boe's eyes grew wide. "Really?"

"What?" I said at the same time. I looked at Blake, unable to conceal the injury in my face.

Blake shook his head at me and clenched his jaw. "RJ, you and I are going to have a little chat after dinner. Agreed?" His voice was like ice.

RJ smirked mischievously. "I'm sure I would find your antics amusing Blakie boy, but I regret to inform you that this evening I am otherwise engaged." He looked over at Boe and winked. Boe grinned devilishly in return. "I'll take a rain check. How about a gammit match Sunday?" Blake turned away from RJ and stared at me motionlessly. "Since Athens is back, I guess that means you're coming out of retirement." Blake continued to ignore him. "You used to love gammit," he told me. "Convince Blake to play so that you can see a superstar in action?"

"Superstar?" I asked doubtfully, unsure to whom he was referring.

RJ held out his hands. "Yeah, me. I know it's been a long time and you've been *traveling*"—Blake fidgeted in his chair—"but you must know who I am?"

I shrugged my shoulders. "You got me, RJ. Who are you?"

"I'm probably the most famous person on the face of this planet, that's who," he replied arrogantly.

I let out a skeptical snort. "Yeah, okay," I replied sarcastically.

"Seriously, I am." RJ looked indignant.

"Not that I believe you, but why are you the most famous person on the face of this planet?"

"Athena, do you really not know?" Boe said incredulously.

I shook my head.

"I'm the best gammit player in the world," RJ declared proudly.

"Uh, what's gammit?" I asked hesitantly, sure that I was going to receive a few looks of disbelief.

RJ let out a breath as if he just remembered something. "That's right, I forgot you can't—" He stopped mid-sentence as Blake narrowed his eyes at him. "You can think of gammit as a cross-pollination between chess and soccer."

A crease developed on my forehead as he changed the subject. "Imagine an enormous chess board with each position being played by a Supra, with the exception of pawns. A single gammit team can be made out either four or seven players. You can play with a single set with four players or you can play with a double set in which case there would be seven."

"Seven?" I asked, knowing that there were eight positions if you didn't count pawns—two towers, two knights, two bishops, a king and queen.

"The king is not a player," RJ clarified.

"Where does the soccer part come in?" I asked curiously.

"The ball is moved around the board by kicking it."

"It doesn't sound all that different from plain old soccer."

"It's actually quite different. The players' movements are restricted by their position. The tower can only move in a vertical or horizontal position and the bishop can only move diagonally and so forth. Also, moves can only be taken consecutively, like in a chess match, but the game happens so quickly that you can hardly tell."

"So, the objective of the game is to get the ball into some sort of goal?"

"Basically, you have to smack the ball into your adversary's king."

"What happens if two people land on the same spot? In chess, one player would be removed from the board. Does that apply in gammit?"

"This is where the fun happens." RJ rubbed his hands together gleefully. "When two players move to the same board space to gain possession of the ball, they have to duke it out to stake a claim."

"Duke it out?" I said, puzzled about what he meant.

"The ball is electro-magnetically charged and will hover a few feet above the dueling pair until one of them kicks it into play. Using only their feet, the two players attempt to fight the other off so they can take control of the ball and steer it in a desired direction."

"Can I play on Sunday?" I asked excitedly.

"No." Everyone turned to Blake when he spoke.

RJ looked at me apologetically. "Gammit is only played by Supras, Athens."

"That doesn't sound fair. How come?" I whined.

"We're the only ones who can wear gammit boots."

"Gammit boots?"

RJ swiveled in his seat and hoisted his leg up. "You've seen these babies, right?"

I recognized the boot and remembered how Blake and RJ descended into the lunch hall at the College.

"Why can't I wear those?" I pressed, determined to play.

"Because it would probably break all the bones in your legs if you did," RJ replied definitively. "There's a pressurized system inside that allows us to defy gravity. I should have mentioned that most of the action in gammit is played a few feet above the ground."

My shoulders shrank, evidence that I was very let down. "And that's not the only reason. Even if you could wear gammit boots, you wouldn't be fast enough and you don't have a boT to anchor you. Communication with our sTell:R boTs is how the game's strategy is communicated throughout the match."

"I got it. I can't play. Thanks," I said stiffly.

RJ held up his hand innocently. "Hey, I'm sorry, but it's really fun to watch." He leaned back in his chair to look at Blake. "Come on, I'll have some guys from the team come out. If I tell them you and Fields are playing, they'll show up ready to rumble just like old times. What do you say?"

"Athena, you haven't touched your food. The only reason I am enduring RJ's presence at all is because you said you were hungry," Blake answered flatly.

"How can I eat with you watching me like that?" I said uneasily.

Blake pursed his lips and slowly turned to look down the center of the table.

I picked at my food and bit the inside of my cheek, realizing the weight of RJ's words. He asked Blake to bring Fields to play, which could only mean that Sammy was a Supra.

"You want Sammy to play too? I asked RJ offhandedly.

"Oh, yeah. It should be interesting if he does."

I grimaced at the revelation, remembering how Sammy often feigned an aversion to sports. What a faker!

There was something else that nagged me and I really wanted to know the answer.

"RJ, how old are you?"

"Eat. Athena," Blake ordered.

"I'm not hungry anymore," I said quickly. "RJ, how old are you?" I asked again, desperately this time.

"We're leaving." Blake stood abruptly and pulled my chair back.

"But I'm not finished," I protested.

"You're not eating," he said, frustrated.

"Yes, I am." I scooped a mouthful of spaghetti into my mouth.

"You can finish eating anywhere you want but here— Buckingham palace for all I care—but we're leaving. Now."

"Blake, you're being such a jerk." Boe stuck her tongue out at her brother as he gave her a menacing look. "Don't worry,

Athena, we'll have girl talk soon. I *promise.*"

"Bye guys," I said, standing rigidly.

RJ raised his glass. "A toast before you leave." Boe raised her glass too. "First, welcome back," he told me, "it's been too long. Second,"—he looked at Blake—"and more importantly, to failure Blakie boy. You're much more affable with her around."

Blake took my arm as we headed out of the dining room. "See you Sunday. Make him come, Athens! He won't say no to you."

We left the dining room and I saw that oC and vI followed us out. Looking over my shoulder, I guessed vI was still miffed at me because she gave me a look that sent shivers up my spine. oC, however, was doing an awkward skip behind us and looked like he was on cloud nine.

"Goodnight, Athena. Hope to see you very soon," the warmhearted boT declared.

"You're taking me home?" I asked Blake worriedly.

He didn't answer my question but led me out the front doors.

"Bye oC," I called over my shoulder, debating whether or not to address the other one. "Bye vI."

I shouldn't have bothered because she turned her head in disgust and raised her hand—silently telling me to talk to it.

"As much as I would love to dine with the Queen tonight, I would much rather spend time alone with you." I bit my lip nervously, waiting for Blake to say something. "Wait, do we still have a Queen?"

Blake's lips twitched. "Yes, we do."

I cocked my head. "Who did Prince William end up marrying?"

I asked, curious.

"Not you," Blake answered, pressing his lips together to restrain a smile.

"Very funny. Are you going to tell me where we're going?"

The last rays of sunlight fluttered around the horizon and I buttoned up my jacket as Blake's car came into view.

"It's getting late. I should take you home."

"No!" I cried.

"Athena,"—Blake took hold of my arm and pulled me toward him—"your family is going to get suspicious if I keep you out much longer."

"Who cares?" Laying my hands flat against Blake's chest, I looked at him imploringly. "What are you hiding from me?" I asked apprehensively. "Why don't you want me to tell Sammy about you? No one else in my family would care so I know that it's only him you're talking about."

"Not just him, Athena. There's your father, too."

"Vas?"

Blake nodded his head slowly. "Your father remembers everything," he said slowly.

"What?" I couldn't believe it.

"It's only you and Sof who don't remember." Blake's face was strained, his voice uneven. "Neither Sammy nor your father will be keen about us."

"Why can't I remember? Why would they feel like that?" I whispered, confused.

"Let me take you home," he said, bowing his head. "I'll

explain later."

"No."

"I'll come back for you tonight."

"I don't believe you. Don't leave me," I said quietly.

Blake's lips spread into a private smile, but it didn't touch his eyes. "You calling me a liar?"

I frowned. "'There is a smile of love, and there is a smile of deceit, and there is a smile of smiles, in which these two smiles meet'. I'm not sure which smile I'm looking at."

"'And there is a frown of hate, and there is a frown of disdain, and there is a frown of frowns, which you strive to forget in vain'. I promise to come because I'm sure I'm looking at the latter."

I should have known better than to quote William Blake, remembering that Boe said he was one of Blake's favorites.

"All right," I conceded, moving toward his car, but Blake didn't follow.

"It would have been so much easier if you didn't want me." I stopped and turned to him. "Why did you have to want me?" His voice was tense and he spoke as if he was talking to himself. "I tried, Athena. I did try, but you kept drawing me to you."

He spoke to me like a supplicant wanting absolution. I reached up to cup his cheek, trying to soothe away the pain in his face.

"What are you talking about?"

"When you ran from me today, I was sure that it was over. I know all too well how lives can be transformed by simple words unspoken or gestures that go unmade. I've seen it happen. I've made it happen." Blake closed his eyes and looked to be remembering something he wished he could forget. "All I had to do was let you go and it would be finished. Today, on my family's estate, I decided then and there that my words, unforgivably spoken, would be *good-bye.*"

Tears stung my eyes and, unable to speak, I breathed, "No."

"But then you came back, like you always do, and I was given another choice—another chance I didn't deserve to keep my *soul.* God help me, I took a leap of faith, thinking nothing immediate was threatening us."

I put my fingers against Blake's mouth and his jaw went rigid at my touch.

"I'm so…happy that you did." That's all I said. I prayed he saw what I meant in my eyes, because the word wasn't enough to express how I felt.

We zoomed through the City and the tightness in my stomach only increased as we drew closer to my home. I tried to convince myself that it was hunger, ashamed at my level of neediness, but I knew it was because I would have to part with Blake soon and my body reacted to what my heart knew all too well.

I dug my nails into my arms and set my jaw, as we pulled up to the landing dock. The car door slid open and I climbed out, knowing Blake would be around to offer unnecessary assistance by the time my foot hit the ground. He didn't disappoint. My childish pride never let me take his proffered hand, but regardless Blake always held my arm and planted his palm against the small of my back to lift me out of the vehicle.

"What time will you be back?" I asked, keeping my voice even.

"Late. I have some unfinished business to take care of."

"Does it have anything to do with RJ?"

Blake led me toward the entrance of the building.

"Don't come down to meet me. I'll come to your window," he explained, ignoring my question. He stopped just outside the main doors and pulled something out of the inside pocket of his jacket. I recognized the small blue book. Blake stepped toward me and held it out for me to take it.

"You gave it to me because you wanted to tell me something," he murmured softly.

The red ribbon.

"Why are you giving it back then?" I took the book and Blake held onto my wrist, rubbing the tender skin beneath it.

"I want to *tell you* something," he whispered.

"Oh…" I replied, reaching around his neck, certain that I would remember the moment for the rest of my life—my first kiss—but Blake's hands slid away and his lips barely brushed the top of my head.

"Till tonight."

Then he was gone. Crushed with a feeling I couldn't quite place, I stood motionless for a few moments before I made my way inside.

¤ XVII ¤

D E R K U ß B Y G U S T A V K L I M T

Walking toward unit 537, I took deep breaths trying to slow my breathing. My accelerated heartbeat had nothing to do with the elevator ride, which I still hated, but had everything to do with my out of control, volatile, hormones.

I tucked the book inside my jacket before I entered. Coming through the door, my stomach gurgled as a mouth-watering aroma filled my nostrils—reminding me that I was starving.

"Guse, that you?" Pork Chop's voice sounded from the kitchen.

"Yeah!" I called out, climbing the stairs in a state of complete distraction.

Sitting down on my soft bed, I removed my jacket and held the blue volume in my hands—venerating the object as if it were holy. My fingers trembled as I peeled open the book where the red ribbon divided it.

My eyes fell slowly onto the page and then I understood. Emily Barret *Browning*. I found the first word, then read the first line and that's all I could do. I threw myself onto my bed, buried my face into my sheets and screamed. A nuclear bomb detonated inside me and I flailed my limbs wildly—my body seeking the release it needed. I turned over on my back, wrapping the thick sheets around me and kicked my feet madly. I looked like a person who had caught on fire and had stopped, dropped and rolled.

"*Whatever* are you doing?" Pork Chop's amused voice gave me such a start that, while I tried to unfurl the mountain of blankets around me, I fell mercilessly onto the floor.

"Don't you knock?" I asked irritably, raising myself onto my hands and knees.

"I did. You must not have heard it," Pork Chop replied in a smug tone.

I didn't have to look in a mirror to see that my face was as ripe as a tomato—I felt it flaming just fine.

Pork Chop crossed her arms. "And what may I ask is the cause of this delirium?"

Carefully hiding the small book within the folds of my sheets, I dumped the bundle back onto my bed.

"Today's Friday and I don't have to back to the College for two whole days," I said quickly. It was partly true so the explanation came easily.

"Sorry to break it to you Guse, but the weeks have changed since our time." I narrowed my eyes at her. "We have four day weeks now instead of five. Not much to complain about is there, but the week starts on Wednesday and goes until Saturday. You can do this entertaining happy dance thing tomorrow night because you'll be back at the College bright and early tomorrow morning."

I lunged for a pillow atop my bed and threw it at her. Pork Chop stuck her tongue out at me and ducked out the door as my feathery missile fell short. "Dinner's ready by the way," she said, sticking her head back in. "And, another thing, Vas wants to talk to you about spending. Can I say that you are a total hypocrite? I can't believe you scolded me for wanting to blow Sammy's money."

"What are you talking about?" I asked, genuinely bewildered.

"Don't play dumb, Guse."

"I'm not!"

"So, the shopping bags and shoeboxes downstairs do not belong to you? Splendid! I really like the cropped tweed jacket. Since the stuff isn't yours, you won't mind that I've taken the liberty of putting a few items in my closet and will be wearing them tomorrow."

Pork Chop ran ahead of me as I rushed out of my room and down the stairs, eager to see what she was talking about. I dashed through the kitchen and stopped dead in my tracks. There was literally a mountain of shopping bags crowding the entire living room, all prominently displaying a familiar emblem. I knew where everything had come from—*Boe!*

"I didn't buy this," I protested as Vas walked in behind me with his arms crossed.

"No?" He looked at me reprovingly. "I believe all the items are addressed to an Athena Ellias." Vas turned and looked at Pork Chop. "Sofia, is there two Athenas living under this roof?"

"Father, I don't know anyone by that name. We have a witch who lives on the third floor, but her name is Gustav, who had better get punished for this." I opened my mouth indignantly. "Do you know how much all this cost? She's at least got to work for it!"

"Pork Chop doesn't know what she's talking about. I didn't buy this damned stuff," I interjected, giving my sister the evil eye.

Vas raised his arms briskly, ever wanting to intervene to prevent a storm from breaking out.

"Are you telling me that all these items were free?" He waved his hand, silencing an outburst from Pork Chop.

"Yes," I said firmly, as my mind conjured up ways to get Boe back for this.

Vas tilted his head to the side. "Can you explain to me why they were free?"

Pork Chop let out a huff and crossed her arms, fervently waiting to rebuke what she thought was going to be a lie.

"Well, *Dad*," I said emphatically, articulating that I was explaining myself to him and not to my irritating sister, "I went shopping with a friend from school today and she insisted on buying all this." Vas furrowed his brow. "She said she owed me because, for some strange reason, she thought she was in my debt because...I helped her with something at the College."

"You let her buy all this for you? Athena—"

"No! I said I didn't want anything. She bought it behind my back."

The determined look Pork Chop wore on her face faded. She didn't trust my word, but she knew that I was a good enough liar that I made sure, if I had to lie, I could back it up with evidence. If I said I didn't spend Sammy's money, she conceded I must have been telling the truth because it would be too easy to discover if I wasn't.

"You're going to take it all back. When you help somebody you don't expect them to repay you for it."

"I didn't expect anything!" I said defiantly. The disappointment I heard in Vas' voice hurt, so naturally the emotion I expelled was anger to cover the insult. "I don't even want them. Tell Pork Chop"—I looked at my sister menacingly—"to return everything she took because I'll be glad to bring it all back."

"She can't return them, Dad. There's no refund or exchange from the store they came from. I think I should just get everything. That should be punishment enough for Guse, who clearly lacks an ounce of self respect—"

"Whatever! I'm not the one—"

"Enough!" Vas ordered icily. "I don't want to hear this. Both of you just go to your rooms." Pork Chop and I started to talk over one another. "I said go to your rooms now!"

We both recognized the sternness in Vas' voice, a voice we knew all too well, and neither of us waited to be told again.

Bursting through my room door, I immediately went to the balcony and prayed that Blake was already waiting so he could take me away. The cold air gave me an unfriendly welcome as my window slid open.

"Blake!" I called out into night—the sun had long since set. "Are you there?" Only the sounds of the city answered. My shoulders drooped as I realized he hadn't come yet. Walking back inside, the walls of my room made me feel claustrophobic. I tried to find something to distract my mind—to make me think of anything besides the violent urge I had to strangle something—someone. I dug through my blankets to retrieve the blue book and commanded my bookshelf to appear. I wasn't ready to read it so I gently slid the missing volume into place and touched the red ribbon that peeked out from the top. I smiled to myself thinking that Blake was the best kind of therapy because he could expel anything from my mind. He cured all the minor neuroses that plagued my psyche. It was ironic because he really only replaced them with another one—an infinite all encompassing neurological disorder—himself.

How much longer would he be? I let out a breath as I glanced at the clock. It was already late, nearing nine o'clock. I decided to pull out the William Blake volume from the collection, finding a melancholy way to pass the time, when Sammy's voice sounded from the speaker.

"Guse, let's eat."

I frowned, contemplating whether or not to go down to dinner. It didn't take long to decide—my stomach growled fiercely and made the decision for me.

As expected, dinner was eerily quiet. Pork Chop and I weren't really angry at one another, per se. We were just too proud so neither of us wanted to relent first, even though the source of the quarrel was completely trivial.

Vas sat at the head of the table with Sammy on the opposite end and I sat across from Pork Chop. Neither of us looked up from our plates as we stiffly stuffed lasagna into our mouths. Vas and Sammy carried on a light conversation, straining to ease the tense atmosphere around the table.

"Athena, I've been meaning to ask you, what happened to your hands?"

It took a few seconds to register that Vas was talking to me. "I fell. I'm fine," I replied dourly.

"Guse, Sof tells me that you're in for the Governor's Gala. I'm supposed to lie and tell you that's it's going to be loads of fun when really the effect of the entire evening is death from boredom."

I didn't look at her, but I heard Pork Chop's fork clank down on the table. Sammy winced. "But you gotta come. After I've delivered my momentous speech," he said sarcastically, grinning at Pork Chop, "I don't know if I'll be able to endure the evening without pulling out every single hair off my head, unless of course you come and distract me by pulling out your own."

I bit the inside of my cheek, trying to contort my features into a frowning expression to hide the amused one that had crept onto my face. "Ha, ha, Sammy. I hate to inform you, however, that I will *not* be attending."

A second didn't pass before Pork Chop cut in. "Dad, the College has this dance on the night of the gala and it's really important for students to go in order to integrate themselves into the school community."

"That's a bunch of crap!" I snapped.

"Are you guys to argue over dinner now?" Vas said briskly. "Just keep quiet. I already have a headache from your bickering. Can't you just talk among yourselves calmly instead of shouting like this?"

"We're not shouting—"

"This is how we talk, Dad," I insisted, finishing Pork Chop's sentence.

"People don't talk like that," Vas replied, still annoyed.

I couldn't help but notice how Pork Chop and I rolled our eyes simultaneously and slumped down in our seats; she was a twin and a nemesis at the same time.

No one spoke while we waited for Vas to finish his dinner. We weren't allowed to leave the table until he had—this was a rule we followed since childhood. I crossed my arms rigidly, as he took an excessively long time to consume his food and drink.

When he stood, finally finished, Pork Chop and I shot out of our seats like canon balls. Without a word, I headed out of the dining room and was just about to dart up the stairs when Vas' suitcase, sitting beside the library doors, caught my eye. Like the magazines Pork Chop gave me earlier, the newspaper was covered with moving images and I recognized the name boldly written across the front page. Tucking the paper under my arm, I ran up the stairs.

There was still no sign of Blake so I sat down at my desk and turned over the newspaper. The article on the front page was about *Dresden* Corporation. It wasn't a coincidence that the company bore Blake's last name because I went on to read that the Dresden

Family controlled over eight-seven percent of the shares. It was one of the largest industrial companies in the world and owned the patent for some kind of hydrogen fuel technology. The CEO, Johan Dresden, had apparently vetoed a proposal to manufacture weapons leaving its rival, *ViAno*, in a favorable position to secure a merger to produce alternate forms of military hardware. The article continued to say how ViAno's CEO, Lorne Leger, had no comment when, at a recent press conference, he was asked about suspicions that his company's technology was being used by a terrorist group known as WiiGiis.

I dropped the paper back onto my desk. I thought Pork Chop said ViAno was some sort of environmental company. I could understand why Blake didn't like Logan if what the article said was true; their families probably hated each other. It baffled me to imagine either of them involved with such serious matters. What was harder to understand was why either of them liked me—I felt like an insignificant kid.

I thought back to the car ride with Logan and remembered his amused smile and his charming demeanor. Could he possibly be involved with WiiGiis? My eyes grew wide as I remembered how apologetic he was when he saw that I got hurt that day, as if he were in some way responsible. He was Sammy's friend, though, and it didn't make sense if he was a WiiGii who hated Supras. Things kept getting stranger and stranger and I was lost trying to keep up. I hated not knowing. I hated being in the dark. I was a Platonist if I ever knew one—there was nothing more that I wanted than to climb out of the cave of ignorance. I wanted to know the truth, look it in the face, even if it meant I would have to deal with a painful reality.

Knowing I had only one source of information, I stepped back onto my balcony to look for him. I let out a frustrated breath. *Where was he?*

I decided to take a shower, hoping to calm my nerves. I don't know how long I stood frozen in the tub, but by the time I got out the skin on my fingers was wrinkled. I didn't change into my pajamas but put on fresh clothes instead. Untangling my wet hair with my fingers, I went over to my bookshelf to pull out the volume I had chosen before Sammy called me to dinner. It was nearing eleven now and Blake still hadn't arrived. I closed my eyes for a moment and let out a deep breath, reassuring myself that he would come. I set the book down on my desk and let it fall open to a random page.

"'The Angel.'" I whispered the title as my fingers ran across the yellowing parchment.

I dreamt a dream! What can it mean?
And that I was a maiden Queen,
Guarded by an Angel mild:
Witless woe was ne'er beguil'd!

And I wept both night and day,
And he wip'd my tears away,
And I wept both day and night,
And hid from him my heart's delight.

So he took his wings and fled;
Then the morn blush's rosy red;

I dried my tears, and arm'd my fears
With ten thousand shields and spears.

Soon my Angel came again:
I was arm'd, he came in vain;
For the time of youth was fled,
And grey hairs were on my head.

I felt cold, like the breath of a ghost had swept over me. I read the last lines again and then again, unable to take my eyes off the words even though they brought the sting of tears. The rational side of my mind reminded me about what I had desperately wanted to deny. I couldn't fight time and, as sure as the sun would rise tomorrow, I would age and die much, much faster than Blake.

Supras didn't age normally. Boe said it was possible they were even immortal. The face of inevitability showed itself to me and the pain was crucifying. There was no one better to tell you the tragic element of every mythological tale out there that told the story of a god and a mortal falling in love. Both desperate to keep one another, they are never able to escape the bonds of Fate that separate them. A salty pool obscured the poet's prophetic words, but the meaning was scalding and a mallet was smashing my heart in.

Water was soaking into my back from my wet hair and my hands moved on their volition to slowly braid the drenched mass. Another tear trickled down my face and plopped onto the open book.

Then his soft hands pulled mine away. My fingers fell limp the moment he touched me. My heart had been so weak just a moment ago, but in an instant it started to beat with such force that it became the mallet that now struck my very soul.

I could feel the tickle of his fingers as his hands resumed the task of braiding my hair. The cold I felt hadn't been just internal, but external as well—the chilly night air was sweeping into my room through my open window. Blake finished the braid and let it brush down the side of my neck. He placed his hands softly over my shoulders and leaned down, pressing his lips against the bare side of my neck.

"I'm sorry I'm late," he whispered apologetically. Blake held still when I didn't reply. Reaching over me, he closed the small blue book that I had left open. Blake swiveled my chair around and his hands came up to my face. I roughly shoved them away and threw my arms around him, burying myself against his chest. I didn't want him to see me crying, if you could call it that, and I needed to feel him. I needed him in ways I didn't understand. Crushed against him, I smothered the thoughts that were plaguing my mind. Blake had come, as promised, and that's all I wanted to think about.

"I'm fine," I said hoarsely. "Let's go." With all the strength I could muster, I peeled my face from him. I couldn't meet his eyes but grabbed his arm and headed toward the window.

"Will you tell me what you're thinking?" he asked quietly.

"I want to go and…be alone with you. That's all." I spoke to him with my back turned, trying to pull him forward.

"If I asked for your help, would you give it to me?"

I stopped at his request, worried by his somber tone. "Of course," I answered without hesitation.

"Then help me." I creased my forehead, anxious about what he could want. "Help me ease this…pain."

"Pain?" I fearfully turned to look at him and found his jaw clenched.

"Do you know what it does to me—to see you like this? It's a kind of dying that no words can describe. Tell me what's hurting you. Tell me what you want. *Help me.*"

The answer was so simple and yet I doubted I would have had enough courage to speak the plain truth if not for the desperation in Blake's voice.

"I just want you." I barely breathed my answer, but the reaction on Blake's face told me that he heard my words, as if I shouted at the top of my lungs. He pressed himself against me in a heartbeat and fastened his arms around my body.

"I'm yours, Athena," he said fervently.

My body turned to liquid. I pulled back a little to reach up and feel his face, wishing so very much that my touch could wash away the hard edge that shrouded his features. There was always a tension in Blake that never completely disappeared; it was as if he was constantly on guard.

I couldn't help but smile as he kissed the tips of my fingers.

"That smile of yours drives me to complete and utter distraction. Do you know that?" I shook my head. "It's genuine but uncertain, torn between a happiness I pray for and a doubt I can never seem to extinguish." Blake cupped my face and leaned down forcefully. "You drive me mad."

I thought it sinful how his frustration touched my heart.

"You know you remind me of a ballet dancer," I said, raising my eyebrow at him.

I was sure that the randomness of my statement would have caused a more obvious reaction in anyone besides Blake—he simply raised his eyebrow in return, indicating that I elaborate. "Do you know what I'm always reminded of when I see a ballet dancer? That being graceful is painful. Their art is dedicated in its entirety to deception. They are willing to ravage their bodies in pursuit of something beyond themselves. It's beautiful."

"So how is it that you look at me and see dancer?" Blake asked coyly.

"I see deception," I replied quietly, scanning Blake's face, ardently looking for a trace of a reaction, but he remained steadfastly stoic. I frowned. "See, you're proving my point. Your ability to conceal is beyond compare."

"I would disagree. There is no one whose thoughts are as elusive as yours." I shook my head, contesting his statement.

Before I got a chance to offer a rebuke, Blake's car appeared and he leapt onto the edge of the balcony holding me securely in his arms.

"It's a night of inconceivable beauty, Athena, and London waits for us."

I looked up and over the dashboard and thought that he was right. The night sky was bright with a full moon and not a lone cloud in sight. I was just about to ask where we were going when the car began to descend and my stomach lurched. Puzzled, I looked at Blake and found his eyes fixed on me.

"The past few hours have been stifling you know?" Reaching

over, he brought my hand to his face. Kissing the underside of my wrist, his lips were anything but gentle. "You're the only air I can breathe," he managed to whisper, as the moisture from his mouth soaked my sensitive flesh, making my body hot.

Giving my fingers a final reverent kiss, Blake slowly returned my hand. I was sure that I was going to die if he stopped touching me.

Please touch me. Touch me. Touch me.

It seemed like forever before the car pulled to a stop. My eyes trailed up the tall tower and rested on London's most familiar face. Big Ben. Blake's arms were around me before I could ask why we stopped there.

"You look…displeased. Not interested in taking a tour of the tower?" Blake's lips twitched as I puckered my forehead. Taking a tour was the last thing I wanted.

He left me for the briefest moment, before returning to wrap a wool blanket around me. "Up we go then."

I saw the familiar blue glow underneath Blake's boots and, shutting my eyes, wrapped my arms around his waist. I cringed as we rose and buried my face against his chest, desperate to feel solid ground again. I took a peek out one eye and my gut dropped violently—we were halfway up the side of the tower.

"Can you, uh, go faster?" I asked shakily. I had seen the kind of speed he could reach and thought we should have reached the top by now.

"You're not afraid, are you?" he asked.

"No," I replied firmly. "You would never drop me." Blake sounded serious so I replied in the same manner. I didn't want him to think that I doubted him because I didn't.

"Are you sure about that?"

Hearing the teasing in his voice, I jerked my head back to look at him.

"Blake, you wouldn't!" I exclaimed.

"Of course I wouldn't," he reassured me.

My stomach lurched as we plunged down a few feet before we stopped in mid-air again.

"Blake, stop it! It's not funny," I said, tightening my grip around his waist.

Blake furrowed his brow and peered down at his feet. I followed his gaze and saw that the blue light coming from his soles was wavering. The pain in my stomach was more acute this time as we fell farther. "Blake!"

"I think there may be a malfunction," he said calmly, cocking his head as we stopped again.

"What!" I cried, wrapping my legs around his waist. "I don't believe YOOOOUUUUUUUU!"

We fell fast, gaining speed as we descended, and I was sure that the pit of my stomach had been detached from my body. Everything I felt was physical, like the discomfort of riding a roller coaster, but not for a second was I afraid. I trusted Blake completely. I just wanted to wring his neck for his idea of a practical joke.

It took me a few seconds to realize that we weren't falling anymore; the landing was so soft that I barely registered the impact. I opened my eyes and was taken aback to find that we weren't at the base of the tower but at the top, with London's skyline visible over

Blake's shoulder. I pulled my head back and grabbed the lapels of his jacket.

"That wasn't funny."

"No, it wasn't," he muttered. Blake shifted me on top of him and all the ire I felt faded because his eyes were burning. My legs were still wrapped around his waist and our bodies were pressed closely together. I curled my fingers into his hair and made a silent vow; I was going to kiss him. Determined, I brought my mouth closer to his, but he deftly peeled away my legs and set me upon my feet. Blake held me at arms length for a second and then jumped off the tower, leaving me slighted and alone.

I stood, unable to move—the rejection paralyzed me—and I was angry. He always denied me what I wanted the most. Blake was always the one to pull away.

He manifested in front of me carrying the blanket he had wrapped around me—I lost it when we fell. He stepped forward and put it around my stiff shoulders. The air was cold at the top of the tower, but my body was warm—desire was scorching my veins and it made my blood boil. That was it. I narrowed my eyes and threw down the wool wrap.

"Blake! Kiss—"

The world evaporated beneath the power of his kiss. His lips were as hard as bone and I shuddered as he hungrily groped my body. Blake's hands slipped beneath my shirt and tightened against my bare flesh as he flattened my back against the tower's hard surface, just as the mighty clock struck midnight. The boom that echoed through the city was nothing compared to the force wreaking havoc inside me. I wrapped my fingers in his hair and kissed him passionately. I had never kissed anyone before—I couldn't remember if I had—but my body seemed to recall things my mind could not because when my lips moved against Blake's, it felt like they knew the solid mould of his mouth.

One of his hands cupped my cheek and pulled me harder against him. He slightly broke the kiss and pressed his thumb over my lower lip, silently supplicating for me to open my mouth—a barrier that still lay between us. Blake kissed me fiercely enough that he could have spread it open, but it was as if he wanted me to surrender myself. Then I understood. He was holding himself back, waiting. I let my mouth fall open and then I believed Blake's words in the car; he kissed me like he needed me to live.

I couldn't breathe, but I didn't care. My lungs, on the other hand, were screaming in protest. Sensing that I needed air, Blake moved his kiss off my lips and gave the nape of my neck a gentle bite before he planted his mouth on my throat. I was desperate to get oxygen into my system. I was scared that I was going to pass out—the pleasure was so acute—and I didn't want this to end. Blake abruptly leaned away, slammed his palms against the stone behind me and pulled in an audible breath against my neck.

"Don't stop," I said pleadingly, holding his face in my hands. "Blake, I want you."

He straightened and pressed his cheek against the top of my head.

"You don't know what want is."

He had said that before, but this time he was dead wrong. I knew what it meant.

"Then show me," I said boldly, sliding my free hand down his back, desperate to feel him. Blake closed his eyes and shook his head, but hastily wrapped my legs around his waist. I was sure he was going to concede and eagerly lifted my mouth to meet his, but he didn't kiss me. Instead, Blake pressed me against his chest and jumped backwards off the tower.

He ran through the city, zipping in between cars, and I silently wondered where we were headed. All I wanted was for Blake to stop and kiss me again, but there was no sign of him slowing. At first, it was thrilling as we raced through London's streets, still very much the London I knew and loved, but I was forced to close my eyes as a wave of dizziness hit me—I was certain that it had more to do with Blake's hands, dangerously high up my thighs, than with the motion of his running.

When Blake finally set me down, it took a moment before my eyelids slowly fluttered open. I instantly became self-conscious. We were at the heart of London in the middle of Trafalgar square. It was only past midnight and the city was still alive. A few stragglers and stray couples lined the streets and the square.

"What's the matter?" Blake asked, inquiring about the glower on my face.

"Don't you care that people can see you—saw you running like that?"

Blake gave the slightest shrug. "It's dark, Athena. All people see is a blur in the night and tricks of the imagination."

I sighed at his nonchalance. "Why are we here?" I asked, scrunching my face into a displeased expression. I wanted to go back to the tower. I wanted to go anywhere where we could have privacy. Then I knew what he was about. Blake had taken me to a very public place on purpose. He didn't want us to be alone.

"I thought we could walk around the city for a while. Just you and me."

I narrowed my eyes at him. It was hardly just the two of us. Blake reached down and tried to take one of my hands, but I pulled it back and hastily stuck both of them in my pockets.

"Why don't we go somewhere more *private?*" I suggested, eyeing the people who passed us.

Blake tucked his arm under mine and moved to head out of the square.

"After all the information you tried to pry out of RJ, I thought you would like the chance to ask me some questions of your own. To use Boe's expression, let's walk and *talk.*"

I knew there was no point in pressing the matter; Blake wasn't going to take me anywhere remotely secluded and, besides, it was an offer I couldn't refuse.

I pulled a hand from my pocket and drummed my fingers across my lips, musing over what question to ask first.

"How old am I?"

"For all intents and purposes, you are seventeen."

"No, I'm not."

"Nineteen."

I cocked my head crossly. "How old was I when you knew me *before?*"

"Older," he said calmly.

"How old?" I was worried about his answer.

"When your father originally brought you and Sof here, you were already past adolescence."

My mouth dropped open. Blake reached over with his free hand and gently pressed it shut.

"Tell me the number," I insisted, fluttering his hand away.

"What does it matter?"

"It matters to me," I replied stubbornly.

"Athena, you've always been sensitive about your age. You're not getting a number out of me. I'm vetoing this one."

Urgh! I hated that word.

"How long were we together?" I inquired, shifting the gears of the conversation.

"Six hundred twenty-two days, five hours, thirty-two minutes, ten seconds and four milliseconds. That includes the first day I laid eyes on that enchanting, somewhat aloof face of yours to the day…you left."

I turned to look at Blake, wearing an expression torn between skepticism and disbelief, but it quickly changed because he looked dead serious.

"How long have I been gone?"

"It's complicated."

"That is not an answer. That's an excuse. How long?"

"For you or for me?" he asked soberly.

I creased my forehead. "Is it different?"

"The rate of time isn't the same," he explained.

I remembered how Pork Chop was only gone for about a week,

but when I arrived in the future two years had already passed by. "You've been gone for as long as you've known Sammy."

That was a little under three years.

"And for you?" I asked, my voice barely a whisper.

Blake pulled me against him and pressed his cheek against the top of my head.

"Longer." His hands found my face and he leaned back to look at me. I wanted to remember the look in his eyes at that exact moment forever. On the day I died, I wanted to see those eyes. He laid a tender kiss on my forehead and then continued walking. "Much longer. Next question."

I wanted to know, but I couldn't find the strength to pry him for the answer. The pained look he wore was too much and I decided to let it go. For now. The night was young and I didn't want to cast a shadow over it so soon.

"How was our first kiss like? Our real first kiss?" I asked slowly.

Blake reached over and grabbed the hand I had removed from my pocket and kissed it gently before entwining it with his.

"I can't answer that," he said smoothly.

I stopped walking and gave him a reproving look. "If this question and answer session is going to be anything like that night at your house, then I'm not participating." I tried tugging my hand back, but Blake held it tightly.

"I can't answer that, simply because every kiss is like the first for me. And if you would so honor me, may I please hold your hand?"

When oC told me that Blake could be a poet, I had had my doubts, but in fact, the boT was right; Blake was a master of words and he dodged my questions cunningly.

"Why can't I remember it?" I asked, a serious tone creeping into my voice.

Blake let out a breath. "Have you forgotten it already? It took place mere minutes ago."

I grumbled irritably. He knew I didn't mean *that* kiss.

"You know what I mean. Why can't I remember anything that happened and Vas can?"

Blake ran his fingers through his hair. "It's complicated."

"There you go again. Stop saying that. What's complicated?" I demanded.

"Everything," he replied gravely.

"That. Is. Not. An. Answer."

Blake looked down at our locked fingers. "There were things that happened before you left…bad things," he finally confessed. "There was a…*process* that would allow you to forget. Your memories were isolated and removed. Permanently. We thought it was for the best."

"Who's *we?*" I asked through clenched teeth, squeezing his hand angrily.

"It doesn't matter. It was a decision I insisted on so you can blame me and me alone." Blake's face was expressionless.

"How could you…do that to me?" I couldn't mask the tremble when I spoke.

"I don't regret it," he answered sharply. "Believe me, you wouldn't want to remember."

"Why not?" My body felt numb.

"You just wouldn't. I'm leaving it that. Next question," he ordered, turning his gaze out onto the city.

I thought of my next question and my stomach clenched, as palpable as turbulence.

"Why didn't you come with me? Sammy went back with Pork Chop, but you stayed behind..." I looked away from Blake and stared at the ground, scared to read what his face might reveal.

"I couldn't," he answered bluntly.

"Couldn't or didn't want to?"

In silence, he steered us up one of London's winding streets, as my whispered question lingered in the air. The echo of our footsteps on the deserted road was the only sound to combat the deafening quiet.

"Both," he declared.

"Both?" I choked.

"I had to stay for reasons I don't want to discuss. When you left it was supposed to be good-bye because"—Blake dropped my hand and walked away—"I wasn't sure..." he paused, "You weren't supposed to come back."

"Why wouldn't I come back..." My voice trailed off. My heart cracked. "You didn't want me back." My palms were still sore but I dug my fingernails into them, wanting the physical pain to distract me.

"No, I didn't," he admitted slowly.

I nodded my head. "I see."

"Athena, it's hard for you to understand because you don't remember, but things were different then. Not to mention it was dangerous for you—"

"You don't have to explain, Blake. I get it. I think I'm starting to understand your antagonism toward Sammy. I guess a lot of time has passed for you and your feelings have faded, naturally, and then he goes and brings me back and now I'm like…an old flame that you feel responsible for."

"An old flame?" Blake's indignation was violent. Grabbing my arms, he shook me roughly. "That's not—"

I thrashed my head from side to side and threw my hand over his mouth. "Don't. It's okay." I brushed a stray tear from my face with my free hand and prayed I had enough strength to get through what I had to say. "Blake, you don't have to feel *guilty* because it's not the same for you anymore and…I know you care for me and don't want me hurt, but at the same time I know you just feel responsible for me because you're too honorable. Please, you don't have a duty to protect me—"

Blake yanked my hand off his mouth and brought his lips forcefully over mine. The pressure was so intense that my body instantly peaked with desire, but he quickly wrenched me away and looked at me with fervent eyes.

"Let's get one thing straight." Blake's voice was harsh, his lips moved over mine. "On a night long ago, on a night like tonight, I asked something of you." His eyes roamed my face. "'I ask of you neither eternal love, nor fidelity, but simply…the truth, unlimited honesty…*if you love me less you can never have loved me.*' Do you know what you said when I spoke Bonaparte's confession? You told me to think of his words—my words—as your own, because they captured something you could never express yourself." Blake placed a reverent kiss on my jaw. "We both asked for truth. And since it is in my power to give, I tell you now that it's impossible for me to feel…less."

"But you said you didn't want me back," I said in small voice.

"Athena, I told you, you have no idea what want is. What I wanted was for you to be safe. For you to be happy. But then there is a want—a hunger—that I cannot discern from need. And that is how I want you. Do you know how long I've waited, knowing there was only a chance you would return? How can I make you understand? How can I open your eyes?" Blake's eyes were molten. "There's nothing in the world that I want—nothing in the world that's worth living for besides *you*. You. Are. My. Raison d'être." Blake's face was stricken and it killed me. "Life without you is just incidental—a colorless, meaningless existence."

I gently grabbed the lapels of his jacket. "If all that's true then didn't you miss me? How long were you really willing to wait? What if I had come back as an old lady?" My face fell, as I remembered the disheartening words of William Blake's poem.

"Long after the beauty of youth has gone, long after the desires for the body have faded, the true face of love is revealed," Blake said in a voice that was warm and low.

My lips tightened into a hard line as I mentally scoffed at his words. It was easy for him to say that considering he was probably never going to age. "I never doubted that it would be worth waiting for you. You see I had tasted this"—Blake ran his thumb across the bottom of my lip—"and I knew I could wait forever for your kiss."

"Even if I was missing teeth and looked like a wrinkled old prune?" I tried really hard to keep my sarcasm at bay, because Blake's words were so heartfelt, but it came out before I could stop myself.

"Yes," he urged. "Because all I want is you, in any size, shape or form." He quirked an eyebrow and cocked his head. "Perhaps, you wouldn't have wanted me if you returned to find a haggard old man?"

My lips twitched into a small grin. "Touché," I murmured.

I understood what he meant. My life had become that in which his life was necessary. I just needed him to be—the fact that his face rivaled that of an angel was incidental.

Blake spun me around, grabbed my hand and walked briskly down the cobblestone street.

"Where are we going?"

Before he could give me an answer I heard a piercing scream. I looked over my shoulder to where it was coming from and saw a flicker of yellowish light. "Shouldn't we do something?" I asked.

"No."

I looked at Blake, disbelieving the callousness of his reply.

"We have to help her," I insisted. I didn't know who *her* was, but I could discern that someone was in trouble and we couldn't just walk away. "Blake—"

"No," he answered sharply.

I had to jog to keep up with his fast pace.

"Why not?" I demanded.

"I'm not leaving you. That's final." I dragged my feet, trying to pull him to a stop. "Athena," he said my name warningly, "we're going one way or another. We can do this the easy way or the *hard* way."

I clenched my jaw as I saw that ruthless spark in Blake's eyes. I understood why everyone treated him so deferentially—how even Boe and RJ were hesitant to push him too far—but I was doggedly determined to match his obstinacy with my own stubbornness.

"If you won't go help than I will." Digging into my jacket pocket, I pulled out the silver tube that Richard gave me the day of the WiiGii attack on the College.

Blake snatched the little device out of my hands. "You think you're going to save the world with *this*—a tazer dart?" he hissed.

"Hey, give it back," I cried.

Blake stuffed the tube in his jacket pocket and picked me up like he was carrying a child. I may have been determined for him to go and help, but I couldn't help but feel aroused by my movements against his body. Blake sighed, aggrievedly, and set me down against a wall.

"What am I going to do with you? If I hadn't been here, you would have gone running into the night to face some unnamed danger thinking some toys are going to protect you?" His voice was edged with anger; similar to the time when he rescued me in the lunch hall.

"We have to help," I protested.

"No, *we* don't. I don't care about that girl in the laneway. I don't care about the man three streets away. All that matters is right here." Blake shook me. "All that matters is that you are here, in my arms, with me—safe."

The scream started to fade and I panicked. "Go help her," I said urgently. "You said that you could never refuse me." My eyes darted anxiously across Blake's face. "Go help her!"

The muscle in his jaw pulsed violently. "Don't move!" he growled, before disappearing around the corner. I was tempted to run up the street after him, but his words were like a hammer that nailed my feet to the ground. My pulse raced as the screaming stopped and I desperately listened for sounds of confrontation, but couldn't hear anything besides the sounds of the city.

I fell back against the wall as Blake reappeared. My eyes quickly fell to the bundle he held effortlessly in his hands. The young girl, with dark reddish hair, was whimpering. Her wrists, covered with an array of bracelets, shielded her face, as if to deflect an attack. The sight of her made my chest tighten, not only was she a small thing, making her seem all the more helpless, but she was also missing a sneaker. Blake's jacket was wrapped around her, but I could see that the shoulder of her shirt was torn.

"She's not hurt," he said briskly, answering my unspoken question.

I followed him without a word as he headed down the street. When we reached the square, Blake gently sat the girl down on a bench and stood rigidly. I took a seat next to her and cringed, knowing Blake was still quite angry with me.

"Are you all right?" I asked the girl, as she ran her fingers through her hair nervously.

"Yeah, I think so." Her voice was a deep tenor, a characteristic that belied her small frame. She held up her hands and shook her head. "I don't what happened. They came out of nowhere." She looked up at Blake. "Thanks, man, for, uh, helping me back there."

I was surprised by how calm she was. "I'm Kris by the way."

"I'm Athena," I said, feeling awkward because my social skills were always under par.

Blake tilted his head to the side and gave Kris an expressionless look. "Blake," he offered coolly. I was slightly comforted by the fact that my skills were much more developed than his.

"You know, you look familiar," Kris said, turning to face me. She puckered her forehead and started to bite a nail. "Do we know each other?"

"I don't think so," I replied. She didn't look familiar and I was pretty good at remembering faces.

Kris crossed one arm below her chest and rested the other one on top of it as she tapped her cheek with her index finger. "Do you go to the College?"

My eyes widened in surprise. "Yeah, I do."

"That's probably where I've see you then. Cool," she said nonchalantly, nodding her head. "Well, thanks again." Kris gave a light wave with her hand and started walking away.

"It's sort of late. Do you want us to take you somewhere?" I called out, stealing a look at Blake, who had his arms crossed with a displeased look on his face.

"Nah, you don't have to do that. I'm not parked too far from here."

"We don't mind," I insisted, walking toward her without getting Blake's approval.

Kris ran her fingers through her hair. "Kay, whatever."

It didn't take long to reach her car. The prestigious emblem on the front of the hood shouldn't have surprised me; Pork Chop told me that kids who went to the College were wealthy.

"See you around school."

"Yeah," I replied, waving ineptly as she got into the driver's seat. Kris gave a small wave from inside the car before she drove off.

"I believe this belongs to you."

I turned around and found Blake holding what he called a tazer dart. I reached out and retrieved the silver tube and tucked it back inside my pocket. It was funny, but I never went anywhere without it.

"Don't be angry with me," I implored. "I'm the one that should be angry. What were you thinking? I don't need to be watched like a child."

"Watching a child would be much easier I assure you. They're limited in their ability to protest." Blake's voice still had a hard edge.

I let out an aggravated breath. "I can take care of myself, Blake."

"I see how you take care of yourself, Athena," he snapped.

I heard the purr of an engine and turned to see Blake's car pull up behind us. Blake wrapped his hand around my arm and walked me toward the passenger seat.

"Where to now?" I asked, sliding onto the soft leather cushioning. The car ascended as soon as the doors slid shut.

"I'm taking you home."

"No! Why? Are you punishing me?"

Blake chuckled mirthlessly. "Punishing *you?*" He leaned his head back against the car seat and closed his eyes. "What am I going to do with you?" he murmured to himself.

I shifted myself toward him and caught his neck around my arms. "Anything you want to," I whispered fervently.

Blake's hands came roughly around my waist and he tugged me closer. I was thinking of how we could maneuver ourselves around the car when he growled in frustration. His door slid open and he pushed me back into my seat.

"I'll be right back," he said briskly, and then dropped out of the car.

"Greetings!" A rush of cold air filled the inside of the vehicle as oC flew into Blake's seat.

"Why did he go?" I asked anxiously.

oC twirled his robotic hand. "He just wants him off your tail. He won't let it get too out of hand, knowing that you're close by."

"What are you talking about? Someone's following us?" I twirled around in my seat to look out the rear window, but the lane was empty.

"I thought you noticed," oC replied, regret creeping into his voice. "It doesn't matter anyway. I'm going to take you home and Blake is going to meet you there."

"Who was following us?" I demanded, wondering why anyone would want to do that.

oC sighed. "I'm always putting my foot in my mouth these days. Is there a chance you would...let it go?" You could tell from oC's voice that he knew that I wouldn't. "Are you going to tell Blake I told you?"

"Not if you don't want me to." oC shook his head. "Then I

promise. My lips are sealed."

"It was Logan Leger."

"Logan! Why would he be following me?"

oC shrugged his shoulders innocently. "I haven't the slightest clue," he said, his voice raising a pitch.

"You're such a bad liar, oC. Tell me."

"It's not for me to say," he offered pleadingly. "It's something you should take up with Blake because I will not divulge anything further."

"Fine. I will," I snapped.

oC's face brightened as if he just remembered something of great importance. "Weren't you proud of vI today? You must have noticed how civilly she behaved at dinner." I held my hands in my face, filled with frustration, as the ever-animated boT changed the subject. "Athena, are you all right?"

"Yeah, just peachy oC," I mumbled.

"Just checking. Anyway, I thought it would be nice if you could come by the house one of these days and spend some time with her."

"With who?"

"vI of course," oC answered eagerly.

"Why would I do that?" I asked, baffled by his proposition. "I have a keen interest to live now a days."

"That's all in the past, my dear. vI wouldn't hurt you and it would be nice if the two of you got along."

"And why is that?" I questioned him warily.

"Athena, I must confess something to you, but you mustn't

tell Blake."

I was like a dog hearing the ring of a bell; my ears peaked. "You have my word, oC."

"It's just that I miss vI terribly," he confessed. "We're rarely together these days because Blake and I are almost always with you and he won't let her come along. If you two could grow to…tolerate each other, then I'm sure Blake would let vI accompany me again."

I furrowed my brow, uneasy about what the boT just said. "Exactly how much of the time are you with Blake?"

oC tilted his head, confused by my question. "I don't know what you're asking. I'm always with him," he replied off-handedly.

My face fell, blanched and then burned red. "Always as in all the time."

"Naturally. I am his boT. Where else would I be?"

I couldn't bring myself to look at oC, as I remembered how Blake had kissed me all night.

"Were you with him…*tonight?*" I asked, knowing my voice was uneven.

"Athena, I'm sorry!" he exclaimed. "I didn't mean to embarrass you. When I say I'm with him all the time, I mean I'm always within a certain radius. Rest assured, when the two of you are alone you have complete privacy."

I bit my lip so hard, I was sure I was going to draw blood. I was utterly mortified at the boT's assurance.

"The only time I have with vI these days is when you're at the College," he continued, trying to abate my chagrin. "But that might very well change if Blake wants me with you even then."

"With me? What do you mean by that?"

oC's shoulders shrank. "Blake is thinking that he wants me to tag you all the time now.

The crease on my forehead was so deep, the Grand Canyon paled in comparison. "Tag me?"

"When Boe showed you kO on her sweater today he was tagging her. When Supras are out in public their boT's condense into tags like that. Blake wants me to do the same for you, especially after the attack on the College."

"What! No! That's an invasion of my privacy," I cried. "oC, you wouldn't! Would you?"

"Please don't hate me, Athena. What can I do?" he said helplessly, shirking away.

"You can say hell no, that's what," I shot back. "Wait a minute, what do you mean Blake wants me tagged *all the time* now?"

"This sort of leads us back to why I brought this up in the first place—"

"oC, please tell me you haven't been tagging me," I said, grinding my teeth.

"No, I haven't been. Not exactly." I glowered at him. "I've followed you, but haven't tagged you. And before you offer one word of censure regarding the former, I must declare that I had no choice in the matter because I must go where Blake goes."

"What are you saying?"

"From the moment you arrived on London Bridge, he's been following you and has rarely been more than a block away."

"oC, are you serious?"

He nodded his head earnestly. "He sits outside your bedroom window night after night, just to be on the street where you live."

I turned my head away as my tear ducts started to fill. For someone who rarely cried, I was abashed at how easily I felt the sting of tears these days.

"oC, can Blake hear us now?"

"No," the boT whispered. "I've temporarily put a sound barrier around the car."

A grin spread across my mouth; I found oC's deception amusing. "Don't worry, I won't tell him anything you told me."

"Thank you, Athena. *Thank you.* Sometimes Blake can be… scary."

My grin grew wider. "Tell me about it, oC."

He let out a breath. "He's so on edge lately and his constant dour mood is exhausting. vI would be endlessly berating him for being so grouchy, but she hasn't been around and I've never had the gumption to say the things she would say. vI would never admit it, but she not only misses me, but Blake as well, which is why she made such an effort to be good at dinner today. I know vI can be difficult sometimes, but you have to remember that she is such a proud, feisty, lady boT. The very fact she's trying to prove herself is a remarkable step forward."

I remembered how jovial oC looked after dinner and could tell he truly missed his companion. Touched by his deep sentiment for vI, I decided to grant his request, although ever fiber in my being dreaded her company.

"All right, oC. I'll give it a try, but if I see one pincer, I'm throwing in the towel."

"Agreed."

As we approached the familiar red brick building, I thought back to the morning when I found myself asleep in my bed. I didn't remember dragging myself onto it in the middle of the night and it had been the same two days ago, when I cried...

"oC, when I fell asleep last night—"

"It was Blake," he whispered.

"The night before that..."

He was silent for a moment. "A girl was grieving for her lost mother and cried herself to sleep, alone and inconsolable."

I should have been ashamed knowing they had heard that, but instead I felt numb.

"Thanks for the ride," I said quietly, stepping out of the car.

"A boT and a Supra are so closely connected that when one feels something the other cannot help but feel the same." oC lowered his head, unable to meet my gaze. "You should know that you broke two hearts that night," he murmured.

In that instant, I sensed my own connection—deep and moving—with the tender boT.

"I give you my word, I'll try with vI. I won't let Blake keep you guys apart."

oC's robotic smile was filled with light and lent its warmth to my tired eyes.

The back of Blake's car was soon nothing more than a tiny speck—oC had floored the pedal. I realized the reason he was so eager to be gone because Blake flew over my head and landed on the dock as graceful as a fairy.

"You can't go through the front door now can you?" he said sinuously, holding out his hand.

It was past two in the morning. I was sure everyone was asleep, but there was a good chance I could wake someone if I tried sneaking in.

"Where have you been?" I asked, creasing my forehead, as he pulled me against his chest.

"Waiting for you," Blake replied smoothly. "You took longer than I expected. You didn't have a particularly interesting conversation with oC, did you?" he asked suspiciously, pushing me inside my bedroom—it had taken no time at all before my feet were firmly planted onto my balcony. I wanted to ask him about Logan and I wanted to fume at him for insisting that oC tag me, but as Blake walked deeper into my bedroom the last thing I wanted was to talk. I slid my arms down his chest and wrapped them around his waist. I raised myself on my tiptoes.

"Blake," I breathed, reaching up to touch his lips to mine.

"This is goodnight." Giving me a perfunctory peck on the cheek he pulled away and stepped back out onto the balcony.

"Wait! What do you mean this is goodnight?" I couldn't help but cringe at the neediness in my voice. I decided to ridicule myself later for my lack of pride—right now I didn't care if I had to beg for Blake to stay. "Can't you stay a little—"

"I said goodnight," he replied firmly.

"Are you still angry with me? Is that it?" I asked, perplexed.

Blake shook his head. "Athena, there is a line that I'm not going to cross." Blake drew an invisible barrier with his hand separating the balcony from my bedroom. "So, it's best that we end the evening here."

"I don't want to say goodnight." I ploughed toward him, crossing the imaginary line he had just drawn.

"You don't have a choice."

I squared my shoulders; Blake's obstinate tone only made me more determined.

"I'll stay out here the entire night then," I declared, crossing my arms.

"Suit yourself." He rose off the balcony and moved away.

"Won't you come inside for a little while longer? Come on. You've been in my bedroom before." Blake cocked his head at me. "You stepped inside just now and earlier tonight you came in. What's the big deal?" I promised oC that I wouldn't tell Blake that I knew he had been in my room the past few nights. My cheeks warmed at the thought of Blake seeing me sleep—of him laying me in bed.

Blake came forward and leaned across the railing. "That's not the line I was referring to—between the balcony and your bedroom." I heard something when he spoke that made me think he was straining to keep his voice even.

I puckered my forehead. "Then what do you mean?"

Blake let out an audible breath. "I mean there's a line between me and your...bed."

My pulse had been like a rowdy racehorse being held back before a race. When Blake uttered his grating reply, the gate was thrown open and my heart took off at full speed. As a jockey, I was struggling to gain control of the wild animal that threatened to send me into cardiac arrest.

"My bed?" I asked shakily.

"Athena, we're not—"

I grabbed his shirt collar and cut him off. "We don't need a bed." Blake wrapped his hands around my forearms as I slid my hands tightly around his neck. "Blake, please," I entreated, knowing he was going to push me away. "Just a kiss. A real kiss goodnight."

My plea had no effect because he withdrew from my grasp. "No," he uttered before he flew down toward the street and vanished.

"Blake!" I called out after him. Ugh! I kicked the balcony's metal rails in frustration. He said I drove him crazy. Well, he drove me to a point so far beyond crazy that no human study could categorize it.

Unwilling to concede defeat so easily, I hoisted myself onto the balcony and sat on the railing with my arms crossed. oC's information was indeed handy; I knew Blake wasn't really gone. I dangled my legs and raised my eyes to the sky—unwilling to look down. My fear of heights only made the knots in my stomach tighten. Time ticked by and the back of my legs began to feel numb. I was so sure that Blake would have given in by now and reappeared, but he hadn't. I blew air in between my stiff fingers and momentarily closed my eyes. There was no way I could outlast him. It wasn't cold enough for frostbite but I was still susceptible to hypothermia. If he hadn't come by now, it was a pretty sure sign that he wasn't going to come back. The thought of throwing myself off the balcony altogether had crossed my mind but I promised Blake that I would never pull anything like that again and I would also have to explain how I knew he would be watching, breaking oC's confidence.

I just didn't get it. Why didn't Blake want to be alone with me? I thought it was maybe because he was trying to be a gentleman—a rarity to find—but I had a feeling it was something else.

Maybe it was me?

I had a frightening lack of experience with the opposite sex and my insecurities were as heavy as Sisyphus' boulder. Maybe I was doing something wrong? Maybe I was doing something Blake didn't like? Feeling vulnerable on the rail, I swiveled my legs around to head back inside my room. It was as typical as a spy on a stakeout—the target only appeared as soon as the watcher determined they wouldn't show. Startled by the dark figure in front of me, I nearly fell backwards off the metal bar.

Blake leaned toward me and grabbed the rail on either side of my leg, encasing me between his arms. "A kiss and then goodnight." The huskiness in his voice urged me to protest, but the discernible edge made me think again.

I nodded my head in agreement. "A real kiss," I whispered.

Blake let out a breath and set his jaw—like he was bracing himself. "You do want to kiss me, don't you?" I asked, bothered by his wariness.

Standing between my legs, Blake clutched the side of my thighs. "Too much," he said gratingly.

His kiss spoke to the contrary however for his lips didn't match the feverish movement of my own. The more I curled myself around him, the more restrained his kiss became. It wasn't difficult to pull away from him because he already seemed detached.

"Am I...doing something wrong?" I asked, fixing my eyes on his unmoving chest—a contrast to the rapid rise and fall of my own. "Should I be—"

"You should be asleep in bed," he said abruptly. I opened my mouth to speak, but he quickly placed his hand over my lips. "A kiss goodnight is what we agreed." With my legs still wrapped around him, Blake lifted me off the railing. I tried with all my might to secure my hold around his neck, when for the briefest moment Blake lay with me in bed, but a second didn't pass before he threw my covers over me and gave me the slightest kiss on the forehead. He was gone an instant later, followed by the rapid closing of my window.

I threw off my bed sheets and ordered it to re-open. Expecting that it would, I nearly smacked my face into the colorful glass when it didn't. When the window remained firmly shut after a second command, I knew that it was Blake's doing. Balling my hands into fists, I stomped across my bedroom floor. I wanted to scream. For the second time that night, I threw myself onto my bed and, smothering my face into the soft moulds of the duvet, let out a piercing shriek. Coming up for air, I turned over to stare at the ceiling and realized that Blake could still hear me from outside my bedroom. I couldn't address him directly, but I wanted to let that complicated Supra know how frustrated I was with him. I hoped my delivery was convincing enough that it sounded like I was venting aloud as opposed to talking to Blake directly. I gave my pillow a few good stabs before I finally lay my head against it.

"Blake, you're going to be the death of me!"

¤ XVIII ¤

W H A T ' S   T H I S ?

I could barely keep my eyelids open. Although there was no sun, I opted to done my sunglasses for mainly one reason: I didn't want Pork Chop to see me doze off while she ranted.

She came down to breakfast wearing one of the new designer pieces that Boe purchased for me, insisting to Vas that I couldn't return them anyway. I was too exhausted to find adequate content to start an argument so all I had managed was a dour, "Whatever."

My passivity seemed to fuel Pork Chop's angst because once inside the car, away from Vas and Sammy, she kept going on and on. I replied to all her snide comments with, again, an automatic,

"Whatever," which only aggravated her further. It didn't take long before I was on the verge of sleep, at which point I stopped responding all together. I wasn't sure how long it was until she noticed that I wasn't listening.

"What the heck?" I bellowed grudgingly, as Pork Chop gave my drooping head a smack—bringing me back to the land of consciousness.

"Wake up. We're here," she said briskly.

I groaned as I recognized the College's familiar façade. It may have been a beautiful building, but it was a penitentiary all the same.

"I'll be here at seven to pick you up."

"What!" I exclaimed.

"You heard me. If you don't want to wait, find your own ride home."

The car took off before the passenger door fully slid shut.

"Siblicide is evil. Siblicide is evil. Siblicide is evil. You mustn't think about siblicide," I muttered to myself.

"Killing your sister would be most unbecoming." I shot around to find Logan standing behind me with his silver roadster blocking traffic a few cars down.

"What are you doing here?" I asked, confounded by his sudden appearance.

"I wanted to talk to you alone." His gaze trailed down my body and rested on my feet, but I didn't move my eyes away from his face. "At least, as alone as he's going to let you be."

"Logan, why were you following me yesterday?" I blurted out without pretense.

"He told you it was me?" Logan scratched his chin, sounding surprised. "What else did he tell you?"

"Everything," I replied hastily.

"So, he told you *nothing.*" He smirked, bemused. "Interesting. Dresden has decided to break some rules but not all of them. But then again, he wouldn't want to tell you about me."

"Tell me what?" The warning bell that marked the commencement of class matched the blaring ring in my head.

Logan looked down at me feet again before pressing on. "Let's just say we've known each other for a *long time.*"

"What?" I rasped, astonished; Logan had known me when I first travelled to the future?

Any trace of teasing in Logan's eyes, vanished. "We were more than just acquaintances, much more."

"That's not possible," I breathed, my cheeks reddening.

"It's the truth and deep down you know that." He stepped toward me. "The first day we met, couldn't you feel it?" he whispered urgently.

His ocean blue's eyes bore into me and I couldn't help but remember the warmth I felt toward him when he had joked with Pork Chop and I. As I searched Logan's face, I felt a violent pang in my stomach. The look he gave me was unmistakable, a look a man gives a woman and not one a friend bestows upon a friend. It shocked me that I even recognized it.

"It's okay that you can't remember." His voice jagged with anger. "It's because of what he did to you."

"Logan, I have to go." I turned, scared of what he might say, but he caught me by the arm.

"I'm sorry to tell you like this, but I don't know when I'll get another chance." He pulled me closer. "You asked me to do this because if you ever returned you weren't sure Dresden would have the balls to do it himself."

"Don't talk about him like that," I ordered, hating the way he spat Blake's name.

Logan was irate at my reproach. "You begged him you know," he muttered coldly. "You begged him on your knees to keep you. But he threw you away. Then you pleaded to keep your memories, wanting to remember. Wanting to…suffer." Logan's eyes were so bright they were almost clear. "Instead of giving you a choice, he brandished the sword of absolution and thought that when he severed your soul he was giving you peace. He didn't give you anything. He stole what was rightfully yours and made sure that if you ever looked at him again, you would look through untainted eyes."

"You're lying," I admonished, shaking my head fervently.

"Dresden's already drowning you," he sneered in disgust.

"Stop it. Blake is none of your business."

Logan tensed, looking like I had just punched him in the gut— he hated when I said his name.

"He didn't even want you back," he snapped.

It was a thought that still plagued me and tears welled in my eyes. "Sammy was going to leave you behind, but he couldn't do it to Sof," he went on. "You should know that you wouldn't even be here if it weren't for your sister. No one else could bring you back except for Sammy—a gift from his genius father, Jovan Feldenheim."

I recognized the name; Boe had told me about the infamous scientist who mysteriously disappeared.

"Why didn't Sammy want to take me?"

"He thought it would be safer. But he couldn't do it. After two years, there was still a part of your sister that lay closed off—a room in her heart that he couldn't enter and couldn't ease open as much as he tried. She missed you everyday, even when she didn't know it. Sammy missed you too," he was quick to add. "How could he not? Sammy adores your sister and can't help but love you in turn. He says the pair of you are but two parts of an apple—fallen from the most improbable tree—and that you complete one another. The sister that you wanted to kill a few moments ago loves you a lot." Logan's voice dropped. "So very, very much."

My bottom lip trembled as I took in his words.

"What do you want from me?" I said thickly. "And you haven't explained why you were following me."

Logan moved to cup my face, but I backed away, frightened because I was sure I knew the answers to my questions.

"I wanted to keep an eye on you," he admitted.

"You wanted to spy on me," I countered, angered by the invasion of my privacy.

"I didn't know what Dresden was up to. He was enraged when Sammy brought you back. Livid. They fought you know. Sammy told him to go to hell—rightly so I might add. If Dresden didn't want you then it was simple; he could leave you alone. Sammy told me the same thing. He didn't want history to repeat itself for your sake and your sister's. So, that was what we were supposed to do; leave you alone. But I couldn't. Thank god for Sof because I'm sure Sammy would have never let me close if she didn't trust me."

"She trusts you?" I gave him a skeptical look. "Pork Chop doesn't trust anyone."

Logan rubbed his chin. "Your sister and I have *always* been close. She was naturally drawn to me when we met again and even though Sammy didn't like the relationship, there was nothing he could do about it; he can never say no to her. He warned me, though, that I couldn't do anything to jeopardize her happiness and, if I did, he wouldn't hesitate to take steps to…silence me."

I raised my eyebrow questioningly; Sammy was hardly prone to violence.

"My cousin is one of the most affable people I've ever met, but when it comes to Sofia Ellias, there's a cutthroat quality in him that makes even me uneasy," he explained.

"Your cousin?"

Logan nodded. "Lucky for me that blood is thicker than water, because when you finally came, he agreed to let me see you, if I promised to leave the past alone. I hadn't planned on telling you any of this, but Dresden broke first, the selfish beast that he is."

That was it. I wasn't going to listen to him insult Blake like that so I pivoted around on my heel and headed toward the main entrance of the College, aware that the unloading dock was empty, with the exception of a few students who were running because they were late.

Logan was in front of me in a blink and my eyes grew wide.

"You're a Supra, too?" I exclaimed. "But that doesn't make sense. I read about the WiiGiis and ViAno and—"

"That's all speculation." His tone was one of indifference.

"Because you're one of them." I stated this as a matter of fact.

He let out a breath. "Unfortunately, yes."

I creased my forehead. "Unfortunately?"

"It makes things difficult for us," he replied guardedly.

I gulped audibly and the corner of Logan's lips turned up.

What did he mean *us?*

"Sammy made one thing clear: that I could play the role of friend in your life. He didn't think another Ellias needed to deal with having a Supra as a…*partner.*" I desperately wanted a bucket of ice water to throw over my face. "And since Dresden was adamant about keeping his distance, Sammy didn't think it would be a problem so long as I agreed."

I couldn't meet his eyes. "What exactly does *difficult* mean?"

I had never seen Logan nervous, he was always arrogantly collected, but now he fidgeted uneasily on his feet.

"Ask your sister," he replied slowly.

I narrowed my eyes, thinking of all the things Pork Chop had hidden from me.

"I will."

"You're late."

His announcement startled me.

"Yeah, I am." After a moment of silence, I moved away. "Thank you, Logan," I said earnestly. "Nobody seems to think the truth matters, but it does to me."

"I know," he replied, gesturing for me to stop. "That's why I came here today. I'm not going to try and deceive you with falsehoods. I'm not going to make you think I'm something that I'm not." I gave him a warning look, but he pressed on. "Leave her alone. That's what Sammy told us. But I never wanted you gone. *Never.* When Dresden made his move, I decided the gloves were off; I wasn't going to lie to you anymore and...I agreed with Sammy to steer our relationship down a *platonic* course." Logan grabbed my face and I couldn't peel his ironclad grip away. "That's all changed now. And he knows it."

"What did you tell Blake last night?" I stammered, tugging at his wrists.

"To stay away from you. That you could be happy here and that you weren't going back."

"What did he say?" I asked anxiously. "Did he say he was going to send me back?"

My question maddened him. "Don't do this with him," he entreated harshly. "He'll break you again and again until there's nothing left."

"Stay out of it, Logan. It's not your concern." Remembering how cold Blake had been when he left my bedroom made me angry.

Logan released me. "When I saw you for the first time that morning, fifty-two years had passed since I last set eyes on your face." His voice was rich with emotion. "When I knocked on your door, I prayed that it would open and a spell would break—the magic you had trapped inside me would dissolve, like a drop falling into a sea and I could move on." He ran his fingers over his suddenly worn face as be backed away. "I wanted it over. You have no idea what's it like to live a lifetime needing someone." Logan let out a breath. "You should know what I discovered that day," he murmured, looking like a poor man, about to spread his dreams at my feet, and I could not bear the thought, sure I would be unable to tread softly. "It was cruel when the door slipped open because I knew it was never going to be over. All I saw was an endless chain of lifetimes without her and I thought death would be sweeter."

Pain. I felt pain that no drug could diminish.

"Logan, I'm—I'm sorry." My words came out all slurred. My memories were gone, but I was filled with emotions that I couldn't place, and something was splitting inside me as his tortured eyes found mine.

Our entire conversation had taken place in public; students had brushed past us, vehicles had honked and maneuvered around his car—blurred images I registered in the periphery of my mind—but standing across from Logan, he was the only person who existed in my world, the two of us engulfed in a small haven where the rest of the universe didn't matter. In this place, I would have rushed to him and twined my arms around his neck, offering him comfort and assurance. But that world, unreal and elusive, seemed to contract as I moved to go to him. The borders closed in with every step and when we finally stood face to face, the only thing that remained was the barrier between make-believe and reality.

"Good-bye, Logan," I breathed and turned my back to leave.

"Au revoir, Athena."

Biology was lonesome without Boe. While Ms. Spaltor finished up the unit on the human spinal cord, I couldn't help but constantly glance at the vacant seat across from me. It seemed like much longer than three days had passed since Boe had greeted me with her infectious smile and warm wave. I missed her. But I missed Blake more. I needed to see him. No matter how hard I tried to focus, I couldn't dampen the ache that I felt in my chest after seeing Logan. And I couldn't stop thinking about what he had said. *Fifty-two years.* Which meant only one thing to me—Blake was old, older than my own father.

It was awful because I needed to concentrate. I was so behind with all my schoolwork that if I didn't catch up quickly failure would be inevitable—and failure was a word I refused to acknowledge in my vocabulary. Vas always told me that to fail meant only one thing: you hadn't tried hard enough—hadn't worked hard enough.

As I tightened the laces of my sneaker, readying myself for gym class, I decided that Pork Chop picking me up at seven might not be such a bad idea. A couple hours in the school library would do me good and offer a much needed distraction. My emotions were volatile these days and I didn't feel like myself. I felt like a stranger in my own body. Although I wanted to see Blake badly, I needed to be isolated for a while with just me, myself and I.

Besides, oC told me that Blake was usually close by, but I wagered that it wasn't the case today because Logan said we were alone.

"It's terrible what happened to Corinne. I heard the arm was reattached but they say doctors aren't sure if her muscles will ever achieve the kind of precision they used to."

My heart stopped as I caught wind of a conversation between two girls exiting the change room.

"It sucks because she was such an awesome archer. Have you heard the details?"

"Andrea told me it was some sort of freak accident involving jet-racers."

The backs of the svelte pair became nothing more than a blur, as I stared after them. When I heard them speak of a severed arm, I could think of nothing except the WiiGii who had tried to kill me. I remembered their tortured cry and my body gave off a shiver. Then, thinking of the handsome girl I encountered in the very room in which I stood, the hairs on my arms rose. Surely it was coincidence; two entirely unrelated events.

Realizing I was about to be late for class, I pulled my hair into a messy braid and darted out to the complex. I didn't want to run laps today; I didn't have the energy for it.

The bits of information I overheard left me feeling unsettled, but as Mr. Ballin announced the new athletic unit, I attributed all my suspicions to my over active imagination and instead prepared myself for what I was sure to be an interesting gym class. Today we would be fencing.

By some cruel twist of fate, Tia was assigned as my fencing partner. When Mr. Ballin called out our names, I didn't try to hide the look of repulsion I wore. Tia on the other hand was thrilled, but it wasn't the kind of delight experienced by someone who actually liked their partner. It was a devious kind of excitement—anticipation for the pain she was going to inflict upon me.

There are three kinds of weapons in fencing: saber, épée and foil. I had only ever fenced épée and foil, so I was relieved to find that Tia and I would be fencing épée.

I put on a pliable pair of fencing pants over my shorts and pulled on a supple jacket. I noted how the design of fencing attire had improved over the centuries. The face of the fencing masks were no longer made out of a steel mesh, but were instead fashioned out of some sort of glass. I wasn't sure if I liked the feature because your opponent could see your face and more importantly your eyes. The eyes could give everything away in fencing. All the equipment appeared on a rack at the far side of the complex with a student's name appearing on a small screen above each fencing suit.

Picking up my glove, I realized that it was right-handed and so too was my weapon.

"Uh, Mr. Ballin!" I called out, turning to find the ever stern-looking gym teacher. "I need a left handed glove and épée."

Some of the girls who were talking quietly beside me stopped and gave me a queer look. Mr. Ballin looked like I had just slapped him.

"Are you trying to be funny, Ms. Ellias?" he asked harshly.

I looked confusingly at my classmates, some of whom started to giggle.

"Uh, no, Sir. I'm not trying to be funny at all."

"Then I don't want to hear another peep out of you."

I held out my hands helplessly. "But, Sir, I can't fence with a right-handed weapon."

"Look, young lady, you've chosen the wrong day to be a smart-aleck—"

"I'm not being a smart-aleck. Sir, I *am* left-handed. I need a left-handed weapon to fence," I insisted earnestly.

Mr. Ballin narrowed his eyes at me and I straightened. I didn't get what the big deal was. Why would he think I would pretend to be left-handed?

"We'll see, Ms. Ellias. We'll see." After giving his chin a few scratches, he turned away. "Let's move it. On piste now!"

I furrowed my brow as Tia and the rest of my class headed toward the grounded strips of metal that lay evenly arranged around the complex.

I scowled; sure Mr. Ballin was going to send me to the principal's office and fail me for the unit. I unzipped my fencing jacket and faced the equipment rack, only to find that a new left-handed glove and weapon had appeared.

"Ms. Ellias, move it!"

I jumped at the sound of Mr. Ballin's voice.

"Coming, Sir." I hurriedly grabbed the gear and jogged over to the piste where Tia stood complacently.

When I fenced in the past, we were required to wear body wires that ran through our fencing jackets. They were hooked up to an electronic machine that determined when a touch was scored. When the barrel at the tip of each weapon was pressed with sufficient force, a hit was awarded. There hadn't been any body wires with the equipment, but I noticed that on the back of each jacket was a small blinking clip. I assumed that this was the mechanism that would detect when a hit was made.

A holographic scoreboard hovered above each piste.

"Fencer's en garde," an electronic voice boomed.

"Since we are short on time there will be no breaks. The bout will go to forty-five points," Mr. Ballin declared, sitting atop a high chair.

Turning to Tia, I raised my weapon and saluted as the other girls beside me did the same. It was customary to salute your opponent and the referee before a match began. Tia simply raised her immaculately shaped black eyebrow in return and put on her mask.

"Prêt," the electronic voice announced. "Allé." The word was barely uttered before Tia came charging at me. There was no time for a parry and she jabbed my arm with her weapon. I tried to mask the pain, but I knew it was written all over my face. The gleeful look Tia gave me as she shoved by me to go back to the en garde line said it all.

Tia's footwork was impressive and beyond fast. As her point collided with my chest, I knew that I couldn't beat her with speed. This was a blow to my confidence because I always relied so heavily on my footwork and was forced to find ways to out maneuver her without relying on my pace.

When she lunged again, I anticipated her direct attack and gave a strong parry carte, but she beat my blade when I moved to riposte and struck me on the shoulder. She came at me hit after hit and I was helpless against her attacks. I tried every parry: carte, sixte, seconde, octave, prime, but nothing worked. She either beat my blade to counter-attack or moved out of the way so quickly that I couldn't hit with the riposte. My lunges were long and hard, but her feet were too fast—she just parried by distance.

I took off my mask for a moment and wiped drops of sweat from my brow. The scoreboard read forty to *zero*. I told myself that I had five points left to score just one. Vas always told me that each and every point was considered a victory so that at the end of each match both fencers were considered winners. But that only applied as long as each fencer scored at least *one* point each.

One point. One victory. That's all I wanted. That's all I needed.

I parried another attack and feinted a riposte to Tia's shoulder. When she moved to take my blade, I dropped my point and aimed for her toe. I was so sure that I was going to hit when Tia stepped out of the way and parried octave. I counter-parried her move, reprised and lunged again, but she evaded my blade and hit me square in the mask instead.

The taste of sweat in my mouth was bitter as I turned briskly back to the en garde line. When a touch was made, Vas said to let it go—clear the hurdle and look directly to the next. With my back turned to Tia, I closed my eyes to concentrate. The score was forty-four to zero and this was my last chance.

Whenever I competed in the past, I always encouraged myself with a saying Pork Chop told me about. It was an obscure Russian proverb that I grew fond of, even though it was peculiar.

Essentially, a man was faced with three paths in life and there were only three. On the first path, he is eaten by wolves. On the second path, he eats the wolves. On the third path, he eats himself.

I remember looking at Pork Chop bemusedly, sure that she was inebriated, but she had scoffed at my befuddled expression and said that the *point* of the story was, *"By god, Guse, 'eat the wolves!'"*

Turning to face Tia, I vowed that that was exactly what I was going to do. The monotone voice said allé for the last time and I propelled myself forward into a fleche. As my feet left the ground, I flicked my blade and struck her on the shoulder. Tia had rushed at me at the same time and we collided into one another. The cracking of our blades sounded like lightning. I couldn't catch my balance and I tumbled to the ground. Ignoring the throbbing in my arm, I shot up to look at the scoreboard. A patch of blood was seeping through my jacket, but I barely noticed. Walking back to the en garde line, I met Tia's shove with equal fervor as I raised my right hand and clenched it into a fist—a fist of victory. Withdrawing my mask, I held up my weapon and saluted my irate partner. It had been a double hit, but I hit all the same. The scoreboard read forty-five to *one*.

I headed out of math and determined one thing: I was going to have to get a tutor. There was no way I was ever going to catch up if I didn't get one. Besides instilling in me an ethic of hard work, Vas also taught me the Socratic value of *"know thyself"* which basically meant know your weaknesses. I was never going to be anything close to a mathematician so I didn't see the point of investing my time in it, but I still needed it as a requirement. Urgh! I grated my teeth at the trivialness of that thing—a high school diploma. I technically already had one.

The table at the northeast corner of the lunch hall was surprisingly empty. Staring up at the ceiling, I was amazed that there was no trace of the huge hole that had been blasted through it when the WiiGiis attacked a mere two days ago. As I took a seat at the vacant table, I sensed the glare of eyes bearing into me.

"Hey!"

"Hi." I looked up to find Kris offloading her schoolbag.

"You don't mind if I sit here do you?" she asked warmly, taking a seat across from me.

"No, not at all."

Kris ran her fingers over face before running them through her hair—a familiar mannerism of hers. "I'm exhausted. I don't know how I'm going to survive through mid-terms." Sitting up, she patted her stomach. *"Burger and fries. Lunch. Load."*

I had been starving since gym class. *"Spaghetti. Lunch. Load,"* I ordered.

"Where's Blake?" she asked casually, as our lunch trays were lowered in front of us.

My heart stopped when she said his name.

"Uh, he's doesn't go to school," I finally replied, picking nervously at my food.

"Figures. He doesn't seem like the type to let people tell him what to do. I wish I could be so lucky. My parents threatened to cut me off if I don't graduate. Honestly, though, the College is a joke. I don't need people telling me what to study or what to read."

Kris bit into her burger and I nodded in agreement.

"It's sort of the same for me. My family is dead bent on sending me here, but the truth is I don't think it's really necessary."

Kris indicated that she felt the same by shaking her head, unable to voice her concurrence because her mouth was full.

"I totally agree," she added after gulping down her food. "Work experience and life experience are just as important and just as essential as education."

"Is this seat taken?"

I pivoted around and was startled to see Richard standing beside me. I glanced at Kris, who looked Richard up and down, before addressing him.

"Uh, are you sure you want to sit there?" I asked sardonically, raising my eyebrow.

He smiled. "Yeah, I'm sure."

I indicated with my hand that he was free to do so.

"I'm Richard Coleridge," he said, introducing himself to Kris.

She narrowed her eyes for a moment before she gave a slight nod of her head. "Kristina James. Everyone calls me Kris."

"I didn't take you to be a Latin lover?"

"Excuse me," I replied, taken aback by Richard's gauche comment.

He held out his hands defensively. "I just meant I was impressed by your Latin."

I realized he was referring to the encounter with the WiiGii and I softened my expression.

"It was nothing. Honestly, I can't claim to know much of the language at all. It was really a lucky guess."

Richard eyed me curiously. "You're too modest," he said kindly.

I puckered my forehead. "Stop being so nice to me. It's weird." Richard chuckled. "Don't think you owe me anything and that you have to pretend to be nice to me," I continued briskly. "I am so sick of people telling me they're in my debt."

"I'm not *pretending* to be nice," he declared earnestly.

"If I recall correctly, the first day we met you wanted Boe to ditch me so you guys could go jet-biking."

"You got a jet-bike?" Kris abruptly asked Richard.

Richard smirked. "I got several."

"Cool," she said biting her nail. "I prefer jet-boards though."

"You board?" He sounded surprised.

Kris nodded. "Oh, yeah."

I looked from one to the other, unsure what to make of their civil exchange.

Richard tilted his head to the side and gave her a probing look. "How'd you get it?" he whispered.

"My dad works for ViAno." A wily smile spread across Kris' face. "Let's just say he doesn't know where his money goes," she whispered back.

"You any good?"

"Not bad." Kris' tone was calm and confident. I could only surmise what jet-boarding was, but I would have bet blindly on her abilities. She didn't seem like the type to claim underserved merit or skill.

Richard crossed his arms. "I would say that we should go boarding sometime, but I doubt you could keep up with me," he said arrogantly.

Kris scoffed and ran her fingers through her hair. "I could take you." She raised a thin eyebrow at him.

"Stop being mean to my friend, Richard," I insisted, trying to partake in the conversation.

Richard held his hand against his chest. "Is she a friend of yours, Athena? If that's the case, then I'll take you out any time you like," he offered fetchingly to Kris. "A friend of a *friend* is also my friend."

"I'm your friend?" I asked incredulously, leaning away to give Richard a queer look. Since when was Richard *my* friend?

"Yeah," he replied softly, "you are."

I puckered my forehead. "Why?"

"Just because," he said casually.

I shook my head. "Because what?" If he said because he owed me, or anything to that effect, I was going to scream.

"Because I want you to be." Replying coolly, he nudged me on the shoulder.

"You're weird," I retorted, pursing my lips. His friendliness unnerved me and I didn't know how to respond to his affability.

"You're the one to talk, Athena," he said lightly.

"You know what's *weird*, Richard?" Kris cut in, cocking her head. "You're nothing at all like I thought you'd be. I mean everyone here has heard of your reputation."

Richard shifted in his seat uncomfortably. I couldn't help but notice how different he was from the last time I'd seen him.

"Reputations often precede—"

Kris cut Richard off. "Yeah, they say you're a jerk."

A wide smile spread across Richard's face—an obvious attempt to cover his uneasiness. "Don't believe everything you hear." He let out a cough—an embarrassed sound.

"I don't," Kris answered casually. "Now that I met you, I can discern that you're a bit of a jerk, but not a total one." She returned Richard's amused grin with a small smirk.

I couldn't help but smile myself. My fondness for Kris was growing by leaps and bounds. She was the type of person who didn't care what people thought and spoke her mind freely. I finally found someone less tactless than me. A person could always use a friend whom they could rely on for the truth. I thought Kris would be a friend like that.

"You gonna finish those fries?"

Without looking at Richard, Kris slid her plate over to him.

"What do you have next period?" she asked me.

"History."

"It sucks that we didn't end up having any classes together." Leaning her elbows on the lunch table, Kris gave Richard an odd look as he popped a fry into his mouth.

"Maybe next semester," I offered hopefully.

After Kris and I said good-bye to Richard, which had been awkward because I was still uncomfortable with him being so nice all of sudden, she offered to walk me to class.

"You up for boarding sometime? I'm really kinda stoked about the idea. Richard doesn't seem like the type to bluff about his abilities."

We headed up the main stairs of the College and I looked at her ruefully.

"I've never boarded in my life," I confessed. "I'm actually not sure what it entails. Is it a cross between skateboarding and surfing?"

"Sorry, how presumptuous of me. Yeah, it's sort of a cross between the two except you don't really board on ground or on water." Kris flattened her hand and slid it through the air. "You're airborne."

My eyes widened with enthusiasm. "Could you teach me?" It sounded really fun.

Kris flinched. "Uh, not sure about that. I don't think I'd be a very good teacher, but if you want me to then I will."

"It's okay," I said holding up my hands. "I don't want you to feel that I'm pressuring you. It's totally fine. I get it. Teaching can be frustrating."

"No, man, I don't mind at all. I'm just saying don't expect too much."

"I won't," I told her, grinning as I offered her my assurance.

"What are you doing after school?" she inquired, just as a group of students shoved into us. "Hey! Watch it." Kris' voice wasn't a shout, but a deep grumble that had enough of an edge to silence the snickering.

We turned to face each other and it was interesting to note the similar expressions we wore—set jaw, furrowed brow and narrowed eyes. I imagined she was telling herself the same thing I told myself, which was the better person walks away.

"I'm locking myself in the school library. My sister's picking me up and she's going to be really late, so I'll be here until nightfall," I replied, shaking off the incident.

Kris raised her eyebrow and smirked. "Fun stuff."

"You betcha," I quipped sardonically.

Waving a quick good-bye to Kris, I turned down the corridor that led to Mr. McGradie's history class and couldn't help but note how my step had a bit of a bounce to it. I expected to eat lunch alone today, but instead found myself in the company of two people whom I actually liked. Who would have thought that I would ever like Richard? Funnily enough, I did.

"*Psst.*"

I halted abruptly in front of the classroom door and looked around to see where the familiar sound had come from.

"Athena." I recognized the voice. Backing quickly away from the entry, I scanned the halls fervently. "Down here." I peered down at the ground and narrowed my eyes to search for him. It didn't help that my eyesight wasn't very good. "No, down *here*." I furrowed my brow, unable to spot him. "On your *shoe*."

It was odd because I heard him say shoe, but instead of looking down at my feet, I straightened and looked up. It was sad how slow my mental reflexes were these days.

"My shoe?" I asked, cocking my head—it was if I didn't know what the object was.

"Yes! Your shoe."

"oC! You're on my shoe!" I exclaimed, finally dropping my gaze down.

"Thank you Athena, I hadn't noticed."

I smiled at the boT's sarcasm and quickly slipped my foot out to pick up the leather pair.

"What are you doing here?" I whispered hoarsely, holding the shoe like a telephone.

"Put your shoe back on!" he ordered.

I noticed how a girl walking by did a double take as she passed me. Realizing that I looked like I belonged in a mental institution, I quickly shook the object pretending that there was something inside.

"Damn rocks," I explained. She gave me a queer look before entering a classroom down the hall. As soon as she was gone I held the shoe back up to my face. It wasn't necessary though because oC transformed.

"oC, what are you doing?" I asked frantically, my eyes searching the now empty corridor. I winced, realizing that I was going to have to walk into history late.

"I promised to tell you when I was tagging you, didn't I? Well,"—he held up his robotic palms—"I'm tagging you."

"Where's Blake?" I asked keenly.

oC's shoulders shrank. His reaction spoke volumes and I knew the answer would be that he wasn't here.

"Blake won't be back until tonight. He asked Boe to pick you up from your place around nine o'clock. She'll bring you back to the manor and Blake will see you there. This is the first time I've ever been away from him. He's taken vI so that I could stay with you."

I nodded my head somberly. Just the thought of Blake far from me made me disheartened.

"I'm so pathetic, oC. Really, I am," I told him gloomily.

oC patted my shoulder gently. "Aren't we all?" he said in a

melancholy tone. I realized he was referring to himself and how much he missed vI.

"Where did he have to go?" I asked, knowing that I didn't have any right to. Blake didn't have to report to me his whereabouts at all times and he was entitled to his privacy.

oC hesitated before responding. "I was not the one to tell you this, but he had to meet his brother."

"Oh," I replied, wincing as I absent-mindedly gave my left arm a rub.

oC's mouth dropped open. "What happened?" His whisper was almost hysterical.

"My arm is just a bit sore from gym class," I said off-handedly.

"You're bleeding!" The boT's voice was officially hysterical.

Blood had soaked through my blouse and a dark red spot was spreading like leaked ink.

"Crap. I should have put on more band-aids." It wasn't a big deal. When Tia's blade broke against my arm, the force cut my skin underneath my jacket.

oC stared frozenly at the spreading stain. I waved my hand in front of his face. "Earth to, oC. Hello?" I shook my head, puzzled by his reaction.

I reached down to fish for some band-aids in my bag when oC yanked my arm and rolled up my shirtsleeve.

"oC, what are you—"

"*I'm a dead boT. I'm a dead boT. I'm a dead boT.*" oC's frantic voice made me worrisome.

"Calm down." I coughed as he sprayed something onto my arm.

"Ow! That stings." Medical supplies erupted from oC's body and I tried to pull away from him. Tiny pincers shot out from his torso, each carrying a small tool.

"oC?" I said worriedly; he looked like he was going to perform brain surgery. The little boT didn't seem to hear me as he continued to shake relentlessly.

"He's going to have my head for this. This is not good. *Not good.*" He sounded so frightened.

"What are you talking about?" I asked bewilderedly.

In no time at all, my cut was cleaned and bandaged so expertly, you would have thought that I suffered from a gun wound. Rolling my sleeve back down and buttoning the cuff neatly, oC finally folded his hands together and hovered while continuing to tremble.

I slowly reached out to touch his shoulder. "oC, everything is fine. What are you so scared about?" I asked gently.

He grabbed the collar of my shirt. "Please! Please don't let him see that." I looked at oC wide eyed, unable to hide how confounded I was. He was begging me as if he begged for his life. "Don't let Blake see *that*." He eyed my arm desperately.

"I don't think Blake is going to blame you for what Tia did to me in gym class. I would say it was an accident, but knowing Tia, I don't think it was, but it had nothing to do with you."

oC shook his head violently. "I should have hacked into the school's communication system and sent a message to Mr. Ballin excusing you from class."

"What! That is ridiculous. Why should you have done that? I didn't want to get out of gym class. I wanted to fence." I couldn't take it when oC started to whimper—it was too disconcerting. "Stop this nonsense at once. If it will make you feel better, I'll conceal my arm from Blake. It won't be that difficult since we're in the middle of fall and tank tops are impractical at the moment."

"Bless you. Bless you, my dear. I owe you infinite thanks."

I was taken aback when oC rushed at me and gave me a peck on both my cheeks and then on my forehead. It was strange, but his touch was unmistakably metallic but also perceptively warm.

"Stop groveling, oC. You don't need to bless me and stop thanking me all the time. I don't like to be thanked," I said awkwardly. I was more than touched at his affection but I didn't know how to reciprocate or respond to it.

"Yes, of course," he replied hastily. "I will not grovel and I will not *thank you.*"

I pursed my lips at the endearing boT. "Do you think you're ready to go into class now?" oC nodded. "Okay, then," I said softly, sounding like a kindergarten teacher speaking carefully to a child who missed his mommy.

oC once again transformed and re-positioned himself on the buckle of my shoe.

"Uh, oC, can't you be a pin or something? Boe explained to me that your visual features are off, but it's just weird having you down there." Without a word and without changing his form, oC moved to the top of my right shoulder and emitted two blue blinks. "Thanks," I whispered, taking a deep breath as I headed toward the classroom door. "Here we go."

¤ XIX ¤

THE DARK NIGHT

There's an old saying, "Ask and you shall receive." Sitting hunched over a chair in the College's library, I found myself a believer. I had found the perfect tutor: oC. Not only was he infinitely intelligent—infinite in every sense of the word—but he also had an endless amount of patience.

I was quite sure that he was running over my calculus question for the hundredth time and yet he was as keen as when we first started, which was hours ago. Already past six o'clock, the library was empty. Mrs. Evans, the librarian, had just come by to let me know that she was going home and warned me that if I left the library I wouldn't be able to get back in because the doors were locked. I was surprised that she was letting me stay, but she said that students were allowed after hours access for as long as they liked.

I had thought it strange that there hadn't been more students around studying. oC told me that kids rarely read books nowadays—libraries had become obsolete. They no longer served a function but were merely manifestations of an idealized form of knowledge—an elitist form of study. It wasn't hard to see oC's point. All my work was saved on files that appeared holographically. Pencils and papers weren't used; everything was written electronically with the stencil Boe had given to me in biology. The closest thing I had to a textbook was something that resembled a really thin laptop that produced holographic images of information.

As I looked around the massive domed library, surrounded by rows of books, I suddenly missed paper. Even magazines and newspapers weren't really made out of it. I conceded that it was probably beneficial to the environment, but I was so at home in the library—like I was in the company of not only the greatest scholars, poets and thinkers but also in the company of great friends. I couldn't remember who had originally said it, but I always believed that books were for more than just reading.

When I told oC this, he simply nodded his head and said, "For some they are. For *you* they are. But today's society is one of efficiency and books simply fall short."

I rested my forehead against the hard surface of the table when oC started to go over my calculus homework yet again, but then he fell silent.

Lifting my head, I gave it a few good shakes. "Okay. Okay. I'm listening." Looking toward where the boT had been hovering, I found that he was nowhere in sight. "oC!" I called out. "Where'd you go?"

I started to hoist myself out of my seat to look for him when I noticed the faint blue glow on my tunic. Kris appeared around a bookshelf and I understood the reason for his disappearance.

"Hey, I thought you might still be here. I just made it. I caught Mrs. Evans on her way out." She gave me a simple wave by wriggling her fingers and draped herself on the chair across from me. "I should have known to stay away from you the moment I laid eyes on you," she said, letting out a deep breath. Taken aback by her comment, my mouth dropped open but I soon closed it shut as I saw her eyes gleam with amusement. "You've already proven to be a bad influence. I'm actually here to *study*."

I rolled my eyes. "You don't fool me for a second. I bet you that you're the top of your class. Don't try to blame your study habits on me."

Kris stretched her arms and leaned back. "It doesn't matter if I am. Studying on Saturday night is lame for anyone."

"Hey! I'm studying on a Saturday night," I said in mock indignation.

"You're a special case," Kris replied saucily. "What are you working on?"

"Calculus," I groaned.

"Why so glum? It's easy." I gave her a skeptical look. "Look, I'll help you, kay?"

"Be warned Kris, if you choose to enter this dark path and expect to see light soon, you will be sadly disappointed. Numbers and me simply do not get along."

"Not with that attitude," she said reprovingly.

I was about to quip a reply when I noticed she pulled out a pen and notepad from her schoolbag, which was covered with buttons, random designs and various nick knacks.

"Pen and paper?" I asked, almost in awe.

Kris raised her eyebrows. "Yeah, I'm a bit old school. We don't have to—"

"No!" I practically threw myself across the table to grab the coveted items. Kris pressed her lips together as if she was trying to restrain herself from laughing. I let out an awkward cough and sat back in my seat.

"I mean pen and paper will be just fine thank you," I said, doing my best to appear nonchalant.

Kris nodded her head slowly. "Okay, then."

It was one of the coolest things I had ever seen. My brain couldn't take any more calculus so Kris and I had taken a break. Remembering the conversation with Richard earlier in the day, Kris asked me if I wanted to see what a jet-board looked like. I thought that she was going to show me a picture or something. I never anticipated that she was going to show me the real thing instead.

She pulled out a flat metal sheet from her knapsack, no bigger than a piece of paper, and tapped it a few times. The thin metal became airborne and unfolded into a board.

"You ride this?" I asked Kris, inspecting the metal surface curiously.

"Yeah, I've been boarding since I was a kid," she replied casually, running her fingers through her hair.

"How does it work exactly?" I stood up and pressed down against it, seeing if it would buckle under the weight. It didn't give the slightest; it felt rock solid.

"It's the same technology used in electromagnetic suits." I furrowed my brow and shook my head, indicating I didn't know what those were. "You know about WiiGiis, right?" I nodded my head slowly. "It's sort of the same technology that their suits are made of. That's why they are so strong. Depending on the suit, a WiiGii could be much more powerful than your average Supra."

"Really?" I asked wide-eyed.

"For sure."

Recalling the snippet of information I heard Kris tell Richard at lunch I wondered whether or not I should ask her about the article I read in the newspaper.

"Uh, Kris, you said that your dad works for ViAno, right?" I asked hesitantly.

"Yes," she answered slowly.

"Well, I remember reading this article in the newspaper about speculations that ViAno technology was being used by WiiGiis. Do you think that's true?"

Kris sat back in her seat and let out a breath. "Honestly, I don't know. I mean it's the same technology, but I don't know whether WiiGiis simply stole it or if they have an inside source."

I took a moment to digest Kris' explanation and decided to wrack my brain about it later.

"You want to show me how to ride this thing?" I asked mischievously, breaking the silence.

Kris grinned. "Nah, not right now. I'm determined for you to get this theorem down pat."

I groaned as Kris tapped the board and shoved the metal sheet back into her schoolbag. "Fine, but I have to go to the washroom. I think my bladder is going to burst if I don't."

Tugging lightly at the small pin on my tunic, I placed oC gently on the table. I didn't think he needed to escort me to the washroom.

"Put a book in the doorway so the doors don't shut," Kris called out as I headed toward the exit.

"I will," I shouted over my shoulder.

It was strange walking through the dimly lit corridors and passing the dark classrooms. As I made my way down the College's grand staircase, I shook my head telling myself that it was only my imagination that made the school seem eerie. I turned the corner and stopped; the light from one of the offices seeped through the glass window and illuminated the dark floors.

Guessing that it was probably the school's caretaker or a teacher working late, I steered myself toward the girls washroom. Then I heard it—a raw unmistakable sound— and my heart stopped. Whispering persuasively in my ear was the voice of caution, but I didn't heed its warning. The halls were again quiet and I couldn't hear anything except the beating of my own heart. I had only heard it for the briefest of moments. It couldn't possibly be what I thought it was. Throwing caution to the wind, I tiptoed toward the bright office, keeping myself hidden in the shadows.

The sound of something cracking startled me so violently that I fell onto my hands and knees. Then I heard the voice clearly and knew I hadn't been wrong.

"We do this my way!" The WiiGii's rasp cut into me like a blade.

"You're not thinking. It won't prove anything!"

Trembling, I started to crawl backwards toward the stairs as the voices started to get louder. There were more than just a few WiiGiis in there. It sounded as if there was an army behind those doors.

"Corinne calm down!"

I put my hand over my mouth to stifle a gasp. It was true. The pleasant young girl who had helped me in the change room was a WiiGii. What's more, she was the WiiGii whose arm Blake had torn off.

I crawled as fast as I could; my knees burned from the friction as I headed toward the stairs. All I could hear was the cumulative rasp of voices over each other and couldn't make out what else they were saying.

The noise stopped and I froze in place sure that they had discovered me.

"It's settled," boomed a single voice, deepening my chills. "The College *will be* destroyed tomorrow. Explosives are already in place and will be detonated at noon. The lives of these students are necessary sacrifices for freedom—freedom from Supra tyranny."

I stopped breathing as Boe's words echoed in my head. *All Supras need to die.*

"No," I whispered.

"Guse!" My heart convulsed as my sister shouted my name. She was at the base of the main stairs looking at me funnily. "What are you—"

"Run!" I shrieked, sprinting toward her.

The door to the office blew open in a flash and nearly collided with my back. I didn't have to look behind me to know the black figures emerged and were coming for us—my sister's expression said it all.

"Run!" I yelled again, but Pork Chop didn't move. At first, I thought that she was in shock or something and that's why she hadn't started climbing the stairs. But as I got closer, I saw that wasn't the case at all. My sister didn't look like she was in shock; she looked like she was bracing herself. Then I understood. She was waiting for me to catch up, unwilling to leave me behind.

As soon as my foot hit the first step, she took off.

"Guse, duck!" I heard her yell. The stairs split into two sets at the first level and Pork Chop and I threw ourselves in opposite directions just as an explosion blew them apart.

"Pork Chop!" I cried, crawling on my hands and knees.

"Guse, go!"

I couldn't see her through the flames and rushed up the stairs, thinking that's what she wanted me to do. Reaching the second floor of the atrium, I looked over and saw that Pork Chop was all the way on the opposite side. She pointed frantically, indicating that we should meet at the end, where the corridors came together. I couldn't recall my legs ever moving so fast before. I wanted to get to her so badly.

As I hurried along, I could see Pork Chop running on the other side of the atrium, far ahead of me. She was racing to get to me, I knew, because she wanted to protect me—that's what she always did. However, this time I was determined to defend my sister and myself and dug into my pocket for my tazer dart.

Just as my fingers closed around the metal shaft, a WiiGii swept over the edge of the railing. As it reached for me, I slashed him with a current from my small weapon and lunged. I expected the force this time and used the momentum to pull me forward without losing my balance. Adrenaline was pumping in my veins, and I sprinted with new vigor toward my sister. I didn't get very far before something grabbed the back of my tunic and threw me to the ground. I was dazed for a moment and I frantically tried to raise myself as two menacing figures hovered over me.

"I'll kill her," one of them rasped.

The WiiGii moved liked an animal readying for the kill and I desperately tried to feel for the silver tube that had fallen from my grasp.

"Wait. We can use her to get to—"

The College's walls rumbled as the atrium's glass ceiling collapsed, distracting both WiiGiis, and gave me the chance to steal a quick glance behind me. Spotting the sliver of metal a few feet away, I inched myself toward it, but there wasn't a need; the pair hissed ferociously at something on the main floor and swooped over the bannister, abandoning me. I got up on my knees and searched for Pork Chop. I put my hand on my chest as I spotted her, already far along and about to turn the corner to make her way toward me.

Then it descended.

"Pork Chop!" I howled, as the WiiGii struck her down. "No!" I screamed. Before I could move, the force of an explosion smashed my body against a marble column and I slumped to the floor.

I ignored the ache as I let out a painful cough. Heaving myself up, I tried to see through the smoke. "Pork Chop," I whispered, just as something came hurtling through the sculpted railing; I was shocked to see the grossly deformed WiiGii. I shimmied away from it and my eyes shot down to the main floor. Relief and anxiety washed over me at once. Surrounded by an army of WiiGiis were Boe and kO, but the little boT looked anything but babylike now. Boe and her boT didn't look like they needed help, but it was still distressing to see the WiiGiis viciously attacking the lissome supra.

Then I remembered oC. The moment of indecision was so infinitesimal that it might not have actually happened. I darted down the hall, not toward the library, but to Pork Chop. I wasn't going to leave her either. I would get her and then we would go to the library to get oC.

I just picked up speed when something grabbed my foot with such force that I saw stars as my forehead hit the marble floor. My head was spinning and I held out my arms trying to find something to steady myself, but all I could see was a blur of black enveloping me.

"Runt," I heard it rasp.

When I struck toward where I thought the WiiGii stood, my hands only hit air. My feet were limp as it grabbed my tunic collar and held me up. Its cold hands moved to my neck, but before it could enclose its deadly fingers, I fell back to the ground, grunting in pain as slivers of glass pierced my body.

"Athena, talk to me."

I opened my eyes when I heard Kris' anxious voice.

"My sister," I muttered as she patted my head. I reached up, felt the thick liquid and knew I was bleeding.

"You got a nasty cut there," Kris said tightly.

"I'm okay. The WiiGii attacked Pork—"

"Don't worry. I've called for help," she assured. I heard a tear and then a sharp intake of breath. "Put pressure here." Something pressed against my abdomen and I winced, the pain too acute that I couldn't cry out. "Stay put."

I panicked as Kris moved away and hopped on her jet-board.

"Help her," I pleaded, my voice stifled. I had to tell her to go help Pork Chop. "oC! Get oC!" I begged.

"Shhh. It's okay. You're going to be fine. I'm going to—"

Something thundered down the hall, and Kris and I turned instinctually. Before I could say another word, Kris was speeding toward the approaching WiiGii.

I pushed myself up against the wall, desperate to call her back; she had to get my sister. But then I saw the flash of blue across the atrium.

"oC!" I called out, crying.

The little boT had just flown into the main foyer and was already transforming.

I gazed down the hall anxiously at Kris, a figure of agility, squatting on her nimble board.

"Kris, come back," I yelled.

She maneuvered herself around the dark figure and smashed the tip of the board into its face, sending it reeling over the railing—I had been right in my estimation of her abilities. But two more WiiGiis quickly appeared and dove toward her. Time seemed to halt as she pulled the familiar object out of her pocket.

"NOOOOOOOOOO!" I didn't recognize the sound of my voice as Kris threw out the whizzing ball just as the WiiGiis rammed into her. The same jet force I had felt before swept through the College and the crash of metal against metal vanished and the sounds of silence descended, broken only by my gasps as I dragged myself toward where I had last seen my sister.

Out of the corner of my eye, I saw the familiar egg shape giving off a faint blue glow. I dimly registered the mass of black metal lying unmoving on the ground floor below and knew that among them would be Boe and kO and somewhere down the corridor would be Kris. But all I could focus on was that I hadn't heard Pork Chop call my name in so long.

The walls of the College gave a violent shudder as another explosion shrouded the building in hot flames.

"Pork Chop," I tried to yell, but my throat was so dry and my strength was fleeting. I was bleeding badly, my body wet all over— bleeding in too many places that I didn't know where to apply pressure. "Pork Chop," I whispered hoarsely. It was a plea. It was a prayer. *Answer me.* But she didn't.

She had been in front of the huge crystal window, which was now broken, the last time I saw her. As the flames spread, I found it strange that my survival instincts didn't kick into gear. Somewhere deep down, a part of me knew that I could die, that Boe could die, that Kris could die, that maybe even oC could die, but I couldn't bring myself to care yet. It was as if I needed to affirm something first before I could agonize over the others.

I finally crawled around the corner and my eyes fell on her limp body.

Barely aware, I gave a strangled whimper. "Pork Chop," I cried out, an inaudible sound. I couldn't find my voice. "Pork Chop, please." The words were barely coherent. They sounded like the moans of a sick animal.

The fire was burning around us and the wind that swept through the open window was feeding the flames.

Lying beside her, I reached up to touch her face. The blood on my hands smeared across her chilled skin as my tears fell onto her soft cheek. I let out a tortured cry as she looked at me with the unmistakable, black, lifeless stare of death. With numb fingers, I closed her soft lids. As the blaze engulfed us, I held my baby sister's body close to me, trying to shield her from the heat.

I loved her too much. If the point of our species was to ensure survival, I didn't understand why we were endowed with this capacity to love. When death was so common among our kind, it was improvident to feel so much if the death of one meant death for the other.

Shifting toward the edge, I knew death was coming. There was no way out except for the open window that lay behind us; we were several stories up and the fall was sure to kill. But I didn't mind. Clutching Pork Chop against my chest, I was dying in agony and praying for it to stop.

The thought of the end made me think of one thing, of one person—Blake—and I wondered what living would have been like. Even now, when the pain was so acute, so consuming, I knew that he could have breathed life into me again. He could have made something of the half-life I would have had. Burying myself against Pork Chop's neck, I cried gutturally, my chest heaving, knowing that in the midst of a cruel universe I had found him— not my other half, not someone who completed me—she lay dead in my arms—but my soul entire. And now I was going to lose him, again.

My thoughts were getting hazy and I knew it had something to do with the pool of blood growing beside me, but the indistinctness didn't dim the pain. Another explosion threatened the College, sending the flames into a new frenzy. There wasn't a choice; I had to drag us out the window or we would burn. Using all my strength, I pulled us toward the brink just as the sky gave a violent rumble and drops of rain fell onto the city. Were the god's crying for me? I thought it fitting that they should, not just because they had mercilessly taken the life of my sister, but they had also made certain that Blake and I would never be together. Death would ensure that.

Almost as painful as my grief was the thought of never seeing him again, of never telling him that I loved him. And I did. More than anything I did. As I leaned Pork Chop's head against my shoulder and slid toward the cool night air, I thought of the small book of poetry and the red ribbon.

"'How do I love thee? Let me count the ways.'" My voice was but a ripple in a storm as I moved closer to the edge. "'I love thee to the depth and breadth and height my soul can reach...'" I could barely speak; the pain was so vicious. "'I love thee freely...I love thee purely...'" Lying down over the threshold, I wrapped my arms around Pork Chop's body. "I love you," I whispered in her ear.

The sky flashed as lightning cracked the heavens. All I needed to do was roll to the side and we would fall. It was painful to breathe, but I wanted just a moment longer to think of him. I wanted to remember that look in his eyes. I wanted to see his face. I wanted the last thing I would ever think about to be his smile. "'I love thee with the breath, smiles, tears, of all my life!'" I rocked our bodies to the side, needing the momentum to roll over because I was simply too weak to do it myself. "'And, if God, choose,'"—I closed my eyes and was filled with only Blake—"'I shall but love thee better after death.'"

Just as our bodies began to fall, I thought it but a dream when I heard her voice.

"Guse?"

THE BRIGHT LIGHT

The light was so bright that it burned, but my flesh didn't care. I was barely conscious and my body felt as if it were in limbo. Unsure if I was awake or dreaming, dead or alive, I desperately tried to find something that could tell me.

"Guse." There it was again; the song of her voice. And then I knew I was dead.

I tried to move toward the sound but I couldn't feel my body.

Was this what being dead was like?

Then it pierced me.

I had never heard an angel roar and the cry of my name was

impaling, waking something inside me that made me aware of the sheets of rain pouring down around me—it was strange because it was as if I moved faster than the drops. Then she moved in my arms. I couldn't understand why this made my heart ache but it did. It beat with a happiness I couldn't describe.

The light grew so intense that it blinded in me in ways that had nothing to do with my sight. I was engulfed in its warmth and I felt *his* hold around me and around her—protecting the precious gift that I held.

My body was brutally jarred as we collided into something and were swallowed by heat. Managing to open my eye a sliver, I saw his face was ablaze. A white angel was holding me. I let my eyes drop shut, not panicking with fear, because I was certain of one thing: the angel was not one of heaven but an angel who the angels themselves envied—my angel. We were together and that's all that mattered.

The high pitch of her voice woke me, but I wasn't annoyed at Pork Chop, who sounded like she was arguing with someone. That was one dream that felt all too real.

For some reason, it was taking me a while to wake-up. It was like I was on that border between sleep and consciousness, but I couldn't convince my body to move. Finally, my eyelids blinked open. I guess that I wasn't awake after all because as soon as I saw his face, I could feel the gentle touch of his hand in mine.

I was dreaming of Blake.

I frowned, displeased that he wore such a glum expression

even in my dreams. Why couldn't he be smiling or better, I thought, kissing me?

The line of his hard mouth softened as be bent his head toward me. Yes, that was what I was talking about. Kiss me.

"Finally, Gustav!" My sister's voice sounded odd—a mix of sarcasm and anxiousness. The bed had a seizure as she threw herself beside me and shoved Blake out of the way. Leaning back, he didn't let go of my hand but looked thoroughly displeased.

"Careful, Sof," he said firmly.

I furrowed my brow in confusion. I didn't want Pork Chop in this dream.

"I hate to break it to you Guse, but,"—she gently slapped my cheek and shut my mouth which had been slightly ajar—"Yes, you're awake. As I was saying," she continued, "I hate to break it to you Guse, but we couldn't do anything about it. The fire was—"

"Sof," Blake said her name warningly.

Pork Chop swatted her hand at him, ignoring his stern tone. My eyes looked from one to the other confused about the exchange. They spoke like they knew each other. This was a weird dream.

"It's your hair, Guse. It's all gone. I'm sorry." She patted my arm somberly. "You're bald."

I stared at my sister dumbly. What on earth was she talking about?

Pork Chop sighed impatiently. "See, you're awake." She squeezed my nostrils shut and clamped down on my mouth, making me gasp for air.

"Fields!" Blake barked. In an instant, Sammy appeared and hoisted Pork Chop away from me.

"Hey!" she protested. "Sammy, put me down."

Raising myself off my pillow, I tried to clear my head. We were in my bedroom. Blake was holding my hand beside me, Pork Chop and Sammy were in front of me and Vas was standing just in the doorway.

"Dad?" I asked slowly.

Vas gave me a weary smile in return. "How's my girl? he asked tenderly.

Something in Vas' face made my pulse quicken. It seemed that my body had finally woken because I felt the light ache that smothered it. It was difficult to move.

"What's going on?" I didn't like the shake I heard in my own voice. Things were getting clearer and it was if something inside me was afraid of what I would uncover.

"Everything's fine," Vas said reassuringly, moving closer.

"No it's not. She's bald," Pork Chop said seriously.

For the first time, my mind registered my sister's words; I was bald! I was sure my face looked stricken as my hand shot up to touch the top of my head because Pork Chop started to wail with laughter.

My body was tight and numb so it took a few moments to calm my nerves as my fingers weaved through my hair.

I gave my sister an evil look. "So funny, Pork," I said bitterly.

Sammy nudged my sister in the gut, trying to subdue her laughter.

"Where's your sense of humor?" she offered. "I'm just playing with her."

My sister looked innocently at Sammy and the sting of salt watered my eyes. It was all coming back to me: the WiiGiis at the College, the explosion, *Pork Chop*.

"Guse, what's wrong?" Sammy asked, sitting down beside me. I shook my head unable to voice what I was feeling.

"Are you in pain?" Blake asked tensely.

"No," I mumbled, squeezing his hand as tightly as I could. He was my anchor.

"It's okay, Guse. We all know you were looking forward to becoming the only child, but, alas, you will have to live with me yet."

I couldn't smile but my lips gave a small twitch. Gazing up at my sister, I knew that we understood each other perfectly. Her tense smirk had all but vanished.

"Alas indeed," I quipped back.

"Boe! Kris!" I exclaimed, remembering the last time I saw my two dear friends.

"Both fine," Sammy said quickly, looking at Blake.

"You two, outside," Vas declared in a grave tone.

Instinctually, I thought he was talking to Pork Chop and I because he only ever used that tone with us. As Blake and Sammy stood abruptly I realized Vas had been referring to them.

I clutched Blake's hand desperately as his fingers started to slip from mine. I didn't want him away from me. Out of the corner of my eye, I saw something lurch beside my bed but I didn't pay much attention. Blake looked down at me and I could see that he was filled with a soberness that made me uneasy.

"I'll be right back," he whispered. I bit my lip trying my best to not look completely distressed. Right back was too long.

"Now," Vas ordered. Realizing that everyone's eyes were now fixed on the two of us, I blanched. Pork Chop looked intolerably amused, with her arms crossed, and Vas looked as stoic as ever.

Shrinking my shoulders, I hesitantly let Blake's hand fall away from mine. Sammy and Blake followed Vas out of the room like soldiers following their general.

Pork Chop and I looked at each other with furrowed brows for a split second after the door slid shut. My sister's ear was planted against the cool metal in a flash.

"What's he saying?" I whispered anxiously.

"I can't hear anything. I need a glass or something." Pork Chop scurried toward me as I desperately looked around for a cup. "Perfect." Picking up a glass of water that sat on my bedside table, she dumped the contents on my lap.

"Hey!"

"Shhh!" she hissed as she held the object to her ear and once against planted herself against the door.

"Well?" I asked eagerly.

Pork Chop scowled. "I can't hear a thing."

"That's great," I muttered. "You could have dumped it on the ground you know."

Ignoring me, Pork Chop leaned against the door with a pensive look on her face.

Resting back against my pillows, I noticed for the first time the holograms that hovered beside me and I cocked my head, trying to figure out what I was looking at. My eyes grew wide as I realized what it was and the holographic image moved faster—it was my heart. As I thought back to the way it must have palpitated when Blake had pulled away, it started pumping faster and faster.

"Pork Chop, turn this thing off," I ordered. She continued to ignore me. I tried swatting at the image, but my fingers simply went through it. "Ugh!"

"Guse, behave yourself," my sister said casually, breezing past my bed and stepping onto the balcony. I must have slept through the day because it was already nearing sunset.

"Tell me how to turn this bloody thing off," I demanded. Looking frustratingly at my sister, my irritation quickly fled as I saw that her sleeve had been rolled back and she gingerly held her arm. It was wrapped in a thin black cast.

"What happened to your arm?" I asked quickly.

Pork Chop turned to face me. "Your *boyfriend* did this."

My mouth simply dropped open. There were so many facets of her statement that bothered me. "You are not a fish Guse, so close your mouth," she said teasingly.

I snapped it shut and pursed my lips. "He has apologized a gazillion times. Considering he saved our lives, I can't really hold it against him," she explained.

"What happened? Do you remember any of it?" Shifting to the edge of my bed, I managed to sit up. Pork Chop waited for me to find a comfortable position before she continued. She knew if she offered to help she would hurt my pride. The Ellias girls were such a proud lot.

"What do *you* remember, Guse?" Pork Chop asked, eyeing me queerly.

"It's coming back slowly," I answered cautiously. There was something about my sister's tone that troubled me. It was as if she wanted to gauge how much I knew before she decided how much she wanted to reveal. Considering I couldn't remember very much, I didn't want to show her all my cards. I couldn't tell whether or not she was hiding something or if she thought I was.

"Did you see what…happened to me?" Pork Chop's voice was strained.

I shook my head. "I couldn't see after the explosion," I replied lowly.

My sister gave me a probing look before she turned to look out over the city. "I don't remember either," she said aggravated.

I could understand her puzzlement. The last time I had seen Pork Chop there was no mistaking that she had been dead. It was strange to see how my holographic heart seemed to physically convulse in front of me—the memory was so painful. Looking at my sister now though, she was the epitome of good health with the exception of her arm.

Pork Chop walked back into the room and let the window close shut. "All I remember is running to you, then something hitting me and then falling. What happened in between is just blank. I've been checked and there's absolutely nothing wrong with me so I don't get it."

"What happened after we fell?"

Pork Chop started to pace up and down the room, twirling

the glass cup she still held. "Blake shot into us." She held up her braced arm indicating how she had hurt it. "It was pretty cool. He was like a freakin missile. That's why he couldn't stop. Poor guy, he blew right through the College. I think we came out on the other side of the building. It's crazy because Sammy says the worst he's got is a backache. Sammy came charging in after him…"

I raised my eyebrow righteously, knowing the time had come for Pork Chop to admit that she had lied to me about Samuel Fields. "I guess you know what Sammy is." I kept my face neutral as I crossed my arms, but there really wasn't a point considering my heart was thrumming madly beside me.

Pork Chop tilted her head at me as her eyes looked to my face and then to the annoying hologram. "Hey, we're even. I didn't tell you about him, but you didn't tell me about Blake either," she said defensively. Damn. She had a point. Usually, I would have pressed the childish issue that she lied first, but for once I didn't want to berate my sister. She was lucky that she had practically died yesterday, or else I doubt I would have been so generous.

"How long have you known?" I asked seriously.

"Sammy told me before we traveled here, but he's never explained why we went back in the first place or why I don't have any memory of being here before. I've tried to pry it out of him, but he won't give anything away." A crease lined my sister's forehead. "It's almost as if he's scared to tell me."

"Scared?"

"Did Blake give you any details?"

I shook my head slowly. "No, but he said Vas remembered *everything*."

"What!" she exclaimed.

"Shhh."

Pork Chop pursed her lips. "There's no point in shushing me because they can hear us clearly."

I forgot about that and cringed, hating the fact that we didn't have privacy when we spoke. My sister didn't seem perturbed, though. I fathomed she had gotten used to having a Supra around by now—she had had nearly two years. I on the other hand had barely had a week.

"When are you going to enroll us in sign language classes?" I muttered.

"I'm going to give Sammy an ear full. He never told me about Vas."

"Are you going to ask our dear old dad about it?"

Pork Chop sighed. "Are you?"

"You first."

"Chicken."

I brushed off my sister's taunt. "So you don't remember *anything* about our previous life?"

"Nope. Weird, huh?"

That was an understatement. Weird did not begin to describe it.

"What are you doing out of bed?" Startled, both Pork Chop and I jumped at the sound of Vas' voice.

"Athena!" Not only did Sammy and Blake return with Vas but RJ and Boe had appeared as well. Running toward me, she gave me a tight hug and covered my cheek with kisses.

"Seriously, Boe!" I tried to pull away but her embrace was so tight. Blake was instantly at his sister's side separating her from me.

"I'm just so glad to see you," she said sweetly.

"Please give Athena her space," Vas said, adamant from the other side of my bed. "Sofia, why did you let her get up?"

Pork Chop hid the glass she had been holding behind her back. "Guse made a pee pee," she said biting her lip impishly, her eyes falling to the large wet spot on my bed.

"What! I did not!" I declared, trying to stand so I could strangle her.

Boe was careful not to press too hard as she held me back. "We all know she's just joking, Athena. We would be able to smell if it was pee."

Her comment only made my cheeks burn hotter. I scowled at my sister as Sammy put fresh bedclothes on the mattress in a matter of seconds, making me realize that he wasn't going to hide his abilities anymore. Living with a Supra was going to take some getting used to, but then, I considered, it would give me some practice.

"I'm glad you came by, Boe," I said nervously, wanting to change the subject. "Thank you for what you did. You could have gotten hurt and—"

Boe waved her hands nonchalantly. "I told you WiiGiis can't touch this."

"Athens, since you're going to have some free time over the next few days, what do you say about watching a game of gammit tomorrow?" RJ grinned mischievously at Blake before turning his gaze on me.

"Yeah, I'd like that."

"Athena, I would prefer for you to get as much rest as possible before you go back to school." I looked at Vas incredulously. *Go back to school.*

Boe patted my hand excitedly. "Since we're technically not going back to the College, I'm going to go back with you." RJ let out a cough in protest. "We agreed the College, RJ. You really should comb over our contracts with more detail because we'll be going to Wollsworth College in the interim while the school is rebuilt."

RJ shook his head and crossed his arms. "We'll talk about this later."

Boe rolled her eyes. "Whatever," she quipped.

"Do I really have to go back to school?" I whined at Vas.

"Yes," he answered automatically.

I groaned at just the thought of that blasted word: school.

"So the College's in pretty bad shape?" I was trying to keep a conversation going to cover the awkward silence that filled the room.

"Yup, but so is half of London."

I furrowed my brow. "What do you mean by that?"

Boe gave Blake a quick glance before continuing. "Let's just say the boys always get to have the most fun."

I turned to look at Blake. The muscles in his jaw ticked as he looked at me intensely.

"What kind of *fun* exactly?"

"RJ and Sammy stellarized iP and lI. You should have seen them." Boe pouted like a child. "I never get to stellarize kO. I was just about to, but then the bomb went off."

"*Stellarize?* Who's lI?" I asked, puckering my forehead.

"lI is Sammy's boT. Didn't you know that?" Confused, Boe looked over to Sammy, who started to whistle and looked at the ceiling with such interest you would have thought we were in the Sistine Chapel. Boe scoffed. "Anyway, to answer your first question, when induced Supras can stellarize their synthesizer causing their boT to harness massive stores of energy." Boe rolled her eyes at my dumbfounded expression. "boTs can become, like, kick-ass arsenals of destruction!"

"Oh, okay," I said nodding my head. I was scared if I didn't feign comprehension Boe was going to smack me.

"But you should see the damage Blake did with the TX. And I don't care what he says, he opted to take the high road with the car instead of having vI acto-stellarize because he knew it would be friggin awesome."

My brain was starting to hurt from all the information it was trying to process. "*Acto-stellarize?*"

"vI's an ac:To boT. You didn't know that either?" Boe asked innocently.

Before I could answer her, Blake swiftly took hold of his sister's lithe arm. "Good-bye, Boe."

"Half of London woke-up windowless last night," Boe said hurriedly, giving her brother a menacing look as he escorted her to the door. "I want one for my birthday, Blake. I saved her life didn't I?" Boe looked over her shoulder and winked at me. All I could do was sigh. That girl was a conundrum if I ever knew one.

"See you, Athens," RJ called out as he headed out of the room.

"Byeee," Boe sang cheerily as Sammy and Pork Chop accompanied them. I waved meekly in return, feeling incredibly exhausted.

My body went stiff as Blake returned to sit by my side. It wasn't his presence that disconcerted me, it was the fact that the only person who remained in the room was Vas and he was staring fixedly at Blake.

"Uh, Dad, I'm sure you know by now, but this is Blake." I held out my hand but didn't take my eyes off my father's face. "Blake, this is my father."

"Yes," Vas replied curtly.

Not for the life of me, could I have ever imagined the awkwardness I would have to endure when I introduced Vas to Blake. My father's estimation was something I cherished very much and I had simply been unready for the two to meet—again. From the look on his face, I could tell my father was not pleased about our relationship.

I swallowed nervously. I hated the fact that Vas had found out about Blake without me telling him first. "Dad, Blake is…sort of…my…well…"

"Yes, I am aware of his intentions." I was certain that my cheeks were going to spontaneously combust from the acute heat washing over them.

"Okay, then," I said nodding my head, wanting the exchange to come to an end. Clenching my jaw, I realized that that my heart was still on display for all too see. I mentally groaned at the fact that it didn't take a genius to figure out how anxious I was. I was tempted to look over at it to see what the organ looked like right before it went into cardiac arrest, but I couldn't take my eyes off Vas whose gaze had not drifted from Blake.

"We have an understanding?" Vas said abruptly.

"Yes," Blake said smoothly, without pause.

Walking over to the edge of the bed, Vas leaned over and gave me a kiss on my forehead. Without another word and without another look at Blake he left the room. I couldn't remember the last time my father had kissed me. His sentiment touched me and tears threatened my eyes. God, I had become such a crybaby.

I felt the slightest pinch as Blake leaned down over me but I barely noticed. Raising my hands to touch his face, I pulled him closer. This is what I wanted. This is what I was waiting for. It was strange because I was sure he was coming closer but his face was becoming hazy. I couldn't seem to focus my eyes.

"Blake," I mumbled, finding it difficult to speak.

"I'm right here," he cooed against my ear, just as my eyelids slid closed.

¤ XXI ¤

S T A Y

It happened again. I was sure I found myself awake, but awake and dreaming, because Blake was not only with me but he was also holding me in his arms—in my bed. I was sure the smile that spread over my mouth would have been much wider if my muscles had been capable. Even though the nearness of his body to mine breathed such heat into my veins, I still felt as rigid as a metal plank. My face was pressed against his chest so he couldn't see my face, but I gathered he knew I was awake. Wanting to hold him closer and to feel him more solidly, I shifted slightly, trying to ease the stiffness in my body.

I should have just bloody stayed still because I barely moved a muscle before he started withdrawing.

"Blake," I managed with a dry voice.

"Go back to sleep," he said softly, already standing to the side of the bed.

I shook my head as vehemently as I could, and struggled to raise an arm toward him.

"Please—"

"Athena, I'll be right here. Just get some rest. Do you need anything for the…pain?" His voice was so strained.

I shook my head more forcefully as he moved down toward me. I knew what he was about to do this time.

"Stop doping me up with all these drugs." Coughing, I tried to subdue the parchedness in my voice. "It's bad for my liver," I said adamantly as Blake continued to lean down toward me. "Please, don't."

Something sparked in Blake's eyes, but I couldn't read the sentiment before he withdrew into shadow, leaving me alone under the rays of colorful moonlight that cascaded from my window.

"Athena, I'm so—"

"Don't you dare say it!" His grave tone spoke volumes and I knew he was going to offer some sort of apology. "What happened is not your fault. I hate apologies to begin with, but especially when I don't deserve them. I should be apologizing to you. I put Boe in danger. She could have been killed. And oC! He's all right isn't—"

"oC." Blake's voice was grinding as he said the boT's name.

"He's not hurt is he? *You* didn't hurt him, did you? It wasn't his fault either." The edge in Blake's voice sent shivers down my spine and I was very afraid for oC. The boT had become very dear to me. "Blake, answer me."

"He's fine," he replied curtly.

With all the strength I could muster I sat up on the bed. In an instant, Blake was at my side pressing me gently back down.

"I want to see him. Now," I said resolutely, struggling in vain against his grip.

"Fine. Just lay down. I'll summon him." My body fell still— not just because Blake had relented but also because his voice was so severe.

Releasing me, he walked over to the window as it slid open before him.

"Where are you going?" I asked worriedly. Just the thought of him leaving made me anxious.

"You said you wanted to see oC. It's either him or me. I won't stand in his presence."

My mouth dropped open at Blake's brutality. I laid my head back onto my pillow, wanting to keep my face out of the moonlight. Blake's resentment toward the boT hurt me and tears filled my eyes.

Blake walked out onto the balcony.

"You can tell oC he need not come then," I whispered dejectedly. I was angry, hurt, and filled with so many emotions I couldn't name, but I needed Blake with me.

Blake immediately walked back in and returned to his position in the shadows as the window slid shut. A tear trickled down the side of my cheek and fell on my pillow while I desperately tried to hold back the convulsing in my chest.

Whenever oC had spoken of Blake, there was no denying how the boT cared about his Supra counterpart. He loved him, so clearly, so strongly, that it probably put some humans to shame that a robot could feel such emotions. But oC wasn't a robot to me. He was a dear companion. He was a friend. He was a person.

I thought of how panicked oC had been when he had seen the wound I got in gym class and I couldn't hold back the sound I made when I tried to gulp down the choke in my throat.

Blake had said that oC was fine, but maybe he wasn't fine. Maybe Blake was too angry at the moment to care about the well being of the boT. Then I remembered his eyes—eyes so soulful you forgot they were mechanical—when he had spotted me in the College's atrium. I didn't doubt they mirrored my eyes when I awoke this morning to see Pork Chop.

I couldn't take it anymore. If I had to beg Blake to stay while I saw oC, I would do it. I opened my mouth to plead, but my window slid open and I saw his hesitant figure slowly zoom into the room. vI hovered just outside the balcony.

"oC!" I hoisted myself into a sitting position and reflexively held my arms out.

"No, no, no, no," oC protested, rushing to my side. "You mustn't get up on account of me."

As soon as the boT was within reach, without thinking, I

grabbed him and pulled him toward me. For someone who rarely hugged people, I found it strange that I did it. But as I held his small robotic body against me, I understood. Hugging oC didn't feel awkward at all. It felt natural—more natural then when I hugged my own species.

"oC, I'm so sorry. It's all my fault—"

"Damn right it is," vI's hard voice bellowed from outside.

oC turned toward a shadowed part of the room, where I guessed Blake was standing, and then to vI. "Don't tell me to keep quiet, oCTon. She's caused all this trouble and she ought to know it."

oC shook his head fervently. "Good-bye, Athena. I think it's time to leave. I just wanted to assure you that I am perfectly fine. You needn't worry about me. All you have to focus on is getting better."

I took hold of the boT's little hand before he could zip away. "No!"

oC tugged my hand gently. "It's okay, Athena."

"No, it's not okay," I said through clenched teeth.

oC once again looked to the shadows before turning to me. "I can see that we're upsetting you. We can discuss anything you like in the coming days."

I took a deep breath, hoping to calm the anger that was building inside me. "vI can you please come in here?" I was so riled up that I was able to suppress the twitch in my mouth as oC's mouth fell open adorably.

After a few moments, vI answered my request by floating into the room with her head held high.

"What is it?" she asked roughly, coming up beside oC, who nervously patted her shoulder before eyeing the dark room warily.

"vI, I would like to apologize to you." I held up my hand to silence oC, who was about to protest. vI simply snorted. "No matter what anyone says,"—I narrowed my eyes toward the back of my room—"I feel I'm partly to blame for what happened. As soon as I heard the WiiGiis I should have gone straight back to Kris and oC."

"Damn straight," vI huffed.

I took a deep breath, ignoring vI's snide attitude. "I know that oC means a lot to you." It took all the willpower to look her straight in the eye. "Which is why I'm asking you to forgive me for putting him in danger." oC's mouth fell open again and this time I had to bite my lip to fight the grin. "oC means a lot to me too and I know he would want for us to be amicable toward one another," I continued. "I'm sure that if you're able to forgive me, then I'm sure that *Blake* would be inspired by your…munificence and bestow the same forgiveness on oC." I gave the boT's hand an affectionate tug as his shoulders shrank after my declaration.

"Done," vI said perfunctorily.

I nodded my head in curt agreement. I think we understood each other perfectly. We both wanted Blake and oC to reconcile with one another. I doubted that vI had truly forgiven me, though.

"It's late," Blake's said tersely, stepping out of the shadows toward my bed.

"*Sir*," vI said mockingly, turning to head out of the room. I knew that vI didn't address Blake so formally and was alluding to the fact that he was acting like a tyrant.

"Good-bye, then," oC said softly as he pulled his hand away from mine and zoomed toward the window, trailing vI. Both boTs stopped and turned just as they flew past the balcony.

"Goodnight, oC," Blake murmured as the window slid shut.

This time my face matched the sentiment I felt—I knew I was beaming. "Don't look at me like that just yet. It's going to take a while for my anger to pass," he said coolly.

His words didn't dim my contentment. "Kiss me." I sighed, holding out my arms to him.

Blake shook his head slowly. "That only worked for the first kiss."

He was still standing out of my reach around the bed, but I knew how to fix that. I immediately pulled off my covers and started moving off the mattress. His hands were pressed against my shoulders in a heartbeat, followed by an audible breath.

I took hold of his wrists as firmly as I could. "Kiss me," I whispered more urgently this time.

"Athena—"

"Kiss me."

As I lay back against the soft sheets, he lowered his head toward mine. When his hands moved, I tightened my grip, sure that he was going to pull away. But he didn't. His fingers traced my jawbone gently and smoothed themselves across my cheeks. And then he kissed me tenderly almost reverently. His lips were so delicate over mine—as if he kissed the petals of a flower.

I threw my eyes open as his hands slid away and he stood abruptly.

"If you don't try to go to sleep, I'll be forced to make you," he said in a low voice.

I lifted the covers that were tucked around me and shifted to the far side of the bed.

"Stay with me," I pleaded, my eyes imploring. I couldn't see his face, but I knew him well enough to anticipate his refusal. "Please stay, Blake. I need you."

He left so quickly that I barely registered his departure until several moments after my bedroom window sealed itself shut.

Rolling onto my stomach, I reached my arm over the vacant space where I had meant for him to lay with me. Looking across the bed, I was a little disappointed that the hologram of my heart was nowhere in sight—I was interested to see what a broken one looked like.

As the crisp night air swept back into my room, I found it entirely contradictory that my body was warm instead of cold— just the thought of Blake returning heated the blood in my veins.

I didn't move, even when he loomed above me standing beside the bed. Half my face was still pressed against the mattress with my arm outstretched across the stark side of the bed. Bending down he gently lifted my fingers and entwined them in his. Crawling next to me, he lay down and pulled me against him as he wrapped my arms around his firm body.

I was so scared to move or say anything because I was sure if I did I would breakdown and start crying from elation.

"Athena, are you all right?" he asked in a tender voice.

For long moments I couldn't respond to his query. I didn't want to make him anxious, but I just wanted to relish the moment, overcome by the fervor of my feelings. Reaching up, I touched his soft skin and ran my fingers down across his neck.

"I was never quite certain but I think God must love me...I thought I would never see you again."

Blake was quiet for a moment. "God has nothing to do with it. If he does, it is not because he *loves*," he replied gravely. I wanted to shake my head, but Blake held my face firmly. "Most people feel the need of something grand, something infinite, like God, but I don't. I see something deeper, more eternal than the ocean, in the expression of your eyes. I know it's not the same for you—"

"It's more," I said quietly. "Much more."

He shook his head slowly, unbelieving. "There is nothing beyond infinity and I'm holding it in the palm of my hand," he whispered huskily.

I shook my head in turn, vehemently disagreeing, but he wasn't playing fair. Blake's fingers caressed my face and brought me closer to him and I lost the train of the conversation. I decided not to play fair either. If I couldn't match his words to express how much he meant to me, then I wanted to show him. I crushed my lips to his, but it seemed I couldn't win either way because my forcefulness was quickly superseded by Blake's own eagerness, plunging me into a rapture that fled all thoughts from my mind.

This kiss was nothing like the one that had preceded it. Blake's lips shifted over mine possessively, the movement fervently matched by his tongue. This kiss, like our first, was raw and feral and, in the moment, made me absolutely certain of one thing: Blake wanted me.

As he pushed himself away and sat with his back turned on the side of the bed, I was absolutely certain of one other thing: I wanted him more than he wanted me.

"Blake—"

"Am I going to have to drug you in order for you to get some rest? You wanted me to stay and...I will, while you *sleep*."

I inched toward him and he let out a breath before moving closer.

"Okay, I'll sleep," I conceded, scared that he was going to stick me with some unseen needle again.

Laying down, he cradled me in his arms and drew the bed sheets up around my shoulders.

"I guess some good came from all this," I said, burying my face against Blake's neck, trying to distract myself from the heated desires coursing through my body. "I'm sure that the WiiGiis won't be able to regroup after this. Many died, right?" An image of Corinne's handsome face made me shiver and I held Blake tighter. "I know you must feel at least a little bit relieved."

"Relieved?" Blake asked inexpressively.

"Things could have gone worse, but luckily everything turned out all right and now you don't have to worry so much. I know it was because of the WiiGiis that you sent Pork Chop and I back. I know you tried to stay away from me because you didn't want to put me in danger, but everything should be fine now." I leaned my head back to look at Blake when he didn't respond. "Right?"

"Athena…" he said my name hesitantly, "it wasn't because of the…" Trailing off, he rolled onto his back and closed his eyes.

"What?" I asked anxiously.

"Go to sleep," he said coolly.

"No." I raised myself on my elbows to look down at his face.

He let out a breath. "The WiiGiis are still very much a problem. Yes, a lot of them died, but some survived. A mere explosion wouldn't have killed them. And there are more of them."

I got a nagging feeling that Blake hadn't been referring to the WiiGiis when he spoke before, but I didn't know how to voice my uncertainty. Instead, I shoved my doubt to the back of my mind and decided to ask something that had been bothering me.

"What happened to Pork Chop at the College? I was so sure that she was…"

Blake laid my face against his chest as I slid my arms around him.

"Just rendered unconscious, Athena."

I wiped a tear from the corner of my eye, remembering her face. I was sure she hadn't just been unconscious.

"Blake—"

"This is not sleeping," he interjected firmly.

"I just wanted to say that I'm in your debt. You saved her life and mine."

Rolling us to the side, Blake gaze downward at me as he quirked his brow. "Any gentleman would be forced to refute that claim and, if nothing, at least declare that we are even." I was about to protest when Blake placed his finger over my mouth. "But I am *no* gentleman," he whispered roughly. "Shall I name the price then?"

I kissed his finger softly before he slid it off my mouth.

"Nothing I have could repay you," I answered. "I'm not sure I can ever—"

"What if you loved me?" His voice was lined with a quiet fierceness that made my heart thrum desperately.

"That is how I feel," I replied slowly. "Don't you know that by now?" I nervously wound my fingers around a piece of hair. "Besides, that is hardly something I can barter with. It's free."

"Then tell me," he whispered demandingly. "Say. The. Words."

"What difference do the words make? Words aren't worth anything." I was restless as Blake's eyes scoured my face.

"Those words are priceless and have *never* been spoken... by *you*."

Nuzzling anxiously against his chest, I feigned a yawn. "I'm feeling very tired all of a sudden."

"Athena," Blake said my name beseechingly.

"'The word *love* has by no means the same sense for both sexes, and this is one cause of the serious misunderstandings that divide them.'"

Blake sighed in frustration. "*That* is something I *have* heard before. I was once quite fond of her, but I've slowly found Madame De Beauvoir quite objectionable."

"Well...it's not something I've heard you say either," I replied guardedly.

"All I can say is *another promise*."

Although I was sure my heart would burst if I ever heard

Blake utter those coveted three words, my lips couldn`t help but twitch into a grin at the thought of me making him promise only to declare them once I had. And I thought Boe was devious.

Even though my aversion to declaring my feelings hadn't dimmed, a small part of me noted how I had become more comfortable with the notion of love. I said the word in my head with little sarcasm lately. My cynical side reminded me that thinking of something and saying it out loud was two very different things and I held fast to my adamant aversion to the spoken word.

The truth is, though, that I couldn't deny that I wouldn't hesitate to give or sacrifice anything for the being that lay beside me. Regardless of the clichés and the sometimes-warranted pessimism of the world, I thought the fact that I would was the essence of living and of being human. Three words couldn't sum that up—couldn't capture how I felt. But I did love him and if he wanted me to say something to that effect then I decided I would.

"Blake?"

"Yes," he answered softly.

"You're the worst kind of bad faith."

Blake brought his face to mine and lay the slightest kiss on my jawbone. "One of these days, I might just have to make you say it."

"I doubt you could," I replied breathily, as his hand roamed down the side of my body.

"I have a talent for persuasion, Athena," he said gratingly.

I doubted my own fortitude when his kisses trailed down the side of my neck. If he kept touching me, I would tell him anything he bloody wanted.

Then I felt the pinch.

"Blake!" I protested, rubbing my arm.

"Now you will sleep," he said smoothly.

I was already starting to feel drowsy.

"You'll be here in the morning, right?" I asked, panicked that he would leave.

"I'll stay the night but if Vas or—"

"Promise!"

"I promise," he declared tenderly.

I leaned against his chest as my mind started receding into the realm of sleep. "So, we'll go play gammit tomorrow?"

"We'll see," Blake replied passively.

"Is RJ really as good…as he says he is?" I was trying to keep my eyelids open, but they were simply too heavy.

"He plays well considering his position is one that suits him— the queen—proud and arrogant. He can match the move of any player on the field at any given time except for *one*."

He sounded like he was miles away.

"What position do you play?" My voice was nothing more than a hum in my ear.

Blake's arms tightened around me.

"The knight."